EMPIRE'S
END

D0669519

X-MEN

EMPIRE'S END

DIANE DUANE

ILLUSTRATIONS BY RON LIM AND BOB McLEOD

BYRON PREISS MULTIMEDIA COMPANY, INC.
NEW YORK

BERKLEY BOULEVARD BOOKS, NEW YORK

If you purchased this book without a cover, you should be aware that this book is stolen property. It was reported as "unsold and destroyed" to the publisher, and neither the author nor the publisher has received any payment for this "stripped book."

For Chris

Special thanks to Ginjer Buchanan, Lucia Raatma, Michelle LaMarca, Steve Roman, Emily Epstein, Mike Thomas, Steve Behling, and Ursula Ward.

X-MEN: EMPIRE'S END

A Berkley Boulevard Book
A Byron Preiss Multimedia Company, Inc. Book

PRINTING HISTORY
Boulevard/Putnam hardcover edition / October 1997
Berkley Boulevard paperback edition / September 1998

All rights reserved.
Copyright © 1997 by Marvel Characters, Inc.
Edited by Keith R. A. DeCandido.
Book design by Michael Mendelsohn of MM Design 2000, Inc.
Cover design by Claude Goodwin.
Cover art by Duane O. Myers.
This book may not be reproduced in whole or in part,
by mimeograph or any other means, without permission.
For information address: Byron Preiss Multimedia Company, Inc.,
24 West 25th Street, New York, New York 10010.

The Penguin Putnam Inc. World Wide Web site address is
http://www.penguinputnam.com

Check out the Byron Preiss Multimedia Co., Inc. site on the World Wide Web:
http://www.byronpreiss.com

Check out the Ace Science Fiction/Fantasy newsletter, and much more,
at Club PPI!

ISBN: 0-425-16448-9

BERKLEY BOULEVARD
Berkley Boulevard Books are published by
The Berkley Publishing Group,
a member of Penguin Putnam Inc., 375 Hudson Street,
New York, New York 10014.
BERKLEY BOULEVARD and its logo
are trademarks belonging to Berkley Publishing Corporation.

PRINTED IN THE UNITED STATES OF AMERICA

10 9 8 7 6 5 4 3 2 1

One

The mountain range was the biggest on the planet. From one edge of the continent to the other it stretched, a chain of sheer and jagged white heights, here and there shrouded thick in mist under the moons, and roofed over with the dazzling stars of the Shi'ar homeworld. A sky full of short-period variable stars that breathed their light in and out like long quiet breaths, or beat quick as hearts.

The observatory clung just under the peak of the highest mountain in the chain, like some small bird trying to avoid the glimpse of a passing predator. Night made it look like just one more outcropping. Indeed, it had been designed so, out of respect for the local environment, one of the few places on the planet still mostly untouched by technological construction: a jagged upthrust "spire" that held the main optical instruments, and another outthrust stone spur for labs, living quarters, and those instruments that didn't care about forms of energy that could be stopped by stone.

Inside the spur was a cube of workspace, which looked like half the other workspaces in that part of the galaxy: mostly bare-walled, crammed with machinery, and unkempt. Desk space was at a minimum; information solids and printed references lay everywhere, mixed in with drink containers, scribers and correcting wipes, and who knew what else.

Avend sighed as he looked at it, despairing of ever teaching his research team to be tidy. But they had so little reason, of late. No one paid much attention to what they were investigating. This, more than any other cause, makes scientists leave garbage around and not pick it up, makes them cranky when strictly physiological reasons are not involved, and sometimes makes them commit suicide.

Avend was not suicidal—not today. For once, something was about to happen that was worth his, and soon others', interest. The data from the probe would be coming in within the hour, if everything went on schedule. Some of his staff had actually started coming in early from their living quarters—an unusual occurrence among astronomers, who tend to be chronically short of sleep at the best of times—and were drifting around with an expectant air, walking in and out of the lab next to Avend's, where the data could be expected to produce itself in one of the secondary tanks.

Avend sat down in the chair behind his desk, as cluttered with work as any of the others, and sighed as the chair—fairly ancient, like much of the equipment around here—creaked wearily under his weight. The problem was not money, as such. The Shi'ar goverment was hardly a poor one; the economies of a thousand planets were siphoned through and into it. But it was a racial trait of the Shi'ar that they could be ruthlessly pragmatic—*callous* was a word some of the subject species used—and they did not believe in waste. Specifically, as applied to research, this principle meant that even though the Shi'ar higher-ups recognized the value of ''speculative'' or pure research, they also insisted that after a reasonable time, say ten or fifteen years, it had better show some results that could be turned to the good of at least *someone* in the empire. Projects which showed no such results had their funding cut, no argument, no appeal.

Research like that which Avend had recently been conducting—specifically, work based on premises other scientists had been laughing at—had an even harder time getting funding. Avend ran his hands through his big unruly feather-crest, rubbed his craggy face, and sighed at the thought of all the other research he had had to lend his name to, research in which he had no interest whatever, to finally get this one piece of investigation done. A twenty-year career in high-energy astrophysics, a few awards, a lot of articles presented, a lot of publication in the usual journals—all bartered away like a string of cash for the sake of this one set of information that might make his reputation or break it.

He reached out to the tank on his desk, pulled a couple of stray scribers off the projection platform, and stroked the tank into life, staring, as he had for hundreds of hours this year, at the vague, difficult image within it. Stars swarmed there, curving gracefully in the peculiar and beautiful double coat hook shape of a barred spiral galaxy: the closest galaxy to the one that was home to the Shi'ar worlds. There were not as many stars visible in the image as were actually there, Avend knew. A lot of dark matter lay between the target and the viewpoint from which the image was taken. But the darkness itself was diagnostic, to Avend, of something going on that needed investigation. He watched the image closely, even though there was no point, like a father watching a sick child.

One of his lab assistants wandered in: young Irdin, with her big pale eyes and fair crest. She said, "Fifteen minutes."

X·MEN

Avend grunted an inarticulate reply. Irdin looked at him, a little pityingly, and wandered out again.

Avend looked at the barred spiral's image steadily, seeing for the moment something else entirely, in his mind: the image of another galaxy, only a little more remote than this one, a matter of another half-million lightyears or so, give or take fifty thousand—the third-closest galaxy to the Shi'ar's own. Avend remembered the excitement that had broken out in the first great observatory where he had been working, twenty years ago, at the news that the heart of the Akh'than galaxy had gone spectacularly quasar. There had been little warning. Some odd energy readings, a lot of gamma and X-ray emission for which there had been no obvious reason. Then, very early one morning—*Why is it always so obscenely early in the morning when these things happen?* Avend thought—the news that the Akh'than core was abruptly emitting something like fifty thousand times its normal output, right up and down the spectrum.

By the time the core had collapsed, six years later, hundreds of papers had been written, some of them Avend's own. Many of them had set his career on its present course. Arguments over the cause of the "core event" were rife, endless theories were postulated; few of them would hold water. Other Shi'ar astronomers got bored with the subject and went on to trendier, "sexier" ones. But Avend persisted, looking at the slowly weakening quasar remnant, becoming increasingly sure that whatever he was looking at, it was not a true quasar.

True, the output had been consistent with a quasar's. But the speed and quality of the collapse was all wrong. Worse, stellar evolution in that galaxy had begun to behave very oddly. It was taken for granted that a quasar's wild output of energy would "overbalance" the energy economies of

6

some of the stars nearest the galactic core, sending them very quickly into nova state. But so *very* many? Nearly half the stars in the Akh'than galaxy had flared, causing the destruction of their planets. Many had gone nova, destroying both their planets and themselves, leaving only rapidly cooling stellar cinders behind them, and nearly twenty had gone supernova—statistically, a most unlikely response to the presence of a mere quasar.

Avend had written some very annoyed papers on this subject. His enemies in the sciences had quickly responded that Avend was basing his conclusions on dubious mathematics (an accusation that had made him fume), and was attempting to rekindle a stagnant career by making sensational claims (which accusation made Avend laugh out loud, severely annoying those enemies; genuine laughter was a weapon whose effectiveness few of them had suspected until it sent them away smarting). No one paid any particular attention to Avend's concerns about goings-on in the core of a galaxy which was, after all, half a million lightyears away. If anything bad was going to come of the admittedly odd behavior in the Akh'than core, it would have happened by now, wouldn't it? The events were five hundred millennia old, now, their images coasting slowly in on the crest of a wave of stale light. *It was a one-off*, popular opinion in the scientific community said. *Interesting, but statistically unlikely to repeat. Why keep harping on it?*

Avend, though, was one of the older school of physicists, one who knew the difference between harping on things and good old-fashioned persistence. He kept thinking about the problem, letting his colleagues think he had put it aside. When it happened again, twelve years later, and a quasar suddenly woke up in the core of the irregular galaxy the

Shi'ar called Orsheh, the second-nearest to them, within two weeks Avend had published his predictions for the energy curves of the object—he was refusing to call it a quasar now—and for the stars in its vicinity.

The other scientists complained that his math was still dubious. It therefore annoyed them that the stars in the area began to behave much as Avend had predicted they would, the "core event" leaving behind it a great scattering of main sequence stars suddenly flared or gone red-giant, or else gone nova entirely, leaving behind much glowing plasma and a few pulsars, but little else. Many of the other scientists dismissed this as a statistical fluke. "Like the first time?" Avend inquired, but his arguments continued to carry little force with the scientific community at large, which rarely forgives one of its own for being right, especially if she or he rubs their noses in it. When they ignored his predictions, and his suggestion that this situation should be looked into before it happened to their own galaxy, Avend did something unusual. He took the matter to the Imperial Science Council, and requested that it be brought directly to the attention of Majestor D'Ken himself.

"Avend?" Another of his assistants was in the doorway: tall lanky Derl, with his ever-rumpled clothes looking like he had put them on with a shovel, and his crest slicked back as usual from being stroked down nervously every five minutes. "Five minutes. The uplink is hot."

"Coming," Avend said, still looking at the old image, the product of stale light. The Imperial Science Council had declined to get involved in what it read as just one more throat-cutting procedural squabble among specialists involved in an esoteric and conjecture-ridden minor branch of the sciences. D'Ken had an empire to tend to, and could not be expected to become involved.

Now, D'Ken was dead, replaced by his sister Lilandra, and Orsheh was a cooler, paler galaxy than it had been. Avend's enemies—no use in thinking otherwise of them now, they had been so cager to see him humbled after his attempt to go over their heads—had quickly pointed out that the Orsheh galaxy had been bizarre to begin with, its core always liable to odd energy flares, probably inherently unstable as galaxies went. That the structure should now be dissolving, resolving itself into a mere shell of a few hundred thousand "brown stars" gone prematurely cold, should surprise no one. Or so they said. It didn't matter anyway. It was all old news, a couple of hundred thousand years gone now. Who cared?

Avend did. He stood up, the chair creaking again as he took his big frame's weight off it. The back of it wobbled. Avend reached down absently and shook the back of the seat a little. It wobbled again, more enthusiastically. He sighed. Stale light, that was the problem. "Live-light" astronomy was possible, but it cost money, which in turn required influence—a lot of both, to push an observatory-class instrument through a space-traversing stargate, when far more vital cargoes and military vessels were lined up outside every gate, all waiting their turn.

Nonetheless, he had managed it. Avend had pulled every string that a long and mostly amiable career had provided him. He had bent the ears of all kinds of people, from members of the Imperial Science Council (strictly socially) to mediamongers, from the upper-level executives of universities, who had been angling for him for years, to colleagues halfway across the planet who Avend knew could be depended upon for nothing but the certainty that anything he told them would be gossip winging its way around the planet within minutes.

He had structured his string-pulling carefully, putting his campaign together word by word and phrase by phrase, like a particularly abstruse paper: an equation, a paragraph of explanation, another equation. Slowly the support had fallen into place. Very quietly, the funding for that necessary instrument had made itself available—for the sources of that funding were waiting to see if Avend's investigation would fail, and if it did, those sources would disavow any knowledge or support of what he had been doing.

He had built the sleek little instrument himself, being unwilling to leave the mechanics even to his most trusted assistants. Avend knew that failure would reflect as devastatingly on them as on him. *My career may indeed be over*, he thought. *No need to end one or more of* theirs *before they've even fairly started.*

It had been a long time since he had been involved in the mechanical end of astronomy, but the need for haste gave Avend little time to indulge his nervousness about whether he was getting the live-light machinery right. Fortunately the technology he needed was mostly off-the-shelf stuff, easily plugged into the platform he had built. It consisted of a mixed array of tachyon- and neutrino-based sensors to augment the various live-light sensors, in visible and invisible spectra, which would be trained on Avend's chosen target: the closest galaxy, the one the Shi'ar called Sorosh, a tight handsome little spiral with its arms coiled close around itself.

The instrument was built, the time laid in when it would be delivered to one of the Shi'ar's programmable stargates. It would be a push-pull gating, one of the most expensive kind. The doorway opened on a patch of space only a few thousand lightyears from Sorosh's arbitrary boundaries, on the Shi'ar side. The probe would be pushed through, and the gate closed. Then, after the probe had done its observations and saved its data, the gate would be opened again, the probe would navigate its way back through—assuming no misfortune had befallen it—and the gate would once more close. There would be no need for it to be fetched back physically; the gate's own support-and-operation framework would relay the data back to the Shi'ar commnets and home to the observatory.

"Avend—"

"Coming," Avend said, and went after the anxious looking Derl into the lab.

All of his assistants were there, standing around the main tank, which had had the drink containers fished out of its projection platform and was now on standby. They all peered anxiously into the cube of darkness, half as wide as most of them were tall.

"Don't tell me it's not working," someone said from the back of the group, as they all watched in silence.

"It's working," Derl said. "You can see that white fringe at the edges. Carrier."

But nothing happened except that shivering of carrier around the edges of the cube. "Isn't it active?" Irdin said softly.

"It's alive," Avend said quietly. "It closes its sensors down for five standard segments after it comes back through the gate, as a precaution against local energy fluxes, radiation, any other phenomena that might overload the sensors when they come up from—"

The cube flared white, blindingly so, even in the well-lit lab, so that a lot of the assistants looked away, startled and blinking. Avend did not look away.

The image jittered to black again, and then for a further few moments shimmered with rogue rainbows, the remnants of chromatic aberration in one of the optical instruments as it complained about heat expansion due to the energy flux associated with having just passed the stargate. "Miserable insulation," Derl muttered under his breath.

"No," Avend said, sitting down in the nearest chair. The panel within his reach was slaved to the probe's command-and-control centers. He reached out left-handed and touched the panel, stroked one of the sets of controls to life. A line of light came alive under his fingers. Avend glanced at the line, then traced off to one side. Another line followed his finger, at right angles.

"It's answering," he said. "Here we go—"

The inside of the cube flared white again, then settled once again to cool blackness with a swath of pale light across it. Avend and all his assistants leaned in to look at it. It was Sorosh, its neat spiral shape all in order as usual—

—except that its core looked paler than usual, and there was a darkness piercing its heart.

Avend touched the controls again. A bar graph appeared off to one side of the image. With his other hand he manipulated another set of lines of light on the controls, drawing a cube-shaped marquee of light around that dark spot.

"What is that?" Derl was saying. "A jet of some kind? Or just a cloud of dark matter?"

Irdin was staring too. "Why are the readings so flat for that area?" she said. "That's the center of a good-sized galaxy in there, there should be—"

The marquee expanded, its edges and vortices mapping themselves out to the edge of the cube. There was no derangement or diminution of picture quality. The imaging hardware was true-holographic in nature, having already stored exponentially augmented images while scanning. The "darkness" became plainer. What had at first seemed a straight dark line now was revealed as a large dark gap, longer than it was wide, somewhat pointed at the coreward end, and thinly fringed with stars. It was not truly a black space—couldn't be, with a significant portion of Sorosh's core still shining normally behind it—but it looked ominous, and decidedly unnatural.

"No dark matter," Avend said, "no more than the usual amounts, anyway." He worked with the control panel again.

They all stared. There was a great starless void torn straight into the heart of the nearest galaxy. The patch or spindle-shaped line which led toward the core was blunted somewhat. The shape looked like that of a sungrazing comet, seen in negative. Some of the assistants were shaking their heads, dumbfounded. Derl was simply standing there with the shocked and frozen expression of a man who finds himself sharing house-room with a ghost. Avend did not believe in ghosts, but he thought he knew how Derl felt.

Once again Avend defined the marquee inside the cube, this time placing it around the head of the grayish "comet," very small and tight. He enlarged the image to fill the cube.

They all leaned in again, stared. In the center of all that emptiness, one star shone brighter than the others which peppered the immediate background. "A big energy flare there," Avend said, almost absently, as he drew the marquee around that tiny point source of light one more time. "Much higher than background. *Much*. Something giving off a lot of X-ray, a lot of gamma—"

The marquee once again swelled to fill the whole cube. More bar graphs popped up on the sides of the image, adjusted themselves, then began to jitter. The cube became one great pale swirl of light—clouds, burning with stars, like one of the great star nurseries associated with intra-galactic hot dark nebulae.

The problem was that stars were not being born here. They were dying. The distressed spectrography the sensors showed, and the great prominences torn out of them, tongues of fire sometimes a tenth the width of a good-sized planet's orbit, were plain indicators of something that had plunged through them. By sheer mass or some other in-strumentality, something had sucked the life and the nuclear fire out of them, and passed on. The derangement of the dying stars' light curves, the energy readings associated with the whole area, were so massive that the graphs the probe was displaying had to be assumed to be erroneous: they were not built to correctly sense such intensities of energy. And beyond the stars themselves something else was in view—something which glowed against the pearly, too-faint light of what remained of Sorosh's core.

Avend drew the marquee one more time, enlarged the image.

Pearly light—and a point of light buried in it, in the clouds of dust and expelled stellar matter, veiled amid the enraged plasma and the dying exhalations of stars. A point source with an energy reading like a galactic core's itself. And around it, emptiness, as if something associated with that point of light drew the energy into itself and did not release it again.

Avend drew the marquee yet again, enlarged it.

Nothing but clouds of desperate light, the point source, and nothing else. Even Shi'ar off-the-shelf technology had its limits.

Avend leaned back in the chair, looked around him at his assistants. They stood frozen, for they knew what a galactic core's readings should look like as well as he did, and this was *nothing* like what should have been there.

He felt for them, but he was feeling unwell enough on his own behalf. Avend had led a relatively gentle life, had been fortunate in family matters, and by and large few things truly troubled him. But now he felt that pressure in his chest, and felt, for the first time since childhood, a fear bad enough to affect his body. He felt the weight of it, the way it clamped down on his lungs and made the simple act of breathing hard.

"They will have to believe us now," Avend said, very softly, and his team turned to look at him, made uneasy by the grimness in his voice. "They will have to listen. There is no other way for us to be saved. None at all."

About a third of the planet's circumference away, it was the fifth hour after sunrise, and the meeting had been going on for nearly four of those. The meeting room was long, high-ceilinged, and its fixtures and fitments gleamed with polished metal and metalglaze. The sun came slanting down through a cleared forceport in the ceiling and had been tracking slowly down the length of the huge central table, on either side of which some forty Shi'ar sat.

It happened every morning, this meeting. Not precisely a levee, but the ruler's daily meeting with an ever-changing group of her major officials. At the head of the table, separated from the others by several yards of clear space, sat a single slender form, dark-crested, looking down the table with an expression that almost no one there had the experience, or the sense, to read as sardonic. In front of her was nothing but a slim, flat electronic notepad. Her elbow was propped on the table in front of her, her chin was resting in the palm of her hand, and her lively eyes were resting, for the moment, on the Shi'ar nearest her, at her right.

"The rest of the précis as shown on today's order of business is essentially correct," he was saying. "The economical projections, in particular, are in line with the fourth-quarter projections which had been suggested by Exordial Affairs for the outer worlds."

Majestrix Lilandra of the house of Neramani blinked slowly, an artificially sleepy look, and said, "So there is no need to fire the new fiscal-ecology prediction team, then."

A slight stir went down the table. "No," said craggy old Yrinx, who had been making the report.

"Good," Lilandra said, blinking again. Yrinx, who knew her well enough to understand the lazy look, glanced away hurriedly and busied himself with bringing up some other matter on his own notepad.

"Yes," he said. "Which leaves us—"

"Finished with this morning's business, I believe," Lilandra said.

"Ah," Yrinx said. "There seems to be one more matter."

She knew what it was going to be. She glanced up, allowing her expression to become less sleepy, and she watched Yrinx swallow. *Good*, she thought, carefully keeping her own face still.

Age tended to come suddenly to Shi'ar in general, after a long middle-age hiatus during which their physical appearance altered little. Lilandra often wondered idly at what point age would suddenly descend on her, most likely during or after one of these meetings, leaving her crest paled and brittle and her skin abruptly taut and drawn over her share of the family's fine bone structure. Not that it would make the slightest difference to her ability to reign over her empire, or in any other way.

Except that perhaps they would then stop asking me the question which I am about to hear once again, she thought. *Ah well. This meeting has gone smoothly enough, for once. It's only fair that they should take the opportunity to try to catch me off guard.*

Yrinx pushed his pad away, as if briefly having the grace to be embarrassed by the old familiar topic, then pulled the pad back again.

"It concerns—"

"The succession," Lilandra said in unison with him. Yrinx looked up, nervous, then looked down again and was silent for a moment.

"Say on, my lord," she said, surprisingly gently under the circumstances, for all that she wanted was to pick up her own pad and throw it at him. "I understand that sometimes forces drive you which seem even more imperative than my will."

Yrinx looked down the table at the thirty-odd other grandees, warriors, lords of the Shi'ar Empire, and other assorted noble and venerable figures. A lot of them got abruptly interested in the shining tabletop, or in their own information pads, or in the sunbeam making its way inexorably down toward the slender, fierce-faced woman at the far end of the table, her chin in her hand and her eyes, cool and thoughtful, resting on them, one by one.

"The good of your Imperial Highness's empire," Yrinx said, "must ever recall us to our duty. And even you, Majestrix, to yours. Though I understand your feelings on the matter—"

"Do you really, Yrinx?" she said softly. "How bold of

you. Do any of the rest of you have the presumption to say so?"

A silence. Yrinx, though, despite the way he was getting cushiony around the middle, and with his sagging, jowly face, was much braver than he looked. "Perhaps I might apologize for imprecision of language, Majestrix," he said, "and perhaps claim to sympathize with your Imperial Highness's feelings—"

"Oh, thrack," Lilandra said, though she did not raise her voice. Several of the more sensitive of her councillors coughed, and one of them dropped his pad on the floor and then nearly sprained himself trying to recover it without committing lese majesty by turning his face away from the Majestrix. He slowly sank straight down in his seat, disappearing under the table about to his nose, and Lilandra kept her face quite immobile so as not to show she was choking with suppressed laughter.

When poor Raith had got his pad again and himself once more upright and composed, Lilandra said, "My lords, I see we must go around this particular *ejh* chase again, but you will know better than to hope I will sit quietly and take it without protest."

"Majestrix," said her Imperial Chancellor-Major, further down the table, "your people find no fault with your reign. The Powers above us know you are the best ruler to grace the throne in many lifetimes—"

"Flattery," said Lilandra, not raising her head, just shifting her eyes toward him, "is unquestionably soft and pleasant to cuddle close to one; but it would be a foolish Majestrix indeed who did not know where it keeps its teeth. I do my job the best I can, Dravian, as my predecessors have done. Even my poor mad brother D'Ken was doing right, by his lights, though gods know he brought us enough disasters in his time. Leave off the compliments, and get to whatever new version of the old song you have for me today.''

"Majestrix, it has come time, it is long *past* time, to do something about the succession. For your people's sake.''

Lilandra sighed.

It was a problem which was not unique to her. Other stellar empires elsewhere had found other solutions to their difficulties of succession. Many were far more agreeable than the system to which she found herself forced to adhere.

What few of the other imperial families had to deal with, though, were the realities of being emotionally entangled with sentient beings of other species. Again and again, over the years, she had found herself thinking, in the slightly cockeyed alien idiom with which she had become familiar over time, *Why couldn't you have fallen in love with a nice local boy!*

But she had not. She had fallen in love with someone so many lightyears away that even Shi'ar data transmissions to that place tended to fizzle out in the middle. Such distances staggered the mind, and chilled the heart which she had thought, once, could not be chilled by such things.

Yet the love was still there, and would not be denied, even through the ironies associated with it—chief of them being that the man whom she loved understood duty too. Indeed, understood it so well that he would not leave his homeworld to come and live with her, no matter how he loved her. And, oh, he did.

Lilandra glanced up. These people knew her dilemma as clearly as she did. They knew she loved Charles Xavier, the head and heart of the human heroes known as the X-Men. They knew she desired no other consort. Yet they would not let it alone. Still they pressed her—and, she had to admit, however reluctantly, with reason. She knew, as they knew, that her people would not accept an heir born of any union between her and Xavier. Even though the Shi'ar admittedly had much reason to be grateful to various natives of Earth—not just Xavier and the X-Men, but the Avengers as well—that would not make her people in their many millions any more willing to accept a Terran as her consort. Their racial pride was simply too fierce. Any heir born of Lilandra and Xavier would be seen as a crossbreed, an inferior, and would most likely become a source of intolerable conflict down the line—civil war, or worse.

All this she knew. All this she knew her councillors knew as well. They were all quite clear about one another's rights and wrongs. But every now and then it was all dragged out again, and would continue to be, until it was finally dealt with.

Lilandra sighed again. "I wish my *people*," she said, bringing the emphasis down hard on the word as she looked around the table at the people she meant, "would look at the various other possibilities for establishing succession which I have suggested to them over time. The essentially nondemocratic nature of the form of primogeniture we practice continues to be a problem, and can backfire horribly. Just look at D'Ken, should evidence be required. I have been trying desperately to encourage our people toward reform of these traditions, but they are slow to move."

"They are slow to change something that works, Majestrix," said a voice from down the table. "Or rather, that works much more often than it does not."

At the sound of that voice, Lilandra sat up straight for the first time in some minutes. Now she was in no doubt as to why its owner was in the room.

"Indeed," she said. "Well, Lord Orien, we now understand your presence at a meeting where it was not otherwise strictly required. I should have realized much earlier on the agenda was about to be tampered with."

The Shi'ar to whom she spoke stood up. Eyes shifted to him. This was something of a breach of protocol before the Majestrix herself had stood to declare the meeting finished.

She did her best to look at him as if he were just another Shi'ar. Unfortunately, this was difficult. As her kind reckoned looks, he was handsome: big across the shoulders, narrow across the waist, muscular without overdoing the effect, and his face struck a pleasing balance between the sometimes too-aquiline features of some older Shi'ar families and the bland or less sculpted faces of some of the newer nobility. Today he was wearing armor, which was his right even in the Majestrix's presence, since he was a fleet commander in the field. She wondered a little at that, though, since wearing armor merely for effect was not usually Orien's style.

"The Majestrix is for once mistaken," Orien said, "though it gives me no pleasure to point this out." Breaths were intaken around the table, making a soft hiss. One did not contradict the Majestrix to her face. Most people took great care to use the roundabout language of diplomacy with Lilandra, both for courtesy's sake and for safety's. She had a temper, after all. However, Orien was not most people, which was why Lilandra was slightly annoyed with him, and had been even before he contradicted her.

He was the council's choice for her: *that* was the problem. He came of noble lineage. He was a brave man, a hero in the field, a more than competent commander, a strategist as well as a tactician. For all that, he was a scientist also, well read, well educated, something of a wit in a dry and understated way. He did not usually take liberties. He knew his status. He knew what people thought he should be doing.

He also knew what Lilandra thought of him, and of what people thought about him, and her, and said nothing to *anyone*. That, in terms of court intrigue, made him unusually dangerous. Hardly anyone can truly resist the opportunity to gossip, to breathe the most clandestine hint of what's going on in their minds to someone. Because of this aspect of humanoid nature, even in those species descended from avians rather than primates, many a court intrigue comes to nothing. In an imperial court, rather than attenuating, whispers amplify. But Orien did not whisper. He kept his thoughts to himself until he spoke them.

Which makes him more dangerous than usual, Lilandra thought, eyeing him as he stood there. There was nothing insolent in the stance, which was as well for him in her present mood.

"Well then, Orien," she said, "shall I send for a mind reader, or will you simply come out with it?"

"Gladly, Majestrix." He did not seat himself again, but gathered the eyes of all the others with his own, as if *he* were running this meeting. Lilandra put her eyebrows up, and for the moment said nothing.

"Astronomers of your people have found something strange going on in the core of the Sorosh galaxy," he said. "The same kind of peculiar stellar behavior as has previously been sighted and reported on in Akh'than and Or-sheh—"

She put her eyebrows down again, nodding very slightly to herself, and starting—for the first time today—to become really annoyed. He was brief, speaking on the subject, but Lilandra had heard something about this matter before.

She looked at the table for a few seconds after he had finished, and then looked up again. Her council watched her.

"Now if there is anything I do *not* need," Lilandra said gently, putting her hands flat on the table, but with a determination which made those sitting nearest her flinch, "it is someone trying to come at their desires by slipping around me the back way. This little faction for whom you're fronting has been pestering the Science Council for years now over this bizarre and apparently ill proven theory. The council has said there's insufficient evidence for concern about the matter, and that should be the end of it. I will not have some minor splinter group trying to fragment the consensus of a body on which we have come to rely for valid and useful information. Such actions can destabilize such a group, which, having taken long enough to get it working together correctly in the first place, I would take very unkindly indeed. I should not like to think, Lord Orien, that you were willing to tamper with the function of an established governmental body simply for your satisfaction in being able to help out some friends who you feel have been badly done by."

"I should not like you to think that either, Majestrix," he said, and this time it was Orien's voice which had a touch of anger in it. Certainly more than protocol allowed. "I would hardly come to you and make claims of the Science Council's error without evidence in hand."

"Evidence of what nature?"

"*This* nature," Orien said, and waved his hand.

In the air over the table appeared the image which had appeared in another cubic viewing tank, a third of the way around the planet, not too long ago. "The scientist who had this image fetched," said Orien, "has gambled his savings,

X-MEN

his reputation, and nearly his whole livelihood on making sure that you see it. He cares nothing for self-aggrandizement or personal power or any of the other things which people around this table will be too eager to accuse him of. He fears for our galaxy's continued life. These images are fresh, Majestrix, much fresher than the stale-light astronomy which is all they have had to go on until now. Something is deranging the nearby galactic cores. It must, at the very least, be investigated.''

They looked at the image for a while, all of them. Lilandra waved at it to rotate it for her better viewing, and though the image had been taken from a single point of view, the obedient and versatile holographic sensors had caught the mass and location of every star within view. The galaxy rotated before her, showing her the pale corridor into its heart and, buried deep in the pallid, pearly clouds there, the object which refused to manifest as anything but a point source of terrible power, an outflux of energy which should have been impossible even were there a particularly virulent black hole there. But this was no black hole, nor white one either.

''Well then,'' she said softly. ''I am no expert, but even I can see this is nothing normal. Whether it is dangerous—that must yet be explored.''

''I hope I have done well to bring this to the Majestrix's attention,'' Orien said.

Lilandra put her eyebrows up again as she looked at him, as he sat. ''That will yet be seen,'' she said. ''Others of a more cynical turn of mind will ask what you might really have been attempting to bring to the Majestrix's attention. Your suitability as a consort perhaps? But we will not speak of that now. If ever.''

Her councillors looked at her covertly. Lilandra reached

out, touched her pad. "Gladiator," she said.

"Majestrix?"

"Bring your colleagues to the council chamber. It seems we have a problem worthy of the attention of the Imperial Guard."

Nothing much further was said until they arrived. The dazzle of their uniforms jarred a little with the cool grays and beiges of the councillors. This was one of those years when clothing colors at court were more subdued, but the Guards' fashions obeyed other rules. There towered Kallark, praetor and Gladiator, in his scarlet. Behind him came Electron and Flashfire, one mostly in gold, the other wearing blue with gold burning in it. Sibyl in her rose, her silver hair flowing, Nightside like her shadow, the pallid blue shadowcaster's skin bound in flowing black. Mentor in his jacket, looking surprisingly casual next to the others, until you saw the implants, like a painful crown of steel. And Commando in his armor, as always a little apart, looking watchful.

Mentor, though, looked most thoughtful of them all, as his eyes fell on the image now rotating gently above the table. "Fascinating," was all he would say for several breaths, and then he looked over at Lilandra.

"Yes," she said, "to coin a phrase. My Guard, we have a problem before us indeed. We are nearly finished here; stay when the others go. My lords," she said, and stood, "the council's up. Go your ways. All matters we have discussed are to be handled as usual. The second-to-last matter—" She frowned at them, then. Frowned at each and every one in turn, in silent warning. They fidgeted as her glance swept around the table, missing only one man there, as if she were too angry to look at him at all.

"It remains as it has done for some time," Lilandra said

at last. "Should I die untimely, it would be your business to select a successor who would appropriately handle whatever problem would have caused my death, and what problems would follow it. I see no immediate likelihood of that. Should the Dark One snatch me out of my bed some night, there would be no guarantee that It might not do so with my heir as well."

She looked around at them, frowning slightly. "However, for the next short while, as regards the succession, you best not plague me about it. Else I'll simply go have myself cloned, and there'll be an end of it."

The sound of intaken breath went right around the table. "Majestrix," Yrinx said softly, "you know our people's feeling about cloning—after the excesses of several millennia ago. There would be the most violent reaction. You might be signing your own death warrant."

"And those of my ministers of state," Lilandra said, "who would be suspected of pressing me to that action? Who can say? So we had best all walk warily, would you not say so, my lords?"

They dared neither to move, for the moment, nor to look at her directly.

"Go now," she said.

They went. Orien lingered by his seat for just a moment, but Lilandra had turned her back. He left too, before the little time he lingered should become noticeable.

The room empty at last, Lilandra turned back to her Imperial Guard and gave them a wry look. "Well, my faithful ones," Lilandra said softly. "You will have guessed where they've left me once again."

"It is hard, Majestrix," Sibyl, the telepath, said as softly. "They cannot easily know the tightrope you walk, or how your needs affect what you do from day to day. They cannot know the stability which the presence of the loved lends.''

"Or which his absence subtracts," Lilandra said, looking up and out the window at the blue day, and the Shi'ar daystar burning in it, shutting the stars away. "No matter. Another time for that. I have a job for you, which I little like."

"You have only to order us, Majestrix," Gladiator said. "We would go to the empire's ends for you."

"Yes," she said evenly, "I know. And so you will, and past them, if I judge the distances correctly. See here."

She showed them the image Orien had presented to her council. A long time the Imperial Guard stared at it, all looking thoughtful. "I am no specialist in astronomy," Mentor said, "but—"

"Oh, the thrack you're not," Nightside said softly, and smiled a little as the others looked at her.

"Now then," Mentor said, "*language*, in front of our Imperial Lady." Lilandra smiled slightly. "I would say that is no recognizable phenomenon."

"Correct," Lilandra said.

"This is then the same phenomenon which has overtaken Akh'than and Orsheh?"

Lilandra blinked at that. "I had not known the data submitted to the Science Council was widely known."

"It is not, Majestrix," said Mentor, looking ever so slightly smug, "but some of us read more than the journals."

Lilandra found herself wondering, not for the first time, exactly how much of the written proceedings of her government and the hearthworld at large Mentor *did* read when he was at home. *If I were of a suspicious nature*, she thought, *I would make sure he stayed out on assignment almost all the time. Fortunately, I know my Guard to be loyal, for I am of a suspicious nature.*

"Well then," she said. "You will well understand the problem, I suspect, if what this small group of scientists has seen is indeed a phenomenon which is recurring serially. This is not something we would like to have happen to the core of our own galaxy."

"I should say not," Gladiator rumbled.

Or the next one over, Lilandra thought, but she was not about to speak the thought aloud. "My chief concern," she said, "is that, to judge by the datastream accompanying this transmission, the stars nearest what seems the center of the phenomenon are going nova and spreading it beyond what might be its normal boundaries."

Mentor nodded. "Like throwing a rock into a pool. The ripples spread. Ripples of energy which tip neighboring stars over into instability."

"Yes. What we must discover, quickly—for our own protection—is whether this process can be stopped. Naturally we will need to consult with the scientists—but at least one possibility suggests itself."

Sibyl looked thoughtfully at Lilandra. "Create a clear zone—a 'firebreak'—around the deranged area, which will stop its expansion and allow time for analysis."

"Have we the technology to carry out 'clearing' on such a scale?" Electron said, looking dubious.

"Surely not," Gladiator said.

"Almost certainly," said Mentor.

They looked at each other.

"It would, of course," Mentor said, "be technology about which the empire as a whole is . . . shall we say, ill informed?"

Lilandra looked at them all, then sat down in her chair again, looking down the length of the empty table. "It really is a good thing I trust you," she said. "Of course our empire possesses weapons we do not readily discuss, even among ourselves. Just the rumors of them are often sufficient." Lilandra remembered some casual Earth-born voice saying, in her hearing, *"The Stealth bomber is a terrific weapon. All you have to build is one. Then you tell your enemies that they can make themselves invisible—and that you've got* thousands *of them! Think of all the money you can save . . .*

She smiled at the memory, but quickly went somber again. "After the war with the Kree, some of our scientists devoted themselves to making sure that, should a race need to be snuffed out quickly—in an emergency—we could do so."

"What kind of emergency?" Nightside whispered.

Lilandra looked at her steadily. "Naturally we all pray we will never have to find out. But our scientists found a way to destroy, not merely planets, but stars. The method apparently damages the carbon-carbon fusion cycle in the stellar interior, making it impossible for it to continue. The star on which the weapon is used goes dark within hours, if not minutes."

"Your Highness is then considering 'pruning' some of those stars," Mentor said, looking at the rotating image, "to stop the spread of the apparent derangement toward the galaxy's core."

"At the very least," Lilandra said. "There are theories enough suggesting that a galaxy can no longer continue as a coherent body with its core blown apart."

"The question is," said Commando, very softly indeed, "can a government, or an empire, continue to cohere after it is revealed that it even *possesses* weapons of this kind? For possession can only imply the intention, eventually, to use them. On someone—"

"That," Lilandra said at last, "only the event will prove. Meanwhile, the weapons will have a healthier use than they might have otherwise. So close to the hyperenergetic area of a galaxy's core, few of those stars will have planets, and almost certainly none of them will be inhabited, so you may work without concern about harming sentients in the area. Take the fastest cruisers available to you, load the necessary weapons, go there, and 'prune' as many of the damaged stars as you may, while trying to get a look at that." She glanced over at the image. It had been cycling through its various magnifications, and now was showing the pearly clouds and that tiny point source. "I want to find out what that is, and to make very sure it will be no danger to our own galaxy anytime soon."

"We will leave at once," Gladiator said. "Majestrix."

They bowed to her, and turned to go.

"Be careful," she said.

Only Sibyl smiled. The others looked stern, determined. They headed out, leaving the single figure in the flowing robes standing in the pool of sunlight, which had finally worked its way down the table to her. Her shadow pooled around her feet for a long time before she finally followed them out, into a world that had abruptly become much more complex than usual.

many miles away—so many miles that trying to express the number any way except exponentially would have given anything short of a supercomputer a headache—a supercomputer was busy with matters nearly as fraught, and much more dangerous.

The Danger Room was dark. Storm stood there alone, breathing softly, listening to the darkness, to the wind. It was no wind of her summoning.

"Ready?" said the Beast's voice from above.

"I don't like this," Iceman whispered, but not so quietly that Storm couldn't hear. He was hanging over Beast's shoulder, looking down at the console with a dubious expression. "It's not a good idea for people to be in there by themselves."

"Storm is not by herself," the Beast rumbled, "either for the reason she would doubtless give you, that her goddess is with her, or for the other reason which should suggest itself, that you and I are here. And most to the point, she is not working alone with the computer, which is the true source of the Professor's concern. Until we are quite certain that the new, ah, software is properly run in . . ."

He let the words trail off. Along with Iceman, Hank McCoy, aka the Beast, had been one of the first five people Charles Xavier had gathered as X-Men. He had also been the first to depart. In the interim—during which he had served with the Avengers, the Defenders, and X-Factor before returning to the X-Men's fold—the original Xavier-programmed Danger Room had been replaced with new equipment, all of it Shi'ar-sourced. Some of it was positively baffling in its apparent simplicity. And then, just two weeks earlier, Xavier had received a software upgrade—which had been delivered in a small four-person craft that the X-Men also got to keep. The craft—which Cyclops had dubbed the *Raven*—was subsequently destroyed during a tête-à-tête with the Juggernaut. The Danger Room upgrade, meanwhile, was dutifully installed by the Beast, Charles, and Cyclops. They were now preparing to test it.

Hank McCoy would be the first to admit that he was of an old-fashioned turn of mind. He liked machinery that he could take apart and put back together again. He was equal to this task with any technology which Earth-based science had been able to produce. Alien sciences, though, were sometimes another story—and the new Shi'ar software was not exactly a mystery to him, but an annoyance. It was much harder than usual to take apart a supercomputer that looked like a small glass brick, in which the data was encoded in the changing energy-states and positions of individual subatomic particles. You needed unusually small tweezers to pick up an electron, and if you dropped one on the floor, the odds of finding it again were slim.

He sighed, reached out to the controls of the computer. The interfaces had been kept much the same as the original ones, but the jobs they did were much more complex than those of the old Danger Room controls. He thought with some nostalgia of the good old days when the threats were fairly simple physical ones, huge metallic arms that came out and grabbed you, weapons that fired. Now things were much less simple. But there was still an elegance to this form of intervention, even if it was a lot harder to trouble-shoot.

"Storm?" he said.

In the darkness, she chuckled. "Old friend," she said, "I can feel your concern. Yet we have been assured that this is perfectly safe . . ."

"That is exactly what the vet said to the tomcat before he—"

"Beast. Activate it."

The Beast sighed, reached out to the controls and stroked down them. This was one aspect of the new installation with which he still felt profoundly uncomfortable. It read thoughts directly from your neural pathways, apparently through your skin, and it translated those thoughts into action. Not necessarily a bad thing, as long as you knew you were always in control of your thoughts. *And who can say that for sure?* thought the Beast. After all, the *Raven* had similar software, and it crashed mainly because it received the thought *Go down* rather than *Land*.

Inside the Danger Room, the wind began to rise.

It howled.

Storm rose into it, smiling slightly. When you had ridden the elements for as long as she had, there came times when you were sure you could feel the influence of the One who stirred them. Half the time it was only your own illusion, of course. The shriek of rage of the cyclone, the contented silky sigh of high-pressure air as you slid through it, the snicker and crackle of ionization in a sky about to let loose with a thunderbolt—these were all expressions of the Goddess's moods, true, but almost never indicators of Her presence in the direct mode. She was rarely so obvious.

Over the speakers, she could hear Iceman and the Beast

expressing their concerns. "Do not worry," she called over the rising hiss of the air, "it would take a lot worse than this to hurt *meeeeee*—!"

The vacuum which abruptly opened up "underneath" her took Storm briefly by surprise. She fell—not the thirty feet or so which was the "real" distance to the Danger Room's floor, but a hundred feet in a second, two hundred, four hundred—toppling, struggling for control again, calling air quickly into the empty place where it had been before. But as fast as she summoned it in, it was sucked out again. It was the worst kind of clear air turbulence, what pilots called "shear CAT." It was caused by the sudden unexpected conflict of two weather fronts, impossible to detect until you were already deep into it, and then deadly. It was nearly impossible to get out of it without first dropping many thousands of feet in a paralyzed aircraft. Storm had long been a student of such brief phenomena. Almost always they *were* brief, the combined curl and trough of a breaking wave of air as it dissolved into small local eddies on its way across a continent, and they had rules and equations which they obeyed. But this one was roaring around Storm like an untamed beast, and she doubted that the mantra $TI = DEF \times VWS$ that the Beast had unearthed for her was going to do much good.

Still, she curled herself up tight while her mind sought command over the air around her. It resisted, which should have been impossible—but this, after all, was the purpose of the Danger Room, to train you for the unlikely, or the impossible, before you met it. Many of the X-Men's opponents had found ways to make the impossible serve their turn in the past. The only way to survive was to prepare for it. And it was all very well to be mistress of the winds, but if you did not closely study the theory behind your mastery, if you did not understand *what* you were doing when you exercised your powers, that mastery might come undone at a bad moment—or succumb to that of an enemy with less natural talent but a better grasp of the scientific principles involved.

Well, Storm thought, and fell and fell through the clear air, while under her the ground started, slowly, to grow closer. Or the illusion of the ground—but she refused to let herself think that way. In any case, the illusion was simply too good, too believable.

$TI = DEF \times VWS$, Storm thought in a slightly defiant mood. She thought she heard the air laugh Hank McCoy's distinctive laugh as it sucked itself away from around her again—a by-product of the telepathic interface of the new software, or Storm's own imagination? *Well, whatever it is*, she thought, *it still has to obey the laws of science.* DEF was the horizontal deformation of the air at a standard pressure level; VWS was an expression of the vertical wind shear between two pressure levels. *That being the case, what if I tried this?*

She threw all her concentration into strengthening the upper-level front, the one whose turbulence against its nether partner had created this terrible roil of air and the suction at the bottom of it which kept depriving her of the wind she needed to soar. More shaking, more roaring in the air around her. The wind tossed her around like a plaything. Storm clenched her teeth so that they wouldn't bang together, and threw more of her attention and desire at that upper-level front, doing her best to move its molecules faster, heat it up. *Increase its heat enough and the violence of the horizontal wind shear will increase too.*

It increased, all right. She fell, and was buffeted, and there was nothing she could do to keep her teeth from bang-ing together, and her own limbs from flailing her body painfully. The turbulence got so bad that it started to generate atmospheric gravity waves—unimportant to her present situation except that they made her dizzy, though if not stopped quickly, even after she stopped the turbulence, they would spread, and some other flier, some innocent pilot, would run afoul of them and rue the day . . .

The air was actively laughing at her now as she fell, and it whipped at her with a good counterfeit of real malice. It was no consolation that she knew it was all Beast's doing. She should have broken out of this long ago now, and was becoming embarrassed. *Some goddess they would have thought me in the old days, could they have seen me having* this *kind of trouble*, Storm thought, gritting her teeth again and pounding her consciousness into that layer of air above her as the ground started to get alarmingly closer. *Come on, heat up. Heat up.*

A tremor of response, no more. But it started to make the slightest difference in the speed with which she fell. Storm no longer felt like a rock dropping unimpeded through the air, but like a craft dropping down into the atmosphere from space, starting to feel the slightest bite of air against her wings, something she could use. The wind was turning slightly more amenable as the clear air turbulence lost some of its concentration, "distracted" by the shift in its temperature, being drained of its violence by the temperatures of the layers of the wave starting to become more similar. The eddies started to break, as a wave breaks on the shore. *Better them than me*, she thought, for the ground was getting much too close. She only had a few thousand more feet of altitude to work with, and she was near enough to terminal velocity at the moment.

For a few moments the turbulence got much worse. The

temptation to pull in on herself and drop just a few hundred feet more was strong, but stronger still was Storm's feeling that even this minor husbanding of strength would be a sort of surrender. She flung her arms and legs out, and with all her strength sought to impose her will on the intractable, shrieking air around her. She almost thought she could feel the Beast pushing back against her, resisting. She laughed into the wind, feeling his resistance slip. *It would be this way as well,* she thought, *for any enemy who found a way to turn my power against me, or duplicate it. Faced straight on, they could not help but fail. I may not be a goddess— but the wind—is—*mine*!*

And the resistance broke. The turbulence came undone all around her, its warp and weave of air and will now unraveled by the pulling of the one crucial string. The ground, rushing closer, suddenly dropped away below her again as Storm soared up, into the burning blue, laughing as she went.

Suddenly it was not blue anymore, but gray, the walls of the Danger Room again. She checked her soar, and hovered there in air which now was once more wholly obedient to her. Through the windows, Beast and Iceman were looking at her, and one other, seated a little lower than they: Charles Xavier.

"Well, Professor," she said, "how did that seem to you?"

"Masterly," he said, "though I still have some concerns about the software. Never mind it for now. Come out, Ororo, and take a look at the readings of the force you applied, and how they affected the forces arrayed against them. They will make for interesting study."

She smiled slightly and soared up to the doorway.

• • •

In the control room, Charles Xavier sat in his levitating "wheelchair," looking thoughtfully at the console, while the Beast lounged back in his chair as Storm came out and laid a hand on his shoulder. He glanced up at her. "Was I nasty enough?"

Storm raised her eyebrows. "Should you ever give up your present job," she said, "equipped with a copy of this machine, you could easily qualify as a stand-in for one of the more malevolent wind elementals in several African religions."

Beast smiled. The Professor looked up, wearing a wry expression, and said, "We must take care, then, that no copies of this machine make their way out into the world. Life is complicated enough already." He pointed at the console. "See there, Storm, the sudden access of power when you started to implement the equation rigorously, rather than merely attempting to control the wind 'by the seat of your pants'—"

A chuckle came from the far side of the room as Jean Grey wandered in, in jeans and T-shirt and with a mug of tea in one hand, glancing at Storm's uniform. "Care to define 'pants,' Charles?—so we can determine whether Storm was working by the seat of them?"

Xavier raised his eyebrows and sighed. "A moment's innocent descent into idiom," he said, "and see what happens. I leave definitions to you, Jean. Storm, you will want to investigate more closely this cerebral approach to the control of the elements with your power. Cerebro has access to the NASA and NOAA weather databases for the raw data and theoretical material you will need. Or you could simply use the Web."

Iceman snickered and got up. "Not with the access speeds around *here*, Prof. The local Net node takes so long to load a page, you'd think someone was painting it on parchment. Better stick to Cerebro, Storm.''

''Be that as it may,'' Xavier said mildly, ''more study would—''

''Charles Xavier!'' said a deafening and echoing voice, so suddenly that they all looked around. It was nothing to do with the mansion's warning systems, no bulletin from Cerebro.

''What the—'' Iceman said.

''Prepare to receive a transmission from the Majestrix of the Shi'ar Empire!''

They all blinked at that. The Beast looked accusingly at the console. ''Have we violated the warranty somehow, I wonder? Or missed a payment?''

''Hush,'' Charles said, and turned toward the source of the voice, which seemed to be coming from the center of the control room.

Storm and the others turned as well, to see the hologram form in the air in the center of the room. It did not quite stand on the floor, and the image, as it formed in a brief swirl and storm of light, was shot through with static artifact, sparklike fizzes and crackles too bright and sudden to be thought of as ''snow,'' unless snow could be set on fire. Within a few seconds, standing there and gazing around at them was the image of Lilandra Neramani, wearing a long, flowing many-colored garment, her arms folded, wearing an expression which suggested that she had been standing there for some time.

''Lilandra!'' Charles said. ''To what do we owe the pleasure? It has been too long.''

''So it has,'' Lilandra said, casting a look over her shoulder which Charles read as suggestive of some impatience. ''The conditions between our two galaxies are not terribly conducive to transmission today, no matter what my technicians may claim to the contrary. Look at the image quality—!''

''Phone companies,'' Iceman said under his breath. ''Go figure.''

''Yes,'' Lilandra said somewhat dryly. ''We can conquer a galaxy, but we cannot get the comm system to work. Some things seem the same all over. X-Men, I greet you. Charles—'' She smiled slightly.

The smile was not so slight that he could not read the meaning behind it. He worked to keep from blushing. ''It is very good to see you,'' Charles said, ''though I am surprised to see you not in the usual, ah, formal wear.''

Lilandra raised her eyebrows. ''Like anyone else in my position, I wear armor when I must,'' she said, ''but, beloved, it will be a difficult day indeed when I find I must wear it for *you*. Charles, I need you.''

Charles looked down at the arm of his chair briefly, considering that the situation was mutual. ''X-Men,'' he said, ''perhaps you would excuse us—''

''No need just yet,'' Lilandra said, the smile going dry again, ''for that is not the mode in which I speak at the moment. There are very strange things going on in the spaces nearby, Charles, and I require professional assistance.''

'' 'Strange' how?''

''You will have to bear with me for a moment,'' she said, ''while I divert all the available power of this transmission to the imagery which will follow. It was relayed to us from the Imperial Guard vessel which I sent to investigate a peculiar phenomenon in the core of the next galaxy over.''

Charles nodded.

The view changed, and the hologram abruptly expanded—so that another room appeared to superimpose itself right over the Danger Room's control room: the bridge of a Shi'ar cruiser. All around them instruments were flickering with lights that Charles's memory of Shi'ar command-and-control consoles suggested meant a state of high alarm. In the center seat sat Gladiator, erect and still, but his stillness did nothing to allay the sense of tension which seemed to emanate from him. ''—have done your bidding, Majestrix,'' he was saying, ''but to little purpose. In the past ten standard days we have 'pruned' nearly fifty stars in this area. At first we thought the pruning was having some effect, but that impression proved to be only artifact, of unknown cause. Our efforts have made no difference to the rate at which other stars in the area are going into flare state, or going nova outright. One of the imperial cruisers accompanying us got caught in such an event before it could make its getaway.'' Gladiator bowed his head. ''They will not come home again.''

Off to one side, the Imperial known as Mentor was working busily at another console. ''Majestrix,'' he was saying, ''this is the best image of the hyperactive area that we can obtain at the moment. Energy readings in that area are well beyond the ability of even my specialized equipment to handle, even at this distance.''

''Is it normal core activity, Mentor?'' said Lilandra's voice.

His laugh was somewhat edged. ''Majestrix, this is an area in which our research has suffered somewhat from neglect. We still know so little about the long-term activity of galactic inner-core areas that our ideas about 'normalcy' therein are likely to be erroneous simply from lack of close observation. In the sense that I have never seen or heard of stellar activity on this level, I would say it is not normal, but that would not be saying much. Imagery coming in now—''

The view shifted again. Clouds upon clouds of stars, backed by yet more clouds of them, stars in such numbers, and yet so distant, that they could only be perceived as dust. This filled the view all around them in brilliance until Charles's eyes started to water. But there was more there than mere scattered, cloudy light. The stars closest to the point of view looked most peculiar. At first Charles, conditioned by an early life's worth of Earth-based astronomy, thought that what he was seeing was some kind of photographic phenomenon, that the blurs and streaks of light associated with some of the closer stars were something to do with the viewing mechanism Mentor was using. But they were not. The stars' outer atmospheres were simply being blown off them, as if they were balls of fog succumbing to a high wind: cometary-looking veils and trails of tortured light blasted back and away from them, stellar photospheres being tattered away, attenuated . . .

They cannot survive, he thought. And Mentor said, ''If others we have seen are anything to judge by, Majestrix, these stars will not survive much more than a few days, perhaps weeks. See how the tails all point away from the one central spot—''

''I see,'' Lilandra said.

''Refocusing,'' Mentor said. ''New image acquired.''

Once again, the brilliance was severe enough to make everyone squint. Charles blinked, tried to resolve what he was seeing. It was more or less taken for granted that the core of any given galaxy was in a state of flux: stars sucking matter out of one another, one gaining mass at another's cost, matter gradually accreting into black holes or objects less describable. Here, though, was something very different, a strange dark zone, with a very small, blinding core of light inside it. Near it were three or four stars, their tormented photospheres all blasting and fraying away at high velocity from them and the core object, so that they redshifted visibly to the naked eye. There was actually some slight movement to be perceived there: the little core of ferocious light, like a burning needle seen end-on, was approaching one of the stars. Charles watched it, though his eyes burned and danced with afterimages.

It took a long time, like watching the moon rise. Slowly the needlepoint of light moved toward the star. The star's atmosphere grew more wildly excited, rippling like a curtain in the wind and blowing off in huge clouds of ionized plasma, any one of which would be sufficient to devour a whole solar system's worth of planets. The curtains of fire were gorgeous, shimmering in ferocious color, an apotheosis that an earthly aurora could only dream of, but they were also a star's corpse-candles, its last cries of light into the darkness. The needle of light grew closer and almost touched the star.

It flared, went nova. The point of light flared too. Everyone looked away. When Charles's eyesight had recovered enough to bear trying to look at anything again, he saw that tiny point of light hesitate, then slowly, slowly turn toward another star.

They heard the sound of Lilandra breathing out, just once, a sound ragged with shock. When she spoke, she had mastered herself again, but just barely.

"Very well," she said. "I will not lose you or any more of my people to this phenomenon, whatever it may be. Mentor, take whatever further readings you require for your continued analysis. Leave a probe there if you like. Then,

Gladiator, bring your ship back to the Throneworld immediately. I will be needing your presence there for other matters. Meanwhile, no shipping from the empire, civilian or military, is to enter that region again until I so order. See to it.''

"As you say, Majestrix,'' said Gladiator, bowing his head to her.

The image flickered out, leaving them all looking at their own control room again, and at the image of Lilandra, all sparked through with intergalactic static. "So,'' she said. "I think you now understand my concern about matters in our neighborhood.''

The X-Men looked at each other, and at Charles. Charles nodded, and rubbed his eyes for a moment, still seeing the little dancing afterimage, green against purple. The Beast, though, looked up and said, "Your definition of *neighborhood*, Majestrix, is novel.''

Lilandra nodded. "But realistic, Beast. From the point of view which takes in the universe as a whole, our two galaxies are the closest possible neighbors, and I believe I have reason to fear for yours as much as for ours. This effect—whatever it may be—seems to be heading out of that neighboring galaxy, and in our general direction. Should it come to us next, the odds seem high that it will come to you immediately afterwards. Leaving aside your undoubted concerns for the welfare of other sentient species in your galaxy, Earth's position two-thirds of the way out into a major arm would not be protection enough for it not to be affected within a relatively short time. I know that present projections suggest that your sun is rather unstable and has a better than average chance of flaring out within the next million years, but should this effect spread into the Milky Way, I would not give the stars in your local congeries better than a hundred or a hundred and ten thousand years before they—''

"Wait a moment,'' the Beast said suddenly, startled out of his usual courtliness, "the next *million* years? I thought we had at least *ten* million! Do your astronomers know something that ours—''

"Hank,'' Charles said, laying a hand on his arm. "Sufficient unto the millennium are the problems thereof. We will count the missing millions after we've dealt with *this:* since if we do not, a few million years one way or the other will no longer be an issue.''

For a moment more, then, Charles sat quietly, still trying to absorb what he had seen. Though there were forces which strode among the stars and destroyed worlds with this kind of abandon, the stars themselves were normally immune to, or exempt from, those forces' attentions. That immunity seemed to be over, though.

"What do you make of it?'' Lilandra said.

"I have absolutely no idea.'' Charles pondered a moment more, and then said, looking doubtful, "For this kind of thing, maybe you would be better served if you called on Reed Richards. His scientific know-how—''

Lilandra shook her feather-crest in a gesture of emphatic negation. "Charles, my people would not tolerate that, not after Richards's unwise involvement with Galactus. In any case, if I must ask for help, I prefer to request it from a source more congenial, to wit, you and the X-Men.''

Charles looked at her a little sidewise—an expression he had picked up from Lilandra herself, the sidelong look of the bird of prey, momentarily bemused by some strange new creature wandering across its field of vision, and focusing on it hard. "Well,'' he said. "We will have to discuss the nature of our intervention in detail, of course. But the immediate answer, I would say, will be yes. Let me consult with the team, Lilandra, and we will work out timings shortly thereafter, for pickup.''

Charles glanced around at the X-Men in the room, seeing Iceman's expression of interest, the Beast's much more intense one, the agreement in Jean's face and in Storm's. ''Meanwhile—'' Charles said.

''Meanwhile,'' said Jean, and whether telepathy or inborn tact was in play, Charles could not tell, ''let's leave these two to finish their call in privacy.''

She headed out: the other X-Men went after her, the Beast bringing up the rear and throwing a last glance over his shoulder at Lilandra's image. ''The next *million*—!'' he was saying softly as the door shut behind him.

Charles settled back in his chair and let it slip over a little closer to the hologram.

''One thing first,'' Charles said quietly. ''This hunch. Are you sure that it is not merely some barely sublimated desire to have *me* in the neighborhood?''

She gave him a look which could have been bottled and sold in major department stores as *Eau de ''Amused Scorn.''* ''Such motivations,'' she said coolly, ''are not to be attributed to the Majestrix of the Shi'ar.''

Charles simply looked at her. She looked back, very much on her dignity. It took nearly fifteen seconds before the dignity cracked, and her rare smile flashed out. So did Charles's.

''After all,'' Charles said, ''since when have you ever 'barely sublimated' your desires, Majestrix?''

''Well,'' Lilandra said, and her smile turned just slightly more wicked than usual. ''That discussion is one we should have on our own time, beloved. But for the moment there is likely to be little of *that*. My Science Council, who have for a long time been avoiding anything to do with the data that we see before us, now seem unable to get enough of it, and their concern over the phenomenon's causes is beginning to spread beyond official circles—even though no leaks have yet happened openly enough for me to take judicial notice of them. Soon, though, the news of what is happening in the next galaxy will start to get out, and I *will* have to react officially. I would prefer to do so by announcing that the problem is solved, thus reinforcing the notion in the subject worlds that the Throneworld is in control of this empire.''

The smile they shared turned rueful. Charles had few illusions about the manageability of an empire the size of Lilandra's, especially when the imperium had been welded together largely by force, and was held together by the threat of more. The ''marriage of worlds'' by which the empire had produced itself, Charles knew, was subject to the same kinds of problems that all other marriages were.

''I cannot promise you immediate solutions,'' Charles said, ''but we will certainly do our best to make them happen as quickly as possible—assuming we can bring sufficient power to bear on the problem. We are, after all, only human . . .''

''Rather more than that, I would say,'' Lilandra said. ''But then that has been the cause of too many problems lately, so I will not dwell on it.''

Someone said something, low-voiced, behind her. Lilandra looked off to one side, annoyed, and said, ''Charles, we are about to lose this connection, I believe. Technical problems. When shall I—''

''This time tomorrow,'' Charles said. ''We'll have the details sorted out by then.'' He paused, and then said, very softly, ''My love—''

Fzzt! went the hologram, and vanished.

Charles breathed in once, breathed out once, then slipped his usual gravity back in place. *Who knows who might have been listening in*, he thought, and went off after the others.

They were all in the big kitchen downstairs, where Jean had gone for a refill of her tea. Iceman, Storm, and the Beast had gone with her. They found Wolverine in the act of raiding the fridge, in the preassembly stages of a sandwich of staggering proportions. Gambit was there as well, muttering imprecations in Cajun French at the new espresso machine, which was making dismal gurgling sounds reminiscent of a free-floating case of emphysema, while refusing to emit anything remotely resembling espresso. "*Sacremént*," he said, shaking it gently, "dis t'ing needs a card trick or two."

"Is it still under warranty?" Iceman said from where he sat at the kitchen table. "Go ahead, give it one for me."

Charles slipped in and went over to the sink, got himself a small cup, then went over to the espresso machine. "You cannot coerce it," he said to Gambit, "it must produce results at its own speed."

"De story of life," Gambit said with only the mildest irony, as the espresso he had been waiting for poured itself into the Professor's cup. "Never mind, I have tea instead. So, what about dis job, Professor? Quick fix, you t'ink?"

Charles sat back with the espresso. "I very much doubt it," he said. "Leaving the problem at the core of the neighboring galaxy aside for the moment, I get a sense from Lilandra's manner that there are other problems closer to home. Perhaps not as, shall we say, cosmically dangerous— but more personally difficult to deal with. I daresay we will hear much more about that when we arrive."

" 'We' meaning who?'' Iceman said.

Charles studied the coffee, or seemed to. Sometimes you did not choose the makeup of a team so much for the sake of a given member exercising their abilities on the problem at hand; sometimes you looked at that team member's effect on the other members. As spur, encouragement, burr under the saddle, catalyst, one member could sometimes move the others to results which could not have been achieved without the total combination.

"To start with, I would say Wolverine. Cyclops. Storm— your experience with the spacegoing Acanti in former times, I think, will well suit you for this business." He paused, drank some espresso. "Gambit. Phoenix. Iceman— and also, I think, Bishop."

Gambit blinked a little. "Spacesuit work, boss. Not usually my cup o' tea."

Iceman raised his eyebrows. "So bring a thermos."

"Smart boy," Gambit said, though his tone was mild for the moment.

Wolverine, though, looked as if he agreed. "Charley, if this is some deep-space thing, what're you gonna need *me* for? Better I stay here an' mind the store. Besides . . ."

He trailed off, though with the expression of a man who knows he's dealing with an expert mind reader, and has little desire to speak his thought out loud—then overcomes the scruple. "The Shi'ar . . ."

"Their political system is hardly perfect," Charles said, "and we have had our difficulties in dealing with it before. But Lilandra is in power, and securely there. We should have few problems at the moment, she thinks, with the political infrastructure."

The others glanced at one another.

"Bets?" Wolverine said dryly.

Charles sighed and sat back in his chair. "Well, all right, Logan; when did the course of our dealings with the Shi'ar *ever* run smooth? But at the moment we have other concerns. We cannot leave them to handle this problem alone. They have already exhausted their own resources, and when that news gets out, the resulting reaction, I gather from Lilandra, is likely to be very destabilizing."

"In the next galaxy over—!"

"This 'pool' is smaller than you think, Logan," Charles said. "A rock dropped into it will produce ripples quickly enough here. Instability in the Shi'ar Empire is to be avoided at all costs. The sooner this problem can be solved, the less serious the instability will be rendered."

"You mean, Charley," Wolverine said, "that as soon as we pull her chestnuts out of the fire—again—she'll be safe. Somethin' of a priority for *you*, I'd gather."

Charles breathed in, breathed out. "Do you believe I would spend the X-Men's resources for that reason only?" he said. "Do you *really* believe that? If you do, Wolverine, I put it to you that you are in the wrong place, and have been for some time."

The others looked at Wolverine, saying nothing.

Logan glowered at Charles, also silent for a good while. "Well," he said finally. "You've already committed us to this thing. I guess it's in a good cause—I'd hate to have the galaxy come undone, or whatever the hell's happenin' over there."

"I intend for us to find out," Charles said. "Meanwhile, I will be in contact with Lilandra again about this time tomorrow, to confirm our travel arrangements. We should all be prepared to head offplanet immediately thereafter. I shall notify Bishop, and call Cyclops back from his shopping trip. Cerebro will have kept copies of the transmission, for anyone who wants to review the material Lilandra sent us. Hank, I wouldn't mind a session with you later, to go over some of the theoretical possibilities and possible explanations for what we saw.''

''I wouldn't mind it either,'' said the Beast genially enough, ''because at the moment, I can't think of any. Perhaps some of that espresso will help.''

''Can't guarantee it'll do anyt'in' for cerebration,'' said Gambit, who had finally gotten the machine to disgorge another cupful, which he handed to the Beast. ''Should raise your pulse pretty good.''

Charles smiled slightly, and looked over at Storm. ''So— one last loose end to tie up. Were you satisfied with the workout?''

''Very much so, Charles,'' she said. ''The new software offers many possibilities, I would say.''

''Yes,'' Charles said, ''it does.'' One by one he saw their eyes turn to him, catching something peculiar in his tone. No matter. They would find out soon enough. ''I look forward to continued exploration of them. Meanwhile, a sandwich would not go amiss. Wolverine, have you left any of the sliced roast beef?''

Logan shook his head. ''Sorry, got the last of it.'' He got up once again to poke around in the refrigerator, paused for a moment, and came up with a package, and a look of narrow-eyed amusement. ''Plenty'a baloney here, though . . .''

Charles smiled a little more thinly, and headed his personal transport over to the nearest counter to get the bread.

Three

The Shi'ar shuttle came slipping down quietly the next evening, right under the nose of NORAD and the various other agencies around the world that monitored Earth's airspace. When a sudden occluded front appeared over Westchester and caused thick fog to completely obscure the sky and slow down the tail end of the rush hour, meteorologists were slightly surprised—normally you needed a much warmer day to produce that kind of result. But no one else was much concerned, for it didn't last long—no longer than it took for the shuttle to land behind the Xavier Institute and pick up its passengers.

Five minutes later, it was slipping up and away through the outermost layers of the atmosphere, the fog was clearing, and the NORAD computers remained none the wiser.

The cruiser was waiting for the shuttle out beyond Mars's orbit. This was a good spot right now, since Mars was close to the sun and the only other thing which could have spotted it, the Hubble Space Telescope, is always kept from looking anywhere near the sun, lest it fry its optics. The rendezvous took little more than a minute. The cruiser buttoned herself up and took herself outward, leaving the solar system for the space outside Pluto's orbit, where it would be safe to open a stargate.

Stargating has certain advantages, Charles thought as he and the X-Men left the shuttle, were greeted cordially enough by a Shi'ar officer, and escorted up to the lower bridge level, the observation deck. *For one thing, it means you do not have to spend five hundred thousand years between leaving for a meeting, and* having *the meeting.* On the other hand, there were drawbacks. The long-term effects of stargates on suns could be debilitating, though the risk was deemed necessary under the circumstances. More prosaically, there was no time to stare out the windows into the long silent blackness and think. During the slightly mad times the X-Men had spent in company with the Starjammers, right back at the beginning of Charles's involvement with Lilandra, the view of endless darkness had been one of the great consolations. This kind of travel was interesting enough—from the technical viewpoint alone, you could hardly call a Shi'ar cruiser boring. But at the same time, the speed with which it moved, and the commonplace certainty with which it came out on the other side, made a ride in a stargating cruiser about as emotionally stimulating as a ride on a crosstown bus.

Charles sat by one of the floor-to-ceiling windows, now, looking out at the only brief glimpse of the inextinguishable starlight that he was going to get on this run. He was thinking of the philosopher who had claimed in one of his essays that the ''annihilation of space'' had done more to make people less human than almost any other change in the twentieth century, ruining their innate sense of scale and connection to the physical world around them. He had concluded, ''If people really want to annihilate space, why don't they simply crawl straight into their coffins? They'll find little enough space there.'' At the time, Charles had discounted the line as the momentary annoyance of a man who should have known better. Then he had begun to have doubts. Now he found himself wondering if the stargates were not merely a symptom of something that had gone wrong with the Shi'ar, but possibly a cause. When you could cross half a million lightyears in a breath, suddenly one of the universe's basic defenses for its inhabitants was eliminated: the vast distances which made war between worlds logistically difficult, usually almost impossible. Intraspecies war had become easy for the Shi'ar. As a result, they had peace—mostly—and relationships with the worlds around them that ranged from resigned cooperation to cringing servility to utter, scalding hatred. *Would isolation be better?* he thought. *Or are the benefits worth the terrible losses?*

He felt the presence behind him, looked up. Jean Grey was standing there, looking out past him as well. "A touch of alienation, Charles?" she said.

His smile was slight. "Hardly that."

"You smell trouble out that way," she said. "So do I."

"From this distance?" He was alarmed.

Jean shook her head, watching as they slipped past Jupiter's orbit, seeing the gaudy belts slip into shadow, the roguish moons wink as they passed on into the dark. "Of course not. The crew—" She raised her eyebrows, folded her arms, and did not look at the various Shi'ar officers up above them on the command levels of the bridge, studiously and efficiently doing their jobs. "They're nervous."

"Any details?"

"No, and I'm not going to violate their privacy without need, as you well know. Just a general atmosphere of concern, trends that have been making them twitch. Apparently the usual intrigues at court have been getting—a bit more concentrated. That much I've already picked up just from overhearing chance gossip."

Charles sighed. Lilandra had been empress a long time

now, but there was no reason to expect that matters would ever get easier for her. The business of rule only became more complex, more treacherous, with the passing years, as courtiers became disaffected, people became dissatisfied with positions they saw themselves as being stuck in, or dissatisfied with the positions of others whom they perceived as incompetent. They would then move to change the situation, often in the deadliest manner possible. The old officer's toast came back to Charles: "To quick advancement and a bloody war . . ." Wars were in no short supply around the Shi'ar Empire, but advancement in the imperial court often did not come in shapes everyone approved of, and that was where the trouble could most easily start.

"Gossip," Charles said softly. *We will have enough of that to deal with shortly, Phoenix*, he finished telepathically.

As if I don't know, she thought back at him. *Well, "sticks and stones," Charles. Have you got anything to be ashamed of in your relationship with Lilandra? I thought not. Then let them say the worst. Slights and insults are like drinks: they affect you only if you accept them.*

He breathed out, a sound not quite a laugh. Storm slipped up beside them, and he looked over his shoulder at her. "That covering fog was nicely done earlier, Ororo," he said.

She smiled, shrugged her cloak back. "The Shi'ar could have done it mechanically—but when there is weather to be handled on my home planet, *I* will handle it. Stargazing, Professor?"

"Of course not," he said, and endured the wry look she gave him in return. "Well. It is hard to avoid—even for so little a time. It brings the memories back, doesn't it—that view?"

Storm raised her eyebrows, breathed out. "Too many of them, perhaps. And it waits, that darkness. Sooner or later, it will be the last thing that all of us see . . ."

"Sounds a little grim, Storm," Jean said mildly.

"Grim? No. Why fight a natural process? Nature is on our side—if we could only see it that way."

Wolverine lounged up beside them, looked out at the darkness for a moment. "Pretty," he said at last. "How soon do we get there?"

Charles and Jean exchanged a look. "Almost immediately, I would say," said Charles.

"Ah, the transitory splendor of the cosmos," said Beast from behind them.

Iceman came up beside him and snickered. "Transitory? Oh, I remember, the sun's going to blow up early."

"Hardly that," Hank said, glancing benevolently over at the young man. "Such a view should provoke far different concerns in the educated man."

"Hafta *get* an education first," Gambit said softly, coming down the stairs from the upper level.

"We must all start somewhere, Remy," said the Beast in a good-humored tone. "Granted, the goal seems more difficult to reach than usual, these days. I have a lovely set of books you should examine when we get home, Bobby. The 1916 edition of the *Britannica*, the one with the engravings. Look under the headings for 'Eschatology,' and don't neglect the quotes from Pascal. 'The eternal silence of these infinite spaces—' "

" '—*m'effraie,*' *ah oui*," Remy said, unimpressed. "You ask me, he didn't get out enough, dat boy. Never went out past de streetlights, I bet. Nervous disposition, him and Proust both. Two of a kind, all dat *thé tilleul,* and all dose *madeleines*—on one big sugar rush all de time, don' know

61

how dey ever got any serious t'inkin' done. You ask me, Hank, you stick to philosophers wit' some *muscle*. And a more balanced diet.''

Hank's mouth fell open. Charles had to cover a smile. The others were less successful. Gambit had never struck any of them as the type to read the great philosophers—or philosophers of any kind—and this little diatribe served to remind them that, no matter how long the Cajun had been an X-Man, there was much about him they did not know.

Before the dumbfounded Beast could articulate a reply, the annunciator system said, ''Passengers please note: Gating in five minutes.''

The ship around them suddenly seemed to get a bit quieter as the engines scaled back their demure hum, preparing, Charles knew, to energize the ship's gating circuitry. There would be no power left to waste on drive when the gate was being kept patent—no more, anyway, than would serve to push the ship through and lock the gate down after it.

The starfield stabilized as they slowed to a crawl just past the orbit of Pluto. The view from the observation deck was wide enough to let Charles and the others look at the way they had come. In the distance, the sun was a point of light no brighter than Sirius would seem from Earth; the heart of the system no brighter than many another bright star.

Off to one side, a faint glitter of light betrayed the cruiser's deployment of the stargate mechanism, a small silvery pod no bigger than the shuttle that had picked them up. Charles watched with fascination as it apparently split in two, longitudinally; then split again, and again, no longer a solid shape, but an angular silvery rim around an empty space. The rim grew wider, the space larger, as the framing elements of the gate divided themselves again and again. Finally, they were looking at a geometrical figure with perhaps a hundred sides, hanging there in the dark.

It stabilized itself for a few breaths until it hung absolutely motionless in relation to the cruiser. A trickle of light ran around the structure, so faint that it might have been reflection from the distant sun.

Suddenly, the trickle of fire became a river, and flared into unbearable brilliance. A circle of actinic light scribed the darkness. Through it, stars were visible; but they were not the stars that should have been visible there.

"All we need now is something to draw some lines with," Iceman said, "and then we can make a big X—"

Remy made a small exasperated noise, and turned away. Slowly the starfield behind them began to move again, at the barest crawl, as the Shi'ar cruiser edged its way toward the stargate.

"Wouldn't like to think what would happen if there was some kinda malfunction right about now and we banged into that," Wolverine said thoughtfully. "Thing'd probably cut us right in two."

"I trust there are any number of failsafes in place," Charles said.

"Yeah, well, I'll just keep my *skepticism* in place for the time being, if it's all the same to you, Charley," said Wolverine, "because all this nice shiny Shi'ar technology can't be doin' 'em that much good at the moment. Otherwise this little trip wouldn't be necessary, and I'd be takin' that trip upcountry I been promisin' myself."

"Hell hath no fury like a mutant whose vacation plans have been put on hold," said the Beast. "But, Logan, I thought you told me that you could not leave until your camping skillet was reseasoned. A matter of some days yet, you said—''

''Yeah,'' Wolverine growled, ''and if Rogue hadn't burned her blasted eggs in it and then left the thing soakin' in the sink the whole day—''

There was a flare of light as the cruiser passed the gate, then darkness again—but not the same darkness. The galaxy in which the Shi'ar homeworld lay was richer in variable stars of all kinds than the Milky Way, especially in short-period cyclic variables. Where stars in the spaces neighboring Earth burned steady, anywhere out of atmosphere, they did not do so here. The stars swelled and shrank and swelled again, pulsing; some slowly, some quickly, some so slowly that the change could not be perceived without long and careful observation. But the skies of Throneworld space were utterly unlike any sky in any other galaxy nearby, and had a glory all their own. Some said that it was this extraordinary vista, a starfield that seemed to breathe like a live thing that had led the Shi'ar out into space in their youth as a species.

Once again, Charles and the X-Men looked out at that pulsing, burning darkness, and Charles did not have to look around at their expressions to know how mixed their feelings were at seeing it again.

''Planetfall in twenty minutes,'' said the annunciator.

They coasted in through the Throneworld system, passing planets which once had been uninhabitable, but now, thanks to extensive terraforming done centuries ago, were densely populated. Some of them, further out in the system, had small, extra ''suns'' strung around them in geosynchronous orbits. Others, closer in, had surfaces largely covered with domed cities, and had been extensively rebuilt underground. All these worlds were merely support planets for the one at the optimal orbital position around the Shi'ar homestar, a yellow G5 primary in benign mode for the moment, its great golden shield of a disk devoid of sunspots. Swiftly and gracefully, the soft hissing hum of the cruiser's engines came back up to the proper note as it locked down the stargate behind it. The cruiser dived toward the Throneworld, coming at it from the night side, which glittered with great concentrated urban areas, more like lakes of light than pools or rivers. Up over the terminator they came, dropping into the atmosphere, the whine of air against the cruiser's body growing.

"I would have thought we would have taken the shuttle down," Bishop said.

Charles shook his head. "No," he said, "we'll apparently land directly at the Imperial Palace." He did not share the other thought going through his mind: that all imperial vessels except the very biggest were built to be able to land onplanet and overawe the locals. The Shi'ar could afford to waste the design time to produce such ships, and the energy to power them. It was another unspoken message about the species which had troubled him before.

Landing took very little time. The curvature of the world bloomed up around them. A planet less world than city, the forests and parks and lakes and seas were very much in the minority—such things wasted space, and for the ruling world of an interstellar empire, what was *needed* were offices. Not that they were not grandly housed. Soon the vista from the observation deck was one of nothing but towers, spires, architraves, colonnades hundreds of feet high, gracefully arched viaducts carrying one or another kind of rapid transit—the delicate, spandreled architecture of a winged race, always striving upward against something that bound its wings.

Down through the towers the cruiser settled, toward a single silver-gray spot among the thicket of buildings. It landed in front of one of the largest of them, a great complex of interconnected edifices which loomed larger and larger as they dropped down, until they finally settled before it and saw plainly how the cruiser was dwarfed by even the smallest of the porticoes that gave onto the landing pad.

Charles sighed, having had his sense of innate scale restored, and not feeling much the easier for it. He turned his hoverchair around to find one of the polite, rather straight-faced Shi'ar officers approaching them.

"This way, if you will, Professor," said the officer, a handsome blond-crested man in the ornate and stylized armor of the Shi'ar upper ranks. His eyes rested on Charles with an expression very difficult to read. Charles had long since learned, as Jean Grey had under his tutelage, to school his curiosity at such times. He did not mentally probe the man. But the sense of sheer dislike from the officer struck him as, if not strictly inappropriate under the circumstances, then perhaps a little odd. He had never met this officer before, would probably never meet him again. The sense of animus seemed overstated.

"Thank you, sir," Charles said, putting the thought aside for the moment, and followed him. The X-Men came after. Charles did not need to see, but did feel, the look that Storm and Jean exchanged behind him. Plainly Jean had picked something up as well, and what it was, there was no telling without asking her. It could wait.

They left the cruiser and made their way out into the day of Shi'ar, coming down a long graceful ramp which left them on the spotless pavement in front of the immense portico of the Imperial Palace.

At the top of the stairs that led up to the portico, a single figure waited.

The effect was illusion, of course, abetted by the fact that she was positioned so far above them. Behind her would be the usual array of lackeys, courtiers, civil and other servants, and all the other hangers-on associated with a great ruler. But Charles hardly cared. He only had eyes for that single shape.

Up the stairs they went. There were no fanfares, no noisy announcements. As far as Charles was concerned, that was just as well. For his own part, his heart was beginning to beat as hard as if he could walk, instead of being confined to an infernal floating wheelchair, and as if he were walking up those stairs as well—bizarre how the further up them you went, the more of them there seemed to be. *Never mind that*, he thought. *There she is. Oh, there she is. Calm down, now, Charles. It's not as if you're a teenager, for pity's sake.*

They came to the top of the steps at last. There she was indeed, dressed more formally than the last time they had spoken, in another of the long flowing gowns, but over it a handsome and close-fitting breastplate and overskirt of the flexible, impenetrable armor which the Shi'ar favored, and holding one of those improbable-looking, multiedged staff-arms associated with the office of the Majestrix. Regal and still, she stood and watched them come.

"Hey, get a load of the Swiss Army can opener," Iceman said softly as they approached.

Sssh, Jean said straight into his mind, so forcefully that he winced a little.

When they were within a few yards, Lilandra handed off the imperial halberd to one of her aides without even looking, went straight to Charles, and reached out to take his hand. He took hers and looked at her. She returned the look, but said nothing audible to him for the moment. He did the same and restrained his smile.

"X-Men," Lilandra said then, "you are very welcome to the Throneworld. Will you meet my cabinet, and then come in and find your quarters and rest a little before we have a briefing about the present situation?"

They murmured agreement. She turned, beckoning them along behind her. "My Minister in Chief, also holding the office of Minister of Peace at the moment," she said, "Yrinx." A craggy man with a gray crest speckled with white bowed to them. Charles looked at his face and received one of those instant impressions that a telepath quickly got used to and learned to trust: *A rock, solid* . . .

"Dravian, my Chancellor-Major." A slender man, calm eyes, difficult to pin down. Something changeable about him, a pleasant affect. *Thoughtful. But very guarded—as if he wants no one to know what the thoughts are about.*

"Eleth, my Minister for the Exterior, and head of the Science Council." A tall, still man who simply bowed, and did not reach out to take Charles's hand, though the others had, in respect for what they knew to be an Earth custom. This man had a sense of near-unbreakable reserve, and (to Charles's surprise, though again he didn't probe) an extremely strong shield around his random thoughts. Charles looked up into that dark lean face, and started to become very curious about what was going on behind it.

But only briefly; Lilandra's voice distracted him again. "Ollikh, the Minister for Interior Matters." *Secret police*, said Charles's memory of having met someone in the position during his time spent with Lilandra shortly after she took the throne, when he believed the X-Men dead. But apparently the job had changed hands. This was not the little, round light-haired Shi'ar man he remembered, but a tall, striking woman, statuesque, with a truly astonishing high dark crest and a face much more aquiline than usual even for the Shi'ar. The eyes in that face were cool, calculating, and at the same time absolutely feral. They fastened on Charles with a look he had once seen on a falconer's goshawk—a locking-on of eyes like targeting radar, preparing for the strike and the tearing which would follow momentarily. And yet she smiled, an affable expression that sorted oddly with the terrible intensity of the eyes and mind. *This will be the one who monitors, among others, the empire's elite assassins' corps*, thought Charles, *and probably other organizations so secret that no one but she and Lilandra know about them*. It occurred to him that this woman, knowing his intimacy with Lilandra, might find that intimacy a threat in the political sense. Yet she smiled.

He greeted her, and Lilandra said, "Fander, my Minister for Preparedness." *Preparedness for what?* Charles thought, and greeted the lady cordially. The cordiality was returned.

For her next meal, maybe, thought Jean, from down the receiving line. *She could drop a few pounds, if you ask me.*

Ridiculous, Charles thought. *Cattiness isn't your style, Jean. Your nerves are showing.*

Absolutely.

She would say nothing more about what was troubling her now, not even silently. Lilandra continued, "Telliv, my Minister-Coordinator for Communications." An elderly gentleman, sharp-eyed, somewhat age-bent, who looked at Charles out of a face and a mind full of thought and laugh lines. And on and on it went, through thirty or forty more names, faces, sets of impressions. Charles filed them all away effortlessly for consideration later, greeting each politely enough, and carefully keeping his eyes away from the one whom he most wanted to look at.

And at last there were no more courtiers or ministers or coordinators left, only the members of the Imperial Guard whom Charles knew of old, and greeted like the sometime allies they were: Gladiator, Flashfire, Electron, Nightside, and Sibyl, a little behind the others as always, watching, smiling slightly.

Charles introduced the X-Men in turn, then turned to Gladiator. "Kallark, where are Mentor and Commando and Quake?"

"On assignment, Professor—they will join us later." *Did Gladiator look a little uncomfortable?* Charles wondered, then put it aside.

"It is a fine enough day, Charles," said Lilandra then, "but let us go in and get your and your people's quarters sorted out. Armor may have its advantages, but the sun is beginning to roast me inside mine."

Lilandra's staff all laughed dutifully at the joke. She looked around at them and lifted a hand in a gesture of dismissal. It was astonishing how all those ministers and cabinet members simply melted away from the portico like snow in the sun, heading into the cooler shadows of the palace. Nonetheless, Charles had no doubt that he and the X-Men were still being carefully watched.

"Well," Lilandra said. "That could not be dispensed with, I'm afraid. Charles, my apologies." She bent down over the personal transport and gave him a gentle hug. Charles smiled a little wryly. It was very gracious, very public and empresslike. But she too knew they were still under scrutiny. Later, things would doubtless be much different.

"And to all of you, friends," Lilandra said, "apologies as well. To keep you out here to be inspected like so many cattle brought to market, when you've come so far to help us—" She shook her head as she led them in through the large doors, to the interior of the palace.

The Beast smiled slightly. "Unfortunately," he said, "government so often has its own imperatives, Majestrix. But we do understand. Now if, as I think, you were going to show us somewhere to freshen up?"

Lilandra chuckled. "You'll be housed near my own quarters," she said, as the Imperial Guard preceded them through the huge main hall, where a statue of Sharra and Ky'thri and their eagles stood, arched in the first passionate and violent embrace of the Marriage. "No point in having to walk half an hour to a meeting and half an hour back."

Charles thought privately that it was also a fine way to keep a close eye on the guests. Not that Lilandra would herself feel any such need, but there might be those in the cabinet who did. "Before we abandon ourselves entirely to small talk," he said, as they came to one of the large turbolifts which served the main hall, and Kallark stepped inside it to check it, then motioned to Lilandra that it was safe, "have there been any new developments in the next galaxy since we spoke?"

They all got into the lift; its doors closed, and it then appeared to hold perfectly still while the Great Hall and other interiors of the palace poured past it, sometimes horizontally, sometimes vertically. The sensation was a little odd, Charles thought, but entertaining. "There have," Lilandra said, "in that stars continue to be destroyed at an increasing rate by whatever the agency is that has been destroying them."

"You still don't know what it is?" Iceman said, sounding surprised.

"Not clearly, no." Lilandra looked slightly put out. "Though our science is advanced indeed, we are not yet omnipotent, and even we cannot completely change the nature and basic engineering of our off-the-shelf technology overnight. Considerable modifications have had to be made to the new probe we are sending into that space, enough to keep it from being destroyed while it sends back its data— let alone while it gets its readings. The amount of energy being released in that area is much greater than any galactic core would normally produce—not as much as if the core had gone quasar, perhaps, but otherwise unimaginable enough, and deadly to machinery not prepared for it. The probe's sensors are having to be 'hardened'; a source of some annoyance to the techs, you may imagine, who devoted much time and pain to making them as delicate and sensitive as possible."

The turbolift stopped and let them out in a wide hallway that was much less sparely decorated than most of those which they had passed—administrative parts of the building, Charles guessed. Again Gladiator and the rest of the Guard stepped out and checked the hallway, then gestured to their mistress that it was safe for her and the others to leave the lift. "When will the probe be launched?" Bishop said as they went out into the hall.

"Within the next couple of hours, I'm told," Lilandra said, leading them down the hall and through a wide, arched doorway. "The techs are anxious to get it out there, but I have suggested that more time taken over the 'hardening' may pay off. Better to get it right the first time than have to send out another probe and waste more valuable time which might be spent in analysis."

She paused, gestured around her. The room inside the doorway was a large, comfortable lounge area with floor-to-ceiling, glass-steel windows opening onto a wide terrace. From it there was a view down into the little park at the center of the Imperial Palace, a vista in which slender trees faintly clouded with the first turquoise buds and leaves of spring embraced a little lake where small black waterfowl swam and sang. "There are personal quarters for all of you opening off this central lounge," Lilandra said, "and if any of you find them unsatisfactory, tell me and I'll call in the architects. The food dispensers over there remember your likes and dislikes, for those of you who've used such dispensers in the past. If you haven't, or if your tastes have changed, tell the machinery so; it should have no trouble coping. Storm, the whirl-bath—what was the Earth name?"

"Jacuzzi is one, I believe," Ororo said gravely.

"That was it. I had my people work on the basic design. You may find it improved. But also I remember you mentioning about the lack of pressure in the shower. You shouldn't have to make it rain in the bath suite again."

Storm chuckled. "Majestrix, I promise to restrain the meteorological manifestations. At least until I have had time to check on your plumber's handiwork."

And Lilandra turned to Charles. "Do you think," she said, "you might spare me half an hour or so, Charles? There are some private matters I would like to discuss before the formal briefing."

"Certainly, Majestrix," he said, trying hard to control his pulse, at least a little, enough to keep his heart from jumping out of his chest. "I am at your disposal."

The discussion took more than half an hour, as Charles had rather suspected. But that didn't matter, as it would be a while yet before the scientists and attendees would be gathering for the main briefing. Charles strongly suspected this was because their Majestrix had told them that she would let them know when she was ready for them, and not a moment sooner. *There are*, Charles thought, *certain advantages to wielding imperial power.* His own thoughts, however, were on certain other advantages, such as, after so long, being able to stroke again, and as often as he liked, the very soft, excessively delicate feathers just above the nape of Lilandra's neck—and hearing her sigh when he did it.

There was much more on his mind. Most specifically, the utter reassurance of finding that, despite all the separations, all the distance, all the piled-up zeroes of empty miles and empty nights, nothing had changed between them. She was still the only one for him; he was still the only one for her. Strange it was, how even when they found time away from their duties and responsibilities to talk, there was always part of each of them, way down at the bottom of each mind, which refused to completely believe that the other was still in love. Yet such a simple thing as a touch of the hand would set all the doubts to rest. *How long will it last?* he thought. *Oh, please, let us not solve this problem too quickly.*

The thought was heretical, and he pushed it aside, embarrassed at himself. When he looked over at her again, she was gazing up at him, and she said, "Charles, I have to tell you—"

"It's imperial business, isn't it?"

"Yes, but—"

"And must we talk shop? Even now?"

"Charles, beloved, you know me better than any other," she said. "You know when I'm worried, I can't refrain.

There are so many lives that have already been destroyed by this trouble. There have been massive evacuations of our own people over in that galaxy—those whom we have been able to evacuate, anyway. For some, we were not in time. Something else for which I shall have to answer to the Two at the end of days.'' She glanced away.

"Lilandra,'' Charles said, "you can't seriously take that weight of guilt on yourself.''

"But I can,'' she said, and sighed, a sound of utter weariness. "I was remiss in not investigating the situation more closely. I cannot choose but admit that. Yet at the same time, *you* know how it is. There are simply not enough hours in the day.'' She leaned her head back and looked at Charles, upside down, oblivious to the humor of the effect. "And you do have to believe the people you work with, after all. You cannot be questioning their motives and results every five minutes, or their effectiveness becomes so drastically curtailed, they might as well not be there at all.''

"The jargon for this in my culture at the moment is micromanagement,'' Charles said. "If it's a vice, we have it too, and I agree with you that it's far better avoided.''

"Well,'' Lilandra said. "The moment's trouble is bad enough; but, Charles, there's worse.''

"I'm sorry,'' he said. "Stars in the neighboring galaxy are blowing up or going dark at the rate of about one per hour, and there's *worse*?''

"The succession,'' she said.

"Oh.''

Lilandra sighed again. "Charles, they are beginning to task me about this on a regular basis. There are a couple of candidates—well, one—who under more normal circumstances would certainly be an excellent suggestion for consort. Unfortunately I do not want him, or any of them. Yet sooner or later . . .''

Charles said, "Sooner or later, they are going to make you take one."

"Or they will kill me for refusing," Lilandra said.

Charles looked down at her in shock. She looked up at him, still upside down, and smiled. The sadness of the smile, and the cockeyed position, made a heartrending combination. "That had not occurred to you?" she said. "In the present state of the empire, nothing strikes me as more likely."

"Oh, but surely the Imperial Guard would never allow such a thing to—"

"They are hardly omnipotent, Charles. All it takes is a moment, as you know. A second for someone to look in the wrong direction—or the right one."

"The right one? Certainly you don't think any of *them* could ever be suborned."

She gave him that sad look. "Charles, even the X-Men have been 'turned' on occasion, struck deep to the mind or the heart by one enemy or another, though fortunately such evils have been temporary. Why would the Guard necessarily be immune? And they might recover, but the effects on me might be less temporary. Indeed, for whatever force would try to handle my Guard so, that would almost certainly be the intended result."

They lay quiet for a few moments, thinking. Charles gathered Lilandra a little closer, if that was possible. "So, this potential consort . . ."

"I will not have him. You are the only consort I want. And the one, of course, whom I cannot have." This time a little bitterness had crept into her tone, and it trailed off in a laugh with a harsh edge to it. "Charles, have I ever told you how I once considered conquering Earth?''

He looked at her in astonishment, and then laughed too. ''Your sense of humor, love, can take the strangest turns.''

''I was not joking, Charles. Certainly Earth's solar system is of interest to us, and worth protecting, for its position in that arm of your Milky Way, in terms of the interstellar trade and attack routes it straddles, all unbeknownst to its people. But Earth is not a subject world, more's the pity. If it were, I might have less trouble making you consort in word as well as deed, if you follow me. I was *that* close to taking a fleet and explaining to my cabinet that there was a threat to your spaces which could most easily be offset by our taking control of them, and of Earth, of course. No one would have argued the point with me, and once we had the administrative end of things sorted out—'' She broke off and sighed again. ''Well, it would have been a poor repayment for your help in the past, as I well knew. So I thought better of it. But it was very close.''

Charles's amazement had passed the chronic stage and was becoming acute. ''It really *is* a joke,'' he said, rather desperately.

''It would have been a good one,'' Lilandra said, rather wistfully. ''I kept thinking about what your face would have looked like when you found out. Rather like it looks now,'' she added, and grinned, a mischievous look.

Charles shook his head. ''I may be the most powerful mind on my world,'' he said, ''and a mind reader, but there are times when even I cannot tell if you're serious.''

She simply looked at him.

''I love you,'' Charles said. ''More than I can tell you, Lilandra. Words, even thoughts give out. I am yours. But as for being consort—''

''I know,'' she said, suddenly serious again. ''We could

make a case that the recent troubles you've had with Magneto and Sinister and the growing mutant situation are likely to cause the destabilization of Earth—''

"They *have* caused it."

"Better yet. I can have a fleet ready to leave in the morning."

"It will leave without me. Lilandra, we have other things to think about."

She sighed, and leaned back against him. "Well, it was worth a try. Charles, they simply will *not* accept you. Even subject races are higher in my people's estimation than Earth-humans. But I will not be forced into choices I cannot stomach, and I will not conjoin for policy—no matter how many of my ancestors have done so—out of laziness, or out of fear of confronting the existing power structure. I will yet bend my people to my will—for my lifetime, at least. After that I assume I will no longer care what they make their rulers do." She smiled again.

"Let that day be a long day off," Charles said softly.

"Well, we will see. Meanwhile, I will hold them off, and the other evil days which besiege us, as best I can. Speaking of which, that meeting is really going to have to start soon, or they will talk about us behind our backs."

"They are talking anyway," Charles said.

She raised her eyebrows as she got up out of the bed. "Is that direct experience? Or simply an educated guess?"

"Telepaths rarely have to guess," Charles said. "It's as if the corridors are rumbling—a low-grade low-frequency rumble. Disquiet, concern, anger."

He broke off, feeling, ever so briefly as he considered it, more than anger: one thread of a pure rage, directed at Lilandra like a spear. Then it was gone, sealed over beyond tracing.

The sweat broke out all over Charles, as if he had seen someone point a weapon at her. She was in the act of reaching for an underrobe, and now she looked at him, but not with surprise. "Hatred," she said.

"How can you feel that?"

She shook her head, the feathers stirring gently. "In my position," she said, "soon telepathy is not required to sense such. This position attracts hatred as a corpse attracts the scavengers, Charles. When I feel it, I welcome it. Shortly thereafter it almost always reveals itself in a form which I can more clearly detect, and deal with, for hatred is mostly irrational. It is the cooler passions I dread in those around me, the reasoned killers. I must have some of them around, to carry out my policy, but they are the tools most likely to turn in my hand."

She sighed. "Come on, Charles, let us put in an appearance. If we can help whatever is ravaging the heart of the poor galaxy next door, that will be well enough for today. Our own problems will have to wait."

"But not forever," Charles said, and prepared to follow her.

In the central lounge, Storm was stretched out on one of the big couches, like a section of a circle, which surrounded a comfortable work area with tables and chairs set around it, and one of the Shi'ar imaging tanks in the middle of it. Wolverine, over by the windows, was pacing and looking darkly thoughtful. The others were off exploring the amenities of their own quarters, or relaxing.

"A good shower?" Bishop said to Storm, coming up behind her.

"More than adequate," Ororo said calmly. "About gale force nine. I must commend Lilandra's plumbers." She glanced at the imaging tank, with which the Beast was playing. "Anything yet?"

Hank threw her a glance. "Two million channels and nothing on," he said.

"You mean you *still* haven't found the Cartoon Channel?" Wolverine said in an incredulous rumble. "Maybe this really *is* a civilization after all."

"Philistine," the Beast said amiably. "The Road Runner has lessons to teach us all. Cheerfulness. Persistence. The usefulness of loud noises in the face of one's enemies, or better still, behind their backs. Ah—"

He broke off suddenly, and the image in the "tank" area over the desk changed suddenly. It filled with darkness, and light, and a spear of darkness at the light's heart—

"Is this what we were seeing yesterday?" Storm said, getting up to look over the Beast's shoulder. "It's much clearer."

"No, dear lady," Hank said, "these images are newer still. The Shi'ar computer security is not all they imagine it to be. Or rather, perhaps they don't expect us to be quite as far along as we are in understanding their systems. These pictures, I believe, are just now coming in. Or so I judge by the fact that the images seem not to have been processed. This is 'raw' light, strictly in the visual spectrum. Infrared will be interesting, and X-ray . . ."

He trailed off. The image had an odd look to it, partly because of the lack of background stars. The sensitivity of the probe had been so curtailed by the technicians that only the very brightest objects were visible in scan. Even so, the light of the stars in the foreground had a flat look to it, like that of the sun seen through a dusty atmosphere as it sinks toward the horizon. The effect only served to enhance the detail of the stars' tormented shapes. This close to the core of the galaxy, any star might be expected to look a little perturbed, somewhat stretched out of shape by the closeness of its neighbors. But most of these were being compressed by immense gravitic and other forces into grossly oblate spheres and ellipsoids, some of them so alarmingly that it was hard to see how they were maintaining their integrity at all. Through the faintly visible hyperexcited gas and plasma filling the space between them, that dark cone was once again moving toward another star.

Storm leaned over the Beast's shoulder, and on the other side, even Bishop, usually so erect and self-contained, leaned in a little and stared in uneasy fascination. "What exactly is happening out there?" he said softly.

"We are going to find out firsthand, I fear," said Hank. "I think it will need to be very soon. Look here."

He tinkered with the tank's controls for a moment. The point of that cone swelled, filled the tank until nothing else was there but the darkness, and in the background, the diminished brightness of the writhing star at which it was pointing. And one other thing. Beast lifted a claw, indicated it. "There."

Storm shook her head as she squinted at the tiny point of light inside the cone. "Beast—how *big* is that?"

He eyed the tank speculatively. "Scale can be problematic with this equipment," he said. "But the resolution is good. I would say—not much bigger than half a million miles."

Bishop's jaw dropped.

Storm's eyes went wide. "Hank—in the Goddess's name, how are we supposed to deal with something *that* size?"

The Beast sat back in his chair and studied the image. "The question's a fair one. But don't look to me for answers. At the moment, I fear I'm fresh out. And I very much wish I *had* found the Cartoon Channel.''

''Surely they would be doing the new 'alternative' cartoons this time of day, Hank,'' said Charles Xavier from the doorway, as he slipped into the lounge in his transport and Lilandra followed him, having changed out of her breastplate affair into a plain sleek black coverall which made her look both handsome and subtly threatening. ''You never cared for those.''

''Their palettes are bad,'' the Beast said, and stood to greet Lilandra. She had walked straight over to the tank, and was examining the image in it carefully.

''Is that the best they have done this time?'' she said.

''It is the best image I have found so far, Majestrix,'' said the Beast, as the others started to drift in from the surrounding rooms at the sound of her voice. ''Doubtless they have others which may produce better results when processed.''

''For their sake, and ours, I hope so,'' Lilandra said. ''X-Men, the Science Council and various other interested parties await our pleasure. Shall we go see what they have to offer us?''

They went out.

The table in Lilandra's briefing room was completely surrounded by nervous people with anxious eyes, who rose to honor the Majestrix as she came in. No chairs were vacant except for those which had been left so for the X-Men, and there was a space for Charles's transport to tuck in, though he noted that this space still left room for Lilandra to be regally isolated down at the end of the table.

The big tank in the center of the table was displaying an image similar to the one the Beast had been looking at earlier, though some of the "grain" had been stripped out of it, and the resolution slightly refined, so that the tiny point of light in the head of the cone of darkness actually had some slight definition to it, a suggestion of a pinching-in at the middle. Charles, as he took his place at the table, peered at the image and wondered why, even when it was still so ill defined, it would somehow still have had the ability to make him feel nervous, even if he had not known what it was doing. There was an unnatural look to the thing. Not supernatural—Charles had some small experience with that type of phenomenon, and this didn't have that mystical "feel." But somehow—the thing he was looking at seemed, simply, not *right*.

"My lords, gentlebeings, let us get started," Lilandra said as she seated herself. "What is the status of the affected galactic core at this time?"

"It is being destroyed wholesale, Majestrix," said Eleth, the Shi'ar who had earlier been identified to Charles as the head of the Science Council. "The largest stars are going brown-dwarf at an incredible rate. The smaller ones are simply being shredded—torn apart, and their energy released into neighboring space, where other stars are being affected by such unusual amounts of X-ray and other high-intensity radiation into the core environment. Several stars have exceeded their Saff'hein radii and are collapsing into black holes. This by itself would not be unusual in a galactic core. Many have such at their hearts—but none have so many. Even should the immediate destruction of stars stop, the core might implode into a so-called 'black cluster.' If it did, there would be gravitic effects on our own galaxy in a very short time. They might be sufficiently powerful to force the two galaxies, ours and what is left of that one, to begin to coalesce."

The people around the table looked at each other in shock. Planetary systems were created in great plenty when galaxies passed through one another—but almost all the systems which might exist at the beginning of the process would be destroyed.

"We will have to put a stop to this, then," Lilandra said, "and I want to hear your best suggestions as to how. First of all, do we know what that point source is?"

"What it *looks* like," Eleth said, "definitely." He touched one of the controls on the pad in front of him.

The image in the tank shifted, going mostly dark. It was concentrated on the head of that cone of darkness, panning along its length.

"This appears to be an energy-gathering field," said Eleth, "of the kind which some spacefaring species use to gather free-floating radicals and atoms for reaction mass for their ships."

"A Bussard ramjet," the Beast said. "A primitive sort of drive-feeder, but effective enough."

Eleth nodded at him. "The field appears to be directed backwards, not forward as would normally be the case for a vessel's propulsion. It may be that the released ambient energy has become more manageable once it has passed a million miles or so from the former star which has released it. Here, though—"

Just inside the tip of the dark cone, there was that bright shape again. The image pushed in and in on it. It started to take form. Charles saw that the pinched-in appearance of its middle was an illusion. There were actually four parts to its body at equal angles to one another, and all joining at the center like an asterisk. The shape burned white with energy and it moved, the separate arms or limbs squirming slightly, as it hung in space.

There was silence down the table. Then, suddenly, Wolverine growled, "It looks like some kinda bug."

Eleth blinked. "Majestrix," he said, "according to your instructions to take whatever other actions seemed wise in this regard, we duplicated our probe three times, though without the sensor 'hardening,' and stargated the duplicates to positions where they could reexamine stale light from the other affected galaxies, Akh'than and Orsheh. Here is an image from Akh'than, after the collapse of its core."

The picture in the tank shifted again. What they found themselves looking at more resembled a very open globular cluster of stars than a galaxy. The core was almost entirely missing. Only a single point of light lay there, very dim.

"Is that a star?" Storm said, sounding doubtful.

"Madam, it is not. It has a very low energy output indeed. At first we mistook it for a dwarf somewhere between the red and brown stages, but it was much too big for that. Other pictures"—the image flickered—"show movement and change in the other remaining stars, but not in that object. Then—" One more image: flick, and the little dim light was gone.

"Did it collapse?" said Jean.

"Yes," Eleth said. "But the gravitic readings are peculiar. Not dense enough for a dwarf, of any kind. And look at this image, somewhat later—"

Flick. Darkness at the galactic core, or in the space where it had once been. But something else was in the field of the image as well. Some kind of geometric-seeming shape. The image animated. The shape moved, blueshifting as it went.

"Self-propelled," Eleth said. "The sensors show it to be rapidly approaching lightspeed. In later cubes it vanishes, suggesting that it has gone superluminal. The last cube—"

He brought it up. The image had gone fuzzy, and blue around the edges.

"Cherenkov radiation," said the Beast. "Not very prolonged. It went to lightspeed fairly quickly."

"Not a natural phenomenon, then," Lilandra said.

"Natural, yes," someone said from down the table. Charles glanced down and saw an earnest face under a shaggy graying crest. "But not a phenomenon, Majestrix. The *problem* is that we have been treating this object like an astronomical object. Which it is not. It took one of my team who started out in medicine and changed disciplines to realize that the energy readings we have been trying unsuccessfully to decipher are not merely light curves and power outputs, but life signs. This is not a phenomenon. This is a creature."

There was some stirring around the table at that. Even Charles, used to periodically being astonished by cosmic or near-cosmic situations, had to take a long breath and think about it for a moment.

"Not just a creature. *Creatures*—"

"Are we sure?" Charles said. "Might we not be looking at several different stages of a life cycle?"

Silence fell around the table as people looked at each other.

"Lord Eleth," Charles said, pushing his hoverchair back away from the table and moving further down for a better look at the tank, "the images themselves are all coordinated as to time, are they not? Well then. This one first, which had previously been thought to be going quasar, and underwent great periods of star destruction like the one we are watching most closely at the moment. That stopped, and it entered a quiescent stage. Now, *that* lasts for a good while, to judge by the time signatures on the images. Then suddenly the object collapses, and another one, different, seeming much more lively in terms of energy, is seen leaving the area. Have we seen a hatching of some kind?''

"If we have," the Beast said, sounding dubious, "is the object presently in the next galaxy, then, the 'larva,' preparing to pupate?"

"Possibly. Eleth?"

Lord Eleth thought about it. "It could very well be. For the second galaxy from which we obtained new images—" He touched his pad again, changing the view in the tank. "Let me run them forward quickly. There, see the stars flaring out? The resolution is too poor on these images to see the dark cone, but the pattern of destruction, working its way into the hyperenergetic area of the core, is the same."

"Run them backwards instead," Charles said.

Eleth blinked, then did so. The corridor of darkness working its way into that galaxy's heart sealed itself over. Very slowly, its stars drifted backwards—

—and one of them, about halfway out from the core, went nova.

"There," Charles said. "I know optical resolution is poor—but does that star have such a moving source of energy near it as we saw blueshifting in the last set of images?"

Eleth worked over the pad a little, focusing in on the nova. "Nothing shows visually," he said, "but—No, wait. Something very faint, it will not come up optically at this range. But the gravitic signature is there, and the blueshift—"

They could see the trace of movement in the image in the tank, though not what made it. "There," Charles said. "Not blueshift. Red, heading *toward* us. Toward the star, of course, in reverse. *From* somewhere else. That may be your life cycle, Lord Eleth. A mobile form—call it the 'adult' for the moment. It inoculates a 'host' galaxy, planting some form of reproductive material in a suitable star. The 'egg' hatches out, and begins eating its way to the core of a galaxy. There it devours stars, absorbing energy—for whatever reason, perhaps simple nourishment—and after ingesting a threshold amount of energy, it goes quiescent. It 'pupates,' to keep the analogy going. It waits, gestates—and then hatches out as the adult, and goes in search of a place to reproduce itself again.''

There was a lot of uncomfortable shifting around the table, the kind of reaction one sees when a large group of people become significantly more nervous than they had been when they started.

"Horrible," said one of the Shi'ar.

Gambit sat back, his arms folded. "We all gotta eat," he said, perhaps more philosophically than necessary under the circumstances. Charles resisted, with difficulty, the urge to cover his eyes and sigh.

"Maybe so," said Cyclops. "The thing I'm worrying about—is this parthenogenesis we're seeing, or sex?"

"You better *hope* it's virgin birth," said Wolverine. "Otherwise you got geometrical progression to deal with. Two, four, eight, sixteen . . ."

Charles felt like shuddering. "One is quite bad enough," he said.

"It might more likely be parthenogenesis," said the Beast, "if only because if this *was* sexual reproduction, the rapidly increasing numbers of these creatures would soon make it impossible for them to reach a galaxy to reproduce. Someone else would long since have been there and done the deed, 'eaten' the desirable, energetic core area, and moved on. At any rate, all we see right now is one, and it is probably the immediate descendant of the one in the images from Orsheh.''

Eleth nodded slowly. ''Majestrix,'' he said, ''the evidence supports the conclusion.''

A long silence. ''We are going to have to destroy it,'' Lilandra finally said, barely above a whisper.

''*Oui, madame*, but who bells *le chat*?'' Remy said softly from down the table.

''A fair question,'' Charles said. ''Majestrix, the X-Men do indeed have tremendous power—but I do not know if every mutant known, all gathered together and working in concert, could affect *that*. We are, I think, in very deep over our heads.''

There were some mutters from further down the table. ''Not that we will not do our best,'' Charles said. ''We are at your disposal, as I said. But I confess that when one is about to attack, finding a weak spot, or a useful way of attacking, is usually first required—and at the moment, I am not sure what that might be.''

Lilandra was nodding. She looked down the table at Ollikh, the beautful, feral-eyed Minister for Interior Matters, and nodded. The woman inclined her head to the Majestrix slightly, then turned her attention, and those unnerving eyes, on Charles again. He felt like shuddering, and restrained the impulse. ''There are some avenues we have been exploring,'' Lilandra said, ''which I wish you to investigate with Ollikh after this meeting. We will discuss afterwards how effective you think they may be.''

''Majestrix,'' said one of the others down the table. *Lord Dravian,* Charles thought, *her Chancellor-Major.* ''This is exactly the point I wished to investigate with you. The developments of recent days have been giving some of our allies pause—''

''I do not know why that should be,'' Lilandra said quietly, ''because if, as I think, you refer to the 'starcracker' technology, the existence of which has recently been revealed to the Science Council and the government as a whole, news of that should not have yet been released to the allies. I know that technological information is the most ephemeral of all kinds, and the hardest to keep secret, but in a situation where its release will be as potentially destabilizing as *this* would, I can only assume that if the allies have found out anything, someone has leaked it.''

A deadly silence fell around the table.

''Someone here?'' Lilandra continued, and smiled a very slight and brittle smile which fortunately only lasted a second. People avoided it as they would avoid looking at the sun. ''Of course not. Pardon a Majestrix's naturally suspicious nature.'' She turned to Dravian again. ''You are thinking—or the others of whom you speak are thinking—this: If the Shi'ar have developed such a thing, have been stockpiling it—we must assume they have, since the Guard went straight out and used it with so little difficulty—then *who* were they planning to use it on?' ''

Silence. ''Well,'' Lilandra said, ''who *knows*? Our empire has only lasted as long as it has because various Majestors and Majestrices have been prepared to be *prepared*—for *anything*. Anything they could think of, and things they could not think of themselves, which their faithful advisors imagined, and prepared for. Who knew what menace might come out of the night? We have enemies enough. As it is, *this* seems more a natural disaster. *Seems,* my lords and ladies—and if I find out it is otherwise, our revenge will be sudden and complete. The species which forged this weapon, if it is one, will wish it had never come forth from the Two, or whichever other god is responsible. Meanwhile, we will investigate how best to stop it."

Lilandra paused. "Avend," she said, "here and now and before my council, who have been less help to you than they might have been, partly because they thought they were so best serving me, I apologize. The funds you spent to arrange that this matter be brought to our attention will be reimbursed immediately, and you have our thanks."

"Majestrix," Avend said, bowing where he sat, "all I wanted to do was serve the truth. This is better far than anything I deserve."

"I think not," Lilandra said, "and mine is the only opinion on the subject which matters at the moment. Meanwhile, we have no time to waste on recriminations or the assignment of blame. I strongly advise you, my lords of the council, not to engage in the usual infighting after this setback to the conduct of 'business as usual' in the bureaucracy of science. Get on with your work. Any further obstruction of this research will not be taken kindly. But one thing. Avend—or Eleth, or any of you who might have an answer—*where has this thing come from?*"

"That is an answer we may never find," said Avend. "It handles energy on such a scale as does no other creature in all the spaces we know or have heard of. But the universe is wide, and just because we have never seen something before, that's no indication that it's not native. Some have suggested that this creature might possibly be native to some other universe or dimension. That might be true, but would not make much difference to our present problem if it were. And again, proof is likely to be hard to come by, especially if we are successful in destroying it."

Lilandra nodded. "A last matter. I desire to know which

of your staff it was who made what may be the most vital connection—that this was a life form.''

A small Shi'ar woman down the table from Avend raised her hand a bit timidly as the other members of her team looked at her. "I, Majestrix," she said.

"This is Irdin, Majestrix," said another Shi'ar. To Charles's surprise, the speaker was the tall young fair-crested officer whom he had met on the cruiser that fetched them. "She is Avend's research assistant, and mine, at the observatory."

"Well, indeed," Lilandra said. "Irdin, you have our thanks, and our congratulations. We will be wanting to hear more about your other researches, Avend, and your other work with your team, when we have more time to discuss them." Lilandra stood up. "Go your ways, my lords. I will call you again after the X-Men have investigated the matter I desire them to look into. Tomorrow, I would say. Meanwhile—you are dismissed with our thanks."

Everyone got up, bowed, and started leaving. The blond officer worked his way over to Lilandra, bowed to her. She turned to Charles, and said, "Charles Xavier, Lord Orien."

"We have met," Charles said.

Lilandra looked at him in surprise. "You have?"

"Lord Orien was kind enough to do courier duty," Charles said. "It was he who picked us up on Earth and brought us here."

Lilandra gave him a very strange look indeed, and turned to Orien. "It was kind of you to do so, my lord, though I must confess some confusion as to why you were doing duty which might have been assigned to someone more junior, someone with fewer pressing calls on his time."

"The X-Men are considered of value to the solution of this problem," Orien said, "and it would have been unfortunate for the empire, and for your intentions, Majestrix, if anything had happened to them in transit. If this''—he glanced at the tank—''is some kind of threat against us by some old enemy, any word of the X-Men's intention to intervene on your behalf could have put them in danger. Under the circumstances, I thought it best to supervise, and see that they came here safely.''

Charles thought he had never heard such good sense stated in a voice so absolutely without revealed emotion, or without any expression which would suggest that the person speaking *believed* anything he had said. What the mind behind that face was doing, Charles could doubtless find out very quickly—but without better reason, he had little wish to push past the cool expression and the radiating dislike. All he could do, at the moment, was bow slightly from his sitting position to Lord Orien, and say, ''Your concern for the empire, and the wishes of your Majestrix, does you credit, Lord Orien.''

It was a little dry. *But then*, Charles thought, *I don't have to show my hand either. Why must he be so handsome?* An unworthy thought. He tried to put it aside. He failed.

''Your research assistant,'' Lilandra said, ''and Avend's. Would you object if she were promoted to research of her own?''

''Not I, nor Avend either, Majestrix,'' Orien said, ''but she would, I believe. She enjoys her work with us, and has said often enough that she feels it will be a while before she'll be ready to go her own way. I would respect that. She's young yet.''

''Very well. But, Orien—make sure she feels adequately thanked. She has done us all a good turn, perhaps saved more lives than she could count if she did nothing else right through the rest of a long life. Let me know if there is anything she needs.''

''Majestrix, I will. Professor—X-Men—'' He bowed to them too as they began to gather around Charles, then took himself away.

Charles looked at Lilandra, picking up a great sense of unease from her.

Paranoia grows on one, Charles, Lilandra said within herself, knowing he would hear. *I did not send him. I had no idea it was he who had gone on that errand. Plainly someone in the government thought it was a good idea that he should have time to get a good look at you. I do not like this. . . .*

Her thought trailed off. Charles waited. Lilandra finally sighed and said aloud, ''Well. Paranoia . . .''

''Even paranoids,'' Charles said, ''have real enemies.''

She had no immediate answer to that.

''Meanwhile,'' Wolverine said, ''what about the eagle-lady givin' us the eye over there? She was sizin' us up like a plate of hamburger.''

Lilandra looked over at Ollikh, who was lingering near the end of the room. ''Let's go with her,'' she said, ''and you will find out why.''

Four

Ollikh was short on conversation. She simply watched them come with that hungry interest Wolverine had commented on, bowed to Lilandra, and said, "Majestrix, shall we?" Lilandra nodded.

With the Guard ahead of them, they made their way to another of the lifts which served that wing of the palace. This the Guard checked, then stepped aside; Lilandra, Ollikh, and the X-Men got in, and the doors shut without the Guard following. "Is this safe?" Charles said to Lilandra, very softly.

Ollikh turned that bright, brittle regard on him. "My own people are watching now, Professor Xavier," she said. "The Majestrix is in no danger. But at present, the Guard are not cleared for the area to which we are headed. No one is, except for the Majestrix, myself, and the specific scientific staff who have been working on the device I am going to show you."

"Device—"

"You will see momentarily," Ollikh said.

The turbolift doors opened. They followed Ollikh down a hallway that, while shining and bright in the Shi'ar manner, was much smaller and lower-ceilinged than was normal in other parts of the palace. She came to the end of the hallway, a blank wall, and stood there. After a moment, the wall went away.

Iceman looked around and chuckled. "Didn't I see this on *Get Smart* once?"

They followed Ollikh through into a large, seemingly empty space, with slick metallic walls and ceiling and floor. The room had no features—lights recessed into the ceiling as bright panels, nothing more. Ollikh walked up to another bare wall, waved a hand at it. It suddenly became much less bare, and a slanted console appeared jutting from it, perhaps ten or twelve feet long, glittering with lights and indicators. The whole business simply materialized in front of her, as if it had simply beamed in.

"The material we keep here," Ollikh said, "is sufficiently classified that we routinely hold it in quantum flux—a dematerialized form which cannot be remanifested without the presence of a mind containing the correct brainwave patterns and associated physiological signals. My mind is one of those. Yours all will be as well."

The hum of restrained power filled the room; very low, very soft, and, to Charles's mind, slightly deadly.

"Well, madame," said the Beast, "despite the resemblance of this impressive array to the Wayback Machine, I must say it reminds me more strongly still of some instrumentation which came with the present installation of the Danger Room."

Ollikh gave him that thoughtful, bird-of-prey look. "Yes," she said, "I know you have some of that technology, since it was I who authorized its release to you. Part of the heart of your Danger Room as it now stands is based in the noumenoextensor, which among other things allows your thoughts to directly affect the room, and the physical effects it produces. Not exactly new technology, but we have been sitting on some of the implementations of it for a while, uncertain whether use should actually be made of them. Now, however, the Majestrix assures me that we have no choice.''

Charles sighed. He had expected to hear about something like this when the Danger Room upgrades first arrived. When the present crisis hit, he realized that he would see it sooner than he'd originally expected, so he was more grateful than ever that the Beast and Storm had had a chance to test the upgrade.

Lilandra looked at them with the expression of a mother giving her children a matched set of twelve-gauge shotguns to play with. ''It is dangerous,'' she said, ''more dangerous than most of us ever suspected it might be. Many of those who tested it in its earlier stages did not survive. Or they did, but . . . diminished.''

''Sounds real impressive,'' Gambit said, lounging against one of the polished walls with his arms folded, ''but what's it *do*?''

''It amplifies the natural properties and abilities of the user,'' Lilandra said. ''If you're strong, you become stronger, and the physical frame is temporarily stabilized and reinforced by various physical and nonphysical means to withstand the strain. If you are intelligent, you become more so. If you throw lightning bolts, you find that you can throw bigger ones.''

''My God,'' Iceman said.

''All real interestin', I'm sure,'' Wolverine said, ''but if this works so good, how come you don't have half the people on the planet usin' one?''

''Its power requirements are fairly extravagant,'' Lilandra said. ''Even this installation, small as it is, requires a power feed disproportionate to its size, nearly a small city's worth on its own. A full-strength implementation will require a power source productive of the same wattage as a small type-O star.''

"Additionally, it is still experimental,'' Ollikh said. "And there are some technologies which are not . . . healthy . . . in too widespread an application.''

"Yeah,'' Wolverine growled, "I just bet. I bet a lotta people out on some of the subject worlds would love to get their hands on somethin' like this too.''

Ollikh did not exactly glower, but her expression began to suggest that she would like to ask Wolverine to lunch, and not in the conventional manner. "Logan,'' Charles said quietly.

"But it does prompt the question,'' said Bishop, "assuming you are about to suggest that we use this device to attack the creature out there—why haven't you let the Imperial Guard use it first? They're your own version of the X-Men, practically, they should be the ones who—''

"That one's easy, Bish,'' Wolverine said. "*We're* expendable—the Guard ain't.''

Lilandra flushed hot. Ollikh acquired, slowly, the slightest smile. Charles gave Wolverine a severe look. "Logan,'' he repeated.

"Oh come on, Charley, you know it as well as I do. The Guard's job is t'protect the palace, Throneworld, an' Lil here. They use this thing an' get nailed, the Shi'ar are out a buncha loyal guardians. That's *real* hard t'replace. Us, though, we're just a groupa aliens.''

Bishop nodded. "A sensible ordering of priorities under the circumstances.''

There was a little quiet at that. Finally, Cyclops said, "Well, since this device has been released for our use, perhaps we should try *using* it, before we become overly concerned about other aspects of the situation.''

Ollikh nodded and said, "One moment." She moved her hands over several of the controls on the console, and the room was very abruptly about twice its original length; down at the far end a dead black wall now reared up. "The target area is ray-shielded, and there is a one-way force field between it and us," she said. "This test area is best suited to projected power, since we are, after all, still in the palace. We are in the process of setting up an area offplanet where the effects of the noumenoextensor do not have to be so confined. Storm, perhaps you would try it first?" Storm nodded. "Over there, then, if you please," said Ollikh, pointing at a spot about thirty feet closer to the end of the room than the area in which the X-Men now stood. "I will put up another force field between you and us—this equipment is a little on the sensitive side."

Storm moved forward to the spot that Ollikh had indicated. Between her and the others, the air began to sparkle faintly as a very demure and understated force field came into being there, stretching right across the room.

Storm looked rather dubiously at the black wall at the end of the room. "Shall I just hit it?" she said.

"If you would," said Lilandra. "We will not activate the extensor right away."

Storm nodded, turned, lifted her arms. A small lightning bolt leapt from her hands and struck the wall without apparent effect. The wall simply absorbed the blast. The crash of displaced air in that smallish space was deafening.

"How strong would you say that one was, Storm?" said Charles thoughtfully.

She tilted her head to one side, considering. "Maybe a million kilowatts' output? Though I tend these days to think of them in terms of electron volts—Forge has been a bad influence, that way." She smiled slightly. "But it is sometimes difficult to rate them accurately after the fact. Let me try for a million flat."

She raised her hands again. Another bolt leapt out, blinding. Once again it struck the black wall down at the end of the room, splashed, and was absorbed. "That is a good refractory," she said, giving the wall a thoughtful look. "What is it made of?"

"Ceramic reinforced with a force field at the cellular level," Ollikh said. "Now. Can you give it another blast of the same strength?"

"Give or take a few thousand volts, yes."

"Then do so."

Storm raised her hands—

—and gasped as she let loose another bolt.

The place went white. Charles looked away reflexively, as did everyone else, at the sudden and unexpected blast of fire. It hit the far wall, and this time there was no effortless absorption. The wall blew apart. Storm staggered back, but as the shards and splinters came at her, another force field stopped them.

Everyone stared. Through the shattered wall, the next room could be seen—it was full of smoke, metal fixtures were running like water, and plastic and other composites had burst into flame.

"Storm," Charles said, "are you all right?" He had heard that gasp as all the others had, but had first caught Storm's sense of utter shock at feeling something she had never felt before.

"Goddess above us," she said, coming back to look at them through the force field wall, "it was like—Professor, I swear to you, that bolt should have been identical to the others! But something—it was as if, as if a door opened—"

"It did," said Lilandra. "Within you. All beings are capable of more outlay of energy than they routinely use. Though you breathe all day, every day, each breath only uses from a third to a half of your lungs' total capacity, the so-called 'tidal volume.' The noumenoextensor reaches into the depths of your mind and assesses what you would be able to do if you had almost infinite power at your beck and call—then gives it to you."

Gambit looked doubtful. "If Storm had 'almost infinite power,' de palace shouldn't still be here, *mam'selle.*"

"You're quite right," Lilandra said, "but the effect isn't immediate. The mind is a skeptic—the human mind doubly so. It must first be convinced, by concrete evidence—like that last bolt. The next time Storm tries this, she should produce a bolt twice that size. And then twice that again, as the mind becomes more and more convinced that what was impossible is possible now. It will take some practice—but all of you will be working at levels far, far above your present ones in a very short time."

"The increase in power," Ollikh said, "is exponential. There is a chance—a better than even chance—that all of you together, with other weapons we are presently redesigning, will be able to attack that creature out there, and destroy it."

Storm stood there, wavering a little. "I blew up your wall," she said, rather bemusedly, to Lilandra. "My apologies. I was hoping for a more focused effect—"

Lilandra smiled. "It will give the architects something to do. Meanwhile, as Ollikh says, we are setting up a full implementation of the extensor on the far side of our third moon out, in the center of a nice barren *mare* where it will not much matter what you blow up, or freeze, or otherwise destroy while getting used to your augmented power. We expect that we will have to move to another location in deep space quickly, as you become more expert, and more powerful. Charles?''

He sat silent, going over in his mind the feel of the sudden access of sheer raw power that had flooded into Storm's mind, the sudden sense of unlimited ability, unfettered confidence—and the reaction, her sudden wobbly-at-the-knees sensation. She was recovering rapidly, though. ''We will have to proceed cautiously,'' he said, ''but, Majestrix, Ollikh, this technology may prove to be of great use. The next few days will tell.''

Lilandra nodded. ''Yes, and swiftly, I hope. Ollikh, have the techs add extra staff to the installation on Safha. I want it ready tomorrow. Meanwhile, would anyone care for some dinner in a while? I am meeting informally with some of the cabinet this evening. The event is officially in honor, or rather acknowledgment, of your arrival, but your attendance is not mandatory, since, like so many of these affairs, it is likely to turn into business.''

''I will certainly come,'' Charles said, glancing around him, ''and I would suspect most of the rest of us will as well. What time, Lilandra?''

''In about two hours. Ollikh will see you back to your quarters.''

''Later, then.''

Ollikh led the way out, and the X-Men went after her, shaking their heads, thoughtful—the Beast first, followed by Gambit riffling through his cards and glancing back at that shattered wall; Bishop guiding the swiftly recovering Storm; Iceman, with a gleam in his eye and a speculative expression; Wolverine, silent and scowling, looking like a thunderstorm deciding where to rain; then Cyclops and Phoenix, arm in arm. Last of all came Charles, hovering silently along, aware of Lilandra's eyes on his back, and of the rank smell of smoke in the air from the half-destroyed room behind the walls. But though Ollikh was well ahead of him, and her own back was turned, he could not lose the image of her cool and hungry eyes resting on them, one after another, as the X-Men reacted to Storm. Her mind had the sense of one with a secret—a secret, perhaps, concealed even from Lilandra or, even worse, one that had been shared with her.

Back in their common lounge about an hour and a half later, people were in various stages of dressing for dinner, either in more formal versions of their own uniforms, or (in Bobby's case, and somewhat unusually) in white tie and tails. "How many times do you get to go to a fancy diplomatic dinner on another planet?" he said, tying his bow tie for about the fortieth time, looking at it in the mirror, and untying it again.

Storm was lounging on the big sofa again, her feet up, wearing nothing yet but a towel and her beautiful hair, still wet from another bout in the shower. Cyclops paused by her, watching Bobby make one more run at the tie. "You feeling better?" he said.

She waved her hand, unconcerned. "It passed. Cyclops, I think it was as much surprise as anything else. Shock— to suddenly be so effective."

He raised his eyebrows over his ruby shades and smiled slightly. Jean came up beside him, and he said, "Whaddaya think, honey? Should I try that?"

"What? White tie?" she said. "Sure. Red cummerbund to go with the glasses? Why not? Bobby, how did you get the clothes-materializing machine to work? Maybe I want an evening gown instead of this." She gestured at her uniform. "I didn't really know what to pack for . . ."

They wandered off together. Charles, already in white tie and back in his hoverchair again, was sitting with the Beast, who once again was examining the various available holos of the core-eating creature in the big main tank.

"Obviously you feel we still have some serious problems," Charles said.

"What, besides the fact that we are operating strictly on theory here, with no hard facts to go on as yet? I should say so. No matter what is done to our own powers, Professor, one basic tactical difficulty remains. No question but that we must attack this creature. But *when* is the best time to attack it? When is it at its most vulnerable? How are we supposed to tell? And exactly *which* way will be the best to attack?"

"I have been considering that," Charles said, "but without experiential data, we are crippled, and will remain so. Still, one can to a certain extent reason from first principles. I would say, first, as to the hows—that of the various kinds of energy we have available with which to attack it," said Charles, "probably the best-suited will be Remy's management of kinetic energy and Storm's manipulation of elemental force; Bishop's ability to redirect anything which is directed at him will also be useful. But, Iceman—for all your occasional concerns about the worth of your powers, Robert, you may be the most useful of all."

Iceman looked up in surprise. Charles nodded. "After all, the creature seems adapted to high-energy environments; if its molecular structure can be slowed down to absolute zero, or near it—"

"Prof," Robert said, "I'll give it a try. But I'm not used to trying to handle a space much bigger than a few city blocks at once. If you ask me to try to chill down something that's—how big did you say? As much as half a million *miles* long, maybe?'' He shook his head. "Even with the power-augmenting gizmo here—not that I know how well it'll work—I can't guarantee performance anything like *that*, or anywhere near the kind of effect that would even slow the thing down. If I were you," he added a little glumly, ''I'd send out for ice.''

"There may be no need," Charles said. "But in any case, this is going to have to be very much a joint effort.''

Wolverine stepped away from the windows where he had been watching the sunset, and came back toward them, hands in jeans pockets, checked shirt open at the throat, frowning. "Still don't like it that we don't know for sure when the best time's going to be to hit that thing," he muttered, ''not that there's gonna be very much *I* can do about it one way or another. But that flyin', mobile form, the adult form—anything that can naturally go faster'n light—well, I don't know that that's a stage where we can tackle it and expect *any* kinda result.''

"Well," Storm said, "the other stages don't look helpful either.'' She got up, folded her arms over the towel. "Consider it. At the egg stage—assuming we can even find it, because that egg would be laid in a star, and for a good while before it hatched—when the egg hatches, the star goes nova. At that point, at least, it would seem to argue that the creature is at a pretty energy-resistant time in its life cycle.''

"And the pupa," the Beast said, "is probably just as difficult to deal with, since it's prepared to enter that state in a galactic core area, which may still be swirling with plasma and radiation of all kinds. Yet it wraps itself up and goes to sleep there, untroubled and apparently unaffected.''

"It may be," Charles said, "that the larva is our best

chance. In which case, we're fortunate, because that's the state we are faced with at the moment. But how long it will remain in that state is anyone's guess. We are moving among imponderables here, and we cannot afford to wait for very long. If it pupates, we will have lost our chance. There's no way to tell how long it might remain so. Even when they get the complete sequence of stale-light pictures from the new wave of probes being sent out, evidence of the last occurrence is not necessarily proof that the creature's life cycle will proceed in the same manner this time. And if it does, and once the adult hatches and starts making its way here, we have no idea what form of superluminal travel it uses. The odds are too good that it will come here. And the destruction it would wreak when it hatched out anew—'' He shook his head. ''I refuse to consider it. We must succeed with the larva.''

''I would very much like some better images of the adult stage, if we can get them,'' Beast said. ''I confess to great interest concerning exactly how the adult manages to insert its reproductive material or egg or whatever into the core of a star, while still protecting it from that environment. Not an easy task.''

Storm shook her head, drifted back toward the door opening into her own room. Charles sighed, looked over at Bobby, who had just finished tying his tie, and was now untying it again. ''It's a shame there isn't a mutant power enabling you to do up one of these the first time out,'' Bobby muttered.

Charles chuckled and glided over to him. ''Here, Robert, let me slip into your mind and guide your hands through it once. Fold over—then wrap—then under and around—''

Gambit came in, in his usual uniform, and sat down at the other end of the table from Beast. There he slumped back in the chair, reached into an inner pocket of his voluminous coat and came up with a pack of cards. They were lodged in a harder-to-reach pocket and were obviously not cards that he used as weapons. Since they ended up being destroyed when Gambit charged them with explosive kinetic energy, he tended to use cheap, off-the-shelf cards for that purpose, storing them in the outer pockets. He held one card up, looked at it thoughtfully, and then put it down and began to shuffle.

The Beast glanced over at Gambit and the cards. "Very nice," he said. "The Ryder 1926 Philadelphia woodcut printing. Where did you find those?"

"Shop in de city last week," he said. "Lady said dey were collectable. I like de feel."

Wolverine came idly over to look over Gambit's shoulder, glowering as he came. The Beast craned his neck again to get a better look at the cards as Gambit laid them out, then shook his head. "Tsk. Feel nice they may, but you've been had, my boy. They're not pasteboard. Scratch the coating—it's not starch, it's matte plastic. Very annoying, but a nice forgery."

"*Ah, salope!*" Gambit said, throwing down the king of spades with a little too much force, so that it fizzled enthusiastically around the edges, but did not actually blow up. He frowned, and then sighed and went back to laying the cards out for solitaire. After a moment he looked over his shoulder, up at Wolverine. "Now dere's somet'in' I been meanin' to ask you," he said. "Since we got here you been glowerin' and grumblin' like Rogue in a bad temper. What's your trouble, Logan? Space travel disagree wit' your plumbin'?"

"Yeah," Wolverine growled. "And this place too. Too clean, too antiseptic, too shiny. I don't trust it. Never have.

Every time we come here, somethin' jumps out from behind the shine and tries to bite us." He took his hands out of his pockets, lifted one fisted hand, clenched it—*snikt*—and the adamantium claws ran out of their sheaths, glittering in the subdued evening-mode light of the lounge. *Snakt*—and back again. "And this time the feelin's stronger than usual. That Ollikh lady—she gives me the creeps. A coupla those guys at the meeting earlier too. Somethin's in the air, and I don't know what. I *hate* not knowin' what."

"Suspicion," said the Beast, "unease. The scourge of imperial courts everywhere."

"Oh, and how many o' dose *you* been at, fuzzball?" said Remy with polite scorn, raking up the cards again, giving them a quick gambler's shuffle, and starting to lay them out again, the singed king of spades first.

The Beast pushed back from the tank. "Via that peculiar form of virtual reality known as 'reading,' my dear Remy—with which I know you must be familiar if you're going to go around shooting your mouth off about Pascal and Proust—many. The courts of Claudius, Nebuchadnezzar, Napoleon, various others. But if kings' heads rest uneasy, how much more an empress's? And in a time of crisis, more so than usual. People who might not have dared move against one in more settled times may find this an opportunity to try their luck at possibly unseating the one whom they feel has been causing them trouble."

Listening to this kind of thing could affect your concentration, Charles found. It had taken him three tries to finally get Bobby's tie sorted out. "Now leave it *alone,* Robert," he said.

"I dunno—it doesn't look right. If I just—"

"Let it *be*." But he probably would have started deconstructing it again had Storm not reappeared at this point, clad in many layers of cool, filmy, flowing white, looking very much like a wandering fogbank. A few moments later, Jean came out in a deep green dress that set off her hair. The Beast, still examining the holotank, felt around him on the sofa, produced a stiff brush, and began putting his fur in order, then stopped. "Can't do a thing with it while it's still damp," he said, and chucked the brush away. "It curls."

A deep soft gong sounded, and sounded again. "The dinner bell," said Cyclops, appearing in white tie and crimson cummerbund, as predicted. Outside the room, a young Shi'ar household officer paused in the doorway, goggled at them all briefly, and said, "If you would follow me, X-Men?"

They did, Wolverine sauntering out last of them all, whistling through his teeth, his hands behind his back, looking around him blackly. Under the quiet talk and laughter of the others, relaxed for this little while, Charles could hear the soft sound following them all down the hallway: *snikt, snakt, snikt . . .*

Dinner was in a room much grander than the conference room they had been in earlier. The decoration was understated, as usual for the Shi'ar, but nothing else about the room was. "My God," Iceman said under his breath, "you can see the curvature of the Earth in here."

"Not the Earth," said the Beast, next to him, as a quiet functionary showed them to their seats.

"Picky, picky."

The seat at the end of the glittering black-surfaced table was empty, but this time there was no great distance between it and the others. Charles was seated directly at its right hand, and the X-Men were alternated with various Shi'ar, but all close to Charles and the head of the table. Most of the Shi'ar were people they had met at the cabinet meeting earlier, and they greeted the X-Men cordially enough.

Servants started coming around with beverages, and conversation began as the drinks were poured, much of it at the X-Men's end of things, having at first to do with the utensils. "Which of these is the fork?" "I hate to break it to you, but this knife has two ends—" "Bobby, leave the tie *alone.*"

Then there was a rustle all down the table, and people stood. Following that lead, the X-Men, save Charles, stood too, and looked down the hall.

Lilandra entered. There was no flourish of trumpets. To Charles's mind, she did not need one. She was dressed, if that was the word—he restrained his smile—in a gown which took Storm's "cloud" effect a step further. It appeared to be genuinely made of blue mist, and billowed like it. Parts of it were translucent, and parts transparent—not the parts one might normally expect. Iceman took one look at her, and forgot to play with his tie.

The company lifted their glasses and wished the Majestrix health and long life, and then wished the same to one another. Charles, though he could not stand, joined all of them in this, exchanging glances with others up and down the table—and found himself looking at Lord Orien. Unnoticed for a second or so, the two of them gazed at each other, glasses lifted, then paused.

Charles did not need the slightest level of telepathic sensitivity to feel the discomfort, the jealousy, the anger. *Nonetheless*, he thought, *why should I be boorish?* He did not move his eyes from Orien's as he drank. After a second,

Orien drank as well, the look in his eyes a salute, the kind that swordsmen give one another before the bout begins.

Only then did Charles turn to Lilandra and say, "Is it committing lese majesty in this galaxy to tell the Majestrix that she looks indecently beautiful?"

Lilandra smiled, just a little wickedly, and said, "Not that I have noticed, or recently decreed." She waved at the servitors, who started bringing the dinner in.

There was a lot of it, in numerous courses, brought in by the servitors on rolling trays, some of which rolled quite happily along by themselves without help. Most of the food was completely unrecognizable, except for something that astonished Charles when he saw it pass by: an utterly mundane roast chicken. The Beast saw it and said, "May I?" He stopped the passing cart, and began to carve off some breast meat.

"Thought that'd be cannibalism, in this necka the woods," Wolverine said, from a few seats down.

"Not at all, Wolverine," said Lilandra calmly. "It's just an animal, and an alien one at that. Now, if I had roasted and carved up old Yrinx there, *that* would be, surely."

"I'm too tough to make much of a meal, Majestrix," said the Minister in Chief. "You would have to be fairly desperate."

"Desperation is the best sauce," Orien said. "After that, it's all a matter of the marinade."

Charles chuckled at that, and co-opted a little of the chicken himself, and chatted with the X-Men and the nearest other Shi'ar, Yrinx and Ollikh. He was surprised to find Ollikh's coolness somewhat warmed by the simple fact of sitting and eating. When she was not standing up and looking intimidatingly statuesque, her whole demeanor changed. Still, those eyes dwelt on the person to whom she spoke with uncomfortable intensity, as if looking for some clue to read. That aside, she was well-spoken and courteous, and actually began to be funny, after she had a little food in her and started to unbend. She even began joking with Orien, and Orien joked back. When Charles joined in, in the same vein, and they began comparing the similarities between human and Shi'ar humor, it started to get outrageous down at that end of the table. Some jokes fell flat, and some had indifferent or mixed effects depending on the species hearing it. But stories involving slapstick worked well, and incongruous situations. Charles told the one about the mermaid and the elephant, and Orien roared, once he understood what an elephant was. Orien told the one about the starship captain and the female of negotiable affections, and Charles laughed until the tears rolled down his face.

And still, he was furious. The second set of beverages was coming around, and Orien was starting another story, when the voice said inside his head, *Charles, I haven't been actively reading you, but you're just radiating hostility. It's becoming hard to ignore. Your mind feels like the outside of a porcupine.*

He sighed, took a drink of whatever the beverage was in front of him—it tasted like carbonated watermelon juice—and smiled slightly. *Jean*, he said, *it's Orien. I dislike him . . . powerfully.*

You have reason.

No, I do not. He has done nothing to deserve my enmity. He is an intelligent man, and an entertaining one. He is honest, as far as I can tell, and certainly courageous and resourceful, or he would not have risen to his present rank in the Shi'ar space service; a thoughtful man, a witty one. Principled, I think, and courteous. Perhaps more so than necessary.

But a rival, Jean said, cutting to the heart of the matter.

No! I do not see him as a rival, because Lilandra *does not see him as a rival. He may be seen by others as a rival, but that is nothing to do with me.*

Yet the horrible thought was still there. *What if someday she had to marry him?*

She was, after all, the Majestrix. She had pressures and duties against which she might rebel, but never for long. One of the things he loved most about her was her devotion, her single-minded attention, to her awful job. She would never be free of it, he knew, until she died—or was overthrown. Of course, Charles reminded himself, she *was* overthrown once, by her sister Deathbird. Charles himself aided her in regaining the throne then. No, she could no more not be empress and live than she could stop breathing and live.

And the truth was that, even if she did try to avoid her duties, they were, while she kept the job, inescapable. If she tried to avoid them, she would be deposed, or worse. Someday the pressures might become too much. Her best intentions, to bend her council to her will for her lifetime, might fail, as good intentions sometimes did. And then someone else would become her consort. Share her bed, for the continuation of the house of Neramani. Possibly, slowly, over time, come to share her heart. She would forget him. She would have to. It would be her duty.

Charles both shied from the awful scenario, and inwardly mocked himself for doing so. *Adolescent terrors,* he thought. *Ridiculous.*

But what if she did?

Charles, Jean said, *there's no shame in occasional bouts of uncertainty. Humans are prone to such. Would you give up your humanity just to avoid looking stupid?*

Sometimes, Charles said silently, *you are too reasonable for your own good.*

I've been well taught, Jean said. *Where do you think I got it from, Professor?*

At that he had to laugh. But meanwhile, there down the table, merry, well-spoken, handsome, intelligent, Orien was telling Gambit some unlikely story, so that even Remy's mouth was twitching a little at the corners. The people from Lilandra's cabinet, the old Chancellor-Major and the rest of them, were beaming at him. Charles heartily wished that the ground would open and swallow Orien, and then instantly felt guilty at the thought.

Charrrrrrrles . . .

All right, all right, he muttered inwardly to Jean, and turned his attention back to the meal. It really was delicious, what there was left of it.

"I would offer you some copper," said Lilandra softly, close to his ear.

"Eh? I mean, excuse me, Majestrix?" And then he blinked. "Copper?"

"Remember? You showed me the little piece of copper, and asked me what I was thinking."

"Oh. 'A penny for your thoughts.' " Charles chuckled. "I'm sorry. The problems before us are considerable."

"Before us," she said, "or in front of us?"

Charles met her eyes. *My love, you are too perceptive.*

We'll see how true that is later, she said to him silently. *Meanwhile . . .* She straightened, clapped her hands. "We are ready for dessert," she said.

More servitors came in, escorting more of the rolling trays with the covered dishes. "What *is* dessert?" said Iceman from down the table.

"Melakh," said Lilandra. "It's a frozen coating of a

sweet fruit juice, and inside, a hot cake soaked in another fruit sauce.''

"Baked Alaska in reverse," said the Beast, interested. "Now how do you *do* that?"

The covered dishes began swinging their lids up in unison, as they had done before. The servitors moved forward to do the actual distribution of the food. And Charles felt, like a knife through his brain, so inimical a stab of coupled hatred and satisfaction that he could barely move—but only for a second. In that second he found that he had locked eyes with Orien. *Now* he probed—finding en passant that the source of the hatred was somewhere else entirely. As usual, there was some crossover of thoughts during the split second of probing, and Charles felt the other man grasp his alarm, felt him tell Charles, without words, that he was ready. Whatever needed to be done—

Charles could not stand, but he could reach out and grab Lilandra's arm, and pull her right out of her seat and down across his lap—just before the blinding line of light lanced across the table from the energy weapon concealed inside the closest of the serving trolleys. Dishes and glasses flew everywhere, shrieks and howls of fear and pain went up— and one enraged curse from Wolverine.

X-Men, Charles cried mentally, *defend yourselves, defend her!* As he probed mentally for the source of the hatred, the one who had launched the attack, he saw that, predictably, the X-Men had not waited for orders. Already ruby-red optic blasts were flying, slamming into the wildly firing serving trolleys and disabling anything they touched. Off to one side, a flung king of spades hit another trolley and blew it into fragments. From a filmy-gowned form up near the ceiling, lightning bolts arced down, melting another of the trolleys into slag. Further down the table, something went *snikt!*—and dived and rolled out of sight as laser fire tracked, stitched through the air, missed. A moment later, an awful shrieking noise like shredding metal filled the air.

Charles was busy trying to track that hating mind to its source. It was wearing a mechanical thoughtscreen of some kind. That screening had slipped for a moment—*Why right then?* Charles thought, while trying to hold Lilandra still. "Charles, let me up—"

This is not the moment, he thought, and held her as still as he could while his mind quested, quested for that source of hate. *Not in this room. Somewhere else. The trace is fading.*

Telekinetic force grabbed a couple of the trolleys while they were still firing and threw them across the room with great force; they accelerated for at least an eighth of a mile, then hit one of the far walls and smashed themselves into spare parts. Several others were abruptly surrounded by great lumps of ice and held immobile, unable to fire, until much bigger lumps of ice fell from above and crushed them flat. Charles looked down at the end of the table and saw Bishop calmly walking around the end seat, while two or three trolleys followed him like disconsolate housepets, firing futilely at him. Well, not entirely futilely; he let them do it for a good few seconds before he turned and gave them back half a minute's worth of their own energy, all in one coherent and deadly blast. Afterwards, there was hardly anything left of them that was bigger than a dime.

Another trolley came through, more quickly, not firing. Charles thought perhaps it was malfunctioning, ignored it. It careened past him, then suddenly turned and made for his hoverchair, reaching out with clawed limbs. The hatred and the satisfaction speared him again. His mind leapt.

From across the table came blaster fire as Orien suddenly

appeared from behind the table and leveled a weapon at Charles that seemed the size of a bazooka. At least it did when you were looking down its barrel.

White fire streamed from it, hit the trolley that was making for Charles's chair. The trolley went up in an explosion that blew the massive table over, blew chairs away, nearly blew Charles away. But the chair held, Lilandra stayed with the chair, he stayed with the chair, and he got, one last time, that acid, tantalizing taste of hatred—then, sudden, and swiftly cut off, rage. Disappointment *Why aren't you dead?*

Gone.

The noise went on for a few minutes as the last of the trolleys was dispatched. Then there was more noise, as guards started running in, the Imperial Guard at their head. "Majestrix!" cried Gladiator, leading them, and the anguish in his voice was terrible to hear.

"I am intact," Lilandra said, pushing herself up off Charles and standing straight. "No, do not bother with me, Kallark, see to the others. I fear some of the cabinet are badly hurt, if not dead. Quickly!"

Charles looked around, taking a mental head-count. "X-Men," he said, "are you all right?"

"All in one piece," Remy said, sauntering down the length of the table toward them. "More'n can be said for some."

"You wanna put up a barbed-wire fence," Wolverine said, standing up with the remains of one of his foes dangling from his claws, "I got the wherewithal right here."

Iceman slid down from the heights of the room on an ice-bridge and looked around him at the wreckage. "Majestrix," he said, "you're gonna need a whole lot of new kitchen appliances. These were pretty badly behaved."

"Believe me, Iceman," she said, "I did not know I had any that behaved this way in the first place."

"Or that way," Charles said, looking at the overturned and smashed table. "That was not merely an energy weapon, but a laser-pumped bomb, I would guess. Meant as a second option to take you out, Majestrix, should the first one fail. And whoever was with you."

"And here is its master," said Storm, coming around from the other side of the table, with Chancellor-Major Dravian in her grip. "Majestrix, I saw him use this—which he tried to destroy afterwards—to activate that one specific trolley." She held up a small remote-control device of some kind. "It then headed straight for the Professor and yourself. I was trying to bring a bolt to bear on it when Lord Orien came up from under the table and blasted it back and away from the Professor's chair."

Lilandra looked at Dravian in silent shock.

"If it had clamped onto you, you would have gone up with it, no way to prevent it," said Orien. "So—" He shrugged, and looked at Charles again with that crossed-blades glint in his eyes.

Charles held out his hand. "I owe you my life, then," he said.

Orien looked at him, and at the hand, and would not take it. But he bowed slightly. "So does she," he said softly. "But there we have no conflict of interests, I think."

"None whatsoever," said Charles. Then he turned to the others. "This attempt may have been Dravian's," he said, "but there is another mind somehow involved. I was not able to trace it." He glanced at Jean. "A psionic damper was used."

"I felt it," Jean said, "but I had my hands full at that point. I'd know it again, though. Cold." She shivered once.

The Imperial Guard began taking away the wounded and the merely shell-shocked. Gladiator came over to where they stood, and said, "We have one dead, Majestrix: Fander. She was shot through the head. Several hurt but fortunately, none too seriously."

"We have a traitor here, Kallark," said Lilandra, looking coldly over at Dravian. "Take him away to wait our pleasure—no premature interrogations. And have him most carefully searched. If he suicides, the guard on whose watch he manages it will accompany him."

"Yes, Majestrix. But—" Gladiator looked unwilling to say it, and said it anyway. "Majestrix—I *told* you we should have been here. Brothers, sisters," he said to the X-Men, "we owe you a debt for this night."

"Doubtless there'll be chance enough to repay it in the days to come," Charles said.

"Gladiator," said Lilandra a little wearily, "there have been many dinners like this before, and will be again. Sometimes, in my own house, I wish to act the hostess, and not the hostage."

"All the same," said Ollikh softly, "security is going to have to be rescrutinized over the next few days, Majestrix. There should be no way this could have happened. If my own staff had been in the kitchens instead of—"

Lilandra frowned. "Most of your staff are terrible cooks, Ollikh," she said. "Nevertheless, you are correct, this must be investigated."

She rubbed her eyes, and suddenly looked very tired and alone. "We have a busy day tomorrow," she said. "The test range on Safha will be ready for you and the X-Men, Charles. Let us forget the dessert course for tonight."

"Lost my appetite anyway," said Remy.

"We'll start afresh in the morning. Gladiator, if you will

escort us back to our quarters, and the X-Men to theirs . . ."

"Yes, Majestrix."

And so it was done. That night, which should have been their first whole night together, Charles slept alone. It was probably just as well, however. He would not have been much use to Lilandra, when the bitter tang of the remembered, hating mind kept rising into his thoughts. Long into the night he lay there in the comfortable bed, his mind questing through the palace, through the city, across the planet. But that mind had hidden itself again—

—and would, he knew, keep striking at her until it succeeded in achieving her death.

Five

Their meeting, early the next morning, was on the somber side. Shi'ar typically believed in the big breakfast as a social occasion—possibly left over from their avian roots, when after a night's quiescence you had to make up as quickly as possible for the lost energy. But breakfast that morning was not terribly social.

Lilandra sat looking rather moodily down into her beaker of morning draft as the X-Men rolled into the breakfast room in uniform. She looked over at Charles as he drew up beside her. "Charles," she said, "have you recovered from last night?"

"I think, rather, the question is, have you?"

"I shall not do that," she said. "I have been with Dravian this morning." She shook her head. "I find it hard to believe—he's been with me since I ascended the throne the first time. All through the madness with D'Ken and later Deathbird. Now, this—I thought there was no one more faithful to me, no member of my cabinet with whom I could more securely trust my thoughts. And now I see to what use they've been put." She shook her head, the feathers stirring gently.

"Why did he do it?"

"Oh, there appeared to be three or four different threads merging. Pressure from some of the other houses, feeling that they should be closer to the throne, his own political ambitions. I suppose it was folly of me to think that such could be throttled by years of loyalty, or that loyalty could not be eroded over time.'' She sighed. "Betrayal—it lives in imperial courts, I know. But it does not mean that one necessarily gets any more used to it with time.''

"No," Charles said. "Well, how is Orien this morning?"

"Orien? I have not seen him. He has duties with the fleet. Right now, he is involved with heavy transport for some of the equipment on the far side of the moon Safha. Some of it is quite massive—it requires a cruiser at least. In fact, one of the components of the extensor and its computer support is a cruiser's singularity engine, the mechanism which enables the deployment of stargates. The power is massive, but nothing else will do. And since the cruiser captain is expected to be expert in the operation of such—'' She shrugged. "There are other advantages. This way, I can keep an eye on him.''

"To what purpose?''

Lilandra breathed out, almost a laugh. But it had a bitter sound to it. "Charles, I do not trust much of anyone today. You are possibly the exception. Possibly.''

The coolness surprised him. *But then*, Charles thought, *why should I be surprised? She has more responsibilities than to my feelings—many more.*

Wolverine came ambling over with a cup of coffee, paused, and looked down at them both, the usually aloof look he wore not in evidence at the moment. "Lil,'' he said, "you holdin' together?''

She looked up at him as if surprised to find a spark of kindness there, and Charles himself was a little taken off guard. "I will manage, Wolverine,'' she said. "Thank you. I appreciate your thought.''

He shrugged. "I been betrayed myself, once or twice," he said, and turned away. "I know what it feels like."

Breakfast finished without the usual comfortable small talk that accompanied such in the X-mansion. Finally Charles said to Lilandra, "Well, what will the schedule be for today?"

"We will make our way out to Safha. There are transports waiting. I encourage you all," she said, "do not be shy about testing your powers to the maximum at this point. There is nothing to hurt on this moon—no valuable real estate, so to speak. Our people stripmined it long ago. When more scenic places to live became available, they relocated without a second thought. Also," Lilandra said, "it was volcanic, at least up until two hundred years ago. Its core has long since quieted and cooled, but you know how it is. People get an idea in their heads that a place is unsafe, and sooner or later the property values drop." She smiled grimly.

"What new data have we on the creature?" said Charles.

"It continues to eat its way into the core of the neighboring galaxy," said Lilandra. "I am told that the rate of ingestion seems to be increasing somewhat. There are several things this might mean. Most specifically, there is a suspicion that it may be about to pupate. Therefore some speed is now required of us. You must get used to the extensor as quickly as you can, and extend your abilities as far as possible within the next few days—if we have that long. No one is sure exactly how long the creature may take to pupate, and it seems safest for us to assume the worst."

"That makes for the best planning," Charles said. "X-Men, twenty minutes."

• • •

The Throneworld was about three times the size of Earth, and the little moon of Safha was at about four times the distance the Earth's moon would have been. The X-Men watched it from the utility deck of the cruiser as the ship dropped gently in.

"What's the gee?" said Beast to the Shi'ar officer who was helping them with their spacesuits.

" 'Gee'? Oh, gravity. About two-thirds of that on the Throneworld."

"We'll bounce," said the Beast, sounding as if he relished the prospect.

"You do that anyway," said Jean. She was braiding her hair preparatory to tucking it into the helmet of the spacesuit. The Shi'ar suits were lightweight, flexible, and unusually pleasant to wear. The material itself was translucent and utterly impermeable to either heat or cold. Inside, the temperature remained a steady seventy-two degrees—or whatever temperature you preferred. The suits were also selectively permeable at the user's will; material could pass in and out of them without breaking the seal. Wolverine was standing off to one side, working his adamantium claws in and out with a kind of grudging fascination. "How does this *do* that?" he said to the young Shi'ar officer.

She looked at him with an assessing expression. "Are you a mathematician?"

Wolverine almost laughed. "Not today."

"Then I don't think I can explain it."

"Probably better that way," Wolverine muttered, walking away to pick up his helmet and settle it in place. "I hate these things."

"Claustrophobia?" Jean said mildly, as she settled her own helmet in place.

Wolverine glowered at her and said, very quietly, "They smash my hair down flat."

From across the suiting room, "Wolverine," Gambit said, as he did up the seal of his own suit, "not'in's gonna make *your* hair go flat. Vanity, it's all vanity."

The barren face of the moon loomed up large in the utility deck's windows and hung there motionless for a moment. Then there was a soft judder as the ship touched down. "All ashore that's going ashore," said Charles, sealing his own suit. "Lilandra?"

He glanced over at the hologram of the empress being relayed down from the command deck. "We are ready, Charles. The scientists and technicians involved with setting up this area have marked out a test grid for you. When you exit, you will see it."

"On our way."

Shi'ar airlocks were as casually elegant as the suits. One moment they were looking at a wall, the next they were looking at empty space. The ship's only concession to the airlock principle was the extension of a slender corridor which now led down toward the dusty pink surface of the moon, each of its ends sealed by a force field. Charles sent the hoverchair down the ramp, and the others followed.

Stars blazed and pulsed above them in the darkness. There was no view of the Throneworld, as they were on Safha's far side, the moon frozen in a genuine satellite's one-face-toward-its-primary position. The X-Men walked or bounced or soared a good way from the cruiser before they paused to look around. It took a moment, as usual, to get used to the peculiar foreshortening of the horizon that you got with a body smaller than Earth, the sense that it stopped sooner than it should.

"Horizon at about six miles, I'd say," said the Beast. "Is that our grid?"

Off toward the horizon, they could see what appeared to be a great pattern of squares, laid out across the emptiness—scored out with energy weapons, it looked like. The pattern went right over the horizon, somewhat broken off to one side by a craggy area, the beginnings of a small mountain range.

"Chess, anyone?" said Iceman.

"Looks more like tic-tac-toe," said Gambit. The pattern did indeed match a tic-tac-toe board, three squares by three.

Off to one side, a small, squat domed building was partly hunched, partly dug into the surrounding dust and rock. "X-Men," said Lilandra's voice, and her hologram appeared standing a little above the dust and the microcraters. "If you look over there, you will see the power facility which will generate the field for the noumenoextensor over this area. For purposes of evaluating the effects, the technicians have laid out a grid with squares approximately one mile wide for each of you to work in. For these initial exercises, it would probably be better if you tried to confine your work to the cube assigned to each of you. That way the techs monitoring your life signs and energy output will be able to assess how well the field is working for each of you, and tailor the settings to you more effectively, so that you can draw on the field more deeply as you feel the need and the readiness to do so. Also, this will help us know how to best feed you extra power later, when we actually go into battle with the creature."

"You're on," said Remy.

"Let's go, people," said Cyclops.

They fanned out across the gridwork. "I will take my

place at the center," said Charles, "so that I can coordinate."

They arranged themselves around him, each at the center of his or her one-mile square. Charles was the only one able to see all of them. The curvature of the moon made that difficult enough. Fortunately, he did not need to see them physically. He could feel them all in his mind, and all their emotions, the various mixtures of excitement, interest, intrigue, skepticism, a certain grumbling background annoyance—that was Wolverine—but everywhere, a readiness to begin.

"Is the field ready, Lilandra?" said Charles.

"Just say the word."

"Then do it now."

And the gasp—

Charles felt it eight times over, and once more for himself. He had not realized how intense the sudden access of power would be when he felt it. *Too used to feeling things at one remove*, he thought, somewhat grimly, and struggled out from under the rush of the others' sensations. The sudden feeling of physical strength increased, of telekinetic talent suddenly extended three or four times beyond its normal reach, of access to a depth of cold he had never imagined, of a universe suddenly much more amenable to having its elemental powers tapped.

It was shocking, in a way. It made Charles look back at the way his own mind had felt just a few minutes ago. The most powerful mind on Earth, he had been called. At the moment it did not feel like he had been any such thing. He felt as if, all his life until now, he had been shut in a tiny, tight closet, exercising his powers only with difficulty. Now, the clarity with which he saw the others' minds was so increased—the grasp, the depth, the focus . . .

"To quote a certain tin can of my acquaintance," said the Beast, *"Bozhe moi!"*

He leapt. Charles watched him go, and saw that the power of the leap had nothing to do with the light gravity. In fact, the Beast had rather reckoned without that. Gambit looked up and watched him go, then remarked. "Was gonna say dat wasn't not'in' Neil Armstrong couldn't do, but I take it back."

Charles smiled. "Jean," he said, "you had better snag him. He's exceeded escape velocity."

She lifted a hand—and the power leapt from her, grasped him like a fist. "Phoenix dear, lighten up!" the Beast said urgently.

"Sorry!" She brought him down too fast, had to readjust again, and again. She laughed a little nervously as she finally brought the Beast safely down to the ground. "Charles," she said, "it's like—like power steering!" And she burst out laughing. "It's like the difference between driving a Volkswagen Bug and a Porsche . . ."

Charles was content to merely watch them for a while: Storm rose up over the airless moon, and shattered and glazed the rock and dust below her with lightning. Gambit flung card after card into the square of the grid around him, seeing the explosions go up ten times, twenty times more powerfully than usual. Wolverine slashed and tumbled and tore, slicing the huge boulders around him with what even for him was unaccustomed ease. Phoenix wrenched a small crag free of the ground in the grid she was in, and balanced it deftly several hundred feet above her head—who knew how many hundreds or thousands of tons' mass, not that weightlessness mattered in this context. Cyclops tested his optic blasts, knocked right over by the force of the first few—then, slowly, learning how to brace against them as his strength grew in conjunction with the power of the blasts.

The learning curve was slightly different for each of them, but Charles watched them learn very fast. Their strength, their power, grew almost visibly over the course of three-quarters of an hour.

Himself, he was almost afraid. There might be no sight of the Throneworld, but it was not hidden from him. He could hear it, like a murmur in a nearby room, the billions of minds, the countless thoughts. He could hear specific thoughts, if he focused on them—anyone's. His range was greatly increased, his depth and power. He found it difficult to handle, somehow. The idea of being too godlike did not appeal to him. He had always felt strongly that, for all the usefulness of great power, you still needed limitation, a point past which it could not go. Omnipotence was not for beings who had not yet learned infinite compassion. Nonetheless, the thought came to mind as he turned to watch Jean set down the crag that she had been levitating; and with a calm that surprised him, she began plucking up others from around her grid, until she was balancing five, six, ten of them—ten jagged mountains torn out of the moon, one on top of the other.

It was amusing. But that nagging thought—the thread—the knife of hatred that had stabbed through his mind last night. He remembered it, and thought, *The others are being tested; why should I not see?* He launched himself on that thought's track, listening. Two billion minds down there, maybe three or four—it didn't matter. A mind might be asleep, or awake, but sooner or later it would think of the last day's doings, even unconsciously. No mind was so blasé or controlled that it could fail to return, again and again, to violent action in its recent past. It would keep coming back to it, reexamining it to see what went wrong, or what could have gone right. *Come on,* Charles thought. *Come on.*

Charles, Jean said inside his mind.

Almost. Almost. Stronger, now. *Not now, Jean, I—*

Charles!

What is it?

It's Scott.

Much more unbearable to look at than usual, the optic blasts were tearing out from Cyclops as he turned and dodged, sweeping his grid box with ruby fire. "Got—a little problem here, Charles—" he said.

"Cyclops?"

"I can't, uh, turn it off."

"But your visor—"

"It's not working—the blasts are too strong, they—"

Oh, no, Charles thought. The one thing that the extensor would not have strengthened or affected in proportion to everything else would of course have been the mechanical aids that some of the X-Men used.

"Cyclops, close your eyes!"

"Already tried that," Cyclops said. "I can't keep my eyes shut. From the feelings I'm getting, there's some kind of imbalance between me and the power."

Only two things had ever been able to keep the powerful beams of force that emitted permanently from Scott Summers's eyes in check: ruby quartz and his eyelids. If neither of them functioned . . .

"Got—a similar problem," said a voice from the other side. The vacuum in Bobby's grid seemed, somehow, much clearer than that in all the others. But then, Charles thought, there was some molecular movement and dust scattering even in the hardest vacuum. From what he could see, the whole grid box in which Bobby now stood was completely complexed with a field of such intense cold that molecular movement of any kind was simply out of the question.

"It was keeping up with me okay, Professor," Iceman said. "But *I'm* starting to get cold. I've got it down to about minus two-seventy—only a few degrees to go to absolute zero—but I'm starting to lose control. Something's going wrong—"

All Charles could do for the moment was let strength flow into the two of them from him, to help them hang on. To Lilandra he cried, "Majestrix, tell the techs to give it five more seconds, long enough for them to make their situations safe—then shut it down! Jean—"

"Let me put these down," she said hurriedly, and directed her telekinetic power at the ground over which she hovered, opened a hole, then glided aside to let the crags she was juggling fall into it.

But then a sudden gasp, not of surprise, but sheer pain. Jean clutched her head, writhing. Beneath her, the ground trembled, shook, ripped wide.

"Bail out, everybody!" Wolverine yelled. The X-Men fled in all directions. Charles gunned the hoverchair out of there, while at the same time trying to get into Jean's mind to lend her the control she needed. He couldn't get in. Something was holding him out, some kind of feedback— and underneath her, the act of will that had tried simply to make a hole to drop the crags in, was tearing straight through the crust of the moon—tearing it wide.

"Shut it down!" Charles cried. "Everyone, get off the surface—get into space! Help each other, quick! Lilandra, get the cruiser off the surface—"

Bobby fled upwards, ice-bridge-borne. The others came after him on powerpacks or whatever else was available.

Charles gunned his chair. "Majestrix, the cruiser, is it—"

The ground shook below them, soundless, as the great rift opening in it went wider and wider. Other rifts cracked away and spread. Over the edge of the moon, the cruiser came lifting gracefully upwards out of a spreading cloud of dust, and darted toward them, catching them all in a tractor beam of some kind and pulling them up and away. It also grabbed the ground-based installation which had been powering the noumenoextensor field and plucked it bodily up out of the moon.

Which was just as well, as the cracks widened, and up through them, boiling magma rose. Not much of it, but enough. It hit the cold of space, and hardened, and more spilled up, oozing through.

Shuddering, with one great fissure driving straight into and through its magma-bleeding heart, the moon Safha began to come apart.

First, though, came the sensation of the shutdown of the field. A sudden collapse. At first, merely a cold feeling— then it refined itself into a sensation of being small and insignificant and alone, much less than before. Then suddenly that feeling was gone. It left behind it nothing but a feeling of blessed normalcy as the tractor beam pulled them all away from the moon in the cruiser's wake.

The cracks spread. Bizarrely, through the cracks they could start to make out the blue gleam of the Throneworld beyond the edge of the shattered satellite.

Through a sudden wave of weariness, Charles could hear Lilandra's voice giving orders, sounding remarkably matter-of-fact for a woman who had just had one of her planet's moons destroyed. "Orien, Fatva, get the fleet out here. Have a cluster of stargates deployed with the far loci extragalactic, and start pushing poor Safha's remnants through them before the tidal effects start building up on the Throneworld. Be very careful about the angular velocities of the material as it comes out on the far side, we'll use it later. Charles, X-Men, are you all right?''

"Dunno if 'all right' would be the words I'd use,'' said Wolverine, growling. "That was nice while it lasted, but—*what happened?*''

"That,'' Charles said, "will take some working out.'' He did not intend to sound grim. But as the tractor drew them all slowly and carefully toward the cruiser's airlock area, he looked over at Jean and read something odd in her face, a strange complex of feelings in her mind. The earlier pleasure now given way to shock, and anger, but wistfulness too, and now, just general upset.

"Lilandra,'' Jean said. "Storm only wrecked your palace. I destroyed your *moon!*''

Lilandra's answering laugh was rueful. "We had hoped your powers would be expanded. I cannot say this is not the kind of result I was hoping for—it is! But plainly we are going to have to keep these exercises out in deep space after this. Orien, is the fleet coming?''

"Responding, Majestrix. A number of ships with stargates ready will be here in a matter of minutes.''

"Good,'' she said. "I want this cleared up swiftly. We're going to have to anchor a small tailored-mass singularity here, to take the place of the moon until we can figure out a way to 'wean' the planet off it slowly. Decrease the mass of the singularity over a period of time, I suppose. . . .'' She trailed off. "Never mind. I saw you retrieve the experimental facility. Is it intact?''

"Oh, yes, Majestrix,'' said another voice, possibly one of the scientists from the facility. "This whole installation has its own gravity and life support. It was designed to be picked up and put down anywhere, and in a hurry. We were a little shaken up, but no one was hurt.''

"Then let's prepare to relocate the installation extragalactic, in the full-power version," said Lilandra. "We were scheduled to start transit toward the other galaxy tomorrow anyway: let us start now instead. We can practice further in intergalactic space, where nothing will get hurt. Charles?"

"I concur," he said, as they came close to the airlock. "If we are going to increase our powers yet further, better to do it away from the Throneworld." Yet, at the same time, that feeling of being cold, small, and alone was assailing him. And anger—that thought, that angry thought that he might just have been able to trace. But not without the noumenoextensor. He needed it.

Charles raised one eyebrow. An interesting concept, that last one—he would have to think about it in more detail later. Meanwhile, "Let's get back," he said.

The team returned to their lounge in a strange mixture of triumph and despondency. "Did you feel that?" they were saying to each other, as if they couldn't believe it . . . and couldn't believe that it was over. "Did you feel that?"

"I felt it all right," Wolverine said. "And I felt it stop workin'." He was sitting there, looking, for him, surprisingly analytical. "What I want to know is, what went wrong?"

Charles, presently nursing a cup of tea, shook his head. "Lilandra's people will have no answers for us for a while," he said. "The usual problems. The technology is new and relatively untested. The difficulty might be something so simple as the fact that it was not built for use by humans, and there has been trouble calibrating it."

"Yeah," Wolverine said. "And that's another question. If they didn't build this for our use, then they built it for theirs. What're these people up to? Who needs that kind of power, normally?"

"It's a fair question," Cyclops said, coming along with a cup of tea as well, sitting down and putting his feet up. "People have been asking it about the 'starcracker' bombs, as well. Charles, what are these people up to?"

"Total galactic domination?" said Bobby.

"They have that. What more could they want?"

"Total domination of some *other* galaxy," Gambit said.

"Ridiculous," Charles said.

"*Is* it?" said Wolverine. "Absolute power corrupts absolutely, that's what we've always been told. I know you like Lil, Charley, we all do, but—"

"She is not interested in more territory," said Charles. Yet at the same time, a flush of unease went through him as he remembered her voice saying, amused, *Did you know that I once almost conquered Earth?*

He swallowed. *But there had been extenuating circumstances—*

Which she would have used for personal reasons, said some other part of Charles's mind. *What would she do if she had pressing* policy *reasons? Or more to the point, what* wouldn't *she do?*

And what about the Kree Empire? a third part of his brain piped in. *Lilandra happily conquered them.*

"I don't think this is germane," Charles said. "We could ask them all day what their armaments policies 'meant,' and I doubt we would get a straight answer—even from Lilandra. She has her own priorities, which is as it should be. But I do not think she means any worlds harm."

"Talk to some'a the subject species out there in the empire,'' Wolverine said. "You might hear different opinions. Ask the Starjammers too.''

That thought too had been itching at the back of Charles's mind, but he was not willing to deal with it now. There were too many other problems.

"Charles?'' Lilandra's voice, but not her person; she appeared in hologrammatic form for the moment. The other X-Men looked thoughtfully at the image, but said nothing.

"Yes, Majestrix?'' Charles said, cautious at the moment, since you never quite knew who was standing just out of range of the pickup.

"The scientists are reporting some changes in the status of the creature at the galaxy's core. It is starting to slow down. Some of them think this might be a good time to attack.''

"We should leave right away, then.''

"So they say, and I concur. If you will meet me in the Great Hall, we will take my flagship and head out. I am having your quarters duplicated aboard. Everything you need will be moved. But I wish to leave within the next twenty minutes.''

"Things're heatin' up,'' Wolverine said as the image flickered out.

"Well,'' Bobby said, "we're just the ones to cool 'em down.''

Jean watched him go off to his quarters to get his things together. *I just hope,* she said silently to Charles, *that we can back up his confidence with performance. You felt it too.*

What do you mean?

The access of power—and then the collapse. And I was very tired afterwards.

Charles had felt that as well, and had shrugged off the

immediate reaction as shock. *You don't often see a moon fall apart under your feet,* he said.

But it was more than that, Jean said. *You remember how Storm felt it after her first try? It was like that. It went away fairly quickly, for me, but—* She shook her head. *It felt as if it was going away too quickly. I don't know—I'm not sure what any of these feelings mean.*

Nor am I, Charles said. *We will have leisure to discuss all this in transit. Let's get ready to go.*

Various members of the Imperial Guard had boarded the Majestrix's flagship with them, and what seemed a whole battalion of scientists and techs as well. Avend and his and Orien's research assistant Irdin were there, as were some members of the cabinet. Among the latter—surprisingly, given his injury—was the head of the Science Council, the tall, taciturn Eleth. "Only a scratch," he said to Charles when asked about the wound-sealed blaster burn on his arm. "Take more than this to keep me away from this trip."

Charles blinked. "But, sir," he said, "the danger—"

"How often," said Eleth coolly, "does an astronomer get a chance to work on anything that looks remotely dangerous? Short of going out and standing in front of a comet." He laughed. "Professor, this thing may be the end of all of us. It may not, if you and your people are fortunate—if we all are. But one way or another, this is a wonder of the universe, and I want to see it up close."

Charles nodded. He knew all too few pure scientists. He admired them when he ran across them. All too often, in his world, people pursued science, not for love or knowledge, but because it was a job. And those who did pursue it for love, like himself and the Beast, were forced to limit it to a sideline thanks to other commitments. To find someone who apparently knew what science was really for always made him feel better.

Charles looked around him. The flagship-cruiser was more like a small city than a warship as such, though it could certainly function as one when it needed to. Right now it was in science-and-investigation mode—not that it was unarmed. Charles knew it was carrying even more of the "starcracker" bombs. They too had been undergoing augmentation over the past weeks, to boost their power and yield. The Majestrix was quite willing to throw them at the creature, in bulk, should the X-Men fail. *We won't*, Charles told himself. But uncertainty dogged him—and the memory of that blade of hatred driving deep into his mind wouldn't go away.

The area of the ship to which he and the X-Men had originally come was more like the central square of a large town than anything else. High above it, an outward-jutting balcony looked down from the bridge levels. Other levels ran around the sides of the great atrium space, leading to crew quarters, laboratories, libraries, computer facilities, and weapons bays. Charles particularly noticed the weapons bays. The people who staffed them were quiet and busy.

He had not seen Lilandra, physically anyway, since they came aboard. Leaving the X-Men to sort out their new quarters, he made his way up to the bridge level on one of the flagship's lifts. He glided out in his hoverchair and looked around the bridge, which was about the size of half a football field.

Various young officers glanced at him, went back to their work. He could hear the hum of thought as they assessed him: *her consort—human—spectators on the bridge, nuisances, how're we supposed to get our work done?* Mixed approval, uncertainty, unconcern, in one or two places, dislike. But always pushed out of the way almost immediately. These were professionals, doing their jobs. They would think about him later.

All except in one place. Before the huge windows that looked out on space, near a free-standing console, stood a tall, straight figure in full armor except for the helmet, his fair golden crest gleaming as he turned.

Orien.

Charles looked at him, swallowed. Then he glided on ahead. *Always better to take the bull by the horns. Or the eagle by the beak, in this case.*

"Professor," Orien said.

"Lord Orien."

"Are your people comfortable?"

"As far as I know," said Charles. "Though I think they're not so concerned about that at the moment. They're much more concerned with getting on with the job at hand."

"Yes," Orien said. "I can understand why, after this afternoon."

"You saw that?"

"Oh, I was there," said Orien, with a slight smile. "It was my ship that pulled you and the research facility off Safha. I transferred here at the Majestrix's order when we returned."

"You must be much in demand as a commander," Charles said.

Orien looked at him, and the smile, slight as it was, went somewhat sad. "There are others I would have preferred to see doing the work," he said, "but life has been busy in the last decade or so for our people. Many of our older officers are no longer with us. The exigencies of command

and battle—these days, younger officers are much in demand, yes. We bear up well under stress, our hormones distract us from other aspects of life less immediate, and there are always plenty of others waiting behind us, willing to take our places when we fall."

"A bloody campaign and a quick promotion," Charles said, half to himself.

"Yes," Orien said, "there's been a lot of that." He looked out into the darkness. "Perhaps more than any of us would have wished. But—" He shrugged. "We do not make policy, we execute it. Our job is to do it as well as we can. In this organization, at least, if one is Shi'ar born and exhibits any kind of talent, it's usually rewarded—perhaps, sometimes, too quickly. But this, at least," he said, and looked out to where a stargate was being assembled, "this is an interesting change of pace. No need to kill—at least, not wholesale. The enemy we hunt is one we may hunt with impunity—at least it is not murder."

"Is it not?" said Charles softly. "Are you sure?"

"What?" said Orien, looking at him, and then nodded. "Oh. I see your point. Though there is no evidence one way or the other yet, there are some among us who have raised that question as well. Can we be sure that this is not an intelligent life form—something, perhaps, in its own way innocent—surviving as best it knows how? Some of our staff have suggested that possibility. Even Irdin, my assistant, has done so. Granted, so have some from the Science Council, a few even from the astronomy end of things. But Irdin was a biologist first, and so she tends to still look over her shoulder." Orien smiled a little more broadly. "It's always hard to give up one's first specialization in the sciences, even when policy or economics dictate you must."

Charles nodded. "I've known people with the same problem. I resisted as long as I could, myself. But sooner or later your work will hunt you down and make you its own."

"So the Majestrix said," Orien said, "when she finished her time with the Starjammers. She did not return with unmixed feelings, apparently, but she did her duty." He looked at Charles, and there was that expression again in his eye: the flourish of swords. You could turn your back on it, or lift the sword in salute in return.

"And what would you have her do?" Charles said.

"Her duty would suffice," said Orien. "It's a word easily bandied about, I suppose, by those who don't understand the ramifications."

Charles bristled a little, but then caught himself, as Orien plainly did not mean him—at the moment.

Orien looked out at the stargate-in-assembly as it became slowly more and more circular. "The succession has always caused trouble for us," he said. "Several times in the last millennium there have been attempts to change the way it's handled." He strolled closer to the window, and Charles went with him, noticing as they went that this would take them well away from any of the other officers who might be listening.

"Since the beginning of the empire, it has been handled strictly hereditarily," Orien said, pausing right by the force field that divided them from the night. "First by descent through the eldest daughter, then through the son, until it was decided that one should not discriminate against the males simply because they could not themselves bear children, and thus prove the heirs' lineage without question. Some have called this folly, but I can't believe we have done too badly, by and large." He smiled, and this time the look was amused. "Though there will always be those who claim that the old ways are best. Then there came a time, oh, a thousand years ago, when the Throneworld had one of those philosophical waves of change that sometimes pass over a culture. A movement began to take shape that claimed that simply allowing, or permitting, the imperial line to select its descendants randomly, in terms of mating for liking or love, was throwing away genetic possibilities that should be exploited. The imperial line began to be conducted, over the first couple of centuries of this period, as a selective breeding program. If there must be Majestors and Majestrices, let them be the best of their kind. The brightest, the smartest, the most fit. Matches were no longer made for policy in the national sense. But now they were made in terms of bettering the bloodline. We became little more than prize stock."

" 'We'?"

"Oh, I am a member of the family," Orien said, "though not in any close degree related to the Majestrix or the present imperial line. Our house is much removed from the Neramani. I think the Majestrix and I may have a great-grandsire or two in common, no more than that. At any rate," he said, "the restrictions on whom a Majestor or Majestrix might wed and breed with became tighter and tighter. Until, finally——" He broke out laughing, a bitter sound. "I cannot believe they did not see what was going to come of this. Finally the decree went forth from the Majestor himself that henceforth there would be no more weddings with other houses, no matter how highly placed or genetically desirable. From now on, the Majestor would reproduce his line only by cloning."

Charles raised his eyebrows.

"At first," Orien said, "when the Majestor died—Arakh,

his name was, a terrible man, but just in his way, despite the blindness of his times—there would be another born of his DNA, physically identical to him, who would take his place. He would be educated with him, sometimes by him, in the art of statecraft. For several generations this was tolerated—indeed, there was nothing much the ruling council could do about it in those days. The Majestor's office was more powerful, and the council's rule in government less so, than it is now. There could of course be no question of his right in line as he was the undoubted inheritor of the Majestor before him, and there was no other issue. After a while, though, it was no longer simply an issue of different persons having the same DNA, the identical body, for generation after generation. Arakh the Eighth decided that he would take matters a little further . . . and never die.''

"Folly," Charles said softly.

"Yes. When his time came, however, he had his brain, his soul, transplanted into an identical clone of himself: young, ready to start all over again.'' Orien shook his head. "Except that an old brain in a new body cannot make anything new. It continues to make the same old mistakes, and also makes more of them, and worse ones, because it now has the hormones of youth powering the canalization of age. It is a dreadful error. The empire almost fell, putting him down, casting out the old order. It was a terrible time for us. Our histories dwell on it with a mixture of horror and fascination. But if there is one thing our people insist on now,'' and he looked at Charles, "it is that the Majestor or Majestrix reproduce in the manner of two millennia ago, not one: that Shi'ar mate with Shi'ar, as Sharra with Ky'thri long ago, and children come to birth who are new, who are their own people, different and unique, but Shi'ar. Do you see what I am trying to tell you?"

"I think I may, Orien—if I may call you so?"

"If I may call you Charles."

"Do so. But otherwise, it might work better if you simply told me, rather than trying to."

Orien looked around him. There was no one anywhere near them; the soft hum of the atrium levels below seemed very far away. He looked at Charles, leaning casually against the force field, and said, "She cannot have you, Charles. If she tries to force the issue, she will tear the empire apart. You will forgive me if I speak bluntly. Any child of your union would obviously have to be brought about with extensive biological and medical intervention. Genetic manipulation, possibly even alteration of the child's DNA, adaptation of it, so that it would be able to survive. That is when the trouble would begin. Your enemies—and you have them here, in plenty—have been waiting for a way to strike most effectively at you. The moment that you and Lilandra seriously began to attempt the production between you of an heir—earlier even, at the moment when you would be formally joined—all the old issues would be raised again. Meddling in the natural course of things, tampering with the royal flesh and blood, descended from Sharra and Ky'thri themselves, sacrilege. And there would be new ones added. Is a Shi'ar child with human genes, even altered human genes, still even Shi'ar? For those to whom such things matter, and there are many, these would be killing matters. For the child, for you, for Lilandra. But first of all for you. You would be seen as the perverter of the right way, the debaucher of the Majestrix's blood. They would kill you the first chance they got, and

possibly exile her—again—and if there was a child . . .''
He shook his head.

" 'Those to whom such things matter,' '' Charles said.
"Indeed. Where do you stand on all this, Orien?''

Orien's eyes turned rather hard at that. "Do not misunderstand me, Charles. I know who you are. I know what you and the X-Men have been to this empire, and what you have done for us. I would be a fool to pretend otherwise. Yet I also know what would happen to this empire should you and the Majestrix ever be formally joined as ruler and consort. And, frankly, it would grieve me to see you killed for so little reason.''

"Whatever else could be said about the reason for it,'' Charles said, "believe me when I tell you that it would not be little.''

"But you have a great purpose,'' Orien said. "Is that not what I hear? To protect the different ones of your world. The powerful ones who have no one else to protect them, nowhere else to go, in a world rapidly turning against them. You are a hinge, Charles Xavier. The X-Man Bishop is proof of that. You are one of those turning points that occur in any culture. Not yourself the door, but the part of it that makes movement possible. If you go to your death over a personal matter—''

"What else is worth going to death over?'' said Charles.

Orien looked at him and his eyes flashed. "I cannot believe that you would truly be so immoral.''

Charles blinked. This was apparently one of those cultural "walls'' that even telepaths hit. "Perhaps I misphrased that. I have been—doubtless, will be again—prepared to die for things that I believe in.''

"Then, depending on what those things are, you have the potential to be noble,'' said Orien. "That is one mark of nobility, one of the few that matter. One may be Lord this, or Chancellor that, and not be any whit the better for it. Nobility lies in behavior. However, what you're saying is that you would allow this part of your life to go forward for the sake of desire, for pleasure, for personal fulfillment—when you know that the greater good lies down another path entirely.''

''I do not know that,'' Charles said. ''Orien. *Do you love her?*''

A long pause. In the face of Orien's previous openness, Charles refused to probe, though there was no avoiding the brief sense of turmoil roiling in that mind so close by. ''It is hard to know if you love someone until you live with them,'' Orien said, ''at least for a little while. I do not speak of the kind of infatuation that strikes at first sight, lasts a while, then fades. I mean the long love.'' He sighed. ''I see the Majestrix on business. I serve her, I obey her orders. I admire her, I like her. She is an intelligent woman, masterful, and still keeps her sense of humor, which means a great deal. But do I love her? Does it matter?''

''What could matter more?''

''Duty.''

And so the circle closed. Charles shook his head and said to Orien, ''Answer me this, then, since we are speaking bluntly. What can you give her that I cannot? I can certainly give her something you cannot. Joy, love. She is the one, the only one, for me. It isn't given to many of us to find that one, to know they are the one. Many things can happen in a life: destruction, death, pain, frustration, loss. But if you have that love, you can live through it. And she has that, from me. What do you have that you could give her in its place when you don't even have that?''

''The certain knowledge,'' Orien said, ''that millions,

perhaps billions of our people, would not die because I was intent on having something, or giving someone something, which would force them to go to war.''

They stood in silence, looking out into the darkness as the stargate came alive. Then Charles said, as lightly as possible under the circumstances, ''Nothing is resolved.''

''No,'' said Orien, making a wry face. ''Who would have thought it would be? Here I stand in my insolence, arguing with the man who they say has the most powerful mind on Earth—a planet which has produced some not inconsiderable thinkers in its time. I am happy enough to have had a chance to state my case, in these busy times, and perhaps done as well as to score a draw.''

Has he? Charles thought . . . but kept that to himself. ''Where *is* the Majestrix?''

''I believe she is down in the war room,'' Orien said. ''Come, I will walk down with you. I am weary of this place today, and my presence is not needed at the moment. Anyway, it will be another hour before we reach the staging area where your secondary testing and exercise facilities are being located.''

They walked away together toward the lift, taking it downward and into the huge entrance hall. '' 'Not inconsiderable thinkers'?'' Charles said, somewhat bemused, as they went along. ''How much do you know about the thinkers of my species?''

''Oh, I have studied their high points, in a general way,'' said Orien, shaking out his crest in the breeze that flowed across the main floor from one of the wall-gardens on the far side. ''It's said, after all, that it's best to know one's—'' He stopped himself.

''Enemy?''

Orien looked at Charles, and actually chuckled. ''Well,

bad old habits of thought will persist, will they not? There have occasionally been moments when we have been on the wrong side of the fence from one another—various forces from Earth, and our empire. Did you know, Professor, there was actually once a time when, if I judge correctly, we were on the very brink of invading Earth?''

Charles's eyes widened. ''Why, how could such a thing ever come about?''

Orien looked at him with an expression of such transparent complicity that even Charles, depressed as he was feeling at the moment, had to laugh. ''Professor,'' he said. ''The Majestrix—'' Orien laughed too, shook his head, and looked up into the air of the big atrium-space as if seeking assistance from some higher power—

—and Charles felt it, long before Orien did anything. The moment of shock, and the moment of choice, in the other's mind, almost identical—though to a trained telepath, easily told apart; the moment of perceiving that a weapon was raised far above, the glint of targeting light, the clear thought in the mind: *Let it happen?* And then: *Let it happen.* A suspended moment, a choice hanging fire—

There was no time to move, to do anything. Orien grabbed Charles, and flung him to one side, out of the hoverchair and down—a tackle that would have done credit to a linebacker. Behind them, the floor exploded. Metal and plastic flew everywhere, smoke burst up, and a ball of fire took root in the hole in the floor and began to grow. Out of the hoverchair, there was nothing much Charles could do but pull himself along, arm over arm, as fast as he could.

Orien was rolling the other way, coming up fast, his sidearm out. He braced himself on one knee, lifted the sidearm, sighted along it, fired—

From somewhere high up came a shriek of pain—someone's last one, Charles judged. The sound at the bottom level scaled up as sirens and hooters went off. People began running all over the place. Hands grabbed Charles and picked him up and dusted him off.

There was not much left of the hoverchair. Several Shi'ar officers came hurrying along with a small device that threw some kind of energy-damping field over the ravening ball of fire sitting in the middle of the floor. It began to die away. Others helped Orien up. He was staggering, and the back of his armor was scorched, as was his crest. All along one side, the feathers had crisped and curled black. He wobbled a little as he pushed away from the others, made a sort of futile brushing-himself-off gesture, and then looked around a little frantically. ''The Professor—''

''Here, Orien,'' Charles said.

They looked at each other through the whooping of the sirens. ''I believe I mentioned,'' said Orien dryly, ''that this situation is complex, and that you had a few enemies here.''

''If I looked like I doubted you,'' said Charles, ''I stand corrected.''

Orien glanced at the officers and soldiers around him. ''Find the Professor another conveyance,'' he said, ''something that will do until a new one can be fabricated. I refuse to allow a mission to save a galaxy to be derailed by some nasty little murder. Meanwhile, find out who that was. Find out who his friends are. I want a report for the Majestrix in half an hour.''

Charles watched him stride off, in command, righteously furious. He felt another stab in the back of his mind. Not hatred, this time, but something more insidious: guilt for his dislike of this man, and that it persisted in the face of what he had revealed himself to be. *Could it be that she would possibly be better off with him than with me?*

The universe started to look very dark.

Six

Another hour's time saw Charles's hoverchair replaced—it was, after all, Shi'ar technology—and the little fleet's arrival at the staging area between the two galaxies.

If the view from Throneworld space had been astonishing, this was more so. Night with stars is something one takes for granted after a while. But a night of total velvety black, except for two bright spiral patches of light diametrically opposite each other, while you hang motionless between—this is something else again. It tends to make the breath catch, the heart beat faster. Fear, amazement, a combination of these, as the eye searches, increasingly, desperately, for the slightest glimmer of light in the empty spaces between. The feelings grow into a massive unease, and it takes a strong mind to break free.

In the midst of this darkness, the X-Men hung. The fleet had withdrawn itself to a safe distance—or what it hoped to be safe. Scattered in nearby space were a series of targets of metal and ceramic and composite, and also scattered all around were the smashed remnants of the moon Safha.

"If I didn't know better, Charles," said Phoenix, hanging there in the darkness in her spacesuit, "I'd think someone was trying to make me feel guilty."

"You do feel guilty. You said so."

"Yes, well . . ."

"They set it up, Jean," said the Beast's voice on the suit radio; he was perhaps a hundred miles away. "Don't let the turkeys get you down. You only did what they asked. It's hardly your fault that the moon had a weak spot. And picture this: It's a hundred thousand years from now. Safha's orbit starts to decay. It cracks apart, falls on them in about eight hundred pieces with enough kinetic energy to turn every piece into a little atom bomb. You did them a favor. Saved them a lot of cleanup later."

"It's nice to have friends," Jean said softly.

"Cyclops," said the Professor from the small capsule in which they had dropped him, more or less like a hoverchair that completely surrounded him, "what sort of shape are you in at the moment?"

"*Twitchy* would be the best word."

Charles bit his lip. Since he was a child, Cyclops had lived in fear of his optic blasts raging out of his control. This could not have been easy. "Scott, I believe you have reason. However, they have redesigned your eyepieces for you. Those new lenses should theoretically control or stop blasts at least a hundred thousand times stronger than your normal best shot."

"If your power is augmented much past that, Scotty," the Beast added, "I for one think we might as well just send you off to handle this problem yourself, and meanwhile send out for pizza."

"Pizza," said Iceman. "I haven't had a pizza in—"

"Must be two hours now," said Wolverine, from a hundred miles or so in another direction—standing on his target, a broad, flat artificial plane of metal, well littered with animated robots, various space junk, and more chunks of shattered Safha. "I saw you messin' with that food machine."

The Beast chuckled. "Wolverine, let us not forget who was caught putting the horseradish in his chile last week: Judge not, lest ye also be judged."

"All right, X-Men," said Charles. "All, report. Cyclops?"

"Ready, Professor."

"Phoenix?"

"All set," she said, but Charles clearly caught her sense of persistent embarrassment, and her determination to do better this time.

"Beast?"

"Quite ready, Professor."

"Iceman?"

"Let's go."

"Gambit?"

"Let de good times roll."

"Bishop?"

"Ready."

"Wolverine?"

"Go."

"Storm?"

"I await your word, Professor."

"And I too am ready. Majestrix?"

"We are observing, Charles," she said.

Orien's voice said, "This is the flagship. Ladies and gentlemen, gods' speed. Noumenoextensor—"

"Answering."

"Start the field at half strength first, please. The Professor will call for increments at will. Twenty-five percent each time, Professor?"

"Yes."

"Acknowledge."

"Acknowledging, flag."

"Activate."

For perhaps a thousand miles in all directions, something happened.

The rush of power came. Charles felt it. This time there was no hum and murmur of billions of minds, though he could clearly hear every ship in the small fleet, the minds in them, almost all bent on the next galaxy. Fear, excitement, and many other states of mind. But except for them, and the X-Men . . . silence. It took a long time for a powerful telepath to get used to the constant background noise. Even though you may never be able to clearly make out the details of what's going on in any one mind, the buzz is always there. But here, nothing. All the minds except those nearby were too far away to hear. It was like the denizen of some huge city going for a walk in a countryside too remote to even have roads or towns, hearing nothing but the wind. Here, he did not even have that. The sense of rest and refreshment was amazing.

But there were other things to think about.

Charles felt the eight minds around him, felt the power rush into them too—manifesting differently in each. To some of them—Wolverine, the Beast, and to a much lesser extent, Bishop—the experience was primarily physical, or had a strong physical component. The noumenoextensor knew, very clearly, what your best-developed ability was, and siphoned its power into that. Muscle hardened, bone reinforced itself, neurotransmitters moved faster or more smoothly. The networking of the mind sped up, the body learned new and more dangerous ways to express itself. Charles saw, or sensed, Wolverine making havoc of the targets and boulders and robots arrayed around him as if they were so much wet tissue paper. He heard the laughter inside the spacesuit.

Of all of them, Bishop was the only one who needed an external influence to get his powers going. And so, he spoke over the radio. "Storm, if you would be so kind?"

"Of course, Bishop," Storm said, and the blast of ionized fire that leapt from her toward him a second later should have been enough to vaporize at least a small chunk of moon. Under normal circumstances, the strain of holding in that much power would have maimed Bishop, if not killed him outright. As it was, Bishop practically shivered with the power of the lightning, and then let it burst free at the nearest fragment, a chunk of rock the size of a split-level house. When the reflected blast hit it, the rock simply ceased to exist. There was not even powder left—the blast had reduced it to components too small for the eye to see.

Storm swung about, did the same directly to another chunk of moon, a bigger one. Several miles away, Iceman was frozen in an ecstasy of power and cold, having stopped all molecular motion in every piece of matter that came near him, within a radius that was nearly thirty miles, now, and increasing every second. "This is it, Professor," he was saying, "this is the way it ought to be. *This is it! Feel it!*"

Charles could. In other circumstances he would have been uneasy, but at the moment, it was good news. "Cyclops?"

"No problems," Cyclops said, between optic blasts. He was carefully and with near-surgical precision carving another chunk of moon into pieces. Then a last bolt swept all the fragments, and blew them into vapor.

"Work to increase the power of each blow, X-Men," Charles said. "Don't scattershot. Amplitude is what we need now."

Miles away, Charles could see and feel Remy skimming

his cards, one after another, with astounding speed, at more of the fragments of moon, blowing them to plasma. He aimed successively at larger and larger fragments, finally taking out one that was easily the size of a minimall.

The Beast leapt and rent as if invulnerable. Stone, metal, plastic, were nothing to him. "Hank," Charles said, "you have other business."

"I am doing quadratic equations in my head, if that helps you," said the Beast, "and normally, I need a calculator."

"Good. Work to see if you can manage to hyperprocess under the extensor's influence. While hand-to-hand may not be something we need in this fight to come, if while engaged you see or hear something that suddenly seems to make more sense than usual, more quickly—it might give us a clue how to defeat the creature."

"I am working on it. I could only wish it were as visual as what Storm, or Cyclops, are doing."

"Visual isn't everything," Charles said, amused. "But you and I will sit down and evaluate the results later. Phoenix—"

This particular piece of my history, Jean thought to Charles, looking around her at the great jagged lumps of stone, *is beginning to annoy me.* She flung her arms out wide, and the power poured from her, scintillating around her until she almost began to glow.

The biggest chunk of rock directly before her, one big enough to qualify as a good-sized asteroid, crumpled in on itself, compressing, fizzing with heat reaction, melting, imploding—until finally it simply vanished in a huge silent roar and shock wave of gravitic forces.

Jean, Charles said, surprised despite himself. *Where did it go?*

I think I squeezed it into its component atoms, she said.

If I can do that to this, Charles, I can do it to something bigger. I can do it—

She turned her attention to another huge moon chunk, began to compress it, pouring out her power.

"Increment at ten-second intervals," Charles said.

That next piece of rock simply winked out of existence. There was another intake of breath from all the other X-Men, but this time there was no sense of shock about it, but instead a sense of fulfillment and release.

Charles blinked. It was not an illusion in the mind, not just a tiny Storm hovering in the darkness, a speck of Cyclops, a hint of Phoenix. Now huge phantom forms were beginning to coalesce around them, forms matching the powers inside the bodies. Somewhere inside those ghost forms the real bodies still moved, but they were hidden, eclipsed for the moment by the glory. Storm straddled the sky like a goddess. Jean floated near her in a nimbus of power. Cyclops, behind Jean, his optic blasts shooting out from him like some angry deity's lightning bolts. Iceman and Wolverine were suddenly huge phantoms acting directly on the targets around them, sheeting huge moon fragments with ice, rending them asunder with claws and bare hands. Gambit flung his cards around him like bolts from the blue, irresistible. Laughter welled up all around Charles as the X-Men attacked the last of the targets, and Charles simply sat and watched, feeling the astonishment in individual minds in the fleet, Lilandra's amazement and concern, Orien's approval and worry—

"Stop increment," Charles said softly. The laughter went on around him, the laughter of gods. There was nothing in the space left to attack.

"We can do it, Professor!" Storm's voice cried—no question, utter confidence. *"We can do it!"*

And in the back of his mind, that stab again. Fear, frustration, and hatred—

Here! he thought. *They're here, whoever it is, they're here.*

His mind fled down that connection, seeking the mind behind it, reaching—

And suddenly the connection broke.

And the giant forms reeled, cried out in pain, faded to nothing. The X-Men, on their targets or near them, collapsed. Not dead, but hurting, minds in shock and turmoil as a somatic connection which had only started to be made was now brutally cut from outside. All were left suddenly small, cold, alone, each one fumbling desperately for a sense of himself or herself.

"Lilandra," Charles cried, "we need pickup now! Something has gone wrong! Bring them in—quickly, bring them in!"

An hour or so later, in the flagship's hospital wing, the X-Men were in various stages of recovery. None of them had been physically harmed, but they were all weak, tired, and bewildered. "Depressed," Cyclops said weakly, "I feel depressed. Why should I feel *depressed*? We all did great."

Bobby groaned. "I feel terrible."

"Can you be more specific, Robert?" the Professor asked.

"Yeah. I feel like I don't want to make so much as a trayful of ice cubes. For *days*."

Charles frowned. This was a problem, as they were likely to be needed again, not in days, but in hours.

"What happened to the noumenoextensor, Charles?" said Jean. "What went wrong?"

"There was some kind of power cutout—or so it would

appear. Lilandra says the techs are still looking into it. It may simply have been a difficulty with feeding the amount of power that you all were attempting to draw. Or some imbalance. It's being investigated.''

"It better be investigated pretty quick," Wolverine said, frowning, " 'cause I don't know about the rest of you, but even though the 'up' was good, the 'down' could kill you dead.''

They all nodded at that. Remy boosted himself up to a sitting position on the bed where he had been stretched out, and said, "Dat's true, but dere's worse. *Mes amis*, I don't *like* me anymore, I t'ink.''

The other X-Men looked at him. "Seriously," Remy said. "Why would I? Look at me now. Little an' weak— why would I wan' to be like dis? I want to be like *dat*. Strong, de power a hundred time, a hundred *t'ousan'* time what it be now. An' de body, strong to take it, de mind, quick. When you been a tiger," Gambit said softly, "why go back to being a mouse? What sane person would wan' to?''

Iceman was nodding. "He's right," he said softly. "What it felt like—like it was working for the first time. Really working *right*. Then, just like that, poof, gone.''

There was an uncomfortable silence in the room. In an unguarded moment, Charles heard Jean thinking, *How alike we sound.* He shuddered. Most of the rest of them were not looking at Charles, and he thought he knew why. But he understood exactly how they felt. That rush of power, knowledge, suddenly gone.

And still, the memory of the knife in his mind.

"Another thing," Charles said, "to add to the general disquiet, since this seems more a time for questions than answers. Someone here with the task force is behind the troubles we're having.''

"I think so too, Charles," Jean said. "I keep getting flashes of someone—something—angry and hating, but the trace has been too diffuse to track clearly."

"I'm glad to hear you confirm it."

"But who are they after?" Bishop said, propping himself up on one huge elbow. "Us? You? Or are we incidental?"

"It is hard to tell."

"But somebody traveling with us doesn't want us to complete this job," Jean said. "Both times we've worked with the noumenoextensor, something has gone wrong. Yet we have to work with it if we're to attack this creature."

"So it would seem," Bishop said. "But if something goes wrong again while we're actually attacking the creature, no matter what the thing itself does, that could be the end of us then and there. I don't like this at all."

"Neither do I," said Charles. "But at the moment there's not a great deal we can do, except investigate what steps are being taken to remedy the situation."

He turned, headed for the door. "All of you rest as best you can," he said. "I need to see Lilandra."

To his surprise, he did not get to see her, and spent nearly an hour and a half discovering that this was going to be the case. Lilandra's staff, to his surprise, were remarkably unforthcoming about where the Majestrix might be located at the moment. All they would tell Charles was that she was busy, and that they would pass on his messages to her. The Imperial Guard also were nowhere to be found.

Charles was not used to being so stonewalled, and it made him slightly cranky. At the same time, there was nothing he could do about it. He went back to the hospital room, and found most of the X-Men sleeping; the exhaustion subsequent to use of the noumenoextensor had caught up with them. Only two of them were awake—one of them reading in an annoyed sort of way from a Shi'ar bookpad, the other with his hands folded, gazing off into space: the Beast and Wolverine, respectively.

"How are you two?" Charles said, slipping in between the two beds they occupied.

"We seem to have suffered least," the Beast said, setting his book down. "It probably has to do with the fact that our specific mutant abilities have more to do with strictly physical traits. Plus Logan's healing factor, of course." He shook his head.

"I was meaning to talk to you about that," Charles said, "if you feel up to it—"

"We're bored outta our minds," Wolverine said, looking up from under his eyebrows. "The rest of the crowd ain't exactly up to conversation at the moment."

"Do you two feel like you will be in shape sometime in the next day?"

Wolverine thought a moment, then nodded.

"I suspect so," the Beast said.

"I was going to ask you, then, if you had noticed any"—he shrugged—"residual effects of the extensor, any leftovers."

"You mean, are we still feeling any stronger or smarter than we really are?" Beast wiggled his eyebrows. "Not really."

"But you were looking unusually reflective when I came in, Hank."

The Beast paused, then chuckled. "Yes, well, but I fear not for any useful reason. I was just thinking—does this creature's life cycle as we understand it remind you of anything, Charles?''

''Well, it is broadly insectile.''

''Yes, but I mean specifically.''

Charles shook his head.

''I was thinking,'' Beast said, ''of parasitic wasps.''

Charles considered that. ''Well, with the difference that their prey is usually live. Though I suppose that you could consider a star 'live' in comparison to the 'dead' matter around it—planets, dust, dark matter.''

''Yes. But I was thinking of something else specifically. I have a friend, a cinematographer, who spent a lot of time working with an independent producer who did a lot of nature films for public television, the BBC, and so forth. He was sent out once to photograph the life cycles of parasitic wasps, I think for an episode of *Nova* or some such. Well, you know the basics, I'm sure. The wasp mates, then starts to prepare a home for its egg about to be hatched. It hunts down its prey, which will be the food supply for the egg—usually some unfortunate caterpillar or fly—stings it, paralyzes it, brings it home to the little hole that it's dug. Then it puts the fly or worm in the hole, lays its egg on the body, seals the hole up, and flies away to repeat the process.

''Well, I said to my friend that this must be fascinating work. And he said, 'Yes, it is, especially when the wasp screws up.' '' The Beast stretched, cracking his knuckles, and folded his hands again, looking at Charles over his spectacles. ''Now, it had never occurred to me that the wasps *would* screw up. I mean, they must reproduce, and one assumes they must be fairly good at this by now, after who knows how many millions of years. And my friend said, 'You have no idea, but they're *not*. Instinct is not quite the razor-edged tool we think it is, sometimes.' And he said that the fact that people are of my opinion was partly his fault, and that of other makers of nature films.

"I told him that I thought he might be exaggerating the case. And he said to me—and I'm paraphrasing here—'You have no idea how many shots it took the last time we did this, to get the right shots of the parasitic wasps to stitch together into one unbroken sequence. And I don't mean the angle of the light being wrong, or missing the creature we're trying to film. See, the problem is that most people see the finished films, and the sequence seems to progress smoothly, from the digging of the hole to the hunting of the prey to the laying of the egg, and the hole being sealed up again. It's not until you start shooting one of these films that you see the wasps digging the holes, and then forgetting to put the caterpillar in them. Or digging the hole, and putting a caterpillar in it, and then forgetting to lay the egg—just covering up the hole and flying away again. Or you see the wasp dig the hole and forget where it is, and fly all over the landscape for hours, looking for it.' "

Wolverine leaned forward, getting interested. "There were apparently endless accidents," the Beast continued. "Wasps carrying the caterpillar to the hole, dropping it in the grass nearby, and not being able to find it again. Wasps absentmindedly laying *two* eggs on the same caterpillar, so there is not sustenance enough for both the larvae when they hatch, and they both starve, half-grown, and die. Wasps who get stuck at the hole-building stage, but who never seem to move on to the next step in the cycle." Hank chuckled. "Well, my friend Bob said to me that the problem is that though instinct gives these creatures a guide, they don't infallibly pay attention to it. And this process of reproduction, which seems so seamless when you watch it in a nature movie, is full of places where it can go wrong—and will do so, very easily, especially if you help it. Bob and the other members of the film crew used to help it, out of boredom, sometimes. They would steal a wasp's caterpillar, or cover up the holes themselves, because they got so frustrated with the creatures, who couldn't do any better. But Bob said, too, that maybe this ineptitude was a good thing. Considering how many parasitic wasps there are as it is, if they *were* efficient, we would be up to our armpits in them. Now, I find myself wondering if this process we've been getting glimpses of isn't similar, if there isn't a place where we could interfere, either by getting in its way, or stressing it, or otherwise changing the rules."

"Oh, *that's* just great," Wolverine said. "What you're saying is, 'Let's make it angry, and maybe it'll make a mistake.' You been watchin' too mucha the Cartoon Channel."

"Not 'make it angry,' but there might be a place, several places, in this creature's life cycle where things could go wrong—and just by helping them to go wrong, we may be able to beat the cycle with less energy output, less danger."

"You mean gettin' away with our lives," said Wolverine. "If that flamin' machine don't manage to kill us instead. Or somebody aimin' at Lil, or the Prof. We're probably next anyway."

"Well," said Charles. He looked over at the Beast, and then said thoughtfully, "Are you *sure* there aren't any residual effects?"

Hank chuckled. "If there are, they're only in memory, Charles," he said. "I wouldn't think that would be enough by itself."

" 'Memory is the gateway to the future,' " said Charles.

"Name the philosopher," said the Beast, and grinned.

Wolverine snorted and said, "Wittgenstein."

The Beast looked over at him sharply. "I thought it was Descartes."

Wolverine looked back at him sideways. "Maybe it was. I made it up."

"*He's* obviously nearly recovered," Charles said, turning away. "You two rest for now. I have some things to look into."

He finally got to see Lilandra later that evening. She was in her quarters aboard the flagship, dressed in black, with a grim and determined look on her face. Charles knew that when she was in such moods, it was wise to stay formal. In the rear of the room, Gladiator stood, watching him.

"Kallark? Good evening."

"Professor," Gladiator said.

"Majestrix—"

"I'm sorry not to have been able to see you today, Charles," she said, looking up from her big shiny black desk, all covered with pads and data solids and printed reports. "It's been a busy day."

"Dravian? Or the second attack?"

"It's more than that. Tell me, have you noticed any odd, or unusual, thought patterns around?"

"Majestrix, I have."

"Why have you not reported them to me?"

Charles hesitated, then said, diplomatically, "I haven't been sure of the source. It seemed premature to accuse anyone without knowing who I accused."

"I see." She sat silent for a moment, and then said, "We are continuing to investigate the attack on you, Charles, but I am not happy about what I am finding."

"Which is?"

"Nothing. The minor officer who pulled the trigger was newly assigned to duty aboard the flagship—a clerk, actually. How he got his hands on a molecular disassociator is not yet determined. Such things are carefully controlled, aboard ship. You cannot just pick a lock somewhere and steal one. And usually they have mindlocks on them, so that a weapon must first be 'conditioned' to the personnel who will use it, and even then a password must be given to the personnel by their commanding officer."

"Interesting."

"It has occurred to me that a powerful enough telepath might have managed to tamper with such a weapon, which is why I was asking about odd thought patterns or traces."

"Majestrix," Charles said, "what I felt, on several occasions, was anger: at you, at me, at the X-Men. Also satisfaction at the thought that something should happen to us, singly or collectively, and frustration when it did not. Nothing more concrete than that."

"Very well," she said, "we will just have to keep investigating matters as best we can."

"If I can help you with that—"

"Thank you, Charles, but too many of my people feel that your presence here means an attempt to meddle in, or bypass, our usual channels and forms of justice. I think we will go on as we have been doing."

She sighed, rubbed her head. "I am sorry if I seem sharp or short-tempered tonight. Much is happening, and much of it seems bad. Have you heard about the star-eater?"

"No—"

"It appears to be starting to pupate."

"Then we are already too late . . ."

"Well, the situation certainly does not look promising for us. But at least the creature has stopped eating stars."

"We will have to find something else to call it, then."

Her smile was wry. "Yes. It is a pity, though. The next stage of its life cycle may be much less easy for us to deal with. We'll make our best speed to the area, though that will not be as fast as I would like. The galactic core areas are so energetic, even under normal circumstances, that gates tend to malfunction there the more mass they must transport. So we will have to gate as close as we can, then go the rest of the way under normal drive. It will take us several days. Time we cannot really spare, but we have no choice. We will be stopping once in each thirty-hour day to recalibrate our instruments—signal degradation is a problem in such energetic spaces—and you and the X-Men will have more opportunities to work with the extensor. Meanwhile, about this attack on you . . ." She sighed. "Gladiator, will you excuse us for a few minutes?"

"Majestrix—" He looked worried.

"Stay right outside. Come if I call."

Gladiator looked at her, but she would not change her mind. He stepped out the door of Lilandra's quarters, and let it solidify behind him.

"Charles," she said after a moment, not getting up. "Tell me the truth."

"Always, my love."

"You and Orien were talking before the attack, for quite a while."

"Yes."

"Were you—arguing?" She did not say, *about me.*

"If it was argument," Charles said, "it was very much in the Socratic style. Let us say that we had a free and frank exchange of opinions."

"And what was the result?"

Charles sighed. "That each of us feels he is in the right

and the other, with the best possible motives, is wrong."

She looked at him in silence for a few moments. Finally she got up and started to pace. "Rumor travels fast around here," Lilandra said. "There are whispers that *you* arranged the attack on Orien, that you were mentally controlling the officer who fired, and made it look like an attack on you to cover the real intent."

"That is outrageous," Charles said softly, "as well you know. If you need me to open my mind to you so that you can—"

"Charles," she said sharply. He stopped; the imperial tone was difficult to ignore. "Of course it is ridiculous. But rumor is always indicative of problems further down. There are many who still believe, despite plenty of hard evidence to the contrary, that this whole business with the star-eater is somehow something I have fabricated, or arranged, so that you and the X-Men will have to be here—but specifically you. Those who believe this kind of thing are all too willing to believe as well that I might be conniving with you at Orien's death. The jump of reasoning to that conclusion eludes me, but there it is. Right now, with matters at a very sensitive stage in several different investigations, I think it might be wiser if you and Orien were not together too much. I am sure that someone is indeed targeting you and the X-Men. I would prefer, however, that you were careful about who might be standing *near* the target, until we can determine who might be doing the firing, and can take them down." She sighed. "Orien is a good and intelligent officer, no matter how negative my personal feelings toward him might be. That you should feel, if not friendly, at least accepting toward him pleases me. But this is the wrong time and place. I would ask you to avoid him."

Charles nodded.

Lilandra sat down behind her desk, sighed again. "I am so tired, Charles. And the behavior of the noumenoextensor has me worried. If it does not function, if the X-Men cannot use it to their advantage, then we will be thrown back on mere physical interventions, weapons and such. That frightens me. I do not think we can win under those circumstances. Yet even if it can be properly tuned for them—and the techs are working on it night and day—they still seem to suffer terribly from its use. I am afraid that use at full power might—well."

She looked up from the desk at him. "They know the dangers," Charles said, before she could open her mouth. "For this cause, they are willing. But if there is anything I can do about it, I will not let them die."

"The problem is, Charles," she said, "in that battle, the extensor will be affecting you too. Caught in its effect yourself, how will you help *them*?"

He was silent a moment. "I am working on that."

She had put her chin down on the fingers of her interlaced hands, and was looking at him from that position. "Do you think you have time for me tonight?" she said.

"Always, dear heart. But are you not afraid of standing too close to the target yourself?"

She laughed very softly, though it was not precisely a happy sound. "Charles," she said, "in my case, it is *you* who may be standing too close. Or sitting, as the case may be. Never mind; if you're comfortable being there, that is enough for me. I did not lie before, when I said I need you. Twenty-eight hundred hours?"

"Yes."

"Kallark?"

The door faded again, and Gladiator came in. "Call Nightside and Electron," Lilandra said, "and have them escort the Professor back down to the hospital wing, or wherever else he wishes to go. Please tell them and the others that when Charles is not with the X-Men, I prefer that he travel escorted. Charles,'' she said, turning to him, ''humor me in this, and when you need to go somewhere, call for one of the Guard. Until we have the perpetrators of these attacks caught, and their motives laid bare, I am reluctant to take any more chances. And I would like to see you at twenty-eight with an expanded version of the Beast's thoughts on putative weak points in the star-eater's life cycle.''

Charles raised his eyebrows, turning the hoverchair as Gladiator stood aside for him. ''Majestrix,'' he said, smiling slightly, ''you do not miss much, do you?''

''Not lately,'' she said, ''and definitely not tonight. Until later, Charles.''

The next couple of days sorted themselves out into a kind of routine, though a difficult and uncomfortable one. The flagship would stargate to a position, then hold there, recalibrating its instruments for an hour, maybe two or three at a time, then stargate again. Under other circumstances, this amount of stargating would be considered dangerous— stargates tended to have deleterious long-term effects on stars—but the usual restrictions had been waived for the current crisis.

Charles and the X-Men noticed considerable tension building up among the crew. They were used to going somewhere with a goal, doing it, and coming home, not this extended long haul. A situation like this, however, made it plain that even the scientific proficiencies of the Shi'ar had their limits. Each time they transited, it took longer to recalibrate the sensors. Arguments could be heard on the bridge. Orien could be heard to raise his voice repeatedly as readings were discussed, and opinions were voiced and slapped down over whether or not it mattered that a reading was five percent or ten percent off the norm. The ship would gate again, stop again, recalibrate—and so it would go until the end of a long day, when the crew were exhausted and could barely stand the sight of one another anymore. There the ship would pause, and the X-Men would have a chance to get out and practice on whatever raw materials they found around them.

As they penetrated into the neighboring galaxy, the business of practicing got easier. There was at least plenty of matter to work with. The fleet was coming in along a vector where there were no populated worlds that anyone knew of. The first stopping-point was well out from a small, unusually green G9 star. It had not been touched by the recent troubles, though it had older ones, perhaps—it had no planets, but it did have a big asteroid belt. Some ways above and beyond this, the flagship positioned itself so that the X-Men could go out and work.

"Professor," Storm said, "you should not do it."

"Storm," said Charles, "I *will* do it."

They were down in the lounge of their quarters, having an argument. Such verbal sparring had become more frequent lately, at least over the last twenty-four to thirty-six hours. They were all on edge. No one seemed able to cut anyone else very much slack. This had been noticed among the Shi'ar crew, who were somewhat amused by it. As it happened, this suited Charles's purposes perfectly.

"If one of *us* wanted to go out alone," Storm said, tucking her legs up underneath her and reaching for a cup of Lilandra's morningdraft, to which she had become rather partial, "you would marshal all kinds of reasons why we should not do it. Unknown spaces. Unknown dangers. It is unwise to work without support. You've told us that many times. And especially in this case, when the noumenoextensor is still not behaving correctly.''

''I know that,'' said Charles. ''But I must do this—must try it alone, to see if I get the results I expect. If I *do* get the results, then we will have this discussion again later, and you will explain to me how you really knew I would be all right, but you were 'just worried.' ''

They glared at each other. The glare was affectionate. ''And if you do not? What are we supposed to do then?''

''Carry on without me,'' Charles said, ''as you have done before, and as you would have to do at any time if something killed me. Storm, why are you treating me as if I were a child, or an invalid?''

She simply looked at him. He glared back. ''I am valid in all the ways that count,'' Charles said.

''Never mind—I was seeing the humor in the phrase, nothing else. Professor, how can you think that your judgment is perfectly clear at a time like this?''

He looked at her. ''You are under great stress,'' Storm said. ''Things are very difficult for you—''

''Lilandra and I are fine,'' Charles said.

''*You* two are fine, yes, but nobody else around here is fine about you, as you know perfectly well. The Shi'ar's feelings are either powerfully for or powerfully against, and you have to know that—you have to be sensing it all day. Jean is having trouble dealing with it. She says there is a constant rumble of mental stress and discomfort about this issue—from you, from Lilandra, from the Imperial Guard, from everyone. And it is not going to get better, not until we deal with—'' She rolled her eyes in the general direction of the core of the galaxy. ''In any case, you have to be experiencing some difficulty yourself in this regard, and the chances of it affecting your judgment, in my opinion, are considerable.''

Charles shook his head. ''All I can tell you,'' he said, ''is that your concern in this particular case is misplaced, though I thank you for it. What I do want to hear from you is this. Have you noticed anything about the others functioning under the extensor that I have not, and which I might need to know about?''

Storm thought a moment, then shook her head. ''Professor,'' she said, ''I still have difficulty believing that we are going to be able to work succcssssfully under battle conditions when the machine has this tendency to cut out without warning. And the 'crash' afterwards is a great concern to me. Each time we use the extensor, we crash harder. A maximum output is likely to leave us maximally put out, as it were. If not dead.''

At this point Iceman and Bishop came into the lounge, looking grim and satisfied. ''Where is Hank?'' said Charles.

''With the Shi'ar scientific team,'' Bobby said, ''and Cyclops is with him. The team is peeved about having to let him help with the extensor, but that's just tough—word came down from Lilandra at about the same time we showed up.''

''Very well,'' Charles said, turning back to Storm. ''Almost all the elements are now in place—''

Professor, Jean said inside his mind, *I'm ready when you are.*

Are you certain no one suspects?

As certain as I can be.

''Correction,'' Charles said to Storm and the others. ''*All* factors are now in place. I should get on with it.''

"I suppose there is no way I can talk you out of this," Storm said at last.

"C'mon, Ororo," Iceman said, "don't be so nervous. It's our best chance at smoking out whatever's going on with the extensor—so it'll be of some use when we finally get where we're going. We can't afford to mess that up— too much rides on it."

"Perhaps," Storm said. "But there is a certain intoxicated or 'drugged' quality to one's experience while using the extensor. It is a peculiar elation that I would not like to become habituated to. But meanwhile, I simply do not like the Professor's plan."

"There is no point in discussing this any further," Charles said. "I cannot continue to subject the X-Men to dangers which might be resolved by me testing the extensor alone."

"But, Professor—" Storm said.

I don't want to hear it, Storm! The others glanced at one another; he was actually broadcasting his thoughts. He continued voice-only: "This is my final word. The chances are very strong indeed that testing the device singly, rather than in groups, is the way to isolate what the problem is. But I will not further jeopardize your lives—or sanity, for all I know—in allowing you to use a mechanism which seems to be giving you all so much trouble."

He turned his hoverchair and headed out. The X-Men looked at one another, their brains tingling slightly with the force of the thoughts Charles had been broadcasting.

"The whole flagship has to have heard that," said Bishop.

Jean's telepathic voice chuckled in everyone's heads. *I certainly hope so. . . .*

• • •

Charles made his way down to the control room for the noumenoextensor, on the flagship's utility deck. There, the Beast and Cyclops were moving from station to station of the a much larger installation of the extensor than Ollikh had shown them: almost forty feet of what appeared to be black glass with multilayered lines of burning light buried in it. Nearly half the installation was alight, throbbing with trails of brilliance that chased each other through the dark matrix that held them.

"Hank, Scott, how is it going?" said Charles as he glided in.

Scott gave Charles an eloquent look of complete confusion. He raised his eyebrows, but said nothing. The Beast said, "The principles are obscure, but not completely imponderable, if you know what I mean."

"I am not sure."

"Well, let's just say that you may not need to be a polymath to operate this equipment, but it helps."

Several Shi'ar officers and scientists were standing around with varying expressions of amusement, annoyance, or moderately well-concealed scorn on their young faces. "I want to thank you all," Charles said, "for your assistance in helping us learn how to better manage this equipment. Working together, I'm sure we will all bring the best out of it."

One of the technicians bowed slightly. Another raised her eyebrows in an expression similar to the one Scott had been wearing. A third simply nodded and went back to waving his hands over the console. "When will you be ready for me to go out?" said Charles.

"Oh, you may as well go now," said the Beast. "Go ahead and get into your suit. The pod's waiting for you. We're going to start you at a somewhat higher level than we've previously been using, and we'll take you up in increments quickly, about once every ten seconds.''

"I think I can handle that," said Charles. "If I can't, I'll let you know."

"Right."

"I will go suit up, then." Charles turned and made his way out of the control room and over to the area of the utility deck where the suits and pod were kept, near the airlock access. There he pulled the suit which had been altered for him out of its rack, and opaqued the suiting and airlock area around him. No one would be too surprised at that. They knew that Earth people had peculiar privacy taboos.

He was listening very hard. All around him the quiet buzz of thought in the ship went on. Here and there he would touch a mind which was more than usually strident with alarm. Several of those belonged to the X-Men. Well, that was normal, and possibly unavoidable under the circumstances. But several of those minds belonged to Shi'ar, or members of other species serving on the ship, and to those he listened with particular interest.

All right, he said at last. *Everything's ready.*

A few minutes later, an empty pod slipped free of the flagship and out into the unending night.

"How long until you arrive at the control position, Professor?"

"Four minutes, I would say."

"Very well. Noumenoextensor initial activation starting now."

Behind the black glass, light glittered and flashed. Cyclops stood back and watched while the Beast moved from one panel to another under the tutelage of the Shi'ar officer with whom he had been working. "Right," Hank said. "The pattern-matching controls first? Then the bioelectricity lock, and the feedback loop, and the brainscan adjustment. How does that look, Tapav?"

The Shi'ar officer looked over the board with a critical eye. "All the energy settings seem as they should be, according to the specs. The important thing seems to be making the inherent energy of the space funnel through the field at the right intensity and speed to feed the enhanced body-power pattern. The aftereffects your people have been experiencing may have something to do with the next part of the process-passthrough, the feedback loop. But it's just a theory on my part—those readings seem right too."

The Beast shrugged. "Theory. But then all too often, when you come to test something, you find that some superannuated theorist dropped a letter or two out of the equations at an early stage, and—"

"Sir," Tapav said, looking injured, "I assure you that *I* am not yet superannuated. And even if I were, I would still be very careful with my letters. Our testing on our own people simply never produced this kind of result. It may have something to do with being a mutant."

The Beast raised his eyebrows. "Wouldn't it be ironic if it did," he said. "Just at the point where you need to have mutants save you and everyone else. Well . . ." He trailed off. "Never mind that. But that's an interesting point. Why *would* our test results look so much different than yours? Our physiologies aren't *that* dissimilar."

"With respect, sir, that's the question our team leader has been knocking his head against for the past several days."

"Doubtless. He and I will probably need to have a chat. I would value his opinions. Meanwhile, show me a set of the calibrations for a Shi'ar who might use this machine.''

''Certainly.'' With a wave of her hand Tapav wiped away the curls and whorls of color embedded in one part of the display. She touched several specific spots on the dead black surface, and brought up another set of coiled and tangled colors. ''This is a Shi'ar pattern,'' she said. ''Mine, in fact.''

''Is it indeed,'' said the Beast, pausing to study it for a moment. ''Why does your pattern go 'up' in the matrix here, and here—while ours goes 'up' there, and there?''

Tapav eyed the pattern. ''Species differences, I suppose. That's basic somatype analysis there.''

''But I thought that the species-specific material, DNA codings and so forth,'' said the Beast, ''was over here.'' He indicated another part of the intricate diagram.

Tapav looked, thought a moment, then shook her head. ''That's a good question. I hadn't done a comparison that way.'' She waved, brought up ''ghost'' images of all the X-Men's readings from the last test, and sandwiched them over one another. The result looked as if a great deal of glowing, multicolored spaghetti had been dropped into the black matrix and frozen there.

The Beast looked at the diagram thoughtfully. ''I think I see,'' he said. ''Possibly, anyway. We will find out. Who has been doing the programming on this project?''

''Oh, there's a whole team, as you might expect,'' Tapav said, ''but our senior research fellow, Argath, did the basic program design, and assigned the various sections of code to the people under him. I don't think there would be a line of code in this project that he didn't personally pass, though he might not have written it all.''

''Well, that's good to know,'' the Beast said. ''Now then—Professor, are you ready?''

"On position," his voice said over the intercom.

"All right, let's go." The Beast waved his hand over the controls, brought up the preset pattern he had prepared earlier. "Extensor active."

Charles reached out with his mind. Far away, he could feel Jean doing the same, and the power available to her waiting mind suddenly increasing. *How are you holding up?* he said.

It's not quite as easy as I thought. The power, it's increasing so quickly.

Ride with it as best you can.

I can hear them now, she said. *Charles—half a galaxy, the minds in this nearest galaxy . . . I can hear them. I can hear them all. All the voices, all the minds . . . they're like the ocean. A lot of pain, out there. A lot of death because of this creature. Stars tearing themselves apart. Whole planetary populations fleeing in terror . . . when they can manage to escape at all. All the lost dreams, the wasted work and lives.*

The Professor bit his lip. *Just listen, Jean. And hang on.*

He waited quietly. Soon it would come—and this time, he would be ready.

And it did come. The knife of hate, driving deep, aimed right at him. This was all his fault. He should pay. He, and all the ones who stood with him. But an additional strand was there as well, bizarre under the circumstances: grief. For the creature out there in the dark—

The power's beginning to waver, Jean said silently. *If this is anything like the last time, it's going to go out shortly.*

I know. Pay no attention to it for the moment. Just hang on the best you can.

—all alone out there. A unique creature, never seen before. It should not be allowed to have this happen to it. It needed a protector.

Charles struck. At the other end, he heard the shock, the astonishment—

—and Jean's cry too, as the power that had been filling her suddenly cut off. But Charles paid no attention to it; he was digging deep. It was going to take a few moments, he knew. Minds did not usually come stamped with their owners' names. Identity lay in imagery. Still, some minds he did know, and this mind was none of them— which eliminated the X-Men, Lilandra, and most of the Imperial Guard. He sorted with brutal speed through the images in that other mind, holding it still though it screamed inside and pounded at him. It was not able to shift him, though. Charles had plenty of practice at this kind of work, and the other had none.

Images of the night with stars, going back a long way to someone's childhood. Back to an old dream of finding out what lived out there, what it thought, what it did. Then slowly realizing that the dream of going to other planets was for others, but not for you. There simply wasn't the money. There were no family connections to help you get into the fleet either. So a career in the sciences, long study in a brutally competitive area, learning the way things work in the body and in other organisms, Shi'ar and alien. But always looking over the shoulder toward that memory of the stars. Then, finally the happy chance to change—

Resistance! Charles pushed against it, surprised at the strength of the mind pushing back.

Let me in!

No, you'll kill it!

The other mind dug its heels in, refused him. Its power

was more than surprising under the circumstances. *Possibly a natural telepath like Sibyl*, Charles thought. *Not mutant, but certainly with much more power than a Shi'ar would normally possess—and a sense that hiding the ability is wiser than revealing it. Persuasive power—power to force someone into doing things they might not do otherwise. Most dangerous.*

Let me in! he cried out with his mind.

No! You'll kill it, was the response. And then utter shock as the truth of the situation came home. *Wait a moment— you shouldn't still be able to, you should be—Who's really out there?*

Charles struck straight in like a spear in the moment's confusion. All around him he could ''hear'' whispered conversations in the dark. The mind which had been having these conversations knew that they had to be kept secret at all costs. But just as secret had to be the power it was bringing to bear on those conversations.

A long, long time back: *''Mother, I want it.''*

''No.''

''I want it. You have to let me have it.''

''No, sweetling, you—''

''You have to. Just do it.''

''Dear one, I—''

''You have to.''

A long pause, and then, *''Yes. All right.''*

That was the first time she realized that she could do something special. She had done it many, many times since, with varying results. It usually worked, but not always. When that happened, usually she stifled her fury at not getting what she wanted, and went on to something else. It had been that way with going out to space. Afterwards, even that had come out right, though perhaps not exactly as she had planned. *That* conversation certainly had not.

"I want you, very much."

"You must forgive me, but truly I cannot."

"But you do want me."

"You are a valuable assistant—a good friend, even. But what you are asking of me is something I cannot give."

"Of course it is. I want you. Be mine, just for a little while."

"No."

"Yes, you must."

"No."

"You must."

A long pause. Then the answer:

"Thank you, but no."

The fury after that refusal had been hard indeed to stifle. But she had, for policy's sake. There would be another time. And meanwhile, life suddenly became much more interesting. Something strange revealed itself in the core of the next galaxy. The Science Council finally investigated it: *he* might have refused her, but there were still things he was good for. They began to get a clearer sense of what this marvel was. She was ecstatic. It was strange life, such as no one had ever seen before, something wonderful to study. And then the Majestrix made her plans—

They were terrible. They were going to destroy it. It wasn't fair. This creature was functioning in the only way it could, in accord with its own unthinkable evolution. How could they be so callous as to simply slay it out of hand? It had killed people, yes, but people died every day. The Shi'ar had killed their millions in the past, and had never looked back with regret. The hypocrisy of the situation horrified her. And then the Majestrix, happily unable to do anything about the "problem" herself, had called in these

X-Men, these aliens with their leader, her lover.

That was when she had moved, as soon as word had filtered down about what was to happen. She knew Argath moderately well, he being an associate of Avend's, and all of them were assigned together to the flagship, her team for its expertise about the creature, Argath for the implementation of his great experiment. Within an hour or so of his coming aboard, she had sought him out.

"It wouldn't be hard."

"It goes completely against the grain. You're asking me to subvert my own research, my own project."

"Just this once."

"It's never 'just this once,' you know that. Are you crazy? What if they find out?"

"They'll never find out. It's not our own people they're going to be using it on, it's these Terrans. They'll think it's some physiological problem, some obscure human thing. They're mutants anyway; they probably have all kinds of internal oddities. That'll be easy to exploit."

"I don't like it."

"It doesn't matter. You have to do it."

"I don't know."

"You have to."

"Well."

"Do it, Argath. You must do it."

A long silence. Then: *"All right."*

Aha, Charles said.

Her scream of fury down the link between them was like a fire in his brain. She struck at him, stabbing at him with her hatred, flailing around in mental fury and trying to do something to him which would kill him. But the knife of hate was not enough. Charles ducked it effortlessly, then struck straight into her mind again with such force that it knocked her unconscious.

Charles? Charles! Are you all right?

I'm fine, Jean. What about you?

I don't feel good, but my brain's still working. Charles, I called and called you.

I was very busy. I'll tell you all about it. Hank? he called. "Professor?"

He de-opaqued the suiting room and glided out, frowning. *Ask the bridge to put a tractor on the pod and bring Jean in. I've finished what I had to do. When you have done that, call the Majestrix. Ask her to have someone go to the quarters of Irdin, the research assistant who works with Orien and Avend, and ask them to have her confined. I believe the Majestrix is going to need to have a little talk with her.*

Seven

The next morning, they stargated again—into turmoil.

The gating took a long time. Orien and the other fleet commanders debated long into the night over whether they should even risk gating again, so close to the increasingly disturbed galactic center. While they were still many lightyears out from the damaged core, and nothing would be apparent by visible light, those sensors that used faster than light particles like tachyons for sensing were reporting tremendous destruction and disassociation of the structures at the core. They also read so much plasma and ambient high-energy radiation that, it was argued, even the rugged hardware of the gates would finally malfunction in the face of it.

But the Majestrix felt that time was becoming of the essence, especially as the star-eating creature had pupated. "No matter how vulnerable it may or may not be," Lilandra said to her captains, "it is at least keeping quiet." So it was, though it could not now be directly sensed except as a gravitational source at the heart of the galaxy, one that was not nearly massive enough to be a black hole or a star collapsing through its Schwarzschild radius.

"Plenty massive enough, though," Wolverine said, looking over a repeater console showing the bridge readings from the utility deck, where he, Iceman, Storm, and Cyclops were waiting for Jean to come in after her own test run on the newly adjusted noumenoextensor. After what Charles had discovered the day before, Lilandra had spoken to the assistants working with Argath on the extensor, and had had them quietly "restore" an earlier version of the mechanism's code, dating from before Argath and Irdin had come aboard the flagship. Those assistants were moving back and forth before the consoles now, watching the readings carefully, while the Beast worked with them and kept a watchful eye on things.

"The mass would match that of a biggish brown dwarf, if I understand these things," Cyclops said, looking out into the darkness. "Plenty massive is right." His face suggested that he was wondering whether, even with the extensor working properly, they were going to be able to affect the pupa at all.

Charles was sitting quietly off to one side, conscious of the conversation going on around him, while he carefully monitored Jean.

They are incrementing again. What do you hear?

All the voices, all the lives of this galaxy, spread across all the stars that haven't been touched by this trouble. It's as it was before—but the power's not dropping off now. Before, it was as if as soon as you tried to extend yourself at all, it would drop away. Not now, though. There was increasing exultation in her mind-voice.

It's not so much all the voices that we want to hear at the moment, Charles pointed out, *but one. See if you can make anything out.*

She was silent. Charles could "see" a little into her mind, but it was difficult to tell exactly what he saw. It was like looking through the wrong end of a pair of binoculars, and perceiving everything very distantly, very small and sharp, but too reduced to make out detail well. The echoes

194

of the trillions of minds of which she had spoken were there, a huge diffuse glow of life and intention and emotion, as impossible to make out individually as the Milky Way was impossible to resolve into separate stars with the naked eye.

Something, she said after a moment. Since she was focusing on it, Charles could sense it as she could, a point source, heavy and compact. But nothing more in the way of detail.

Incrementing again, Jean. Concentrate on it.

The sense of weight and silence grew. Silent waiting. Something was going to happen, but not just now. Not yet.

Is it conscious?

Not at all, Jean said after a moment. *Alive, yes. But not conscious, not sentient.*

"Not right now, anyway," Charles said to himself under his breath. Outside, off to one side, the stargate that the fleet would use continued, very slowly, to unfold itself, glittering in the pale fire of the seemingly unhurt galactic core.

It's waiting, Jean said. *What I'm feeling now isn't a thought. I think it might be this creature's version of cellular memory. The body remembers what it wants to do, what its DNA has programmed it for—if it even stores its reproductive information in anything like DNA, that is.*

Unknown, Charles said. *We may find out. I hope so, if only at the postmortem stage.* He sighed. *One more incrementation coming, Jean. Try one last time. If we can tell this creature to wake up and go somewhere else . . .*

Silence for a few moments. *It has no intention of doing that*, Jean said, *if it ever has "intention" to do anything. Intelligence it may not have, but its body knows where it is. It's warm. It's fed and full. It has to sleep awhile, to internalize the energy. Then, when the time is right . . .*

When? Can you tell? And can you tell anything about whether we've correctly analyzed its life cycle?

Another long pause. *I don't know,* Jean said finally. *Its body, such as it is, is so firmly locked into its present form that its cells—if that's the word for its basic units of internal structure—are more or less denying any knowledge of what comes afterwards. The creature's physiology knows that* something *will come afterwards. But if it were conscious, you would describe its present state as blissful ignorance. We're just going to have to wait and see.*

All right. You should come in, then.

I don't know if I want to, Charles. All the voices out there—surely there's no harm in listening to them for a little while more.

I would not do that just now, Jean. The fleet is anxious to gate quickly once this modified stargate is deployed.

Well, all right. There was something at the bottom of the thought that startled Charles a little: a touch of petulance, almost an intention to refuse. But it was gone as quickly as he felt it. *Some artifact of the extensor, perhaps.*

Maybe, Jean said. *Otherwise, the extensor seems to be working perfectly. No power drop-offs. I think when we come out on the far side, we can safely test it again one last time, as a group, to make sure.*

You're sure you feel all right, though? No traces of that exhaustion?

I feel fine, Charles, she said, and again he heard in her thought that thread of exultation, the sense that things could not go more right—except that they *would,* eventually. It was a somewhat unnerving tone of mind. It seemed to suggest that the universe would not have a chance to do otherwise than Jean expected.

Charles turned and looked over at the Beast. "Back the extensor down slowly, would you, Hank?"

"Will do."

Coming down now, Jean. Let's see how you do.

Slowly, the sense of the overpowering strength of Phoenix's mind began to ebb away. Charles listened hard, and caught a sudden sense of sadness, followed by a flash of anger. *Why should I stop? Why can't I stay this way? This is horrible, to feel this diminution, this loss of what I'm becoming. There must be a way to—*

And the thought smothered itself, aware suddenly that someone might be listening, someone with power to foil its desires.

Jean? Are you all right?

Fine, Charles. It's almost down to nothing, now.

Almost. He listened, listened hard.

Gone, whispered something in the back of Jean's mind. *But not gone forever. And next time . . .*

Silence, then. *Back to normal*, Jean said.

How are you feeling?

Fine. Normal fatigue, not that awful ready-to-collapse feeling.

"That's very good," Charles said aloud, "very good indeed. Come back in." He turned toward the Shi'ar techs working with the Beast, and said to the nearest of them, "Would you inform Lord Orien, or whoever else is on watch on the bridge, that Phoenix is coming back in now? And we'll do a full test of the team when they've finished this next gating."

"Certainly, Professor."

He turned back toward the window, musing, and then glanced up at Iceman, who had been leaning against it. "That perception of warmth. It's as I told you, Bobby, you may be the answer to this problem. Lack of 'incubating' heat might prove to be the creature's weakness.''

Iceman looked out into the night and raised his eyebrows. ''Hope you're right,'' he said, and headed off, back up toward their quarters.

''He's looking a little twitchy,'' Cyclops said, watching Jean, in her spacesuit, slowly making her way back to the airlock.

''That would not necessarily be inappropriate,'' Charles said. ''He has always been somewhat uncertain about the usefulness of his power. To suddenly find himself to be the member of the team on which so much hinges—'' Charles stretched, folded his arms. ''It could make anyone nervous. It might as easily be you, for example.''

Cyclops smiled. ''I'm nervous enough already, Professor. Don't make it worse.''

Jean came up through the force field airlock, stood looking around her for a moment as if things seemed strange, and then pulled off her helmet and shook hair out. Scott went to her. ''You all right?''

''I'm fine,'' she said. ''Scott, it's working right, now. No 'bad feelings' afterwards. I think we might have a chance to pull this off.''

''We will find out in the next few hours,'' Charles said. ''If you will all hold yourselves ready until we know that conditions are favorable for us to test . . .''

''No problem,'' Wolverine said. ''Be a pleasure to go out and shred somethin' after all this sittin' around listenin' to the science guys complain about their flamin' machines.''

He headed out, followed by Scott and Jean. Storm, though, stood looking out the huge windows at the night, and the fractured galaxy hanging in it.

"You're troubled," Charles said. "But it would hardly take a telepath to tell that."

She looked out into the darkness, shaking her head. "We will be approaching the creature, soon," she said.

"Within six to eight hours, Orien told me."

"And we will have a battle on our hands." She turned to Charles, leaned against the window. "Professor," she said, in soft anguish, "you know my problem. I cannot kill."

"Yet I would guess we are going to have to kill this creature," Charles said. "And, Storm, it may be that we cannot do it without your power."

She stood silent and irresolute. He sighed. "Storm, so many trillions, quadrillions of lives, perhaps more, rest on what we are going to have to do. I cannot ask you to change your principles. You must make your own choices. In the event that it is your power which will make the difference—I would ask you to consider hitting Bishop with everything you have, and letting him redirect the power. You would not yourself be responsible for what happened afterwards. I know, it may sound like sophistry, but this is a problem which we will have to resolve. And if when everything else has been tried, *you* are revealed to be the key—"

She looked at him, shook her head. "Charles," she said, "I do not know. The tyranny of numbers . . . I would barely know how many zeroes to put after a trillion—"

"Twelve," the Beast said, "unless you're doing it the continental way, in which case—"

"Hank."

"Sorry."

"But, Professor, even so many lives . . . all the lives that *are* . . . How do they weigh in the balance against one vow taken and broken? I would have to live with that, just as well as with all those lives lost. Trying to work it out by numbers is no solution. Or a false one.''

She was right, he knew. ''Ororo,'' he said, ''let me know what you are able to do, as soon as you can. I cannot get rid of the feeling that much will depend on it.''

She went away slowly, her head bowed, thinking. Charles sat and watched her, and pitied her, but carefully kept the emotion to himself.

The gating progressed without incident, though it was unsettling enough after the fact. Before, they had at least come out into normal-seeming space. Now they were in something that looked more like a view into a mind trapped in a body that had been overdoing the hallucinogens. Great flaming veils of plasma and ionized dust churned and boiled in the space into which they had gingerly made their way. The fleet was holding still again for the moment, trying to recalibrate their sensors through interference worse than anything they had so far experienced. It would be some little while before they could move on.

They were, however, now within several light-hours of the galactic nucleus—or rather, the former galactic nucleus. It was a sparse, dim, pale, torn-up-looking thing, all streaked with tattered gaseous streamers, its stars sick and pallid or already going brown.

The radiation was bad enough that even Shi'ar suits would have had trouble dealing with it. Charles spoke to the techs to see about having them modified as quickly as possible. It was while he was trying to find out how long this would take that a young Shi'ar officer came up to him and told him that the Majestrix required his attendance at a meeting immediately.

He went along readily enough, and found her sitting at her council table, with Gladiator in the background but very much there, watching everyone and everything that moved. Old Yrinx, her Minister in Chief, was there, and her Minister for Science. Lord Orien was present, seated way down at the opposite end of the table from Lilandra, looking as if he would happily have been at the opposite end of the ship.

Lilandra smiled at Charles as he came in, but the smile was somewhat wan. "A busy day," she said. "How did Phoenix's test go?"

"Flawlessly," Charles said, "as far as we can tell. The side effect of abnormal fatigue seems to have been eliminated."

"Good. You will test again one more time then, as soon as the new spacesuits are sorted out."

"Yes, Majestrix."

She sat back in her chair, rubbed her eyes for a moment. "Very well. As regards Irdin, Charles—our people have run brainscans on her to confirm your experience inside her mind. Not that we would ever doubt you, of course—"

Not that you *would*, Charles thought. *But there are always other voices in your cabinet who need convincing.*

"—but we need our own forms of documentation, as I am sure you understand. Obviously your experience was confirmed, and the scans show that she was responsible for the attack on you as well. She used her ability to suborn one of the weapons officers. There are simply a couple of other points about this business I need to have cleared up."

"I am at your disposal."

"Charles, there is one thing I must know first. When Argath changed the code, the programming of the noumenoextensor—did he make that decision consciously?"

"He made the decision," Charles said, "but consciousness and will are not the same thing. It was another's will operating on his which caused him to choose to alter his own code—to hide in it, as we now see, the subroutines which were sabotaging the X-Men's attempts to successfully access the power made available to them by the extensor. The choice was consciously made, but it was not Argath's choice. Nor would he have been conscious of any difficulty about that for some time. It would appear that Irdin's influence has a persistent quality. Once she extends her power in this way, the effects seem to last for some time."

"Will he remember this choice?"

"I think not. If Argath was as set against it as he sounded to be when she began to exert her influence on him, doubtless his mind will have 'sealed over,' forgotten the incident completely—unable to cope with the information that he acted as he had, and not of his own free will, doing something he would normally have found repugnant. I would bear that in mind when you decide what you will do with him."

"What you're telling me," Lilandra said, "is that despite the fact that he contaminated his own code, he is not to blame."

"That is what I'm telling you, Majestrix."

She breathed out. "Irdin's case, however, is rather different."

Charles sighed wearily. "I must agree, Majestrix. She knew the choice she was making. She knew the danger this course of action would cause to the X-Men and others—many thousands and eventually millions of others. The danger did not matter to her. She is"—he threw a glance at Orien—"someone with a cause. While causes can be noble, and occasionally it is right to fly in the face of authority for the sake of a species' or creature's protection, well . . . At the very least I would say she is misguided.''

''She willingly committed sabotage, however, or caused another to commit it, and against his will.''

''Yes.''

''And the result of that sabotage has been to endanger the X-Men, yourself, and my crew, directly.''

''Yes.''

Lilandra rubbed her eyes for a moment. ''This unfortunately seems straightforward enough. Lord Orien—'' She looked down the table at him. ''You resisted her.''

''Majestrix,'' he said softly, and stopped, and then started again. ''I am very embarrassed to have this come to light in this manner.''

She gave him a cool look. ''Doubtless there are various personal remarks which could be made about this, but I will refrain.'' Charles, though, could hear her thinking that she almost wished Orien had succumbed to Irdin. Then he would no longer be an issue as a possible consort for the Majestrix, especially not after this had come out. Her disgrace would have touched him as well. He would immediately have been designated a security risk, too dangerous or unreliable to ever become permanently associated with the imperial house. This thought, though, she kept to herself. There was a vague feeling at the edges of her mind that it was unworthy.

''Majestrix,'' Orien said, ''if it would do any good, I would apologize.''

''For what?'' she said. ''We cannot help where our affection bestows itself.'' The look on her face was even less revealing than usual, and her tone of voice was flatter than Charles would have thought possible. ''It is not your fault that her affection fixed on you, nor any fault of hers that you failed to return it. I would hardly think that this is cause for embarrassment, any more than it is in other quarters.''

She looked at him, and very slowly he looked away and dropped his gaze to the table.

''So,'' Lilandra said. ''Charles. Is she a mutant?''

''I think not. Just an unusually powerful natural talent, along the lines of Sibyl.''

''It would appear, though, that the talent is coupled with a sociopathic streak.''

''While I am fairly expert in the matters of the mind,'' Charles said, ''I am no psychiatrist. I think a professional trained in your people's mindset and particular psychopathies would be needed to make that assessment.''

''This power of mind, though,'' Lilandra said. ''Do you think she is likely to use it again?''

Charles hesitated, and then said, ''Almost certainly. She has been using it since she was very young, as far as I can tell. I doubt she would more easily stop using it than you would stop using an arm or a leg simply as an act of will.''

''With training, can it be controlled? Could she learn to control it?''

''Majestrix, again, this is a question for the psychiatrists.''

''I think not. The question, Charles, is, *does she have a conscience?*''

''If you mean, does she have a sense of right and wrong, then yes. If you mean, is it the usual sense of right and wrong—'' He shook his head.

''Majestrix,'' Orien said, ''there is something to her point of view, distasteful as we might find it at the moment. If this creature is part of nature—and there is no reason to suspect that it is not; we have no evidence that it came from some other dimension or continuum—then as part of the universal ecology, it has a part to play, a role. We may understand that role badly, or not at all, but that does not change that the role is there. Unpopular though it might be with us, it may be that this wholesale destruction or recycling of galactic core material—bright matter, dark matter— may be in its way as beneficial as forest fires are on planets a little less engineered than the Throneworld. They burn through, they clear the way for new growth. We who build houses find them a nuisance and a menace. But the universe tends to have a larger point of view than ours."

"I will not now argue that point," Lilandra said, "though I wonder whether the logic might not be slightly specious. I am not sure how this material can be recycled. What we see before us at the moment is tremendous amounts of plasma, many black and brown dwarfs, and black holes accreting, here and there."

"I would not venture too far into calling this process useless, though, Majestrix," said the Minister for Science. "There is evidence that black holes in the centers of galaxies may themselves invert and go white, spewing out large amounts of matter which later coalesce into stars. A swifter form of stellar evolution, this, than the usual matter of waiting for clouds of gas and dust to accrete. And the plasma that we're seeing is a notable exciter and accelerator of star formation."

She looked at him and sighed. "I really *need* to have this problem made more complex still," she said.

He shook his head. "The truth is the truth, Majestrix. I serve it as I must, including informing you about both theory and fact when necessary. To fail to do so would be psychopathology on *my* part."

"Yes, well, we all find ourselves in a veritable hotbed

of ethics today," Lilandra murmured. "The question is whether we truly have leisure to indulge ourselves in such. Yrinx," she said, glancing over at her minister, "see to it that the psych staff examine Irdin immediately. In-depth scans and a full NP report, by this evening."

"Yes, Majestrix."

"Charles, I would imagine your suits will be ready shortly. Please conduct your last tests. We will move on the 'pupa' as soon as you've done so. You're all dismissed," she said, and got up, waving Charles away with the rest of them.

My love—

Not now, Charles. Not now. There was turmoil in her mind to match that outside. *I cannot, and I must.*

Cannot what?

But her mind was suddenly shut to him, and he would not probe.

With the others, he went out.

Seven hours later they arrived, at last, in the "hot" area. Orien, like all the other fleet commanders, had been nervous enough about bringing his ship into this area to begin with, redoubtably armored as it was. Shi'ar vessels were not designed to routinely handle such high levels of radiation and so many sudden unpredictable shifts in local gravitic stress. But the area, when they arrived there, was unnervingly calm. Local space was full of plasma torn out of expired stars, but that they had expected. Vast quantities of ionized dust and gas flared rose and violet and agitated gold in the blackness.

And there, at the heart of it all, was what they had come to see, and—at least theoretically—to destroy.

The X-Men and Charles gathered on the bridge deck at

arrival time, as the flagship nosed slowly in through the troubled space. Orien was moving constantly from one command-and-control console to the next, looking over his officers' shoulders and generally acting like the archetypal nervous commander. "The gravitic stresses concern me the most," he said to Charles as he passed by him for a moment, looking out into the hectically colored space around them. "There has been so much disruption of mass around here, and at such high speed. This is the kind of situation which breeds micro black holes, and I do not want to take one of those through the hull—"

"Wouldn't necessarily be fatal," Remy said from beside Charles. "Fair amount of kinetic on dat, I'd t'ink— shouldn't be too hard for me to flip one out de way it came, if one came t'rough."

"Yes, but perceiving it first would be the problem," Orien said, "and then you have to think about how *much* kinetic energy it would be carrying. If you could catch it— *could* you catch it?—I am sure you could indeed 'flip it out' without too much trouble—if the cursed thing didn't vaporize half the ship on impact due to carrying too large an intrinsic velocity. Say a hundred thousand miles per hour or so."

Remy looked thoughtful. "Mmm. Maybe not, *homme*."

They all looked out into the darkness. Wolverine in particular was right up against the huge windows, peering. Behind him, Storm and Bishop were looking over his shoulder, and behind them, Phoenix. "Strange," Bishop said, "to see so much light in space."

"The light is always there," Orien said, coming along behind them. "Rare, though, to have so much matter around to reflect it, and to have the conditions, the ionization and so forth, which produce the effect—"

"There," Phoenix said suddenly.

They all looked. "Contact, sir," said one of the Shi'ar officers behind them. "Definitely an anomalous object."

"What's the mass?"

"About a tenth that of the Throneworld."

Orien nodded. The Beast, coming up beside Charles, looked at him with concern. "Judging by the size of the Throneworld," he said, "that could make it as much as, oh, six pentillion tons."

They all gazed out into the dark. It was the nature of the light which at first made the object difficult to see: multicolored, twisting and shifting as gas clouds and brief nebulae tattered across the flagship's path, the light rose and faded without warning. But at the heart of it, occasionally veiled by some auroralike waft of brilliance, something four-lobed lay. It was smooth, and gleamed dully in the light, a dark silvery matte-surfaced object: four rough spheres, partially melded into one another in a pyramidal configuration.

"That's it?"

"That's what we're after," said Jean. "I can 'hear' it a little even now, even without the extensor. Sleeping . . ." She paused a moment, then smiled slightly at her own turn of phrase. "That's not really the word for it. It's nowhere near as conscious as a sleeping person."

"It is much smaller in this form than it was while in its 'ingesting' mode—and much smaller than we had feared it might be," Orien said. "Instruments show it to be no more than, let me see what it would be in your measurement— two thousand miles wide?"

"No *more* than two thousand miles wide," Wolverine said, in a mixture of wonder and irony. "So all we have t'fight is somethin' that three of us, takin' turns, couldn't drive across in less than five days without speedin'."

Orien gave Wolverine a quizzical look, then like the rest, turned back to look silently at the pupa. Lilandra stepped up to join them, and for the moment went almost unnoticed. "It's kinda bumpy on de outside," Remy said. "What is dat?"

"The surface? Possibly a shell," Orien said. "Difficult to say—it is very refractory, difficult to scan through. The initial scan—" He peered at one of the consoles nearby. "It seems to indicate partially collapsed matter. A mixture of normal atoms and atoms with their electron shells stripped off. Inside . . ." He shook his head. "The energy readings are odd."

"When have they *not* been odd where this creature was concerned?" Lilandra said.

"Odd for us, Majestrix," said Orien, "but not for it, I assume."

"Assumptions are all we have to go on at the moment," Lilandra said. "I suppose we must make the best of them." She bent down to Charles for a moment and said, "By the way, we will be dealing with Irdin's case later. I would appreciate it if you and the X-Men were there."

"Very well," Charles said, somewhat absently. For the moment he had no eyes for anything but the silent and enigmatic shape floating out there. "Jean," he said, "can you hear anything at all?"

"Nothing more than just now. A sense of sleep . . ."

Charles nodded. "Majestrix," he said, "that hotbed of ethics you were discussing. I think there may be one more coal of it lying in our way here. I think we must at least try to communicate with the creature, give it a chance to understand our imperatives and take itself away from our galaxies of its own free will."

She looked at Charles, skeptical. "Do you think it likely to be able to 'hear' you, in this state? If there is indeed anything *to* hear you? Phoenix?" she said.

Phoenix shook her head. "Majestrix, there's no evidence that it would be intelligent, as we count such things, when it hatches. Whenever it does hatch. I would question whether we can wait around for that to happen."

"*I* would certainly argue against it," Orien said. "Our ships are battle-shielded and can take a fair amount in the way of radiation and gravitic flux, but they cannot bear them at the present levels forever. I would not care to gamble your life, Majestrix, or my crew's, or those of the rest of the fleet, on the off chance that this creature might wake up and have a nice chat with us eventually."

Lilandra gave Charles a rather regretful look. "I would agree," she said. "I am afraid we are going to have to be pragmatic about this, Charles. The chance of making some misstep, in the name of ethics or kindness, and releasing this creature into our galaxy, or yours, to do more damage—well, that is nothing I would care to have on *my* conscience."

Charles sighed, and after a moment, nodded. "I am not entirely happy about it," he said, "but I understand your position. X-Men—"

He looked around at them. Storm looked troubled and glanced away from him. The others looked at one another.

"We're ready to go," Cyclops said.

"Well," Lilandra said, "we must consider logistics. How shall we attack it first?"

"I think," Charles said, "the X-Men had best make the first attempt."

"Since the second attempt," Orien said, "is likely to involve a large number of 'starcracker' devices and other assorted explosive and destructive modalities, some of which would fill local space with even more and hotter radiation than is here already, I would agree emphatically with the Professor.''

"Professor," the Beast said, "I think for this first run with live ammo, so to speak, I would like to work with the noumenoextensor staff. Keep an eye out for any new problems that might materialize. Not that the last test did not work well. But we are past the testing stage, now. If I'm needed, of course, I'll come out directly.''

"Hank," Charles said, "I commend your caution. It may be wise.'' Charles looked around at the others. "Very well. Let us go suit up.''

Half an hour later they were out in the color-splashed darkness, hanging free in space, while once again the flagship and the rest of the fleet backed away to a safe distance, and the noumenoextensor was warming up. The eight of them, Charles in his pod and the X-Men all spacesuited, were suspended, spaced approximately equidistant around the pupa.

Is everyone ready? Charles asked telepathically.

A chorus of agreement. From the flagship, the Beast said, "The machinery is humming, Charles. Say the word.''

"Go.''

The noumenoextensor field came alive around them. There was a brief stutter of power as it established itself in space already so full of radiation and other forces. Then the field density settled. The influx of power came—

—and Charles felt a terrible relief as the increased power settled into his mind, as he felt his mental reach expand and his scope grow to match it. The murmur of untold trillions of minds in this galaxy, even the faint echo of trillions more in the next, filled the back of his mind. In the other X-Men, he felt again the sudden growth of strength, and the relief, as terrible as his own. *To be this way again. To have it back again, this limitless power, finally.*

He firmly put that relief aside. The others were fairly throbbing with the power the extensor made available to them. Once again those "ghost" forms of each of them were taking shape—forms tens of miles high, slowly growing to hundreds. Perception of one's surroundings changed too. Suddenly they were not dwarfed by their target; it was more manageable now. Big, yes, but not out of all proportion, no longer too big to grasp. They were their own right sizes, surrounding something about the size of a New York City block. Far off in the distance a fleet of tiny ships no bigger than houseflies watched what they did.

If only we did not have to do what we must, Charles thought. *Jean, let us be very sure that this creature is not conscious. If you will assist me—*

They probed; they listened. Trillions of other minds they heard, and they were able, should they have so chosen, to descend into any one of those and "read" it with great clarity. But from the pupa—nothing. Warmth, a sense of waiting—that was all.

I will try this, Charles said, *just once. It costs nothing.*

With all his strength, and with the increased power afforded him by the extensor, he poured the message out at the inert multilobed shape drifting there in space. *We greet you, but you are doing us great harm. You must leave this space and not return again, lest more harm be done.*

No response whatever. Charles repeated it again, and yet again, much more loudly.

"Charley, fer cryin' out loud," Wolverine said, "I'm

pickin' you up on my fillings. If that pile'a tennis balls can't hear you shoutin' like that at *this* range, it's never gonna, and we can't wait. Give it up.''

Charles shook his head. "Very well. We must, I fear, destroy it. The most obvious option is to break the shell, and then deal separately with the interior. Storm—''

She was silent. Her 'ghost' shape, growing, like the others', more solid by the moment, gazed over at him with a troubled expression.

Storm, it's as I said. You must decide now, if you have not decided already. Otherwise, take yourself out of harm's way and let Gambit and Cyclops work.

A moment's hesitation, then—*No.*

Charles nodded. "Bishop—''

"I understand, Professor. Storm—when you are ready.''

Ororo gathered her power, stretched out her arms. Mastery of the elements was Storm's forté, and here she was surrounded by truly terrifying amounts of the "fifth element,'' raw plasma. She called the plasma to her, drew it in. It swirled around her, clung, coalesced in sheets of power like wavering flames, but huge and menacing, a cross between a thunderstorm and a firestorm, all held tightly to her, wrapping itself around her in layer after coruscating layer. Charles thought, suddenly and irrationally, of old tales of cherubim with wings of flame, and wondered whether some ancient poet-prophet had seen, or meant to foretell, a moment like this.

"Bishop!'' Storm cried from inside the whirlwind of plasma that was lashing and whipping around her, striving to get loose, though she was still in mastery of it . . . just. "Are you ready?''

"Ready!''

The light concentrated itself around her, blinding. Then

Storm turned toward Bishop and raised her arms. The plasma flared out around her in wings of fire, threatening, straining away from her—

The raging bolt with which she hit Bishop was one beside which lightning would have paled into utter insignificance. This was more like the furious exhalation of a star, funneled down into a single stream, as if a fire hose spat fire, not water. Bishop took it, his back arched where his "ghost" form stood braced, apparently on nothing. He took it, and took it, and took it, until he began to tremble with the strain, and a low groan began to work its way up out of him as he held on, held on . . .

After what seemed an eternity, he turned, threw his arms wide, and let the blast go.

It hit the pupa, hid it entirely in a backwash of white fire. The fire faded out after a few seconds. All the dust and gas in the area blazed with instantaneous ionization.

The pupa, though, did not show so much as a scratch. It drifted there, gleaming in the brilliance of the newly excited nebula.

Keep at it, Storm, Charles said. *You may need to apply a great deal more power.*

I have plenty to apply, she said, and struck Bishop again and again with bolt after bolt of plasma. He held on to each charge for longer and longer intervals, letting them go only when it seemed as if they would burst him from inside. Each time, a larger blast of power came ravening out of him and struck the great silvery object—and each time, the power simply splashed and sheeted away.

Perhaps more coherent blasts are needed as well. Cyclops—

Cyclops began targeting the pupa with optic blasts, concentrating on a single area near the top of one of the spheres, trying to produce some change, any change at all. But nothing happened. "Jean," he said, "put some pressure on that spot telekinetically. See if you can't get the shell to give while I'm softening it up."

Phoenix pushed hard at that spot. Charles could feel the pressure of it in his own mind, like the beginning of a migraine headache. But there was no result. "Scott," Jean said, "I hate to tell you, but it's not softening. The attractive force inside atoms isn't a weak one, like gravity or magnetic force. Those atoms are packed down tight, nucleus to nucleus, and they don't want to shift."

"Dey still movin', right?" Gambit said. "Lil' protons and neutrons jostlin'. Which means dey got kinetic energy. And dat, *I* can jostle. You two keep workin' on dat spot; lemme add a little spice to de mixture."

He started flinging cards which were also huge ghosts of themselves at the pupa. They hit the target; brief fire erupted again and again at the spot where he struck. But the fire faded and left not the slightest mark.

Everyone at once, Charles said. *The same spot. Pump as much energy into it as you can.*

They did, and space around them flared with multicolored fire. Slowly the frantic burning of the nebulosities around them started to fade, simply because their dust had been blown to its component atoms, and all the atoms ionized, and the ions themselves disrupted, by the huge amounts of sheer force being released in the attack on the pupa.

But nothing was happening.

Charles frowned. *Fire seems not to be the answer at this point,* he said. *Let us see if ice will make a difference. Iceman?*

He was there, like a statue, silent, frowning. Slowly he

stretched out his arms, and said to the others, "I'm going to do my best to concentrate the effect very tightly. But if I slip—"

We will be on guard, Charles said. *Try applying the cold to a spot directly adjacent to the one where Cyclops has been working. The drastic contrast may produce a crack, like putting a cold glass in a hot dishwasher.*

Iceman leaned in with a concentrating look, and held out both hands. Instantly the cold could be felt blasting from him, no matter how carefully he tried to control the effect. Even the intelligent and powerful Shi'ar spacesuits had trouble keeping their tenants from feeling it.

But nothing happened to the pupa.

"Professor, there's no atomic movement at all in the spot I'm affecting," Iceman said after a few minutes. "Not a twitch."

"But the immediately contiguous matter doesn't show any difference at all," Jean said, sounding discouraged. "There's not even a phase-shift perceptible in the shell."

"Stuff would make great car bumpers," Remy muttered, raining down cards on the spot they were working on.

"Except the car would sink to the center of the Earth," said Cyclops. He had been blasting one spot continuously for the past several minutes, and it had not so much as started to glow with the heat.

"All right," Wolverine said, "when all else fails, brute force, huh? Maybe it's like openin' a ketchup bottle. Everybody else tries it and can't do it, then the last one opens it 'cause everybody else loosened it up."

Sound cannot travel in space, but none of the other X-Men could avoid thinking that they heard something go *snikt*—and slowly, the huge "ghost" of Wolverine—no ghost now, but looking quite solid, deadly determined, and a little amused—advanced on the pupa, adamantium claws out. The claws must each have been fifty miles or so long. They flashed down at the pupa—

—and slid off. Wolverine growled, and went at it again, losing the good-humored look. If this object *had* been a ketchup bottle, it would have been in danger of being simply snapped in two at the neck. Wolverine slashed at the pupa, hammered on it, pummeled it, concentrating on areas the others had not tried, in hopes that he might find a weak spot. But after fifteen minutes of treatment which would have made Jean's destruction of the moon Safha look rather tame, nothing much had happened except that Wolverine was nearly out of breath, and completely out of words which could be used in polite company.

All right, everyone, Charles said, *let us pause for the moment*.

They all stopped what they were doing, and hung there in space which was now boiling with their own energies. At the center of it, the pupa drifted, inert and undamaged, though possibly a little shinier than it had been when the process started.

Any ideas? Charles said.

"Yeah. Let's drop-kick the sucker straight into the next—"

Any useful ideas, Logan?

"Let's take an hour off," Wolverine growled, "and see what else we can come up with. Or maybe the Shi'ar want to drop a few of their toys on it and see what happens. We might have done the ketchup bottle trick after all."

No one else could come up with anything better at the moment. "Beast," Charles said on his suit radio, "I think you may as well shut down the noumenoextensor for now. We seem to have exhausted the possibilities for the moment. And if you would ask the flagship to slip in close again and pick us up.''

''Certainly.''

The power drained out of them. There was, as Jean and Charles had earlier confirmed, no inrush of that terrible fatigue. But there *was* a sense of loss, a wordless cry of, *No, I want to stay this way, why can't it last forever?*

Finally they were all hanging there in the darkness, themselves again, and dwarfed once more by the pupa, which loomed above them like some dark moon. Slowly they made their way back to the Shi'ar flagship, silent with disappointment. Last of all came Charles, still hearing in his mind the cry, *I don't want it to stop. I want it to last forever.*

In his own mind, he was not so much troubled by it. But he heard it in all the others' minds too, and he began to be actively afraid.

They went back inside, but they had little time to start their debriefing. Only a very short time after they got out of their spacesuits, one of Lilandra's officers came to summon them to Irdin's hearing.

''Can't we skip this?'' Bobby said. ''I wouldn't mind a few minutes to rest, after that.''

''I did tell Lilandra that we would be there,'' Charles said. ''I do not think this is likely to take long.''

They followed the officer, who led them into the main atrium of the flagship—and Charles was astonished to see practically the whole ship gathered on the terraces and platforms which gave into that great space. All the senior officials who had come with Lilandra were there, her ministers and the members of the cabinet. The Imperial Guard were there as well. And finally she herself stepped up into the paramount place, a walkway reaching out into the center of the atrium from one of the lower balconies. She was clad as befitted the full ceremonial state of a Majestrix: armored, right to the crest, and holding one of the ceremonial halberds—one which looked unusually and uncomfortably sharp.

When she took her place, there was a movement like a breath of wind across a wheatfield as the assembled Shi'ar bowed to her. She waited for it to finish.

"It has been the custom of the Majestors of our line to do justice publicly," Lilandra said, when silence had fallen again. "Though others have broken with that custom on occasion, we keep it, even in circumstances when time might militate against it." She turned her head, looking over at Gladiator, who had come to stand not far behind her, on the balcony. "Bring in the prisoner," Lilandra said.

Gladiator signaled to a group of officers across the room. A few moments later, Irdin was brought in.

There was a slightly wild look about her. Charles knew that Irdin would have been given drugs to inhibit her telepathic ability, so that she could not use her mental influence on those around her. He had a sense, though, of what she must be feeling—a sudden terrible deafness, as the voices you have always heard murmuring at the back of your mind are suddenly gone. Silence, and fear, and nothing but the echoes within your own mind for solace. Irdin stood there surrounded by her guards, her fair crest quivering as she glanced around her, angry, frightened, and uncertain.

"Those whom you have wronged—myself, officers on this ship, and the X-Men—have a right to confront you and see your sentence," Lilandra said. "My judgment on you, after discussing your case with the the officers who have investigated your acts, is that you have sabotaged a security operation of the Shi'ar Empire, or have attempted to sabotage it, for personal reasons. You have assaulted the minds of unwilling persons, forcing them into acts which they would not normally have carried out. You are guilty of culpable coercion, attempted murder, and sabotage. Before your fate is pronounced, you may speak.''

Irdin stared at her with the expression of someone unable to believe what is happening, someone seeing the universe take a turn which should have been impossible. ''Murderer!'' she said at last. ''You dare to judge *me*! You're in the very act of trying to kill something that can't defend itself, that has a right to live!''

''She's got an interesting definition of 'can't defend itself,' '' Scott said softly in Jean's ear.

''And if you can't kill it, you'll kill *me*, is that it? You have no right! And you have no proof—''

''We have more than enough. Your guilt is plain. The evidence of it lies bare in your own mind, where, despite what power you *do* have, you were unable to conceal it.''

Irdin glared at her, sullen, and looked pointedly away.

''Very well,'' Lilandra said. ''As the personification of the law of the empire, without which the empire would fall, we pronounce your fate as codified in that law.'' She lifted the ceremonial halberd, leveled it at Irdin. The point glittered. ''Death is your fate, and to your death you will go henceforth.'' Lilandra grounded the halberd, looked over at the assembled Imperial Guard. ''Take her away,'' she said quietly, ''and let her be turned over to the sergeant-at-arms for execution. Justice is done.''

The room went very quiet. Charles, though, could not help himself: he had to say it. ''Majestrix—can she not be spared?''

"In our law," Lilandra said, turning a stony gaze on him, "she has incurred the death penalty not once, but three times. Were we implementing the law in its most stringent sense, as some of our government have encouraged us to, she would be partially executed twice, and resuscitated twice, then executed one last time. But we are minded to be merciful. Irdin na'Hlemarui, go, and may Sharra and Ky'thri be better disposed to you in your next life than they have in this one."

"I wouldn't be blamin' Sharra and Ky'thri for it," Wolverine muttered under his breath.

As she was taken away past Orien, Irdin turned to him with tears streaking down her face. "It's not fair!" she screamed. "She doesn't even *love* you! She loves *him*! And I love *you*! It's not supposed to *be* like this!"

Orien bowed his head and stood silent.

"Murderers! And you, *Majestrix,* you're the worst of them! You're quite willing to murder me just because I attacked your human troll, your not-consort—*that's* what I'm really paying for, isn't it? He *deserves* to die! He's trying to kill it, an innocent thing, a defenseless thing! Murderers! *Mur—*"

The doors closed behind her, and the silence that fell was profound.

Lilandra turned her attention back to the assembly at large. "Fleet commanders will meet with me immediately in my quarters to plan the next stage of our intervention in this area," she said. "As for the rest of you, as justice has been done, and seen to be done—you are all dismissed."

The room emptied quickly. Finally the only ones left there were the X-Men and Charles. They looked at one another.

" 'Justice'?" Wolverine said. "Huh." He stalked away

toward the doors, shaking his head, his expression black as a storm.

Charles found it hard to look at him. Finally he turned back to the others. "We have plans of our own to lay," he said. "We must analyze our last attack, see if we can work out what went wrong with it, and prepare for another."

"Might be we didn't do anyt'ing wrong," Gambit said quietly. "Might be we're up against it dis time."

He went out after Wolverine. Slowly, the others followed.

Charles came last, troubled at heart, and wondering whether Remy might be right.

Eight

T he mood in the X-Men's lounge that evening was much more somber than usual after the general assembly, and Charles had no trouble understanding why.

Storm sat quietly off to one side, meditating, withdrawn. Gambit had several times come close to accidentally destroying the central table while playing solitaire; cards tossed down with a little too much force had cracked it in a couple of places. Wolverine had gone straight to his room and opaqued the door. Cyclops and Phoenix were off in their own quarters, talking. Not arguing, as far as Charles could tell from the general emotional atmosphere, which was leaking out, but their conversation had been going on for a long time now. The Beast, having stayed only a few minutes, had then gone straight off again to consult with some of the Shi'ar staff who had been working on the noumenoextensor. Iceman was sitting out in the lounge, trying to read, or pretending to read, but he wasn't having much luck: he kept losing his concentration, and gazing off into space with a frown. Bishop was nowhere to be found.

And that left Charles sitting in the lounge, alone and silent.

He had noticed that the others had been having trouble looking at him, being around him, as if the events of the last couple of hours were all his fault somehow. It was an irrational belief, of course, and as irrational for him to take any offense at it.

Yet he too could not get rid of the idea that there was something more he could have said or done, had he suspected the way Lilandra's mind was leaning as regarded Irdin. He could have been more forceful—except . . . Charles shook his head. Shi'ar law was what it was. He could not do anything but tell the truth in response to the questions he had been asked. Justice, Shi'ar justice, had been done. He just wished that Lilandra had not seemed to enjoy it quite so much. But that was a subjective judgment as well. Surely she could take no pleasure in ending a sentient life.

Outside, he knew, the Shi'ar had begun peppering the pupa with high-energy weapons, preparatory to attacking it with some of their other, less-well-known hardware. There would probably be no point in using the so-called starcrackers. Those devices depended on stopping a stellar body's carbon-carbon cycle, and this pupa had nothing of the sort. But there were plenty of other weapons they could use, and once again space outside the great windows was heating up as interstellar dust and gas swirled back into the disturbed area and were newly excited by the enthusiastic discharge of weapons through them.

Charles glided over to the holographic tank in the center of the room and touched it to bring it to life. "Bridge," he said. "Lord Orien—"

"Orien," said a voice, and there he was, briefly distracted in the act of looking down at a console. "Ah, Professor."

He looked very composed; much more so than Charles felt. "Is there any response to the bombardment?"

"Not as yet," Orien said, sounding somewhat resigned. "Though I must confess that after your encounter with the pupa, I did not expect much result so early. We will be scaling up our efforts shortly. There are numerous devices to be used and evaluated for results—pumped-photon bombs, particle disassociators of the kind which were almost dropped on the two of us, strong-force amplifiers. And if all else fails, I am not averse to trying antimatter. Though it always takes so much time to produce it that even though we have our crews in the early production stages already, I very much hope that something else works first. Otherwise we would have to be here for some while to complete production, and you already know my feelings about that.''

Charles nodded. ''Well, if we must . . .'' He gestured at the image of the pupa in a tank near Orien. ''*It* seems not to be in a hurry about anything.''

''At the moment, I would agree. Was there anything else, Professor, or were you just curious?''

''Curiosity only, my lord,'' Charles said, though even as he said it, he realized he was lying. He had much hoped to see Lilandra, unarmored and normal again, somewhere in the background. ''Please do call us if you note any change.''

''Believe me, I will want you to know as soon as I do.'' Orien waved a hand at the pickup, breaking the connection.

Charles sighed and turned away from the tank to find Iceman looking at him speculatively, arms crossed.

''Something, Robert?'' Charles said.

''Yeah. I want to know when I can get out there and take another crack at that thing.''

''I would say it would not be immediately. The radiation out there will soon exceed anything that any spacesuit made anywhere could handle, if it has not done so already. There would have to be time to let it subside.''

''I've had enough of this,'' Bobby muttered, and shook his head.

Charles looked at him. "Of what?"

"Of the way I've been, until now. I want to get out there and *use* the extensor. You know how it feels—we all have. You're more—*you*—when the extensor's working. It's not just more power, it's—" He shook his head, spread his hands, unable to find the words for the moment. "It's just that . . . while I was using my powers, the feeling—" He shook his head again.

"Take your time, Robert."

"There's more *me*," Bobby said, looking increasingly annoyed that he couldn't explain, or that Charles couldn't understand, or both. "And less. A lot of the time, when I'm working, I don't know, I'm afraid. I think, 'Is this power worth anything?' Being able to freeze things, make ice-slides—big deal. But *this*—you can feel the certainty of the power itself. There aren't any doubts about your ability down in your bones, in your cells; they *know* they can do whatever's needed. They don't know what uncertainty is—only what *doing* is. They can do it. I *like* that, Professor."

His expression was almost pleading. "Why shouldn't it always be that way? What are we doing wrong with our powers, normally, that it's not that way all the time?"

Charles heard again that echo in his mind, in the others: *I don't want it to stop, I don't want to go back to being the way I was.* "Robert," he said, "just because this augmentation of our abilities feels good to us doesn't necessarily mean that we're doing anything wrong when we use them normally. It's possible that with careful study, we may find that this device points us toward techniques that we can use to augment our powers naturally—"

Robert snorted. "How long is *that* gonna take?" he said. "All this practice, all this time in the Danger Room, all this''—he waved his hand dismissively—''practice takes so long, the results take forever . . .''

''Instant gratification,'' Charles said regretfully, ''is no more available to us in our chosen line of work than it is in anything else that really matters. If you desire real results, Robert, achievement that lasts, the extensor is hardly going to be the answer.''

''But you *would* say that, wouldn't you?'' Iceman said. ''You'd have to!''

''What?''

''Professor, look! I don't want to make you seem wrong, you're not *wrong*, but this is something new, it can make a big difference! If we could use this all the time, if we could get them to let us take this back to Earth with us—''

''You heard Ollikh, the Majestrix's security officer,'' said Charles. ''I very much doubt they will allow that, for the very same reason that they are allowing us to use it now: because the power it bestows is too terrible.''

''But, Charles,'' came Storm's quiet voice suddenly, ''Robert is right.''

Charles looked over at Ororo, who had opened her eyes, finally, after nearly an hour and a half of silence and withdrawal. ''Storm—how do you mean?''

''We *are* more ourselves,'' she said, ''when using the device. It makes a profound difference to our access of our abilities. Are we not to be the best we can be?''

''Yes, but artificially.''

''Charles, what is so unnatural about this? They are our own powers, merely magnified. Would you tell a near-sighted person that it was wrong to wear glasses because the intervention was artificial?''

''If we could bring this gadget back home with us,''

Iceman said, "it would make a huge difference to all kinds of things. Think about all the trouble back on Earth. Emergencies we can't handle because there just aren't enough of us, or they're too big—floods, earthquakes, stuff like that! And other problems. Magneto. All the rogue mutants running around hurting and killing people—"

"Those," Storm said, "and many other menaces that, if we had routine access to this device, would not be able to harm us anymore. Think of it, Charles. We would not even need to use the device all the time—"

"It would start that way, perhaps," Charles said quietly, "but it would not stop that way." He could hear the echo at the bottom of her mind: *I want to be this way forever!*—and all the more dangerous for her not being conscious of it. The image of that gigantic Storm wrapped in wings of flame, to be easily mistaken for a genuine goddess, towering over something the size of a continent, ready to unleash her power on it, even if only at a remove. It unnerved him.

"Storm," Charles said, "doubtless we will again use this device, because in the present necessity, we must. But I will not recommend that we use it a second longer than we have to. I for one am hearing voices in my mind that I have not heard in a long time—that I do not normally permit myself to hear, because they are inimical to our work. The voice that says, 'What about me?' to the exclusion of others, the voice that says, 'Let it be the way I want,' at the cost of the greater good. I very much fear that more than our powers are being strengthened here—that the forces down at the bottoms of our minds, the childlike or unconscious forces that fuel our powers, are being lent undue strength by the extensor."

" 'Monsters from the Id,' Charles?" Phoenix's voice

was slightly amused, only the slightest touch mocking, as she and Cyclops came back in.

He looked at her. "Nothing quite so blatant, I would think. I am not sure, but—what do *you* hear at the back of your mind, Jean? We all hear voices all day, and telepaths are more likely to hear them than most—hearing them in other minds alerts us to our own. The encapsulated voices of parents, of people in our childhood who had authority over us, friends sometimes—their opinions, fragments of their wills, inside us on tape, as it were. But the tapes do play. The secret is not to be frightened by that fact, but to know that the voices *are* chattering away in the background, and can be guarded against. However, to ignore them altogether is unwise. What *do* you hear, Jean?"

"If it is a voice, which I doubt," she said, sitting down, "it's one that says, 'For the first time, be the telepath you only dreamed of being!' We can't all be *you*, you know, Professor. Or we couldn't, until *now*. Suddenly, when I'm working with the extensor, I have so much more range, so much more power. Do you have any idea where I've been? What I've seen? A billion minds, all held inside me—all those experiences, filling me, flowing over, endless. Endless knowledge, pain, joy, wisdom, folly, all there at once."

"But there is a problem," Charles said, "and this I *have* felt, working under the extensor. The problem is with focus. One must concentrate hard, narrow down intention to the goal alone, keep one's whole heart pointed at it. And soon the goal threatens to become all there is. The extensor gives you the power with one hand, and with the other takes away the *scope* which you possess at normal magnification, the ability to spread your perception wide and judge how and when to act. You begin to be reduced to a weapon. Your will starts to become an accessory, rather than the central part of you which powers everything else. Your power starts to *become* your will."

"Well," said the Beast, coming in, "I had a feeling this little tête-à-tête would come sooner or later. Didn't you, Charles?"

"I had not anticipated it in quite this form," Charles said. "To be all you can be, yes, that I support. But not the 'you' that is an add-on, an annex, one which threatens to swallow the 'you' that you started with, and leave you none the wiser about the change! And if something happens to the 'add-on,' what then? We are a long way from the Shi'ar Empire, on Earth. Suppose we did take the full implementation of this technology home with us, and suppose it malfunctioned?"

"Maybe we could set something up with Sears?" Bobby said.

"After you had become dependent on the extensor," Charles said, becoming a little annoyed now, "you might not find it so funny. Remember earlier, before the device was functioning correctly? The feeling of loss, of pain, and almost of betrayal, as you dwindled down again to what you had been? This was the very thing that you were talking to me about, Storm, a very short time ago. Yet now you're suddenly eager for this dependency. *Listen* to yourselves!"

The X-Men looked at him; and it was not that their eyes were alien—they were all the people he knew. But at the moment, they genuinely could not see what his problem was. And something was missing from them all: a sense of self-sufficiency, of— He was not quite sure what to call it. He shook his head.

"Professor," Jean said, "we have always valued your

judgment. But not even you are right a hundred percent of the time.''

"Perhaps," Charles said. "You must all know that my feeling is that this device, while needed for this present crisis, should not be used any further.''

The Beast turned to Charles. "I was having a look at the Shi'ar's recordings of our little session with the pupa," he said. "The physical readings, power output, and so forth. There are indeed some interesting shifts in people's brainwave patterns, and no way to tell whether those shifts are benign or not. Without further testing and analysis, it's going to take a long time to be sure.''

"We do not have a lot of time for testing at this point, Hank," Charles said. "If we must use the extensor again— as I hope we must not—then we will be using it in full power mode, as we did last time.''

"There weren't any bad aftereffects, though," Scott said.

"Weren't there?" Charles said. "Look at you all now.''

"Come on, *professeur*," said Remy, who looked up from his cards now with a slightly amused expression. "We fight all de time. Jus' one more argument. No news here.''

"But we have never argued about this," Charles said, "and this goes to the root of what we are. We're mutants, and there is nothing to be done about it, even if we wanted to. I would think we have made our peace with the issue at this point. But I am beginning to believe that to rely on a mechanism like this simply for the extension of our powers may make us even less human than we are to start with.''

They gazed at him with what seemed a complete lack of comprehension.

Charles turned to the Beast and said, "You were saying

that you found no evidence of any toxic phenomena in our minds.''

''I haven't found anything recognizable yet,'' said the Beast, ''but the Shi'ar records are extremely complex, and I'm not always sure I'm reading them correctly. The Shi'ar come at brain science from a slightly different angle than we do, and they see the cerebral process as being a rather more diffuse and less centralized thing than it would be in our own understanding. There were some readings not strictly anomalous, but in almost all cases, nothing I've ever seen in us.''

''Well, you would say that,'' Bobby said. ''You weren't out there with it on full, feeling what it felt like. Even when what we were doing wasn't working—still, the way it felt—''

''No,'' the Beast said, ''I was not. Possibly I won't be the next time either.'' He looked at Charles thoughtfully. ''Unless you prefer to stay in, Charles, and I'll go out next time, assuming there is one.''

Charles opened his mouth to say that he would of course go out with the X-Men—and suddenly wondered whether that was the echo in his mind speaking with his voice. *Of course, you must go out and feel that again, but the real reason is to make sure that* they *are all safe, of course.*

The tank chose that moment to come alive. ''Professor Xavier,'' said Orien's voice.

''Orien?''

He was there, looking away from them out into the light-torn darkness. ''We have been using pumped-photon explosives on the pupa for some while now—a considerable tonnage of them. If that object had been a planet, it would have been gone, many times over. But it is not a planet, and if I read the signals correctly, it is not that much longer even to be a pupa.''

''What? What's happening?''

''The energy readings from inside it are increasing. I believe it may be about to hatch.''

The X-Men looked at one another—then, as one, tore out of there on their way up to the bridge.

The gathered X-Men—joined by Bishop and Wolverine—arrived at the bridge to find considerable activity. All the stations and weapons consoles which Charles had earlier noted ranged around the huge atrium space were alive with light, and busy. The atmosphere was one, not of charged excitement before battle, but of a peculiar balked tension.

Orien stood there in front of the great window, gazing out at the night, newly alive with writhing color, the fire of tormented nebulae and gas glowing. His attention was bent on a spot where detonation after detonation was occurring, eye-searing, one after another, like the pop of flashbulbs at a rock concert. ''Orien,'' Charles said, ''are you still firing on it?''

''If it is about to hatch,'' Orien said, not taking his eyes off the target, ''it may be vulnerable—or, at least, so our scientists say. That would be the ideal time to destroy it, if it can indeed be destroyed at all in this manner.''

Out there, fifty thousand miles or so away, the flashbulb-popping of the detonations continued unabated. Charles watched them and shook his head. ''They do not seem to be having much effect.''

''No,'' Orien said, ''I would have to agree with you. I think maybe this time the scientists have been indulging in wishful thinking. But in the face of what we see before us, and what it implies for our own galaxy, there has been a lot of that going around." He looked grim. "I will give it a few more minutes."

Charles looked around at the X-Men, and noticed that Jean was looking absent, slightly unfocused. "Phoenix," Charles said sharply, "you were in rapport with this creature before I heard it at all; in fact, you will have 'heard' it several times now. Are you able to pick up anything?"

She stood there with a listening look. "Not at the moment," she said. "It might have been easier to hear then because of the extensor, Charles."

He looked at her and made sure the instant suspicion which arose did not show in his face. "No need for that at the moment, I think," he said, "but stay alert. If there should be any—"

Jean looked quizzical. "Charles—wait a moment."

There was brief silence around her, while they all watched her—Cyclops with the most concern. Jean tilted her head a little to one side, gazing out into the darkness, and looked bemused.

"It's too soon," she said,

"Too soon for what?" said Scott.

"Don't take me too literally," Phoenix said after a moment. "It's hard to translate, these aren't even images, just impressions. I think it may have been blind before, but that's changing too, something's—" She stopped again, listened. "Charles, there's just a sense of all this being too soon somehow—it's not supposed to *happen* yet—"

The Beast looked thoughtful. "Maybe we *have* managed to disrupt its life cycle a little," he said. "Professor, could it be that all the energy we've been pumping into the pupa and its environment has hastened the process of its hatching? And it's coming out too soon?"

"It could possibly be so," Charles said. "Orien—"

"If so, there is no way to tell whether the fact will operate for us or against us," Orien said. "But we may soon find out." He turned to one of the junior officers who stood nearby waiting for his orders. "Talat, what is happening to the pupa's energy output now?"

"Increasing right across the scan spectrum, lord," Talat said. "Most output is in infrared at the moment."

"Infrared . . ."

"Warmth," Jean said softly. "The first thing we sensed from it, practically. And it's getting warmer . . ."

"What about your rapport with it, Jean?" Charles said. She nodded. "Getting stronger as well."

Charles shook his head, a little concerned by that. He had no mental sense of the creature nearly so acute as Jean's, though he too had sent to it while under the influence of the noumenoextensor. *But I never "received" from it, apparently, as intensely as Jean did. Her rapport with it is deeper, and now it grows. Possibly some side effect of the extensor as well.* Though that thought made him nervous. There was already one side effect of it that he didn't much care for.

"The IR signature is increasing fast," said Talat. "Approaching stellar ignition temperature."

"I don't know if we want to be in the area when it passes that point," said the Beast. "It's likely to be a noisy hatching, especially if it should be inclined to follow the simile all the way, and go into fusion. We have been disrupting it, after all, adding energy to the equation that wouldn't have been there otherwise."

"I had been thinking about that," Orien said. "Talat, tell the fleet to break off bombardment—I cannot see that it is doing any good—and move us well back."

He turned to look over at another console—then stopped,

bowed. Charles looked around and saw Lilandra standing there, in tight-fitting black with selected pieces of armor over it. She looked somewhat concerned, but nowhere near as grim as when Charles had last seen her. With some slight trepidation he met her eyes, and felt the wall behind them, through which she did not want him to probe.

In mind, he backed away, aching a little, but there was no time for that now. "Majestrix," he said, "you seem to have come in at the exciting part."

"The story of my life," she said, not entirely without humor.

"Temperature of the pupa is scaling up fast now, lord," said Talat. "We are backing away. Five hundred thousand miles—"

"Hope it's far enough," Wolverine said.

"It is a gamble," Orien said, as they watched the place where the last of the explosions were rapidly fading away with distance and the end of the bombardment. "At least this distance will buy us a couple of seconds' worth of reaction time, at which point we can be outrunning anything moving merely at lightspeed, and—"

Jean's eyes suddenly widened. "There it goes!" said Talat, turning to the window with everyone else.

A flare of light as white as any of the explosions had been, but more lingering, bloomed from a tiny point on which they had centered. Charles looked at it, then at Jean. Her mind was in turmoil; he could feel, very dimly, some of the sensations assaulting her. "Jean?"

"I'm all right," she said, staggering a little, putting a hand out to Cyclops, who caught her arm and steadied her. "Warm, but my body knows it's not me, it's—*oh!*"

That was more a cry of pain than of surprise. "Magnification on that object," Orien said, and one of the nearby tanks went solid white with fire, which slowly began to fade.

"Mass sensor on that," Orien said.

Lines of colored light began to stitch themselves through the nearest tank, all curving, bending inward to a single source, wrapping themselves around it. Orien reached out and gestured over the tank controls. The center image grew larger, betraying a shape. "Interesting," he said. "It is still keeping the form of the shell."

Jean moaned a little, tried to stand up. The four glowing globes in the center of the tank shivered, stretched, and started to elongate. After a few moments Charles and the X-Men found themselves looking at a larger version of the earlier larval form, the four-pronged asterisk, but with some additions: there were odd vanelike constructions at the end of the limbs.

"A caltrop," the Beast said suddenly. "*That's* what it was reminding me of, and I couldn't remember the word."

"A what?" Iceman said.

"Caltrop," said Charles. "A four-pronged device used to lame horses in medieval times. You would scatter them in front of a cavalry charge. The four-pronged shape always comes to rest with one sharp prong pointing upwards, and has great stability."

At least, he thought then, *it does in gravity.* It was starting to spin slowly.

Lilandra was shaking her head. "What are we seeing?" she said, astonished. "I thought it was supposed to become *adult* now."

"This may be a transitional stage which happens normally," said the Beast, watching with interest. "Or perhaps only optionally. It may only have happened because we added so much energy to its environment." He smiled, but the smile wasn't entirely sanguine. "I'd say that we've interrupted its life cycle, all right. But the trouble with doing such things is that the cycle does then become unpredictable."

They watched it spin faster and faster. "Charles," Jean said abruptly, straightening up again, "this is going to sound odd, but I'm *starving*."

He glanced over at her, and Talat said, "Energy readings are increasing again, lord. Not heat this time. A lot of hard radiation, bremsstrahlung, cyclotron radiation . . ."

The four-pronged shape spun faster yet, until it was visible only as a faintly glowing sphere. The glow paled—then flashed intolerably, with a pinkish tinge, and vanished.

The X-Men stared. "Where'd it go?" Iceman said.

"Talat?" Orien said.

Talat was shaking his head. "We still have it on scan, lord. It's just that optical's no good for something that's moving faster than light."

"Oh, my stars and garters," said the Beast softly.

"Confirming," Talat said then.

"There are certainly enough known creatures which can not only survive space, but travel superluminally by organic means," said Lilandra. "The Acanti, for one. The behavior is rare, but not incredibly so."

"The larva has indeed gone transluminal," said Orien's officer. "Massive output of what you call Cherenkov radiation confirms it. Gathering speed now. The larva is accelerating past our best superluminal speed, Lord Orien."

"How fast?"

"No more than about four times the speed of light at the moment," said Talat, "but it is accelerating steadily. Possibly geometrically, if it keeps up at this rate."

"If it does, it will shortly be out of tachyar range as

well," Orien said. "Tachyon sensing is not much good above two hundred fifty-six times lightspeed. Talat, go after it. Best speed, but keep our distance for the moment. I suppose," he said with a wry look, "that for the moment, we should count ourselves lucky that it cannot stargate."

"I wish we had proof of that," said Charles, "except in the negative sense."

"That may be good enough for our purposes at the moment," said the Beast. "If the creature could gate, it would by no means have taken so long getting here from the last galaxy. Where is it going?"

"Making for the inmost stars of the galactic core," said Orien's officer.

"If it destroys those as well," the Beast said, "the whole galaxy's anchoring mass will be deranged, possibly completely lost. Over time, this galaxy would simply come apart."

Charles rubbed sweat off his face, thinking. The creature had stopped well short of this area to pupate, and until now Charles, talking with the Beast and the Shi'ar scientists about this, had thought it might have been an error of some kind. Now, though, he started to wonder. *If this transitional phase was supposed to happen—we may only have hastened it. There may well be some other change which still needs to happen, that requires more energy still, which is why the creature pupated before reaching it. Not an accident. It has something else to do, something which required energy that, compared to everything that has gone before, will be inadequate.*

"Can you do nothing to stop it?" Lilandra said, turning from Charles to Orien.

"Majestrix, if we take the ships in there after it, we will not take them out again," said Orien. "Our shielding is having enough trouble keeping out the radiation as it is, and the hyperactive areas into which we have so far ventured are *nothing* compared to where that creature is heading. Additionally, there is a massive black hole in the heart of this core. We could not go near it and also expend the power on shielding which we presently require to survive.''

Charles had to say it, though he hated to. ''Orien,'' he said, ''what is the range of the noumenoextensor? How far can it throw its field?''

''Not *that* far,'' Orien said, looking at Charles with a strangely appreciative expression. ''But indeed I appreciate the thought, Professor.''

Charles frowned. ''All right,'' the Beast said then, ''but what about a stargate?''

Orien looked at him as if he were out of his mind. ''I have told you, if we go in there—''

''Not *that* way. What if you open a stargate on the area to which the larva is heading, and throw the noumenoextensor field *through* it?''

Orien's astonishment grew—but he began to grin as well, a hard, canny look. ''Beast,'' he said, ''you are a true scientist—which is to say, you're three parts mad out of five.'' He turned to his officer. ''Get Argath up here immediately.''

It was only a matter of a few minutes before the head of the noumenoextensor project appeared, looking somewhat upset—apparently he had the idea that he was somehow to be belatedly chastised for the misdeeds in which Irdin had involved him. It took a few minutes for the tall, lean Shi'ar to understand that this was not the case, that there was another question entirely to be resolved.

''Oh, no, no, no,'' Argath said after the Beast's idea was explained to him. He was completely horrified. ''The frequencies would interfere with the field generation, it couldn't propagate to maximum effectiveness—"

"How effectively *could* it propagate?" said the Beast.

Orien laughed. "Make that four parts mad out of five. Argath, that's the question. How far can you allow the effectiveness to drop and still guarantee safe use of the noumenoextensor effect for those involved?"

Argath literally wrung his hands, and despite the critical nature of the moment, it occurred to Charles with some amusement that it had been years since he had actually seen anyone do that. "Oh, Lord Orien, I would not dare to let the field fall below ninety percent effectiveness."

"I thought you said the field propagation was holographic," the Beast said. "So that any part of the field can reinforce any other in case of sudden catastrophic loss of signal strength."

"Oh, sir, it is, but the possibility of passing the signal through a stargate introduces all kinds of other complications."

"We pass all kinds of signals through stargates," said Lilandra suddenly, moving out to the front of the group from where she had been examining a console, "and all kinds of fields, some of them a lot more mechanically sophisticated than this one, or so I have been told. What makes this case so difficult?"

Argath threw a terrified look at Charles, and then turned and bowed to Lilandra, positively in an agony of fear. "Majestrix," he said, "it has never been tested."

"This would seem to be the time," Charles said. "I will try it."

"So will I," said Storm. "And me!" said Iceman. "Count us in," said Jean and Cyclops. All the others chimed in as well, as Charles had known very well they would. He put aside a pang of terror for them—thinking as much of what could happen to them if the noumenoextensor didn't work correctly, as what could happen if it did.

"We will have to push you through the gate as well," Orien said to Charles, sounding grim now. "We cannot do it in spacesuits, not under those conditions. You are going to have to go through in an armored pod. Even then, you won't have time to linger. The radiation there will be intense, and the moment it starts overcoming the shielding, we will have to pull you out, no matter what stage you might have reached in your confrontation with the larva."

"Understood. Make sure there is plenty of room for us to move around in that pod," said Charles. "While our 'body doubles' will be acting on the larva for us outside, we will need room to do the same inside."

"You are suggesting the same sort of setup as your Danger Room, in a portable form?" Argath said. "Yes, the field will support it, with a few changes."

"Go make them," Lilandra said. "Hurry."

Argath left in a rush. "Charles," the Beast said, "for safety's sake—"

"Go with him," Charles said.

"Good luck," said the Beast to the others, and sprang off after Argath.

"I would prefer you do this suited anyway," Orien said. "Should something go wrong with the pod's shielding, you would take a massive dose of radiation, possibly a fatal one, before we could snatch you back."

"I agree," Charles said.

"Let us go," Storm said, and dived off the bridge deck, soaring down through the atrium. The others went after her, each in his fashion. Charles stopped Jean as she started to levitate past him. "Phoenix—"

"I'm all right," she said. "But hungry. When we get back after this, I'm going to *murder* a pizza."

"I may just help you," Charles said with a smile. "And with extra garlic. Come on."

He had just time to glance at Lilandra as he followed. She looked after him, longing, but her mind did not call to his. Charles, in pain, kept going. There was work to do.

"I've heard o' bein' behind de eight ball," Remy said about an hour and a half later, looking around him. "Never t'ought I'd be *inside* it."

The comparison was apt. The inside of the armored pod was a perfect matte black, featureless, with no controls that anyone could see anywhere. It was filled with a cool clear light that had no source. "The pod has its own gravity, its own drive system. Just think at it," Argath had told them as the X-Men loaded themselves in through an aperture it had abruptly produced. "It will go where you want, show you what you want."

"Weapons systems?" Bishop inquired mildly, looking around.

"Ah," Argath said, "*you,* I believe."

Bishop nodded, and shrugged his suit into a more comfortable position.

"Good luck," said Argath, and the darkness sealed itself around them.

Storm lifted herself into the center of the pod, poised there. It was about two hundred feet in diameter: very much a Danger Room in the spherical mode rather than the rectangular one. "So the field will affect us inside here," she said, "and we will 'project' our greater selves outside."

"That's right," Charles said, though he was not happy about the phrasing *greater selves.* "Now if we—"

Abruptly the blackness dissolved, to be replaced by what appeared the blackness of open space. They all seemed to be suspended in it. Nearby the Shi'ar fleet hung, the huge graceful ships gleaming in the light of the disturbed galactic core. "X-Men," said Orien's voice, "if you will look approximately 'below' you, you will see the stargate unfolding. We will be ready to push you through, and activate the field, in approximately two minutes."

"Thank you, Lord Orien," Charles said.

A little silence fell while they watched the gate unfold, glittering. "And what happens, Charley," Wolverine said, "if somethin' cracks this pod open and lets the outside inside—all that radiation? How fast are they gonna be able to grab us?"

"I would say fairly quickly," Charles said. "There should be no problem with them putting a tractor on the pod through the open gate. Additionally, *we* can always act on the pod to move it."

Bishop blinked a little at that. "It has a certain 'by your own bootstraps' quality, that idea," he said, "but it should work."

"Orien," Charles said, "what is the larva doing?"

His voice was sounding grimmer than usual. "It is eating a star at the moment," he said. "No, I misspoke. It has finished, and is heading for another."

Gambit blinked. "Like potato chips," he said. "You can't eat jus' one."

"The larva's superluminal capacity has become most impressive," Orien said. "The speeds at which it is moving— they are far above our best superluminals, X-Men. Perhaps fifteen hundred times lightspeed? Seventeen hundred? And still increasing. Nothing but a gate could keep up with it now." He paused. "Almost ready. We will wait a moment for it to finish the star it is presently consuming, and target the next one.''

"How long is it taking to *eat* one of these things?'' Iceman asked.

"At the moment,'' said Orien, "about a minute and thirty seconds. The larger ones seem to be taking two minutes or so. It may have ingested as many as a hundred other stars while we have been preparing.''

They all stared at one another in disbelief. "Oh, come on,'' said Iceman, "it can't do that!''

"Tell *it*,'' Jean said.

"Why don' *you* tell it, *p'tite*?'' Gambit asked.

"Do you think I haven't been trying?'' Jean said. "It's not listening. Imagine you were a hungry baby at the breast, having your lunch, and you heard a strange little voice saying, 'No, don't drink that stuff, drinking that is *bad*'?''

Storm looked troubled. To Bishop, she said, "I think, as regards my part of this attack, we will have to handle it the same way as before. I will do the best I can, but I do not know how long I will be able to keep it up.'' She looked over at Phoenix with mild exasperation. "I wish you had not mentioned babies.''

Charles felt her discomfort, her potential pain—and then felt something else entirely: the rush, the gasp of power. "Here it comes.''

Needless to say it. They all knew. The transfixed expressions on their faces, the stiffening of the bodies, and the sudden flowering inside their minds made that plain.

"We are pushing you through now, Professor,'' said Orien's voice. "It is just starting in on another star. Do what you can.''

• • •

The universe winked as they passed through the gate, through the needle's eye. Suddenly the Shi'ar ships could only be seen through it with great difficulty, and far away. Before the X-Men, around them, everything was filled with flaming gas, streams and tatters of it, and below them hung a star, a misshapen orange one, with something burrowing down into its heart.

It was the larva, dark against the star the way a sunspot is, only by contrast of temperature. "X-Men." Charles said. *"Now!"*

He hurled a mental bolt at the larva which he thought might at least get its attention, if nothing else. Around him, the gigantic ghost bodies of his students came to life, and arrowed down toward the star and the creature as if diving into a swimming pool of fire. Sunstuff splashed about them as they made contact, unharmed. Despite the size of the bodies, the minds and powers inhabiting them felt otherwise exactly as normal. It was exhilarating, heady to feel Storm's huge inrush of power, to feel the bolts lance out of Cyclops more terribly than ever, the cold welling up in Iceman in astonishing depth, even in the face of this ultimate fire; and Gambit and Wolverine felt it too, each in his way, the muscles hardening and claws harder than adamantium ever could be lancing out, the cards itching with kinetic energy that a whole planet might have had locked up in it.

Storm dived into the plasma of the star's tattering chromosphere, wrapped it around her as she had done in open space before. There, she had at least been partially visible. Here, she was simply fire herself, elemental as she had never been before. The laughter that came from within the fire had a slightly unnerving quality to it, as if it were genuinely the fire that laughed, fickle and destructive. "Bishop, are you ready?"

"Affirmative."

She hit him with a bolt which must have sucked a quarter of the stellar atmosphere dry. Bishop caught it, absorbed and held it. "Cyclops," he said, his voice slightly strained, but eager, "if you and Gambit and I hit it all at once—"

"Agreed. Say when."

"Iceman," Storm said out of the fire, "can you lure it out of there? It is hard to affect while it's feeding."

"I'll try." The bolt of cold he shot down at it cooled some of the uppermost gases in the star's ailing atmosphere and actually darkened part of the local chromosphere. Charles watched, astonished and impressed. *Jean,* he said, *are you having any luck communicating with it?*

Nothing. But it's hungry—so hungry. Her voice sounded pained. *It didn't like Storm taking all that plasma. Look at it go, it's heading for the core.*

The creature was tunneling. "Oh no you don't," Wolverine said, and went after it.

He caught up with it halfway down into the star's core— leaned back and slashed with his claws at one of the four "arms," the leading one, which was piercing toward the star's core like some sharp proboscis.

Jean screamed.

The larva whipped around and hit Wolverine solidly, amidships, with one of the other arms. He screamed as his giant form was thrown easily fifty thousand miles up above what remained of the stellar surface.

"Didn' like dat," Remy observed. "Touchy."

Cyclops said, "Good. Gambit? Bishop? All together now."

Optic blasts lanced out. Gambit's cards, each as wide

across as a small planet, flicked downwards. From Bishop, a bolt of force as wide as he was arced at the larva. They all hit at once.

Jean screamed again, more terribly this time—clutched at herself, started to curl into a ball. Charles made his way to her, reached out to catch her where she floated in space, stricken.

Too—close, she gasped. *The rapport—it's stronger—too strong—*

Break it, Jean. Break it!

Can't. The larva— She shook her head desperately. *Or—*

The extensor, Charles thought, cursing inwardly.

The creature was flailing again, as it had when Wolverine hit it. Slowly it turned away from the starcore, began to swim up through the star's atmosphere toward them.

Iceman, Charles said. *See if you can make a difference—*

Bobby clenched his fists, then threw his arms out in a huge gesture at the larva making its way up toward them. Cold, cold like that in the long night before the universe ignited, came blasting out. The larva slowed slightly as it passed through it, then came on through, coming at them.

"Now *what* was it you were saying," Bishop said to Wolverine, "about making it angry, so that maybe it would make a mistake?"

"Might do that yet. But for the moment I'd worry less about *it* doing that than *Ororo*."

For she was wrapping the fire about her again, losing herself in it. Again, from within the layers and layers of ravening plasma, came that odd, remote laughter—and the sense of a bolt being readied.

"Storm," Bishop said, "I am not quite prepared, wait just a moment."

"I am prepared enough," she said, her voice rich with

something one did not usually hear there: impatience. "Time to strike a blow myself."

What if she kills it? Charles thought, and he could hear all the other X-Men but Jean think it at the same time— Jean was in too much pain to think about anything but herself at the moment.

"Hungry," Jean moaned. "Why can't I eat, *have* to eat, something's stopping me, *stop it*!"

"Hey now, Storm," Remy said, "wait a moment now, don't do anyt'in' you gonna regret in de mornin'."

She struck, ignoring them all. Fire poured from her and struck the larva.

It ingested the fire without a second's hesitation. Then they heard it roar, and then it came at her.

Cyclops, Gambit, Wolverine, and Iceman all flung themselves or their powers at the larva at once. It ingested Gambit's cards, and Cyclops's optic blasts, and then it shot fully up out of the star's atmosphere at them and bowled right toward them. They tried vainly to get out of its way.

It hit, scattering them with completely irresistible force in all directions. Then it hit Storm, beyond them, the same way, just as she was attempting to strike it with another bolt. She cried out in pain and fell back, floating helpless. Her fire went out.

Stunned, the others floated there helpless for some moments, and the creature turned and sank straight back toward the star. "What do you mean, 'regret it in the morning'?" Iceman said. "I regret it *now*."

"Got de six-ten split *dat* time," Remy groaned after a moment. "*Sacremént*, what's dis *bébé* made of?"

"Collapsed matter, partly," Charles said, "as its shell was. But it is ingesting more mass all the time. Hurry, make pickup on Storm. Jean?"

Hungry, was all she could whisper mentally. *So hungry. Have to hurry . . . have to . . . catch up . . .*

"She's out of it," Wolverine said, reaching Storm. "Okay otherwise—I think. I don't like how she sounded." He straightened. "I'm gonna have another go at our little starfish there."

"Wolverine, no!" Cyclops yelled.

Gambit was recovering himself somewhat. "*Oui, allez,* Wolvie, we can take it."

"He needs his head felt," said Iceman, groaning.

"No leisure for that now, X-Men," Orien's voice said, "however much we appreciate the thought. You are about to exceed your radiation limits. Argath, get ready to kill the extensor."

"*Orien!*"

Too late—it was done. They were back in the sphere again, being pulled through the stargate. Behind them, the larva was finishing the stellar meal which they had interrupted, and was making its way off to start another.

In a few minutes they were back aboard, and various Shi'ar staff piled into the pod to help them with their spacesuits, and help them out. They needed it—they all found themselves weak—except for Cyclops, who, ignoring his own exhausted muscles, carried Jean in and spent an anxious few moments trying to revive her. When she came around at last, her eyes were frantic, but her thoughts were in such a muddle that she couldn't communicate for some moments.

"Take your time, Jean," Charles said, as Scott settled her on a couch out in one of the small lounge-niches on the utility deck, near the airlock. "The extensor must have incremented too quickly for you, locking you into the rapport."

She gulped. "It's not that."

Lilandra appeared in holographic form, with Orien behind her. "Charles, are you—"

"I am all right, and I think the others are, by and large." He looked at the other X-Men standing around him. They looked battered, but not too badly so. "But Jean seems to be having a problem."

"Not me," she said. Yet certainly she did. She looked most peculiar now. Almost eager—and at the same time, frightened. She gulped again. "We have to leave," she said.

Everyone stared at her. "Leave?" said Lilandra, puzzled. "We cannot do that! If we lose track of the larva, we will—"

"No, Lilandra, you have to leave right now. Have them take the fleet away. Far away. Take it away quickly!"

"But *why,* what's going to—"

Charles went straight into Jean's mind and did his best to make sense of what he found there. As Jean had said, they were not images. Impressions, yes. If you were deaf, and dumb, and blind, and still were trying to describe things to someone, you would work in terms of the senses you had. Heat and cold and hunger, the intelligence on the other end of the "connection" definitely knew. It had some vague sense of the passage of time, of *now* and *not now.* On the cellular level, it had some kind of memory—though not of particulars, but of abstracts. Close to its body was nested a comfortable core of power, which was growing as it was fed. Soon that power would become available to it.

Charles was not sure exactly what was implied by that feeling—but he suddenly felt, as Jean had, that discretion was definitely going to prove the better part of valor today. "Majestrix," he said, turning to Lilandra, "for your people's sake, order them to stargate out of here. I don't think there's a great deal of time.''

''See to it,'' Lilandra said to Orien. In the hologram, Orien could be seen to turn and begin hurriedly snapping orders at his officers. They scrambled in all directions, and one set of consoles some way above them in the atrium beyond the bridge deck started to become very busy indeed.

''It will take some minutes,'' Orien said. ''The gates are sensitive to this environment, and the power settings will be very unstable if we—''

''I would just cope with the instability, if I were you,'' Charles said, catching, through Jean, the increased sense of something impending, something about to happen, something waited for, for a long time.

Three minutes passed. ''The gates are almost ready, Majestrix,'' the report came. ''Thirty seconds.''

''Very well. Prepare to—''

And then it happened.

Nine

Tachyon production way up, lord,'' Talat said suddenly from his console. "Very high. *Much* too high.''

A peculiar groaning, rumbling noise, just at the edge of hearing, went through the fabric of the ship. The Shi'ar crewmen standing around, and the bridge crew still visible in the hologram, all sank perceptibly where they stood; then, bizarrely, bounced up again. The X-Men, all out of the pod-sphere now, looked around them and out the utility deck windows with astonishment.

"What's the matter with the gravity?" said Scott, hurrying over to take Jean from Charles, and alternately sagging and bouncing slightly as he came.

"Massive gravitational disturbance," came Talat's voice from the bridge, now sounding very frightened indeed. "From the core, washing out in big waves. That was the first crest. More are coming."

"The only thing that propagates faster than light in realspace is gravity," Orien shouted. *"Where are our gates?"*

"Up to the bridge, everyone," Charles said. "There may be some way to help."

He was already heading that way himself. But there was to be no time for that either. "Gate's ready, lord," came another voice from the bridge, not Talat's.

"Go! Get us through!"

The circle of space which did not match their own suddenly winked into being in the great frame of the gate. The flagship flashed through it, and off to one side. The others followed it through, angling away.

A pillar of utterly blinding white light, looking solid as a pillar of stone, burst out through the open gate. Charles knew there was nothing in space for light to reflect from, not anywhere near the correct amount of gaseous material or dust to cause a beam of light to look like a beam. However, no one seemed to have told *this* light that. Like a sword, it burst out with them into the space into which they had gated—and the last Shi'ar vessel, transiting the gate as it happened, vanished. A moment later, the beam vanished too. It had destroyed the gate from the other side.

Charles swallowed and made his way up to the bridge with the others at his best speed. The problems with the ship's gravity stopped for a short time, and then started up again, so that Charles's hoverchair nearly grounded itself a couple of times on the way up to the bridge, and a couple of times nearly banged itself, and him, into the ceiling of the lift. He was glad to get up there with the X-Men, and to set it down on the floor of the bridge at last.

The place was in pandemonium. Lilandra stood there, hanging on to a railing near the main command-and-control consoles and watching the officers try to get the ship under control. "We can do nothing but ride this out," Orien was shouting to her over the alarms hooting and howling through the upper levels of the atrium. "The gravitic waves coming from the core area are more than powerful enough to overwhelm our own systems if we try to maintain status quo through them."

"All right. But what has happened? Where is *Mehe'ri*?"

It was the last ship that had been in the gate when the light burst out.

"Gone, Majestrix. I am sorry."

"What *happened* to it?"

"It did not have enough warning," Orien said evenly. "We had just enough, as it was. I can only hope that even now we are far enough away. Here it comes!"

They looked back. Slowly, the light at the core of the galaxy behind them grew.

Fire. A single core of it: something like a star, but more blinding, somehow more intense. "Talat, put the analytical recorders on that, in Sharra's name, or Avend and his people will be up here ripping our crests out in minutes. We may all be about to die, but let us at least have enough knowledge about it to make them happy before it kills us."

Storm was gazing out at that furious light with an expression compounded of terror and, Charles thought, desire.

"What *is* it?" Lilandra said again. "What destroyed *Mehe'ri*? And the stargate?"

"I think we are privileged, Majestrix," said her Minister for Science, coming up onto the bridge deck. "We are seeing one of the universe's great mysteries, and for the moment, have survived the terror of it. I would say the core of the galaxy has just gone quasar."

The bridge crew looked at one another. Lilandra, and the X-Men, looked out at that light. "We always wondered what caused this kind of thing," the Beast said softly. "No one had the slightest idea. Suddenly, a galaxy's core would go mad—just start radiating from what seemed a point source, like a star. Hence the name, out of '*quasi*-stell*ar* object.' One of the ugliest words in the language, if you ask me, but nonetheless an astonishing thing. Amazing amounts of energy from those point sources, like a whole galaxy's output concentrated in one area. Now I wonder," he said, looking out at that eye-hurting point, "if all quasars are *these*."

They looked out in brief silence at the terrible light. Charles found himself wondering if all of what they saw was light at all; whether some of this awful outpouring of energy was in superluminal particles. Living beings did not normally see such things, since one could not generally be near such an explosion and still remain alive. The eye naturally would not register such, but other aspects of the human body might. All Charles knew was that the light made him afraid, and that the fear felt strictly physiological, like cold, and had nothing to do with reason—though later, it might.

"It could be," said the Minister for Science. "A great deal of mass, all concentrated artificially in one area—former stellar mass which in the normal course of things, if it accreted, would go over the event horizon and make a black hole of itself. But it is prevented from doing so, somehow, by the creature ingesting it all. Then, when it has had enough for its own physiological needs, whatever those might be—it *ignites* it somehow, converts all that mass to energy."

Charles looked over at Jean, still unconscious in Cyclops's arms. "That is what she felt, I believe," he said, "though her own perceptions were muddled enough, and she was deeply enough in shock, not to be able to make better sense of what she felt. No matter—she warned us just in time."

"*Mehe'ri* was not in time," Lilandra said bitterly. "Well, the Two shelter them; *we* can do nothing for them. What *can* we do?"

"Look," Storm said suddenly.

How she saw it first, Charles could not tell. *Unless*, he thought, *she too is acquiring some kind of rapport with it. Something to do with the extensor. Oh, heavens, I hope not.* In Scott's arms, the unconscious Jean stirred restlessly, moaned a little.

Out of the terror of that sudden light it came soaring. It seemed slow, while it was still distant, but the illusion began to disperse as it came closer. It was still four-lobed, but the lobes—blunt and rounded in the pupa, spiked and finned toward the ends in the larva—were now backwards-raked four-vaned wings. One wing reached forward and three of them back in a more rakish configuration of the caltrop shape, very sharp and stylized.

Charles, looking at them, thought of the warp-cycling vanes that some species in the Shi'ar galaxy employed for controlling the superspace fields they used for propulsion. Except that none of those ships had vanes ten thousand miles long. The creature glowed with light of its own, and sheened back light from the quasar behind it. As it passed them, even though it did so at a distance of perhaps a hundred thousand miles, the glare of it made them all avert their eyes, and all the surfaces of the remaining Shi'ar ships were combed with the black shadows of their various superstructures as it sailed by.

It passed them by without so much as a pause. Accelerating, it began to diminish into the intergalactic darkness like one more star. Not a wandering star, though: one which definitely had an air of knowing where it was going.

The Shi'ar galaxy.

"Follow it," Lilandra said, as Avend came up into the bridge to stand and gaze at it with the others. "We can do nothing against it for a day or so more. It is swift, but not swift enough to cross all those lightyears in a day, not even at the speeds it was developing when it was still a larva. At the best of its speeds that we've seen, Lord Orien, how quickly could it reach the fringes of our galaxy?''

''Not one day, no, Majestrix. I would say, possibly three.''

She blinked.

''The only time we saw it cease acceleration, Majestrix, was when it was about to ingest a star,'' said Lilandra's Minister for Science. ''Until we have evidence to the contrary, it would be wise to assume that it can, in extragalactic space, accelerate to much higher speeds than any we have so far seen it obtain.''

''It didn't move this fast in those other galaxies, though,'' said Iceman. ''The ones that you saw back at your lab.'' He looked over at Avend.

''That's true,'' Avend said. ''Either its life cycle normally compresses as its lives go on—and that could be linked to its cumulatively escalating mass between stages—or else it has become artificially compressed by the energy we have added to its personal ecology.''

Lilandra looked grim. ''So that our attempts to stop it have in fact made it *more* deadly than it would have been otherwise?''

''We don't know that for sure,'' Avend said hurriedly.

''But there are those who will certainly reach that conclusion,'' said Gladiator, from behind Lilandra's chair.

She nodded. ''Well,'' Lilandra said, ''we have built our nest, and now we must hatch out what we find in it. Keep pace with the creature using the stargates, my lords, and do not under any circumstances lose it. We will have time in the next day to make another stand. Perhaps we will find this form more vulnerable than the last ones have been. If not, we will have to start formulating other plans, for this creature must by no means be allowed to enter our galaxy and begin another cycle.''

Orien and the others nodded. ''X-Men,'' Lilandra said, ''you made a noble attempt. Will you make one more to-morrow?''

They looked at her, somewhat weary, but ready, Charles thought. Only Storm, still looking out into the darkness after the creature, did not respond. '' 'S what we came for,'' Gambit said. ''Wouldn't mind a crash 'n' burn, though.''

Lilandra nodded. ''I think I understand you—and I would not mind one myself.''

Singly and in twos they headed off, Scott last of all, with Jean. Lilandra paused by them, and said, ''Cyclops, if you will permit, I will ask our medical staff to look at her.''

He glanced over at Charles, who nodded. ''Thank you, Lilandra,'' Scott said, and went off, stepping carefully as the gravitic waves still propagating through the area made the ship's gravity go strange again.

''Charles,'' Lilandra said, ''if you could spare me some time for a consultation, I would take it kindly.''

''Majestrix, of course.''

They made their way down to her quarters, Gladiator trailing behind at a discreet distance. They discussed what they had just seen as dryly as if they had been reading someone else's report on it rather than seeing a galactic core annihilate itself in a second. ''That will be all, Gladiator,'' said Lilandra wearily, as they came to the door and it paled for them. ''I will send for you later.''

''Majestrix,'' he said, and bowed, with a look at Charles. Then he went away.

They went in and the door opaqued. Charles sat there, going alternately hot and cold inside—and suddenly she was on her knees beside his chair, her arms around him and her face buried against his neck. "Well," she said, rather muffled, and sounding very unhappy, "now you have seen me be afraid in front of my whole ship, and I must say, I do not care for it. What *is* it about that light? It ran ice down inside my bones."

"Majestrix—"

She looked up, pulled away slightly, with a hurt look on her face. "Never call me that, Charles," she whispered. "Not here. Not in *these* circumstances."

"It is just that—it has been a little while since I saw you."

"I thought—I stayed away. I thought perhaps you did not wish to see me, Charles, to be with me, after the—after the judgment. I saw your face."

He looked away from her, then realized that that was not helping matters. He looked back again, took her hands. "My love," he said, "I thought perhaps *you* did not wish to see *me*, knowing how my face must have looked. You were not the only one who was judging. And for that, I am sorry."

She laughed, a brief, somewhat bitter sound. "Well, for all our power, and all our alleged wisdom, we are fools, my dear. I should have known there were no conditions on your love for me. There are none on mine for you."

"I should have known that too."

They held each other for a long while, and came to know it better yet.

Much later, she said to him, "What will we do now?"

"Go on with what we're doing," Charles said.

"If we do not manage to stop this creature—"

"We will."

"Charles," Lilandra said, "it is not like you to go into

a situation without examining and accepting all the available options. We may be fools, but we are not stupid. If we cannot stop this creature, then I will almost certainly be executed. My people can be very intolerant of failure, especially in situations like this."

"*Executed?* But no one has the power, the right—"

"Oh, it would not be *called* execution, and certainly there is no legal power to allow such a thing," Lilandra said, looking at him dryly, "but there are always ways to remove a ruler who is proving ineffective."

"If you think for one moment that I will allow that to happen . . ." Charles said. "And the foolishness of it. As if killing you could make any difference to what was going to happen to them!"

"Yes," Lilandra said, "the irony would not be lost on me. Nothing else would be lost on me for much longer either. They would do it, nonetheless, to buy themselves political stability for the time the empire would have left to it, before our galaxy collapsed. A matter of some hundreds, maybe a thousand years or two, you might think, but our people are used to taking the long view. Then"—she looked at Charles—"there is no question but that the various expansionist lobbies woud begin looking toward your galaxy. In fact, they would start *now*, with an eye to moving our administrative and other power bases to your galaxy well before ours began to collapse."

"No one lives by choice in a burning building when there is a perfectly good building to move to next door," Charles said. "But the creature seems likely enough to head for *our* galaxy right after yours. What would be the point?"

"Their argument," Lilandra said, "would be that there is always the possibility that it will go somewhere else. It might head for one of your two small cousin galaxies, the

Magellanic Clouds, or for some other galaxy past you in the Local Group of twenty-eight. They would do it simply because it would make them feel better. It always feels better to be doing something when the dark closes in.''

'' 'Whatsoever work your hands find to do, do it with all your might,' '' Charles said, '' 'for the night cometh, in which no man can work.' Though it would have been another night he was speaking of. But Lilandra, what if they *did?* Earth has no way to defend itself against the might of the Shi'ar Empire, should they turn their eyes our way. No, we will just have to beat this creature, and that's all there is to it.''

''I wish your certainty were as contagious to me as it is among the X-Men,'' Lilandra said. ''How are they, Charles?''

''Phoenix . . .'' He shook his head. ''I am greatly concerned for her. Though she is a telepath of great power, she is still young, and to a certain extent unprepared for the extra power which has been thrust upon her. She retains the memories of the creature that took her form and died, but memories are not the same as experience.'' Charles chose his words carefully. Jean Grey's telepathy and telekinesis had seemingly increased mightily years earlier, to the point where she eventually went mad with power, calling herself Dark Phoenix, and eradicating an inhabited sun in Shi'ar space. Lilandra had been forced then to condemn Phoenix to death; she eventually sacrificed her own life. But, as it turned out, that was not Jean Grey, but a very real duplicate created by the Phoenix Force. The original resurfaced months after Phoenix's demise. She eventually acquired all the memories of what happened to her doppelgänger, including going mad with power.

Charles shuddered. Those were not happy memories.

Shaking his head, he said, "The extensor is a two-edged sword."

"I know," Lilandra said, and for a while she would say nothing more. "Can you break her free of the influence this creature seems to have on her?"

"We will have to," he said. "If we do not—" He shook his head, and gently and idly stroked the feathers at the back of Lilandra's crest. "Again, the sword is two-edged. If she becomes too deeply in rapport with the creature, and we succeed in destroying it, she might die as well. Yet at the same time, her understanding of the creature has told us things about it that may be vital to its destruction, and may yet tell us more. She is dancing on the edge of that sword, and she knows that she is. I cannot simply forbid her to do so, no matter how fearful I am for her safety. But, that aside, I do not know that she would pay any attention to me if I did. She is an X-Man—and would remind me of that, forcefully."

"They are not children, Charles," Lilandra said. "They are adults."

"But they *are* still my students. I have a responsibility to guide them—"

"And to know when to stop."

Charles nodded, looked over at her.

"It is not going to work, is it?" he said after a while.

" 'It'?"

"Let us say," Charles said, "that we survive all this. That the miraculous happens, and we find our way through this crisis. On the far side of it—we still have your domestic problem, and I do not see any way in which it can be easily resolved."

"No problem worth solving, I think, can be easily resolved," Lilandra said, getting up out of bed and moving slowly to a chair, over which her bedwrap lay. She threw the wrap around herself and went over to the great dark window full of moving stars. "But, this one . . . I wish I could simply go back in time and rewrite my people's history. Save that they would then no longer be my people. They are, as I am, occasionally pragmatic in the extreme. That pragmatism has been forged in the fires of a very difficult history, during which other forces to which we should have succumbed still did not destroy us somehow. We have survived. However, we have brought a certain cruelty out of the forge with us, a tendency to eliminate the apparently unfit first, and ask questions later."

"But one may still work to reform the cruelty."

"Sometimes, I have been doing so. Other times, it is wiser not to tamper. My handling of this crisis will be extensively analyzed and examined, if we come home."

"When we come home."

"Very well. But no matter how I handle it, there will still be those who will say that this entire situation would have been better handled had you not been here. They will suggest that my judgment was influenced, even contaminated by yours. That your presence endangered others of my officers and staff." She came back and sat down on the edge of the bed, giving Charles a resigned look. "The truth will not change their opinions. What did you tell me, once, was a saying of some of your people: 'My mind's made up, don't confuse me with facts'? But there are problems other than their bigotry and inflexibility. Let us realistically consider the logistics of it, Charles. You have your own work, duties you need to perform which, even stargating aside, make it inconvenient for you to stay here—if you would stay here, which I doubt."

"I know," he said.

"They will press me, if I really desire to continue this relationship with you, to abdicate," she said. "I will not do it. I am a child of the Neramani. I was raised for this work. It is in my blood, if not my bones. I have held the throne and lost it, and held it again. And having lost it, having been forced out into the universe which is not your home, will bring home to you as few other things can the *value* of your home, of being among your own people after being in exile among aliens, no matter how well-intentioned they are."

"But you always have a home with us. You know that."

"Where you are, Charles," Lilandra said, leaning close to him, "that is heart's home to me. Always. But the mind and the body have their own requirements for a home as well, and real trouble begins when *all* their needs diverge. And my mind's home is here, I fear. Duty has its own song to sing, as you know, though you may curse it between the choruses." She sighed, bowed her head. "I am as torn as you are."

"Perhaps not in the same way," Charles said. "I may not have a whole empire to rule, but I have a planet to assist, a home to help guard against those who would ruin it. I have little enough help in that work. So for the time being, at least, I must stay where I am." He reached out to take her hand again. "If there is such a thing as fate," he said, "a power that plans and plots our lives, then it has given me a hard enough part to play." He laughed a little. "And placing us two so far apart from one another in our jobs, our lives, and still causing us to feel the way we feel about each other . . . one would hope, in such a case, that there was a good reason for it. Yet at the same time, whatever the reason, I feel that I should bear up as well as I can, and be as heroic as I can manage under the circumstances, no matter why we are this way—for pride's sake.''

She nodded, looking out the window. ''Charles,'' Lilandra said at last, ''my people will not be shifted toward our position. I speak as if they will, sometimes, in angry moods. But in quieter reflection I think I know otherwise. It's we who must shift. I will not be able to put my government off forever. Sooner or later they will require me to take a consort. Sooner or later, as I grow weary, or old, I will cease to argue.''

''Not old,'' Charles said. ''Never you.''

She laughed. ''What a courtier you are. Oh, I will, Charles. Soon enough the feathers will go brittle and pale. You at least have *this* advantage.'' She stroked the top of his head with a slight sad smile. ''You lost your plumage in your prime. No one will be able to tell the difference from *that* direction when you begin to fade. But age comes to us all, Charles, and weariness. Sooner or later, they will wear me down, and a day will come when that they *have* done so will not matter that much to us. Entropy is running in the universe. Sooner or later it catches up with us.''

''I know of a wise man,'' Charles said, ''who used to say that, for just that reason, you should never look behind you. Look forward, and keep your mind on running the bases.''

''A wise man indeed.''

''And for the moment,'' he said, ''I think you are simply tired. We all are. Think what we have been going through, in these last days. This resigned mood, so unlike you, whatever you say about some of your moods being angry—it may just be skewed blood chemistry. When did you last eat?''

She looked at him, and started to laugh, very softly—but the laugh had tears at the edges. ''The perpetual enthusiasm of the younger races,'' she said, ''the perpetual certainty that things *will* work, despite all the evidence to the contrary. Very well, Charles. Let us by all means eat, and then we will sit down with the X-Men, and the members of the Science Council who are here, and go hunting ourselves a miracle. *What* was it that Phoenix was asking for, before you went out into battle?''

''Pizza,'' Charles said. ''I will speak to the food processor, and show you. Afterwards—well, life is indeed full of the miraculous. After we eat, let us see if, here or elsewhere, we cannot find some more of it.''

Charles went down to the quarters that had been assigned to Scott and Jean. He hesitated, then knocked.

A moment later the door cleared. Scott was standing there, looking rather haggard. ''May I come in?'' Charles said.

Scott gestured him in.

Charles glided past him to the bed where Phoenix lay. One of the Shi'ar medical analysis units sat near the bed, its console silently reading out physical and mental status in graphs of softly colored light. Charles looked at it, recognizing some of the readouts readily enough from their congeners on the consoles in the Danger Room. Many of them seemed to have been set to different baselines than the ones he was familiar with. He could make little sense of them at the moment; he would have to ask the Beast about the new settings when he saw him. He did not need the readouts, though, to tell him what he most wanted to know: that Jean was unconscious, but not profoundly so— the ''hum'' of a mind going about the business of a state somewhere between sleep and dream was present. There were occasional faint images spiking through the unconsciousness—detectable, but too faint to "read" clearly. To Scott he said, "Has she spoken?"

"Not out loud, no," Scott said. "I heard her speak 'inside' once—you know the way she'll broadcast a little, sometimes, when she's distracted by something, or upset."

"What did she say?"

"She said she was hungry. She said it several times." Scott sat down near her bed, reaching out to take her hand. "What are we going to do?"

Charles looked at her, thoughtful. "It's a difficult question," he said. "I had given some thought to trying to break her out of the rapport; it would seem to still be in place."

Cyclops nodded. "Can you do that?"

"I think I probably could. But if I do that, there is the chance of losing a weapon against the creature."

"And if she can't pull out of the rapport, and we kill it?" Scott said. "What then?"

"I think we both have our suspicions," Charles said evenly. "On the other hand, what if we do not stop this creature? I know some of us may not be terribly sanguine about the structure of the Shi'ar Empire itself, Scott, but think about all the lives, all the many lives living around all the stars there. Sooner or later they will be wiped out, destroyed in the inevitable gravitational collapse and destruction of their galaxy. Sooner or later they will all die, or most of them, because of what we were not strong enough to do."

"And what about her?" Cyclops said, jumping up out of the chair—then catching himself in the violent movement, and moving more carefully afterward, as if afraid he would wake or disturb her. "Why does *she* have to be the one to make this sacrifice? Why does it keep *having* to be her? Why does she keep having to be the one to put her life on the line for us?''

"Because," Charles said, "that is her gift. How *else* do you expect someone with such powerful telepathic and empathic skills to act? She would accept this burden willingly, were she conscious, and you know it."

Scott turned away, his face bitter behind the ruby sunglasses. "When it's her own choice, that's one thing," he said. "And it's something I've never been able to argue with. But when someone else makes the choice . . ." He turned back to Charles. "When *you* make the choice for her—that's something else entirely."

Charles shrugged. "I can only invoke a tired old strategy," he said, "and ask, what would Jean say about this situation were she conscious?"

Scott sat down, let out a long breath, and just paused that way for a little while, as if listening. Then he looked up at Charles again. "There are times," he said softly, "Charles, I swear, there are times . . ."

"Understood," Charles said.

Cyclops, after a few more breaths, laughed, and said to Charles, "Not much point in telling a telepath what you're thinking, is there?"

"Not when it's obvious. But I really do understand," said Charles. "There's little enough genuine expression in the world, even of anger, much less of appropriate anger. You have a right to be angry, I'd say. So have I, at seeing my students suffer as they have done while battling this creature. The only question that remains for the two of us is what we do with that anger, how we get past it, or make it work for us. At the moment, I know what I have to do with it. I have to prepare strategies to make the next fight a more effective one. And you will have to fight again. Nor do I think Jean will be able to join us. It may be, though, that she has something more important to do.''

''You mean, as some kind of ringside commentator.'' Scott made a wry face.

''She may possibly be able to tell us better where to punch, yes. We can do the rest. But the point now is to try to work out when she might be conscious.''

''So you're not going to try to bring her out of it.''

Charles looked at the quiet form lying on the bed. She turned, shifted slightly. That sight alone relieved him a great deal; at least the state of consciousness was not pathologically profound. ''For the moment,'' he said, ''I would judge not. It is often better to let such things proceed naturally, rather than indulge one's weakness, and meddle just for the sake of doing something. If she is in some state of consciousness which lends her any significant perception of the creature—well, I would rather not disturb that state, lest on awakening she lose something she could have told us otherwise. It will be at least a day before we need to meet the creature in battle.''

''Do you seriously think we're going to be able to do anything to stop it?''

''We will have to attempt it. The adult state is as yet untried. It may have vulnerabilities which are not presently obvious. Certainly the Shi'ar have their own intentions. I believe one of the fleet ships is preparing now to stargate to a position well ahead of the creature, though still in intergalactic space, and lay a large spread of gravitic and other energy mines in its path, along with various other devices they used on the pupa without result.''

''They're not going to try that right *now*, I hope.''

''No,'' Charles said, ''though some of the younger officers are eager enough, considering what has happened to their sister ship. Orien, though, saw immediately that it would be wiser to wait until the X-Men are ready to take the field again tomorrow. If their attack can be combined with ours, all the better. And if the creature becomes, shall we say, unduly annoyed, by their attack—we will be in a position to defend the fleet.''

Cyclops let out one short laugh at that. ''We hope.''

''Yes,'' Charles said, ''emphatically, we do. In any case, this potentially combined attack will give us an idea of what vulnerabilities the adult creature may possess. But for the time being, let Jean sleep. If she comes to for long enough to speak more than once, I will hear it and look in on her. Right now—''

He probed gently at Jean's mind, and heard nothing but that carrier ''hum'' of mind, and above it, a great quiet with echoes running through it—not sounds, but a mental effect like the rippling light that one sees on the ceiling of a room with a window overlooking sunlit water. A dance and waver of light, of life, but giving no clear indication of what color the water might be, or what swam in it.

''I would say the rapport continues, all right,'' Charles said, ''though it is possible that the intensity of it is diminishing somewhat. We will see. But in the meantime, don't tire yourself out, Scott. Make sure you get some rest as well. One of the others will sit with her when you need a break. Logan, or Hank, perhaps.''

''Might be better if it wasn't Logan,'' Scott said. ''It always pains him to see her hurt, or out of action. Sitting with her might make it worse. Especially if she senses it. You know how she reacts to distress.''

''True,'' Charles said, ''but it's for that reason that I *would* suggest Logan. Never mind, it's not important. Just make sure that you get some rest eventually. And, Scott—''

Cyclops looked at him. "If you're going to tell me it's going to be all right," he said dryly, "don't bother. Whatever else being an X-Man is about, it's rarely about being all right."

Charles thought briefly of the situation with Lilandra and Orien, then raised an eyebrow, and chuckled. "So young to be a cynic," he said. "But never mind—for there are days when I might just agree with you. I will be back later."

Some hours later, Wolverine came into the lounge to find Storm gazing out into the darkness again. He sat down on one of the nearby sofas, throwing a look toward the hallway door that led out of the lounge to Jean and Scott's quarters. It was shut, and had been for some time.

"No change," he said, to Storm or to the air, it was hard to tell which.

"No change," Storm said. She came away from the window, came over to sit by him. "Logan, have you had anything to eat? You look terrible."

His face worked in a way that suggested he felt terrible but was not about to make the admission. "Well," he said, looking up at her from under his brows, "what about you? You don't exactly look like your usual serene goddesslike self either."

She stood over him, folded her arms and tried to look haughty—but as he looked steadily at her, Storm gave up and smiled, a somewhat ragged and weary expression. "Does it show that much?"

"Well, if you were thinkin' about takin' out an ad that says, *I'm tired and I have a problem*, save your money."

She laughed, a slightly sad sound, and walked back over

to the huge windows at the rear of the common lounge. "Ah. I will, then."

"Is it Jean?"

"Yes," Storm said. "And no."

Then she shook her head. "I want to do it again," she said, "to use the extensor. The sooner, the better. The last time—" She shook her head. "Logan, you can't imagine what it was like. To *be* the star. There's something about what I do—it's always been hard for me to describe, but I think I'm understanding it a touch more clearly. When you control the elements, there's always a feeling as if there's something else—something more worth achieving. I mean, *control* is all very well, but—" She shrugged. "Think of it as a relationship. In a relationship, you don't want to control, you want to be in it, of it. You want to be so *in* it that you don't even notice it as a relationship as such. Except idly, the way you notice that you have a name. When I raise the wind, or bring the rain down, or work with plasma, or the other forces of the universe that we think of as elemental, there's always a desire to be in them, *of* them. Not separate, but part of their whole. I got close, there." She stood gazing out into the dark, very still. "Very close. It felt like it's never quite felt before."

"Ororo," Wolverine said, "it ever occur to you that maybe there's a reason for you to be the way you are? That you may be *meant* to be separate? That if you stop bein' separate, you stop bein' Storm, bein' Ororo? You have a right to do that, y'think?"

She looked at him with some surprise. "If *I* do not have that right, who *else* possibly could?"

Wolverine looked at her dourly. "Relationships," he said. "Funny you should mention those. Has it occurred to you that some of us like bein' in a relationship, friendship, with you, and we wouldn't like it a whole lot if it stopped? That we might find it kinda difficult to be best friends with a thunderstorm or a blast o' wind? It's *you* we're friends with, your personality. It's *who* you are, not *what* you are. If y'stop becomin' a *who*, and start becomin' a *what*, how'm I supposed to have a relationship with you? And who says you're allowed to just throw somethin' like that away?''

She looked at him as he continued: ''And the rest of us. Course you're closer to some of us than to others. Normal, in any big group o' people workin' together. But if you get lost in bein' a *what* 'stead of a *who*—what about the people you're closest to? What do we tell Rogue an' the others when we get home? Sorry, Ororo's decided to become a force of the universe full-time? Gone off to become a sheet of plasma or somethin', but she sends her best.'' He snorted. ''Storm, throwin' away a personality like that, just for the pleasure of it—it's suicide. Or close enough. If you're not killin' the body, you're killin' the *self* inside it. That's the *sui* in fronta the *cide*—even I know that much Latin. I heard some shrink say once that the rules for suicide were that you weren't allowed to do it while you had a living parent, or a living child, or a living spouse, 'cause of the pain it would cause them. Well, you got at least one person who stands *in loco parentis* to you, Storm. Think how Charley would feel. Not to mention the rest of us. A lotta people round here love you. Be real sad to see you throw away the thing that they all love.''

Storm turned to look at him again, and her eyes flashed. ''This is all too easy for you to say, Wolverine,'' she said. ''What did *you* feel out there?''

He breathed in, breathed out, and walked to the window himself. *Snikt,* and *snakt*, went the adamantium claws as they briefly worked in and out. "Power," he said. "That creature—it was tough." He smiled grimly, a look of approval. "Tougher'n I thought. I thought I shoulda been able to make stellar calamari rings outta the thing. But—the *power*. The feeling of being a thousand miles tall, stronger than I ever could be, the feeling of being able to do anything—nearly." He stopped, shook his head. "Still love to know what that thing's made of. But the feeling that, if I could just hang on a little, if they'd just turned the extensor up a little bit higher, I coulda taken it. Hell, I coulda sliced up the core of that star, hydrogen, metal, and all. I coulda cut it up like an orange. There's nothin' I couldn'ta done."

"And you tell me," Storm said, "that it's not good to let a personality slip away. But that's a thought you had *afterward*. Did you have any thoughts of that kind *during* the experience? Did you have any thoughts about *why* you were fighting, or simply *that* you were fighting? It was simply very good, wasn't it? And that was all you wanted to think about."

Wolverine glanced up at Storm, hard-eyed. "It's always a danger," he said. "Always easier to fight than to think. You think I ain't aware of that?"

"I'm sure you are." Storm sighed. "And here we are playing devil's advocate for each other. But in the end, it's going to come down to whether we do what others want for us, or what we want for ourselves."

"It *will* come down to that," Wolverine said. "But there's a difference. Start doin' what you want for yourself to the exclusion of everything else, and you stop bein' part of a team. And you're one of the team leaders, Storm. You steppin' down? Is the position open?"

She looked a little blank at that.

"You need a personality to lead a team," Wolverine

said. "And think about this: What'll happen when you go under the extensor again, and you find that big feeling of being a star, or whatever—and you don't come back?"

She laughed a little scornfully. "Come, Wolverine. Where would I go to?"

"Where Jean's gone, maybe," he said. His expression went very dark. He would not look at Storm. "You want to take that risk? It's suicide, like I said."

Storm paced over to the window again. "I'm sorry, Logan," she said. "You cannot understand what it felt like."

"Another o' that shrink's games that he used to talk about," Logan said. " 'Nobody Knows the Trouble I've Seen.' And the important part is that 'Nobody Knows': they can't possibly, because they weren't there, and so on. So you say." He made a scornful face. "C'mon, Storm, you don't have to be able to shine to recognize a star. If you think I'm stupid, just come out and say so, but don't say I can't *understand*! I understand better than you know. It's just that I think I have my mind made up." He looked out into the darkness too, got up and started to pace. "I *love* that feelin'—being ten thousand miles high, being the most dangerous thing around. Invincible. Someone's been ripped up as many times in fights as I have, you think I wouldn't love bein' that way all the time? But I'm still human, Storm. And I know there's too big a price to pay for bein' invincible, if you stop bein' human as well.

"Somethin' else," Logan said after a moment. "Remember Dark Phoenix? It's real easy to laugh that one off—it wasn't really Jean, it was only some energy creature that looked just like her. The thing is, *that was Jean*. In all the ways that mattered, that person was Jean Grey. She talked like 'er, acted like 'er, walked like 'er, *smelled* like 'er. But when the power got t'be too much, she lost it. She wiped a star. She almost wiped us.''

Logan? Charles's voice suddenly seemed to fill the air around them.

"Yeah, what, Charley? I'm a little busy right now."

Too busy to see Jean?

"What, is she—"

She woke up about twenty minutes ago. Come on in.

He got up and headed down to her and Scott's room at a run. More slowly, wearing a dark and reflective look, Storm followed.

Jean lay there on the bed with Scott holding one of her hands. One by one the X-Men hurried in and sat or stood around the bed, looking down at her, smiling, grinning, wearing expressions of immense relief. She blinked up at them, a little bemused. "I haven't been out that long, have I?"

"Jean," Charles said, "we have been somewhat concerned about you."

"Oh, come on now," she said, and then Logan came in, and she saw the look on his face. "I'm all right, really—I *am* all right!"

She started to try to get up. Scott, with an ease apparently born of long practice, pushed her down again.

"Do you remember anything from your unconscious period?" Charles said to Jean. "Specifically, anything regarding your rapport with the creature?"

"It's very low-level at the moment," Jean said. "Barely a dim buzz in the background. I can hear it—it's getting hungry again. Or, rather, it's not this stage of it, the adult stage, that's hungry. It's remembering forward, anticipating the hunger that's going to come."

"Jean. Is it intelligent at all? Is there *any* way we can make contact with it?"

"No, Charles," she said. "The rapport is strictly one-way. If it registers me at all, it's as some strange kind of brain-damaged larva it's carrying inside it. It's somewhat disturbed by my presence, but it doesn't know what to do about it. Its evolutionary processes never prepared it for anything like this. So it's quite willing to go ahead with its business, and ignore me. It's only when it's actively interfered with, I think, that it begins to react."

"So I noticed," Wolverine muttered. "My ribs still ache, even though it wasn't my own ribs that got hit."

"What's it going to do next?" Iceman said. "Though I think I know."

Jean nodded. "It's going to lay its egg. It only lays one. Already it's sniffing out the right star. It's so strange, Charles—the creature's drawn to suitable stars the way a moth is to a candle, but it's not so much a question of the light as the frequency. It senses the star's spectrography as if it were a smell, perhaps even like a pheromone. It's drawn to core stars of what I think we would call Population One. It likes the scent of overexcited stellar coronae, such as you get in core areas. And it can smell micro black holes—it knows that those indicate a good nesting area too. There's one, there's a micro, in the Shi'ar galaxy—I'm sure it smells that. I could, while I was dreaming—being inside it. An odd iron scent, like train tracks: a dark smell, an edgy smell, with power hanging about the edges of it."

"How long do we have?" said Scott.

Jean shook her head. "Not long. It'll come to the fringes of this galaxy soon, I think."

"Sometime tomorrow," Storm said, "if what Lilandra said was true."

"Yes. You'll know when you're close. It'll speed up."

"Faster than it's going now?" Bishop said, incredulous.

"I don't think I'd get in its way, Charles, if I were you," said Jean.

"Well, we are going to get in its way shortly, whether it likes it or not," Charles said. "We must try again to stop it."

Jean shook her head. "It's going to be interesting trying," she said, "but I'll do my best. It's possible that if one attacked it telepathically—"

"We may have to try that, you and I," Charles said, "but I prefer that we save that option for last, and I prefer that *you* not attempt to participate in this next fight at all. You are still too weak, and we have no idea how that rapport, when reestablished, would affect you if you were also trying to fight."

"Charles, I'll be all right—"

"You will *not* be all right," Logan said, sitting down next to her and glancing over at her. "Charley, tell her she's not gonna be all right."

"I have told her, and will keep on doing so. Jean, if you argue, I will refuse to listen, and if you attempt to go anyway, I will crawl out of this chair and sit on you."

"I'd be tempted to sell tickets," the Beast said mildly. "What kind of currency are the Shi'ar using these days?"

"Hard, I am certain. Never mind that now. Jean, one more thing. Did we make any impression at *all* on the creature when we fought it? If we had had more time, would we have been successful?"

Jean frowned. "Possibly. It didn't like when everyone was hitting it at once. It was uncomfortable. And when Logan hit it—" She glanced at him. "That really bothered it. Energy attacks, it has some experience with—at least it can understand them. But direct application of kinetic energy—not just your kind, Gambit, but plain old physical force, just being *decked,* or having someone try to deck it, that felt unutterably weird to it. It makes sense, though. When would there usually be anything big enough to interfere or even interact with the creature physically?''

''On its scale,'' Iceman said, ''jeez, you'd practically have to chuck a planet or something at it—''

The Beast looked unusually contemplative, even for him. ''I wonder,'' he said. ''What would happen if you did chuck a planet at it? No, make that two planets. Catch it between them, whack the planets together—'' He clapped his hands, creating a small *wham.*

Charles gave him a surprised look. ''Where are we going to find the power to do that kind of thing? Even the Shi'ar—''

''Well, let them work on it,'' Hank said. ''But isn't it possible that where more elegant solutions may fail, brute force might triumph?''

Charles made an amused *hmp* noise, then said, ''Well, every option must be investigated, I suppose. If you want to go talk it over with your scientist friends down on the utility deck, be my guest, but—where are you just going to pick up a couple of spare planets? And they would need correctly opposing intrinsic velocities, and...'' Hank opened his mouth. ''Never mind,'' Charles interrupted. ''I leave it entirely to you.''

''He's just jealous,'' Iceman said with a smirk. ''Jean broke the Shi'ar's moon, so big-brain has to go and break something bigger.''

''Oh, very droll, Mr. Drake,'' Hank said with a roll of his eyes.

''Jean,'' Charles said, ''the creature. After it lays its

egg—if it gets that far—what then? Will it lay another?''

''I think it might normally,'' she said, looking doubtful, ''but I get a feeling from its body memories. Charles, it's so strange: its cells, if that's what they are, remember the way they should be, but also they know how they are, and how they will be later. As if human cells not only had a DNA blueprint inside them, but could read it as well. But this creature has a lot more energy bound up in it than usual—I think because of the various attacks on it.''

''Do you mean that you think it's going to lay more eggs?'' Bishop said.

''No, but I do think it's more fragile than it was. I think we've been stressing it to the point where it's not going to reproduce as effectively as it feels it should. Again, those body memories are pretty strong. The creature doesn't really like the way it is now. There's a feeling of discomfort, of things not being right.''

''Maybe den it can't lay an egg at all?'' Gambit said.

''I wouldn't bet on that,'' said Logan.

''No,'' Charles said, giving him a look, ''nor would I. But it is also a possibility that we must consider—and it would be a welcome one. One thing, though: What happened to the parent of this one?''

''It died, Charles. When the creature lays its eggs, it packs literally every available erg of energy into it. Afterwards, it's burned out, wasted, like a salmon after it's swum upstream and spawned. The adult might have only lived a few days afterwards, or a few hours—it was nothing more than a shell. Probably it fell into the star where it laid the egg, or was subsumed into it some other way.''

Charles shook his head. ''It seems sad, in a way.''

''I don't think it seems sad at all,'' said the Beast. ''It's probably just as well. Otherwise, as I said before, we'd be up to our armpits in these things. The way they disrupt the galaxies they use—it's a good question whether more ordinary organic life would have even originated in any of the galaxies, if there were more of these creatures. Now that you look at it, of course," and he started to get that pondering expression that the other X-Men knew too well, "maybe this is why most life evolves on planets associated with stars in spiral arms, rather than near their cores."

"This line of reasoning shows signs of becoming dangerously metaphysical in a very short time," Charles said, not without good humor, "so I will leave you to it for the moment. Jean, you said that the creature was still hungry, but ahead of time, as it were, on behalf of the larva to come."

"I think so. I don't think the adult will damage any more stars; it may not be capable of doing so. It's charged very full of energy as it is, and if it needs to 'top up' its supply, maybe it can do so through those big vanes on its wings. I'm not sure what they're for."

"Manipulating subspace, I would suspect," said Hank. "But catching it and stopping it to make tests would seem to be impractical."

"Got *that* in one," Wolverine said.

"Well." Charles looked around at them all. "Jean, you must get some rest. We will be catching up with the creature in about eight hours, meeting it at the point where the Shi'ar are preparing their attack."

"They're going to pump *more* energy into it?" Jean said, sounding alarmed.

"Well, they must try, to satisfy their own hypotheses, after all. But we will be doing the same thing, won't we?"

"I suppose we will."

"All right," Charles said. "Enough. Jean, rest. We will

have another tactical meeting, a couple of hours before attack time. If the creature did not like the way we hit it all at once, we must find a way to streamline and concentrate that process—managing our attacks in such a way as to exert maximum pressure, and hold that pressure for maximum time. That may make the difference. Meantime, let's all go get something to eat.''

The X-Men started to head out. Finally the only ones left were Jean and Scott, and Logan. Wolverine looked over at Cyclops, and said, ''Y'know something I've noticed?''

''What?''

''Charley keeps sayin', 'This'll make a difference,' or, 'That might make a difference.' ''

''And you get the feeling,'' Scott said softly, ''that he doesn't really know what's going to make the difference at all.''

''Yup. Neither does anybody else. Fun, ain't it? And what if *nothin'* makes the difference?'' Wolverine said.

Scott shook his head, and turned back to Jean.

Logan gave her one last look, relieved, but still troubled, and went away.

Five hours later, the X-Men met with Lilandra on the bridge of the flagship. Orien was standing near the windows, looking out at where the remains of his fleet were spaced equidistant from one another in the darkness between galaxies.

''Report,'' said Lilandra.

''Majestrix,'' Orien said, looking at her and then at Charles, with a nod, ''this space is now sown so thickly with mines, energy weapons, and other devices of destruction that if a conventional battle fleet came through here, even shielded, within a matter of minutes it would remain only in the form of wreckage. Understanding that what we must now deal with is more powerful than a fleet, we have overdone it somewhat as regards the weaponry used. We are, in fact, now running practically empty except for the self-recharging gunnery like the main needlebeam batteries. It is probably a good thing that we are close enough to home to call for backup, should we need it.''

''So you're just assuming this thing's gonna fly straight through your minefield?'' Wolverine growled.

''Oh, we make no such assumptions, Wolverine. The attack array as a whole, and every weapon individually, is mobile and steerable. If the creature changes course, the entire weapons field will change course to match.''

''But they're gonna have to do it real fast,'' Wolverine said, ''and they can't possibly move as fast as it can.''

''Fortunately we can see it coming from a long way off,'' said Orien, ''and we think we can slow it down. Professor, we have had time to do analysis on the last batch of recordings of your fight with the creature. The vanes are indeed subspace manipulators. Around the creature, they generate a thin skin of space in which the speed of light is normally many times faster than what it is here. We can disrupt its field as it comes through. In fact, that will be the first thing that happens to it, out at the edge of the weapons array: it will lose its skin and be forced to shed all that speed as kinetic energy, and heat and light. As soon as that happens, we hit it with everything we have; then so do you. The edge of the 'braking' field is far enough away, and deceleration will take long enough in both time and distance, that you will have plenty of time to work before the radiation associated with the initial attack can catch up with you.''

''Okay,'' Iceman said, ''but what if *it* can see *us*?''

''Certainly it will not be able to work out the function

of these devices," Orien said, "even if it can perceive us."

"I don't know," said Jean, who was with them, though still leaning a little on Scott. "It may have gotten a little bit shy of things that go *boom*, after the last time. We'll just have to see. Being slowed down the way you're describing, though—I don't think it's going to like that much. More interference . . ."

Charles shrugged. "We have no choice. If we're to bring it to battle, it must first be slowed down. My compliments, Lord Orien, the plan is elegant. X-Men, are you ready?"

"We're ready, Charles," Storm said. "I will be concentrating on fueling Bishop. Bishop will hit the creature with whatever power he has from me, Cyclops, Gambit if possible, and the Shi'ar as well."

"We have one shipboard energy weapon dedicated for you, Bishop," said Orien, "and it will be on constant feed and under your control. Call for whatever you need and you will have it instantly."

Bishop nodded. "It will be interesting to see what effect the mixture of energies from plasma and optic blasts, and your needlers, will have."

"Gambit will also attack directly," Storm said, "and Iceman will hit the creature as well, attempting to do low-temperature damage to the vanes—if it cannot make better than lightspeed, neither this galaxy's core nor any other would have anything to fear from the creature for a long, long time."

"There are things I can hit it with too," Jean said, "that would—"

"No," said Charles. "You need to sit this one out."

"I have to at least stay in rapport with it, Charles! That we agreed on. If I could just go out and be with everyone else—"

"The first, yes. No more. *Must* I crawl out of this chair?"

"Charles, it's simply not fair. To the others, as well as to me. Everyone else is going to be out there—"

"Jean," said the Beast, "I'm not. I will be of more use in here, keeping an eye on the extensor with an eye to our particular needs; this is where I can best fight. You can do more good by staying in here and monitoring the creature. We need to know its reactions. If you're knocked out again, and we can't tell how well we're doing—then there's little point in any of this. We may as well just go home and write our wills—and since I haven't yet even *begun* to decide who's getting my record collection, this is an unacceptable alternative. Also, one or more of us would have to break off the attack to make pickup on you again, possibly at a crucial moment. Let's just do as the Professor suggests."

Jean frowned, but subsided. "All right," she said. "But I don't like it."

Orien's officer Talat came up. "Lord," he said, breathless, "the creature is approaching. Coming fast now."

"Phoenix?" Charles said.

"I know." She glanced at the ceiling, then shook her head. "It doesn't notice anything. It's just humming along, coming toward us." Her look at Charles was somewhat melancholy. "I'm getting hungry again."

"Send out for a pizza," he said, "and sit down. We'll go out there and do what we have to."

He turned, the other X-Men turning to go with him. "Majestrix," Charles said.

"X-Men, Charles," Lilandra said, "go well. Do well. For if we do not do well here—"

She said nothing more, only bowed to them.

Hurriedly, they left the bridge and headed down for the utility deck.

Ten

Seven gigantic forms hung in the darkness between the galaxies, at the fringe of one of them, looking out into the long cold night. Beyond them, in the immense distance, hung another galaxy that looked normal. They knew the darkness that truly lay at its heart, though, and they knew that the light they saw would not last. The light behind them might not last either.

"I can feel it," Iceman said in a low voice. "It's better than it was last time."

"Concentrate now," Charles said. "Don't let it get the better of you." But his concern was that it was already doing so. "Status, Orien?"

"The creature is entering the edge of the 'tanglefoot' field," Lord Orien said from the flagship. "It should start dropping velocity very shortly."

From far away they could see the flicker and dance of light, a point of brilliance that blueshifted as it made its way toward them. It was faint at first, but it did not stay that way for long. *How many thousands of millions of ergs' worth of energy*, Charles thought, *were likely to be released when a body of such size and mass suddenly came out of faster than light mode and was forced to discharge all that velocity as other forms of energy?* It was the kind of question that Hank would love, as it had many zeroes implicit in it.

The blue light got brighter, fiercer. At its core a single bright actinic-blue pinpoint rode, like a star itself. Under the influence of the field generators the Shi'ar had left in its path, the skinfield around the creature failed and it began to dump all its velocity. Hard radiation and terrible light streamed from it, and a high, thin, faint screeching sound started to wind itself through the back of Charles's brain as he sat in the darkness with the X-Men, a ghost or parody of himself, two thousand miles high.

The problem was that Charles did not feel like either a ghost or a parody. Increasingly he found himself experiencing the sense that *this* was the right size to be, that his normal self, barely a speck or a molecule by comparison of size, was in fact the *abnormal* one. That his broken, crippled body was but a temporary aberration, just something he had had to endure until the extensor came along and made him the right size to hear a whole galaxy, or the vague ruminations of a creature that could eat half the stars of a galaxy's core and come away none the worse for it.

He had been fighting this feeling as hard as he could. But the song of the cosmos was in his ears: not only the countless thoughts of the beings of the two galaxies between which he hung, but more distant minds, inexplicable, tantalizing. How many other galaxies was he starting to "overhear" now? If he concentrated, he could dip into some of the sources of those strange, inhuman, fascinating thoughts. This was a kind of travel that made mere crude physicality no longer an issue, and the fact that one could not walk became a joke, a trifle. Increasingly, Charles wanted to turn away from the present distractions and concentrate on hearing it *all,* or at least trying to. It was cruel to have to spend this time working to destroy the incoming creature, when there were so many more interesting things to listen to—and also, he had to try to keep the others on track. But more frequently, Charles wondered why. Under the influence of the extensor, they, like him, were becoming more themselves than they ever had been.

He shook his head and tried to steady himself. There was still a job to do before he could indulge himself in the travels of the mind that he so craved. Closer than the strange thoughts of other galaxies was the upscaling moan-shriek that was beginning to fill his mind: distress, discomfort. *Complaints*, he said silently to Jean. *Listen to that.*

I don't like it, she said. *I'm not sure something's not going wrong.*

With the others, Charles watched, and he listened. Around the creature, the flicker and flash of the Shi'ar energy weapons began, like silent distant flashbulbs popping. In silence they watched—except that, for the others, the silence was also becoming less.

"That thing yellin'?" Wolverine said. "How'm I hearin' that?"

"Yeah," Iceman said. "It's getting loud—Phoenix, are *you* sending that?"

No, she said. *I think it's started to listen to the frequency we think on, as a result of hearing me. Again, it's not really doing this consciously. The creature's pretty adaptable, some ways. Stimulate it and it responds.*

"I've noticed," Wolverine said. "We'll see if I can't stimulate it a little more."

It's not communication, though, as we would think of it, Phoenix said. *It's not really aware that we exist as such. But it does have an urge to cry out to the universe that it's coming. Or that there's something it wants.*

"It wants us to stop, from the sound of it," Bishop said. "I could almost feel sorry for it—except I have difficulties feeling sorry for something this big and this blindly destructive."

The screaming scaled up as the flashbulb-popping effect got brighter and closer, concentrating on the one spot. It looked like a very small globular cluster, of the sort which hung in a halo around the Shi'ar galaxy, and also the Milky Way. But those clusters burned steady rather than flashing and burning out like this. "Orien?" said Charles.

"No effect that I can perceive," said Lord Orien. "The creature is progressing through the field at what seems a normal enough rate of deceleration, so the weaponry might as well not be there." He sounded both amused and grim. "I tell you, if I had to wage war against someone, I wish I could have several of these to lead the way. After one of them had passed, my enemies would have nothing left to use on my main force."

"Always assuming," said the Beast's voice from the utility deck, where he was monitoring the noumenoextensor, "that the creature did not first turn on your own forces, in the manner of some of Hannibal's less controllable elephants, and decimate them first. It is an interesting thought, though. Was this a weapon once? Everyone thinks of doomsday *machines*—what about doomsday creatures?"

"I would hope not," Charles said. "Once turned loose in your neighbor's galaxy, the creature might wreak havoc indeed. But what happens afterwards when it, perhaps, turns around and comes back to snack on *yours*? That would not be a chance that I'd care to take—and if some species did, in the depths of time, I'm sure they have by now long since paid for their folly."

Still the creature's light blued as it came shrieking toward them through the night, the cry of its mind becoming steadily more unsettling. "It's only doing about point seven of lightspeed now," said Orien. "Decelerating rapidly."

"It'll still be some seconds, then, before it reaches us," Charles said. "Twenty, I would say."

"Still decelerating."

It was coming toward them now, seemingly faster and faster even though they knew it to be slowing. But as its apparent size increased, the illusion would not go away. It grew, a swelling point of light, throbbing with the remaining energy being bled off it as heat and radiation and visible light all up and down the spectrum. It came like a disastrous comet, trailing a purple fire of ionized dust and dark matter as it slowed. Its shape began to resolve into the familiar caltrop configuration. It was tumbling, though, not coming in straight as before. It looked out of control and confused, and that scream scaled up further, sounding angry.

"What kind of mistake you t'ink it'll make dis time?" Gambit said to Wolverine, grinning a hundred-mile-wide grin.

Wolverine glared at him. "A big one, I hope."

"Better get ready," Charles said.

The others were. Storm wrapped all the free plasma in the area around herself—not that it was present in such concentration as in a star's immediate neighborhood, but galaxies produce stellar wind just as stars do, and the wind, whether stellar or otherwise, was something that Storm could use. Relentlessly she gathered space's hidden fire all around her, wrapping it layers deep, grasping it in both hands like whips of lightning. "Bishop," she said.

"Standing by, Storm."

Remy watched the creature come. "Prof," he said, "Orien say it's dumpin' its speed partly as kinetic, *oui*?"

"Yes, and as light and heat—it has no other way to rid itself of the excess. Huge and strange it may be, but it remains as liable to the laws of conservation of energy as we do.''

"'S pretty well charged up, *neh*?'' Gambit said, and grinned again, making a pushing-his-sleeves-up gesture which was amusing considering that his sleeves were elsewhere, inside his spacesuit. ''If I can shift all dat kinetic out of it at once—''

''If you manage *that* successfully,'' Charles said, ''I for one doubt that there would be much of that creature left, no matter what it is made of.''

''Worth a try. Let me take point.''

''It's a possibility we'd discussed,'' Charles said. ''Go on, then. Cyclops, Storm, Wolverine, Iceman, you others all prepare yourselves. Bishop—''

''Right,'' Bishop said. ''Orien, have your 'spare' ship start blasting me now—I'll see what Gambit pulls off. Perhaps I'll pitch in in the middle of things if it looks like he needs help.''

'' 'Help,' '' Remy snorted. ''Don' know about dat, Bish, but you wanna add your strength to mine, you go right ahead.'' That slightly feral grin again, directed at the creature this time.

One of the ships hanging nearby in the night—if fifteen thousand miles away could be considered ''nearby''— lanced out a needlebeam that struck Bishop exactly. He flung his arms out wide, as if slightly astounded by the energy pouring into him. ''Pour it on,'' he said. ''I'm going to need it.''

The creature plunged closer, its scream getting quieter suddenly. ''That's kinda strange,'' Iceman said a little suspiciously. ''Is it gonna do something?''

I'm not sure, Phoenix said. *I think it may simply be feeling a little more normal now that it's lost most of the ve-*

locity it was carrying—all that velocity that it suddenly had to bleed off, whether it liked it or not.

It was coming closer and closer, burning blue. That bright four-armed spark tumbling closer, only a little of the subdued shriek of power now coming out of its heart. "Five seconds until it will be within your close attack range," said Orien. "Four seconds. Three. Two. One."

Storm trained her bolt on Bishop. It was not as massive a one as when she had had a whole star to wrap around herself, but potent enough. Bishop held it as long as he could, as that white, tumbling spark of light came toward them, swift, swam huge above them, attempted to flash past them.

"Gambit," said Charles, "give it a try!"

Remy, taller than several continents laid end to end, towered up over the creature and flung at it an archipelago's worth of cards. He threw a deck's worth, as if he intended this one game of fifty-two pickup and nothing else ever again. Flashes of intolerable light broke out along the surface of the creature's body as the cards struck the four outflung limbs, the vanes of the wings hanging back. The creature screeched with pain and anger, flailing as it tried to turn toward the source of the attack.

"Keep moving around, Gambit!" Charles said. "Don't let it—"

Too late. The creature had already figured out at least partly where he was. It swam toward Remy, ungainly but purposeful, wrapped a limb around him, then another, somehow leaned back where it hung in space—so that Charles was suddenly and bizarrely reminded of a major-league pitcher ready to put one right over the plate—and flung Remy's giant self out into space with laudable economy of action.

"Give me some more power!" Bishop was saying to the ship which was fueling him. "Cyclops!"

Cyclops turned a barrage of optical blasts on Bishop. Storm turned her bolts on him as well.

"Iceman," Cyclops prompted.

"Hitting it from this side," he said. The temperature dropped to near-absolute zero on the far side of the creature. It lashed about it with its arms, and shrieked more desperately, if possible.

Bishop finally let the force inhabiting him go. It hit the creature square amidships, right where the four wing-vanes met. The force of the blow he struck was enough actually to stop the creature in its path and push it a little way backwards.

The scream scaled abruptly up. *Rage!*

If it's going to make a mistake, Jean said, sounding shocked and pained herself, *this is when it's going to happen!*

The creature tumbled a little back and away from them now, flailing about itself as white fire from Bishop's bolt surrounded it, pushed it back—but did it no other harm they could see. It shrieked more loudly.

Hungry, Jean said. *It's getting frustrated. It knows it needs to get out there and lay the egg that's going to hatch out and eat.*

"That's a pretty good trick," said Wolverine. "Iceman, I'll stay out of the cold; don't mind me. Let's see if this critter dislikes rough 'n' tumble as much as it did the last time."

"Don't mind rough," Gambit gasped, now himself tumbling in space, trying to slow down and get back into the fight. "I'll help."

SNIKT! came the sound—not that the sound was possible

in space, but neither was it possible, in the strict sense, for Wolverine to stand half a planet high in the darkness. He waded in.

Charles watched, and tried to choose his moment. *Beast, he said, you need to start incrementing the extensor now. Wait for my signals, though.*

I will.

Go.

Wolverine fell toward the creature, grasped it, grappled with it. It turned and shook, screeched and flailed. Wolverine struck at it with his claws. It tried to fling him away as it had Gambit, but he had one gigantic arm clenched around one of the four wing-vanes, and was hanging on like grim death while he sliced and struck with the other. *It hates this,* Jean's voice said in Charles's mind. *It really hates this.*

I know. Prepare yourself to strike it. I know you're not extended, but we need all the help we can get. Prepare.

I am.

You can ride piggyback on me when I strike.

The Beast incremented the extensor again. To Charles's eye, all the others suddenly seemed to become more solid than they had been—more real. The light of the two galaxies shining from so far away, the light from the ships closer by, suddenly seemed *less* real. Charles felt the strength fill him, felt his mind come awake, alive. Again he heard the song of two galaxies, one near and one far away. The second more anguished, its song partly a dirge; the first one still more innocent, though how long that would last was a question.

Charles tried to clench and grip the force of his mind all together into one fist, a fist that would strike in the one right spot. It was difficult; the shrieking was getting louder.

But that terrible sound was in some way a key to where he would need to strike.

"You guys gettin' ready?" Wolverine said, between panting breaths. "This thing's gettin' pretty frantic here. I can't make much of a dent. Not any dent, really. You're gonna have to try to hit it too."

On the far side of the creature, Iceman was turning and bobbing and weaving above it, keeping his cold carefully focused on one side of it and away from Wolverine.

"If I were you," Wolverine said, "I'd hit it with everythin' at once. I'll let go and kick away."

"Yes, but try to cut it again first, Wolverine," Charles said. "Beast, increment!"

The extensor went up again. Once more there came that blast, that gasp of power, stronger this time than any of them had felt it. They all swelled, they all grew. Wolverine pulled back a clawed fist and punched deep.

A desperate shriek, followed by a scream from Jean, pierced them all. *Now!* Charles cried, and struck the creature with the fist of his mind. The others struck as well. Storm, to his astonishment, threw her bolt, not at Bishop, but directly at the creature. Bishop turned loose all the new force he had had pumped into him by first one, then another of the Shi'ar fleet cruisers. Gambit rained down cards, each one exploding with the force of an atom bomb on the creature. Cyclops fired optic blast after optic blast, like a red sun suddenly deciding to go coherent, the bolts so terrible that there was no looking near them, let alone directly at them.

Jean moaned softly. This was Charles's only indication that things were working. *Now*, Charles said, *now again!*

They all hit at once—and Wolverine lifted that clawed fist again, and said, "This time for *real*."

He drove the fist in.

Increment! Charles said.

And the claws pierced the creature.

A sudden silence—then a final scream that went through every one of their minds like a knife. Jean was stunned into silence by it. Charles reeled. The creature flung Wolverine away from it and came barreling toward Charles's ghost form.

Wolverine flung himself in the creature's path, trying to wrestle it out of the way, but it shook him off as a terrier will shake off a rat. It went for Charles again.

One more time, groggy and dazed though Charles was, he took aim at the creature with the fist of his mind, and struck. *Jean! Jean!*

But she was not there to help. The others, still dazed from the previous attack, could do nothing either. And then from the far side came a blast of cold like a breath of God's own winter. It gripped and seized the creature, and struck Charles motionless with the sheer venomous absolute-zero fury of it. The creature shook, flailed its limbs, and shot away toward the Shi'ar galaxy again, gathering speed as it went, accelerating with astonishing speed toward superluminal status.

They all drifted, moaning, in the dark of space for a while. Finally Charles managed to pull himself together, and felt about him in mind for the others.

Gambit?

"Here . . . just."

Wolverine? No answer at first. *Logan!*

"Unghhhh," he said after a while. "Thought I knew what a Minnesota merry-go-round was. Seems I missed a coupla lessons."

Not as many as you think. You marked it, Logan. First

blood—though to what purpose, we still have to determine. Bishop?

"Conscious, Professor, but I wouldn't say much more than that."

Storm? A long pause. Storm?

It was some moments before the answer came. "I harmed it."

No, Charles said. *Your own ethics aside—I can heartily wish that you had.*

"Charles?" It was a cry over their spacesuit radios, this time. "Charles!"

"Lilandra," he said aloud. "We could not stop it. It just brushed us aside, even with the extensor notched up almost to the top. Only Wolverine got close to hurting it—and I am not clear how he did that."

"Attitude," Wolverine growled, and then moaned a little at some ache in his unbreakable bones.

Charles found himself wishing he could bottle that attitude and sell it. He would be a rich man after the arms dealers finished beating a path to his door. "But it does not matter," he said after a moment.

"No," Orien's voice said a moment later, "it would seem not. Majestrix, the creature is back on course. We have thrown everything at it that we can. It was not enough. We must call in the full fleet, and try to make one last stand inside the galaxy. We do not have enough power to call on out here, and we are out of weapons. We must return home quickly, resupply, and go out again."

"Give the order for it," Lilandra said dully. And then, in her mind alone, so that only Charles would hear, she said, *Charles, what can we do?*

Not give up, he said. *Never give up. Make sure of its course, leave ships to tail it, to precede it on its way, to keep us warned of where it goes and what it does. Return to the Throneworld, as Orien says, for more weapons. And try again. There are still a couple of options.*

Her laugh was bitter. *You never do give up*, she said.

There is too much to play for, as you know, Charles said.

"What's the score, Charley?" came Wolverine's voice, sounding tired, but still game. "We goin' after it?"

"Yes," Charles said, "at a somewhat reduced pace, for the moment. Back to the ship, all—and well done. We'll do better the next time."

At least, Charles thought, only slightly desperately, *I hope so.*

They made their way slowly back to where the flagship's tractor beams would pull them in.

The meeting with the full Science Council and the rest of Lilandra's councillors back on the Throneworld was a dismal one. Charles would have preferred not to attend it, but he had no choice—especially since the military, angry that their advice about the creature had not been taken, or had been taken too late, were now in full cry about what should be done. Everything, Charles could see, was going to be the X-Men's fault. They had used the extensor wrongly, or not well enough, or they had been afraid to use it correctly.

I do not know why we bother to help them, he thought privately to Lilandra after a while.

Reflex? she said inside her mind. *They are a quarrelsome lot. But they are in fairly subdued mood today, Charles. You should see them normally.*

He snorted, then when some of the closer grandees around the table looked at him, did his best to make it look like a sneeze.

The arguments went on for the better part of three hours.

No one was able to come up with any better solutions than had been proposed already, except for brute force. "Now if you *do* have a couple of spare planets with approprate intrinsic velocities lying around . . ." the Beast said.

Several of the Science Council got interested looks at the suggestion, and Charles began to worry. As it turned out, they *did* have such planets, though not "lying around," and the discussion of available kinetic energy and moment of inertia and other abstruse subjects nearly turned the air blue with its intensity. Charles, grateful for an excuse, chose that moment to go out and look for a drink of water, wondering who they had been planning to use the planets on.

Lilandra took the opportunity to follow him out briefly. "When one thinks of the end of one's universe," she said, getting a drink of water herself, "or one's world anyway, one does not usually imagine it this way, as a prolonged administrative argument."

"No," he said. "I admit you're right. How long until we go out into space again?"

"Oh, the process has started already. Orien has taken a secondary flagship and gone out with specific recommendations for reweaponing the fleet. They will need to set up the tanglefoot field again. He hopes to increase its intensity this time, and make the creature dump its velocity more quickly, with an eye to destabilizing it. It did seem to be in more distress when we stopped it that way."

"Yes, but it's moving faster now, isn't it?"

"Unfortunately, yes," Lilandra said. "So now we will have a last heroic stand in our home galaxy."

"Heroic it may be," Charles said, "but I do not think it will be our last. And not here. We must at least try to guide the creature further away toward the other side of the galaxy, away from your people on this side."

"Charles, there is little to choose between the sides. Our galaxy, unfortunately, is very completely colonized. And how would you lure it?"

"By making a light like the right kind of star? If we can work out what that might be. Still, we must be responsible about this. If the creature can, it must be diverted toward the path where there are the fewest worlds. It will kill a star in which to lay its egg, I know. This may not make that much difference, but if it is choosing from an available range—"

"It seems," said the Beast, wandering in, "according to Jean, that the creature is searching for a particular unstable line in the stars' spectrographs. Such a star would probably tend to flare."

"Are you talking about proper flare stars," said Charles, "or just ones that do so randomly?"

"Not the true flares, the blue ones that go red, but microscopic-level flares. Kind of like our sun, which flares, but not enough to destroy their planets, or scour off the life on them—just enough to prompt the occasional cosmic-ray storm. The creature would seem to prefer stars with this one line in their spectra, this weakness in their structure; which when stimulated—"

"The star would then flare controllably? Interesting," Charles said. He looked at Lilandra. "In birds, it would be the equivalent of an egg tooth. In untoward circumstances, the larva would be able to escape without too much energy being released."

"So it might be. Charles, you should go in there and share that thought with them."

"Not that they seem to be in much of a mood to listen to me."

"They were not listening much to me either," Lilandra

said, in the authentic voice of an empress ignored. "Plainly I am considered to have handled this whole thing badly. Were it not for the fact that soon someone will jump up to assassinate me, we would be hearing about it even now."

Charles flushed hot. He had heard thoughts of that kind among the council this morning, and had written them off to anger and desperation. He had not suspected that Lilandra had heard them too. "No matter," he said softly. "We will cheat them yet, my love."

"*Should* I cheat them?" she said. "Have I *not* handled this badly?"

"Ridiculous," Charles said, and took her hand. "Majestrix Shi'ar, never doubt yourself. Never."

"This is an interesting turn of mind for you, Charles. The self-examining one, always turning over the rock of the self to see what might be crawling underneath."

"I know what lies underneath *your* rock," Charles said, "and nothing crawls there. As for motives, right now mine are simple: to save a galaxy or two. Yours must lie in that direction as well."

"Where your motives go, there go mine also, my love," Lilandra said. "Let us go back in there and see if we can't whip a little more sense out of them. But do you really think—"

"Hush," said Charles. "Let's go make it so."

Arguments went on for a long time over whether the empire as a whole should be notified of what was happening to it, but here at last Lilandra prevailed, insisting that if millions of people might be about to die, they had the right to know about what was killing them, no matter what instability this might cause in the empire as a whole. Then began the implementation of the logistics, already partly in hand, of gathering together the armada and arming it adequately for the task ahead.

Orien, speaking to Charles via holographic transmission from the other Shi'ar vessel, was doubtful about this aspect of the preparations. "As I told you, before we sowed enough ordnance in that thing's way to take out an entire fleet. Now we have a greater fleet assembling than the small one we set out with, and half the fleet commanders have private agendas which almost all mean that they dislike anyone coming down from above telling them how to arm their ships. So there are all too likely to be 'omissions' which may cost us dear in battle, unless these people are carefully watched. Additionally, I like taking all those ships into that turbulent space even less than I liked it before. We have several micro black holes in the core of our galaxy, as you know, and various other anomalies of the kind routinely associated with cores. We will lose more ships— possibly many more.''

"It seems the price which must be paid," Charles said. "Though heaven knows, none of us would prefer to pay it.''

They studied for a while the transmitted hologram of the structure which Orien thought to implement in their defense. "We will slow the creature down, englobe it, and rain fire on it from all sides," he said, "and you must do what you can to make life difficult for it in the middle.'' He paused, turned his head to listen to something that one of his staff was saying, and then looked back at Charles again, running a weary hand through that stiff golden crest of his. "The creature has apparently found the flare star it prefers," Orien said. "It has made a sudden course change and is heading for that star like an arrow.''

"Any planets?''

"Mercifully no, but that is the only good news here. The creature will reach it and begin laying its egg in a matter of an hour or two, perhaps. How long it will take to hatch, we have no idea. We must turn all our attention to marshaling our fleet. Here is the second part of the plan." He made an adjustment to the tank display, and a second "globe" of ships, three layers thick, appeared around the star in question. "We will englobe the star as well, riding shield to shield if we must, to keep the creature from getting at it. Perhaps, as the Beast suggests, we can disturb the creature's breeding cycle at that point. If the egg cannot gestate, that would finish this menace forever." The words were hopeful, but Orien's expression suggested that he was more skeptical. "Meanwhile, we have begun evacuating the populated worlds in all the nearby systems, for about fifteen lightyears around. Gravitational effects will of course begin to propagate immediately. Light will take longer, but—" Orien shook his head. "We are a mighty empire, it is true, but, Professor, the logistics of evacuating a hundred billion people, even with stargates, are nightmarish. It will take at least a day or two." He shook his head again. "It would be a miracle. If we successfully move all those living beings without ourselves killing as many of them in the process as the creature would have, then that will be a miracle indeed. Sharra and Ky'thri will be with us as they never have been before. But I am afraid we might have to move them again, regardless, if the core effects are as severe as they were in the last galaxy. And where do we evacuate them *to*? Your galaxy is not necessarily any safer than ours at this point."

"Nonetheless, there must be places where they would be welcome." Charles started considering the options.

Orien looked at him. "Professor, may I tell you something?"

"Feel free."

"I have previously had petty thoughts about you. Your motives, your reasons for being here—I am ashamed of them. I see the selfless way you are endangering yourself, your team, for our people's sake."

"Not just for yours," Charles said. "I am altruist enough, but you may assume that there is at least some pragmatism operating here."

"Just the fact that you say that," said Orien, "belies your case, Professor. Never mind. I apologize for my past pettiness."

Charles was oddly moved, and a little embarrassed. "While I thank you very much," he said, "we have more vital things to think about."

They went back to studying the map again, and made a few minor changes to the plans for the englobement. Finally, Charles looked up from the plans, and sighed. "I have been thinking about what you said," he said to Orien.

"I hear a 'but' coming," said Orien, with a slight, sad smile. "The mind and the heart disagree?"

"Yes," Charles said. "I perhaps owe you an apology as well, on those grounds. When all this is over"—he found it very hard, but he said it—"I may resign in your favor."

Orien's eyes widened slightly.

"Yes," said Charles. "But I will *not* stop loving her."

Orien looked at him for a long while without saying anything, and finally shook his head and laughed just once. "Well," he said. "Maybe it is good that one of us should."

"You need not tell even small untruths to spare my feelings," said Charles. "This is, after all, one of the penalties of being a telepath of my power: one tends to hear much more than was intended.''

''I know,'' Orien said. ''Let us get back to our work . . . and we will share our thoughts in more detail, when all this is done.''

They had, it was estimated, about three hours before the creature arrived at the star where it seemed intent on laying its egg. Above and around the Throneworld was assembling the greatest armada that the Shi'ar Empire had ever seen gathered together in one place.

Charles at first tried to keep count of how many there were—after four thousand, he gave up. Such a collection of spiked, ferocious-looking armament he had never seen before, and never wanted to see again. He and the X-Men looked into the tank and saw the great assemblage forming over their heads. Their reactions were mixed.

''All those guns,'' Storm said softly, watching one particularly large battlecruiser come in.

''They are ships of an imperial navy,'' the Beast said. ''They must be able to defend themselves.''

Wolverine snorted. ''Yeah, well, in a place like this you don't really get a sense how much defendin' themselves they been doin' until they get everythin' together this way. They're all pretty much new ships too, ain't they?''

''Keeping your navy new is usually a good idea.''

''Yeah, well, if all this is here, what's going out in the empire, I wonder?'' Wolverine said. ''Kree rebels're prob'ly havin' a field day.''

''I believe,'' Charles said, ''there is some measure of unrest.'' He had heard this from Lilandra, the evening before. Even a small power's forces do not go unnoticed when they are suddenly withdrawn from their usual theater of operations. And the Shi'ar forces were scattered far and wide throughout their galaxy, sometimes in places where they were welcome, often in places where they were not—such as the former Kree Empire's territory. Their sudden recall to other duties had definitely been noticed. Some of the outer planets which had been looking for an excuse to make their presence felt on the galactic stage one way or another now seized their opportunity.

"There are cities burning on the outworlds," Lilandra had said to Charles, wretched, late the night before. "It cannot be helped. Even we cannot be everywhere at once. All our available resources must now be turned to attacking this creature, stopping it here." She laughed a little bitterly. "Though some of my counselors, now far gone in fear, are beginning to suggest foolish things. That we should keep our forces in place where they are, because the galaxy will not fall apart *that* quickly after the creature has done its will with the core."

Charles had shaken his head at that. "Are they unclear that the gravitational effects will propagate immediately, regardless of the limitation of lightspeed?"

"Some of them are, and are still too afraid to move anything, lest our empire crash about our ears. Others just do not know, and possibly don't care, or are just too afraid to change the status quo." Lilandra sighed, sat down on the bed again, slipped her light wrap around herself and shivered, though the room was warm. "Charles, could it be that if an empire cannot hold itself together without armed might being shown in every corner, could it be that really we do not deserve to be an empire at all—that we would be right to let things fall apart?"

Things fall apart; the center cannot hold . . . said the echo of the Yeats poem in Charles's mind. "I have heard it said," said Charles softly, drawing her to him, "that empires have a term of life just as human beings have. A time comes when it makes no sense to try to prolong them. Their vision is lost, or the meaning of it is lost. There is a saying, that one shall not strive 'officiously to keep alive' what has had its hour in the starlight and is ready to pass."

"It is a philosopher's thought," Lilandra said, "and none of my counselors would believe it for a second. Yet now we come to the test of it. We will either save our galaxy, and spend many years restoring the order lost at the fringes, or we will all go down together, all in the same burning house. How many other empires has this creature destroyed, I wonder, over the millions of years it has been journeying?"

"It does not know," Charles said. "It knows nothing of empires. To judge from what Jean says, it may recognize no life forms except itself. It knows only its own life. It has no relationship with its offspring—it dies when its egg is laid. It knows no others of its own kind. It perceives our interference with it only as some blind force doing something to it that it can't understand. Think of the sorrow there; for all we know, it has been wandering the galaxies for how many millions of years, looking for someone, finding no one, because it's just too big. Too big and too strange to interact successfully with anyone here."

"And you have tried."

"It does not know that other creatures exist, so when we try to speak to it, it doesn't hear. It is a deafness made more profound by the fact that the creature afflicted with it doesn't even know that sound exists. No. I am afraid that we will have to destroy it."

"Or die trying," Lilandra said.

• • •

Charles stirred uneasily in his hoverchair at the memory. "We're going to have to go out again, of course," said Bishop. "And indeed, last time we were a little more effective than we've been so far. But . . ."

He trailed off uncomfortably. Wolverine, who had been gazing into the tank, now glanced over at him. "We did become our powers," Wolverine said. "And it's just like Jean said, there's always the chance that you'll lose it. I lost it. I went nuts out there."

Storm shook her head, and said, "I struck it myself." She had said little since they came back in after the attack. Plainly she was still in shock over her own actions.

Bobby said, "The extensor being turned up high didn't seem to have hurt me any."

"Your cold saved us, that's true," Charles said. "But it saved us only because you *became* your power. Storm, you *became* the storm, the personification of the fire and the plasma. Wolverine, you *were* violence for that little time—clawed, inimical. Bishop became the gunnery conduit, and little more than that. And I was just a mind, the fist of the mind, ready to strike. Gambit, you became explosion. It was a near thing. You all came back. But when we do it again, we are going to have to turn the extensor up that one notch more. And Jean is still not conscious."

"X-Men," said a voice out of the air, via the tank, "we are about to stargate to the attack area. The creature is approaching. Please get ready."

They got up and started to prepare.

It was a small star, a type F, slightly greenish. Around it, to the viewer who might suddenly have appeared out of space nearby, were many small dark specks. The star's disk, if you looked directly at it, was peppered with them, in an extremely regular pattern. Out in space, past the limb of the star, the careful viewer could see glitters where the star's light blazed on tiny specks of metal: the biggest ships of the Shi'ar armada.

Charles stood on the bridge of the secondary flagship with Lilandra and the X-Men, looking out the window at the strange sight. In the tank, it was clearer. The light of the star was muted until it was little more than a perfectly round pale green nightlight, and all around it, in a pattern corresponding to the vertices of a geodesic sphere, were the ships of the Shi'ar fleet.

"They have not yet put up their shields," Lilandra said to Charles, "except for what they need to protect themselves from the star itself—they are practically in its corona, after all. It will take a fair amount of energy to bring the shields up to opacity, let alone to the point where they will stop a physical object."

"Second globe now forming," said Orien's voice. He appeared in an auxiliary tank off to one side, standing and looking out the window of his own ship. Young Talat, who had been his second-in-command on the main flagship, now stood a little behind the X-Men and Lilandra, looking both proud and rather nervous, having been given command of Lilandra's ship for the first time. "My own business lies elsewhere," Orien had said earlier, on moving to the other flag. "The Majestrix's safety is important to me, but I am also concerned with making sure that this rather hazardous operation goes off smoothly—and I prefer to be in a position where I can make sure that happens, and not have to worry about whether the Majestrix's position on board my ship will prevent me doing something slightly dangerous."

"In the second englobement, you mean."

"That's right, Professor. This particular business is hazardous enough that I do not desire the Majestrix's person to be too close. At the same time, one must see to it that morale is maintained among the staff.'' *Not to mention discipline*, Charles nearly heard him think, though it was more his expression which betrayed the thought than anything else.

''The noumenoextensor is still aboard this vessel, though,'' Charles said.

Lilandra nodded. ''I must tell you that Argath has been increasingly advising against its use. He is once again claiming that the radiation and other interference from the overexcited stars, this close to the core, are likely to cause problems.''

''Worse'n the ones we been havin'?'' Wolverine said. ''That's hard to believe.''

''Apparently so, Wolverine. I would not like to cross him in this. If your decision is to go out, then go you must, but be warned. It may not work the same way it did before.''

Charles said nothing to that at the moment, only looked over at Phoenix. She had come out of her coma a few hours before, but Charles was not able to get rid of the impression that she was still far from herself. Jean had an odd faraway look about her, and when you spoke to her, there was a moment's pause, as if she had to disentangle herself from some other set of thoughts before being able to answer. It was the rapport with the creature, of course, and Charles was still reluctant to disturb it. Still, the thought of what would happen to Jean when the creature died remained very much on his mind. ''Jean?''

''I'm hungry,'' she whispered, gazing out at the night.

Talat was watching another tank in which the creature's course was being projected. After a moment he said, ''Majestrix? Perhaps twenty minutes, if it maintains its present speed. But it has been accelerating steadily for a while now.''

''A result of our tampering?'' said the Beast.

''Perhaps. I do not know if I care to indulge in any more,'' Lilandra said. ''But I also do not know that we have the choice. All we can try to do, this time, is attempt an intervention slightly more passive than the recent ones. If you are right, and simply keeping this creature away from the star will mean that it does not lay its egg—then that will end its menace here and now.''

''But what if it simply goes off and tries to find another star like this one?'' Bishop said.

''Of this type? It will find none such,'' Lilandra said, and her face went rather grim. ''You may reassure yourselves on that count. There are no stars of this type left in our galaxy. I have seen to that.''

The X-Men stared at her. ''None'a dem had planets, *hahn*?'' said Gambit.

Lilandra raised her eyebrows. ''Two did. We evacuated them. Fortunately they were not heavily populated, and the very irregularity which this creature is seeking in a star's spectrum seems to have the side effect that such stars do not often develop planets. But even if they did,'' Lilandra said, ''you must be clear, Gambit, that in order to save the many billions of lives threatened by this creature should it reproduce, I would have done far more if I had had to.''

''Approaching fast now, Majestrix,'' said Talat. ''The creature will reach the star in approximately four minutes.''

''Bring up the tanglefoot field in the creature's path,'' Orien ordered over the intercom. ''Make it drop its velocity.''

The gathered fleets raised their shields. ''Creature is decelerating now, Majestrix,'' said Talat. And indeed, in the tank it could be seen slowing, even at this scale.

Charles winced at the sudden shout of pain, by voice and in his mind, as Jean fell to her knees. The forced deceleration of the creature was much bigger than it had been last time. It was intended to be—and it was affecting Jean too.

"It doesn't—" Jean said, gasping, her arms wrapped around her stomach. "It's—"

Charles could feel the creature's frustrated fury through Jean's rapport with it. It did not know that anything was interfering with it, but it was nonetheless desperately angry. That dreadful sense of hunger was still there too, and getting worse now. Mixed with it were weariness, a lack of understanding, a *Something's been going wrong lately* feeling, a kind of mute annoyance with the universe for repeatedly failing to behave as usual. Astonishingly, the creature actually began to accelerate again.

"How is it doing that?" Lilandra said. "It should not be able to—"

"We have a very determined creature here, Majestrix," said Orien, sounding equally determined. "Inner englobing fleet—shields to secondary and synchronize."

Everywhere the green star was not directly behind the line of sight, beams of light struck out from the thousands of ships englobing the star, binding them together in a single structure. "Those are the axes along which the opaquing field will propagate," said Orien. "We will completely block the star's light away. Secondary englobement fleet will provide the shield which physically denies the creature access."

"Blocking the light is a good idea," Beast said, "and it might confuse it, but you'd better hope that, this close, it can't sense it directly by feeling around in space for the difference the mass makes in the local spatial structure. Otherwise you're going to—''

''Twenty seconds now,'' Talat interrupted.

The Beast watched the tank intently, along with everyone else but Scott—he was trying to help Jean. But she was shaking her head, there on her knees, pushing aside his attempts to help.

''I can't,'' she said. ''I can't, it can't, it has to, it wants to—''

''Hang on, Jean,'' Charles said, sliding a little way into her mind to try to lend her some support. ''Just let it pass over you. It has other things to think about.''

''It does. It wants—'' Suddenly her voice rang out clear and anguished. ''It wants to die, it just wants to get this over with and die! Let me die,'' she cried. *''Let me die!''*

It was the creature's voice—all the voice it would ever have—speaking through her, Charles knew, but the effect was unnerving, and Scott looked at her and turned away hurriedly, his face working with discomfort. He'd lived through Jean dying once—Dark Phoenix taking her own life right in front of him—and to hear her talk like this could not have been easy for him. Still, he continued to kneel by her, holding her hand. Charles could feel Scott's mind trying to comfort her through the rapport that husband and wife shared, and Charles joined his efforts to Scott's.

''Let me die, let my child be born, let it eat, let me die!''

''Ten seconds. The creature is now traveling at point four lightspeed,'' said Talat, sounding nervous. ''Lord Orien, I don't know if—''

''Neither do I,'' Orien's voice said, grim. ''But we'll find out. Primary and secondary englobement, shields to opaque.''

The star completely vanished as the shields came up.

Nothing else visibly happened, though there was a slight tremor in the tank image, as if great force was being exerted out there in the darkness. "Five seconds."

"What?" Jean said, sudden and shocked. "Where—wait a moment—oh!"

"Three. Two. One. Impact!"

The image of Orien in the tank jittered and went out. From one side of the sudden darkness where the star had been, violet fire plumed up where the tiny bright white speck had impacted it. The speck bounced, but in front of it other lights bloomed—not just the artifact-light of the Shi'ar shields absorbing the impact, but also the white-yellow explosion of some of the ships helping to generate the shield, unable to stand the creature's impact and protect themselves. The ships exploded, the light of their destruction flowering swiftly, and as swiftly going out as the wreckage and gases were overlapped by the remaining ships' opaquing fields.

"Close up, there!" Orien said. "Redistribute the pattern! Hurry!"

Slowly the pattern started to reestablish itself, the holes closing. The physical denial field flared briefly purple again as it came back into being. The creature, tumbling, slowed, then stopped. Jean screamed out loud with its rage and pain. "What's the matter?" she cried. "I want to have my baby! I want to die! Is it so much to ask?"

The creature backed away—started to take another run at the shield. "I know it's there," Jean said. "I don't care why it looks like this, I know it's there, the cradle, the grave—"

The creature flung itself at the shield. Again the terrible purple plume, like sheet lightning, again the terrible tiny blossoms of white-golden light, explosions, gas and fragmented hulls and instantly frozen atmosphere twinkling out into the endless night. And the creature bounced back again, and once more Jean screamed. It was a terrible sound, ragged with fury and frustration, and all Scott could do was hold her while she thrashed, still clutching at her stomach, one with the creature, unable to stop being that way.

"Form up!" Orien shouted. "Regroup, hurry, it's trying it again." But they could not form up again as quickly this time—too many ships had been destroyed in the last attack. With terrible slowness the points of light in the strategic tank crawled together, started reassembling the geodesic sphere form.

The creature paused and turned. Charles and Lilandra watched, and so did the X-Men, all but Jean, still on her knees and moaning, and Scott, down on his knees with her.

It turned.

"It's leaving!" Talat said. "It's leaving, sir!"

On her knees, arms hugging herself desperately, Jean began to laugh: a ragged, terrible sound. "Just let me die. I'm *going* to die. *I'm going to*—"

There was a moment's breathless silence—and then, from a standing start, the creature flashed toward the englobed star one more time. "Accelerating. Point five lightspeed. Point six."

"Where's the tanglefoot field?" Orien roared.

"Not functioning at best effectiveness, lord. The star's corona is affecting it. Point six five."

"Look out!" Orien cried, but this was not an order that he expected to be obeyed. Even if he had issued a coherent order, it would have been too late.

The creature struck the outer englobement.

A whole side of the force field globe blew out, unable

to impede the creature. Hundreds of tiny spots of light broke out across the globe's virtual curvature. The creature hit the inner globe, and there was nothing the ships could do. Another few hundred tiny explosions, and the creature dived past the remains of the fleet, through the greenish light now streaming out without anything to stop it. It dived straight into the heart of the star.

All the remaining ships of the fleet looked on in shock. "*Now* what?" Talat muttered. "What in Sharra and Ky'thri's name do we do *now*?"

From Phoenix came a great cry of relief and pain and joy, all confused together. She fell, twisting out of Scott's grip, and lay on the floor, gasping. "Done," she said. "Oh, thank you, whatever powers there are! Done, done!"

"What do we do?" Lilandra whispered, gazing at Jean in horror.

Charles paused only a second. "Crack the star."

"What?" Lilandra said, astounded.

"Crack it, Lilandra! If we could not interrupt the creature's life cycle one way—"

"I concur," said Orien, as his image shimmered back into being in the tank. "Why should we wait for this creature to reproduce itself normally? We know it will be invulnerable then, or near enough so."

"Very well," Lilandra said. "Take action, Orien. If we are to be assassinated for malfeasance, let it be a malfeasance that will be sung of with awe."

"On your order, Majestrix," Orien said, "with pleasure."

Lilandra turned away from the tank while Orien was busy giving orders to clear what remained of the Shi'ar fleet away from the star. To Charles, as she rubbed her hands together nervously, she said, "If this does not work, Charles—"

"It will be the extensor for us all again," he said, looking around him at the X-Men. Storm looked unnerved, and so did Wolverine and Cyclops. Bishop's expression was as phlegmatic as ever. Gambit had assumed the *Who me? I don't care* look which, to those who knew him well, meant he would have preferred to be any number of galaxies away, but was not about to admit it. The Beast looked resigned. Iceman actually shrugged.

"All fleet craft," Orien was saying, "withdraw to fifty thousand miles. I will insert the device into the star in two minutes, repeat, two minutes."

Charles made his way over to Jean, settled his chair down beside her. She was recovering herself a little now, sitting up on the floor, shaking her head. Tears were running down her face. Charles reached out to take her hand.

"Jean—"

She shook her head at him. "It died, Charles. It was happy to die. That was all it wanted of the world, to do what it was made to do, and be burned away with its child at the end of it all."

"What about the egg?"

"Oh, it's in there. I can feel it." She gave him a pained look. "And now you're going to kill it too."

"I do not see that we have any choice."

"Neither do I," said Jean bitterly. "Do what you have to. I'll brace myself."

"One minute," said Orien. "Professor, how is Phoenix?"

"Conscious," said Jean, "if not well. Thanks for asking, Orien."

"If you pick up anything that we should know about," Orien said, "I would appreciate it."

"Nothing right now," Jean said, her forehead wrinkling slightly, "but a hunger that's sleeping."

"Insertion in thirty seconds. The device will be activated ten seconds after that, as soon as it exits the chromosphere."

"So we won't have to use it again," said Iceman, a little sadly.

"What? De extensor?" Remy shrugged. "Well, Remy won' miss it. How many times can you be ten t'ousan' miles tall an' lord of all you survey 'fore it starts to get borin'?"

Wolverine looked at Gambit in total incredulity. "You're so full of it, your eyes are brown, you know that, Cajun?"

"He may still have a point," said Storm slowly, "though boredom would not be the problem for me. I find the device too much a temptation for an ex-goddess." She gave a look to Wolverine that Charles swore was filled with gratitude. "If I had had to use it once more—"

"Inserted," said Orien quietly. Charles turned toward the tank again. So, gradually, did the others, looking at the green star. "Probe is in the chromosphere. Descending."

Charles looked back at Jean. Scott was helping her up to stand again. She had that peculiar listening look on her face that most telepaths had. She shook herself suddenly. "Tickles," she said.

"Was that a thought from the egg?" Charles asked.

"No. An itch. Something itchy passing by."

"At maximal level," Orien said. "Activating."

They all looked at the star.

For a moment it did nothing. Then, slowly, faint dark blotches began appearing on its surface.

"Carbon-carbon cycle shutdown confirmed," said Talat, glancing down at one of his readout consoles, then looking back toward the tank again. "Propagation of the effect will take some minutes."

"It itches," Jean said, sounding bewildered. "It stings. This is bad, this isn't right."

"Implosion is beginning," said Talat. "The fusion reaction in the star's core is shutting down."

"It's not right," Jean said again. Then she frowned. *"No!"* she cried suddenly.

Talat, looking at his console, turned away from it—then hurriedly swung back again, like a man who doesn't believe what he sees. "Lord Orien," he said, "do you get a core reading of—"

The tank went white.

"It's bad for that to happen," Jean said, looking off into empty space, with a mild, bemused expression on her face. "Now I'm *very* hungry."

There was no star at the center of the tank image anymore, only blinding light, huge clouds of swirling gas. At the center of it all, something very small and dark started to grow, and to glow. It had four lobes, which stretched and felt around it feebly at first, then more strongly.

"Very hungry," Jean said, with some relish.

"Brace for the shockwave," Talat was shouting, "the grav field won't be able to maintain through it!"

The shockwave hit, and many people and things fell over, or fell down. Lilandra wound up in Charles's lap. In a no-nonsense manner he caught her before she sprawled out of the chair entirely, and set her as upright as he could in his position. "Hank," he said, "Jean, your best estimate. Was that response something we caused, or a contingency plan that the organism itself carried in case of being planted in a star with a bad fusion reaction?''

The Beast shook his head, spread his hands. "Your guess would be as good as mine. But neither would be as good as Jean's opinion, I'd say."

They turned to Phoenix. She shook her head. "It knew it didn't like the way that felt," she said. "But, Charles— either the shortened gestation, or something we *did* do, has had a definite effect. If I thought the other one was hungry, *this* is almost giving me stomach cramps. This baby is starving, and it is going to do much more damage to this galaxy's core than the last one."

"Unless we stop it," Charles said. He looked over at Lilandra.

She drew in a long breath, then nodded. "You told me," she said, "that another use of the extensor was too dangerous. That it might cost you your lives, this time."

"It might," said the Beast. "The EEG and other mind- and body-related readings from Charles and the X-Men have been becoming progressively more atypical as usage has increased. Indications are that the device has some cumulative effect on the neural pathways, and the cumulative effect increases geometrically each time—"

"Even after we found out how it was being misset due to Irdin's tampering?" said Lilandra, horrified.

"Even after that. In fact, Irdin's misunderstanding of the way the machine worked may have actually worked to vitiate the more toxic side effects," said the Beast. "It is as the sages say: 'Oft evil will will evil mar.' ''

"*Which* sages say dat?" said Remy.

Hank ignored the question. "As it stands now, there have been increasingly toxic effects on all of us who have used the device. If I do indeed turn it right up—"

"If doing so stops this creature from killing any more galaxies, not least among them our own," Charles said fiercely, "I would count my life well spent. But I cannot make that decision for everyone."

He looked at the X-Men. They looked at one another. "The problem," said Wolverine, "is that we can't be sure that that's what's gonna happen. If I knew I was gonna die to save the galaxy's life—sure, I'd do it. But if we're just throwing ourselves away . . ."

Bobby, who had been so eager to get back into the machine's influence, now suddenly looked rather more concerned. Remy glanced over at him, pulled out his deck and began riffling through it; cut the deck once into his free hand, slipped the rejected cards underneath, and picked one off the top pile, then displayed it.

The ten of spades. "Oh dear," said the Beast.

Remy shrugged. "I'm in, den. If I'm goin' out, I go wit' a blast. How 'bout you, Bish? 'Today is a good day to die,' *hahn*?"

Bishop rumbled, "I do not believe there are *any* good days to die—but there are definitely good causes in which to do it, and good company. This is the best of both. I'm ready."

"Certainty," said Storm after a moment, "is something I have had to do without often before. It seems a bad moment to start insisting on what the Goddess so rarely gives on any subject whatever, let alone life and death. I will take my chances, and see what adventure She sends me."

Wolverine frowned. "Course I'm not gonna sit this out, y'understand," he said. "Just that—never mind. Jean?"

She looked very pained indeed. "It's going to head right into the core," she said, "and have itself a real feast. I've seen too many stars die because of uncaring hunger. I never

328

want to see it again.'' Charles wondered if she referred to the creature, or to her memories of Dark Phoenix destroying the D'Bari star, or both. Probably both.

Next to her, Scott stood up and faced his teammates. "It isn't the first time we've been willing to give our lives for something that may have no tangible results. How many times have we fought to save a human race that would just as soon see us lynched? We've made a career out of it. The fact is that there are lives at stake. We can do no less than everything in our power to save them. Let's do it.''

"Then this is our time," said Charles, looking at Lilandra. "Majestrix—wish us well.''

She bowed to all of them, a gesture one does not usually see from monarchs. Talat looked astounded, and then concealed the look as quickly as he could.

"Inform Lord Orien of what we intend, if you would,'' said Charles. "I suggest that you set us out in the pod, via stargate, in the new larva's path, and push the noumenoextensor field through it as before. I would not worry overly about the radiation,'' he added as Talat opened his mouth to object. "Leave us out there until the job is done. We will check dosimeters later.''

"If they haven't melted down,'' Iceman muttered.

"Yours? Hah! Remy believe dat when he see it,'' said Remy, as they headed off toward the utility deck. "Now, Bête, you tell me *what* sages? I t'ink you just make all dis stuff up.''

"Of course not, lad. It was Tolkien, I believe. The problem is that you spend too much time with your playing cards and not enough time reading.''

A rude noise followed the Beast down the stairs. Talat stared, wondering what to make of it, and then turned and very pointedly did not look at the Majestrix—at least not until she had had a chance to wipe away the tears.

The pod was very dark while they waited to be pushed out into space. The Beast had wanted to go with them, but Charles had convinced him that the place where he could do most good in this fight was the one in which he had most practice: supervising the noumenoextensor's settings.

"Turn it right up," Charles said to the Beast, now, over his spacesuit radio. "All the way up. We've tried it at all the lesser strengths, and it hasn't been enough. We've tried all the other stages of the creature's life cycle, and we've only been able to affect even the most vulnerable of those at the highest strengths."

"And if it burns you out?"

"Then it does. There is no more time to waste in testing the ifs and maybes of this situation."

The dead matte black of the inside of the pod went away to show them, suddenly, the wild stars of the Shi'ar galactic core. It was another area all flung about with tattered veils of flaming gas and nebulae, a place of chaos with mad stars burning through it—and soon to become more chaotic still. "Ready, Charles?" said the Beast.

Ready.

"Good luck, all."

And with great suddenness, Charles Xavier was the largest thing in all these spaces.

The stars were toys, mere baubles. He could have hung them on a Christmas tree—and indeed, the fiery gas trailing from one of them to the next looked a little like neon tinsel. His mind filled again with the muttering of the populations of two galaxies, and he heard them all, could move from mind to mind, knowing its inmost thoughts with perfect clarity. Oddly, this did not horrify him.

He was a god. A crippled god, perhaps, but there is an archetype for that, after all.

Around him other gods hung in the darkness, a company of Olympians, though perhaps somewhat preoccupied ones at the moment. Destroying fire burned from the eyes of one, streamed at her will around the slender body of another. A third was ice itself. A fourth was the dark anvil of the gods, waiting for whatever force might be struck down onto him, waiting to turn it back on its source. One was a sardonic-looking deity with a handful of fiery cards, ready to deal. Still another was fury, clawed, seeking its prey. Yet another was thought itself, the power of the mind—

—and at the moment, a mind burning with a terrible hunger.

Ahead of them, in the darkness, a creature something of a size with themselves was making its way toward a star. It sank itself partway into the atmosphere of the star and began to feed, sucking the core of the star dry until it started to collapse into a cinder.

Maybe we should interrupt it before it gets started, said the anvil.

Likely t'make it ornery, said the card-dealing god. *Bad 'nough when it's in a good mood, Bish.*

I like the interruptin' part, said the god with claws. *Worked pretty good last time. Now, with the power turned right up, it oughtta work better.*

A Wolverine huge beyond estimation stalked toward the creature as it lifted itself out of the drained star. It turned as if to regard him—though with what, there was no telling—and turned away, heading for the next star lying nearby in the galactic buffet, no more than a few hundred million miles away.

Wolverine grabbed the creature by one of its four loby limbs, pulled it close, and lifted one fist.

SNIKT! A noise that could have destroyed any planet with an atmosphere solid enough to conduct sound. Wolverine lifted the massive adamantium claws, drove them deep into the central part of the creature.

It screamed. Jean screamed with it. The creature writhed, strove with Wolverine—then hit him squarely in the face with one of the free lobes. He tumbled, knocked off balance.

The creature fled, heading for that next star. *Oh, the hunger*, Jean said. *It's going to do it all over again!*

We have to stop it! said Cyclops. He and Storm went after it, all afire, optic bursts and star plasma whipping at the creature, driving it on and away.

It felt their fire, turned to meet them, and started to fight. The crippled god watched this with some concern. *It has learned to strike back*, he thought. *It learned this from us. We are creating something here which may be infinitely more dangerous than all the forms of this creature which we have fought so far. If this hunger is not stopped—*

I do not think it can be stopped, said the other god who was thought as well, though fiercer thought than his own. *Yet nonetheless we must find a way to break the cycle, to—*

She stopped suddenly.

What?

Not to stop the hunger, she said. *That will be futile. All its instincts direct otherwise. Any attempt to stop it, it perceives as an attack.*

Yes?

But if one were to make it hungrier—make the hunger

worse—It can only process so much mass at a time.

The thought was enormous, in the original sense of the word. So many lives were at stake.

But still—

Do it, he said to her. *Do it. I will feed you power. We all will. Bishop!*

Yes, Professor?

Prepare yourself to be the gunnery conduit again. Storm, Cyclops, fire everything into Bishop that you can. Phoenix, can you accept their channeled energy to add to the power you will need now?

It will take some work, but yes. Wolverine, no more attacks. Think to me. Think hungry!

Hungry—?

Remember that sandwich? How many layers did that thing have? Wouldn't you like one now?

Shi'ar may be able to move planets, came the muttered answer, *but they can't make pastrami. I been dreamin' about gettin' back to our own fridge and putting together a sandwich about the size of—well, that.* He pointed at the creature.

Dream it. Get hungry! Make it hungry! Gambit, think Creole food.

Never stop doin' dat anyway, chère.

Massive waves of hunger began to fill local space, borne on Jean's thought. Charles wondered when he had last had a really good meal. He handed this hunger on to Jean, and became briefly astounded at how it grew in her mind, how ravenous and unfillable a thing it was when it left her. Hanging there in space, she flamed with the power Bishop was channeling her from Storm and Cyclops. Backed by their power, she drove the desperate hunger straight into the creature, like a spear.

Force had meant nothing to it. Persuasion had fallen on deaf ears, understandable enough when a creature with no ears and no idea of sound is involved. But this it understood. It was ravenous—more so than it had ever been before.

It turned on the nearest star and sucked it dry with horrifying speed—then darted toward the next one.

The ships of the fleet were drawing in close, not knowing how to read what they were seeing. *Stay back*, Charles broadcast to them. *Don't get involved with this!*

The creature had finished another star, was flashing along to the next. Partly in Jean's mind, partly in the creature's, Charles could feel the insatiability of its hunger, how the mass flowed into it, became a comforting core.

Keep it up! Jean cried. *Cyclops, Storm, I need more!*

They fired power at her through Bishop until she glowed with it like a star herself. She was not massive enough for the creature to notice, fortunately. It was already finishing off another star and heading for another.

Keep it up! cried Jean.

Another star, and then another and another, and the creature began to slow down.

No! Jean cried, and forced her hunger, all their hunger, onto it, into it.

It believed her. It believed the hunger. It kept eating.

The corpses of stars, gas excited to fire, matter and nuclear metal in globules and lumps, littered that whole space now. The area was becoming very excited. Nearly everything glowed some color or other, to Charles's concern.

Will it have the good grace to make itself sick, or perhaps die of eating, before this galaxy's core goes quasar with all this stimulation? For even in their present godlike forms, he had no assurance at all that they could survive being this close to a quasar when it went off. *Never mind that at the moment. Hunger.*

Enough. Enough.

No! You must eat to survive. Eat!

Hunger.

It ate. Sucked another star dry, and another. Then it started to rebel again. *Enough.*

No! YOU MUST EAT TO SURVIVE!

The imperative, being after all its own, prevailed. It ate. Sucked another star down to the last gasps of gas and moved away from it, slowly, but unable to resist the hunger, and started to eat another. Sucked—

—and then all of space went white. The light they had seen from a safe distance, last time, that terrible quasar fire that ran fear down into the body through the eyes that saw it.

Except that a few seconds later, they all still existed. Charles now feebly remembered that he was Charles Francis Xavier, that he had a body, and that it was hanging around here, somewhere, in a spacesuit, soaking up radiation at what was probably not a healthy rate. "X-Men," he said, and did a hurried mind count. Everyone was dazed— particularly Jean—but all were alive, and all were looking back in astonishment to the source of the light—a dwindling point source at the heart of a spreading cloud of gas.

"Wha' happened?" Wolverine said.

"It ate too much," said Bishop. "All that mass—it didn't have time to process it, however it does that. Its insides went critical."

"An' it blew up," Gambit said, impressed. "Jus' one problem."

They looked where Remy was looking—and Charles gulped.

There was something dark growing at the heart of the white spark which had been the creature. Darkness boiled there. Something odd was happening to the light around that darkness. It was reddening, as gas and matter rushed toward the blackness—

No, Charles broadcast telepathically to everyone he could. *Oh, no! Everyone get away! Get the ships back!*

"What?" said the Beast. "What is it?"

The darkness was collapsing in on itself, faster and faster. Growing. Matter spiraling in on it. And the core of it, the creature which had ingested so many stellar masses but had been unable to digest them—all those masses were still there. Collapsing together past the Schwarzschild radius into a full-blown black hole, the sort that the core of any galaxy would be proud of. A big one.

And hungry.

Charles was about to ask Hank to bring them back to the ship, when he saw, with a start of horror, that that might not be a good idea. Talat, concerned for the X-Men perhaps, had let things go on for a little too long. Whatever the cause, the Majestrix's ship was caught in the whirling pattern of gas and torn stars which were making their way downward and inward toward the still-growing black hole and its event horizon. Time dilation effects were starting already. The ship looked drawn out, somehow longer than it should have. And the cries of the minds caught in it were running slow, a horrible drawl, through which Charles could nonetheless hear and recognize one in particular.

Ccchhhhaaaaarrrrrllllleeeesss!!!

Lilandra—

But she could not hear him. Gravity already had its grip on him and the others, on the pod where their real bodies rested. He too would be cycling down into that dreadful darkness quite soon, along with all the rest. It would at least be a unique death—if that was the right word for a process which would at least take millennia of objective time, if in fact it ever truly ended at all. Event horizons were difficult to describe correctly, in terms of their effect on the living mind—though it occurred to Charles now that he would have much leisure to formulate a description. All the leisure there was.

He looked ahead to Talat's ship, the alternate flagship. *Jean, there must be something—*

Charles, it's too strong, I can't—

Then another shape flashed past them, not being pulled down into the maelstrom, but diving into it, accelerating fast. It swung around the first ship, almost its twin, and fastened tractor beams onto it. It shifted course and began to labor back up the gravity curve. There was no chance of the second ship escaping, none whatsoever. *A desperate attempt*, Charles thought, seeing the tractor beams themselves bend and warp in the influence of the growing black hole. But they held. They held, and the first ship whipped around, slowly at first, then faster, slingshotted around by its anchor to the other ship's mass, and to a very slight extent by the movement of the maelstrom itself.

The first ship flung free of the whirlpool of matter being sucked down into that final darkness. *Go*, Charles shouted at Talat, *get her out of here, give it everything you've got!*

Something wrenching grasped him, flung him toward the escaping ship. The ship dissolved itself around him.

He was inside with the others, sprawling on the utility deck, gasping for air, gasping with horror and relief. Hank had managed to activate the Shi'ar teleportation system and bring them in once they were past the event horizon. Charles tried to boost himself up on his forearms. All he could see was the second ship through a portal, almost the twin of this one, vanishing, slipping down into the darkness.

Orien.

ORIEN!

No answer. Not on this side of time, nor this side of space, and possibly in no other time or space anywhere. For if you have spent a million millennia dying, but are still not dead, when will you catch up with your afterlife?

After a while there were hands on him, helping him back into his hoverchair. The X-Men stood about him, or in a couple of cases sat on the floor, trying to recover. Nearly everyone else was doing the same. The ship's alarms were whooping mournfully as she accelerated away from the new black hole at the galaxy's center, accompanied by the shattered remnants of the Shi'ar Grand Fleet.

Charles was profoundly tired. He looked up after a little while to see Lilandra, Majestrix Shi'ar, looking down at him. It was hard to read her face, but fortunately her mind was more accessible.

Well, my love, I seem to have made it back. But not by any accomplishment of my own.

Don't be ridiculous, Charles. You destroyed the creature. Our galaxy, and yours, are saved. Much death has been prevented because of what you did.

Yes. But not only I, and the X-Men. Orien . . .

She bowed her head. *Yes. I saw.*

A good man, Charles said softly. *And a liar.*

A liar?

He let her hear the words in the man's own voice, the response to "I will not stop loving her": "Maybe it is good that *one* of us should." Offhanded, casual, humorous, and definitely a lie.

A noble liar, said Charles, *and better than either of us deserves.*

My love, let us go home.

Yes. Wherever home is. And then Charles started to laugh softly, so that Lilandra and the X-Men looked at him very oddly indeed.

"Charles?"

Charles wiped the tears out of his eyes. "I could just *murder* a pizza," he said.

Eleven

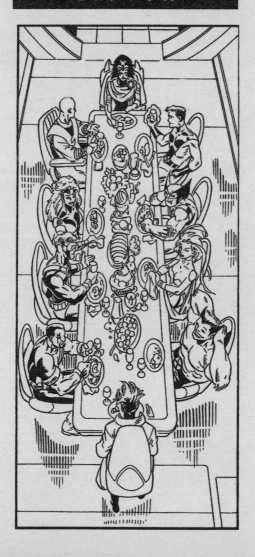

he night before they made planetfall on Earth—quietly, in a little Shi'ar shuttle which brought them down into the backyard of the Xavier Institute without any fuss—there was a serious dinner aboard Lilandra's ship.

There had been some talk about a massive welcome on the Throneworld, but the X-Men had wanted nothing to do with it. "After all those dirty looks we kept gettin' while we were there," growled Wolverine, "they think they're gonna make nice with us now that they think we're legit?"

So they sat at the long table in Lilandra's main meeting room, and there transpired a genuine feast, mostly of Remy's making. Even the star-eating creature could not have ingested the amount of dirty rice he produced, not to mention the *poulet sauvage,* the red beans and rice, and numerous other Cajun specialties. Certainly the amount of chile in everything would have slowed it down, or so the Beast claimed.

"More likely speed it up," said Remy laconically from where he sat opposite Lilandra, in the cook's place of honor. "Increased peristalsis. Ring o' Fire, one of my friends calls it."

"Well," Lilandra said, "before we set you all down on your home at last, the scientists tell me that the black hole is settling in very nicely, and will do the core area no serious harm—not for the next hundred thousand years, anyway."

343

"At which point it will no longer be any of *our* problems," said the Beast. "Is it developing that characteristic spindle shape? You know, the 'particle accelerator' formation."

"Not as yet. They say, give it another thousand years to stabilize. The important thing is that the creature is gone, and we know what to do, now, should another one ever turn up. Our own telepaths, with enough training, can handle the creature or its kindred."

"It took a while to find out," said Bishop, "and it seems so simple, in retrospect. But then, trial and error. And we, like the wasps the Beast used as his paradigm, were likely enough to make mistakes along the way."

"We got it right at the end," Wolverine said, "which is what counts."

"It really was the end too," the Beast said. "The debilitating effects of the extensor should pass. But if we'd gone in one more time, or even for another fifteen minutes or so, we might not have been so lucky."

Wolverine smiled. "Ain't luck, fuzzy, it's skill. Pass me some more o' them red beans, Cajun. You really got the recipe right this time."

Gambit grinned lazily.

Meanwhile, Lilandra said to Charles privately, *other matters have become . . . less troublesome for the moment.*

Oh?

Well, with the demise of so promising a candidate—her thought was purposely cold and ironic—*my counselors have decided to let the issue of the succession alone for a little while. They are, of course, in the process of looking for someone else as promising. There are no such others alive—except for the one they will not accept.* She smiled slightly. *And for the time, there the matter stands. Unless, of course, you wish to change that.*

How, beloved?

By staying with me on the Throneworld.

Charles smiled slightly. *I'm afraid I have a responsibility to the X-Men and the Xavier Institute. It will be a long time before school is out, I fear. I must stay where I am. There is a planet to protect, and the young and powerful to educate. And why should I be the one who moves? Come to Earth and live with me. Let tiresome rule of a quarrelsome empire rest with someone else. We have plenty of room in the mansion.*

Lilandra looked down the table. Gambit had pushed his plate aside and was playing solitaire, and cheating. The Beast was making spritzers with a wine too noble for such usage. Cyclops and Phoenix were feeding each other forkfuls of red beans and rice. Iceman was chilling a bottle of wine with his hands. Wolverine and Storm were whispering in each other's ear and chuckling at Phoenix and Cyclops. Bishop was brooding.

Room you may have, she said silently, *but better save room there for those who need your help from day to day. Those who save your world on a daily basis. As for me—many have died to keep me in the position I hold. Poor thanks to them if I slip out the side door for my own pleasure. Duty, Charles.*

Duty. He made a face, then let it slip away.

Would I love you, if you were otherwise? Hardly. Would you love me, if I so easily let go what was mine? Not likely.

The Empress of the Shi'ar smiled at Charles Xavier. He flushed hot. *It must be the wine*, he thought.

"Duty will come tomorrow," she said, "with the dawn. And as for the rest of your thought—let's go find out."

DIANE DUANE is the author of a score of novels of science fiction and fantasy, among them the *New York Times* hardcover bestsellers *Spock's World* and *Dark Mirror*, *The Book of Night with Moon*, the very popular Wizard fantasy series, and the Spider-Man novels *The Venom Factor*, *The Lizard Sanction*, and *The Octopus Agenda*. The *Philadelphia Inquirer* has called Duane "a skilled master of the genre," and *Publishers Weekly* has raved, "Duane is tops in the high adventure business." Duane lives with her husband, Peter Morwood—with whom she has written five novels, including the *New York Times* bestseller *The Romulan Way*—in a beautiful valley in rural Ireland.

RON LIM got his start on the alternative press comic *Ex-Mutants*, then moved on to prominence as the artist on Marvel's New Universe book *Psi-Force*. He has since lent his artistic talent to a variety of comics, including *X-Men 2099*, *Spider-Man Unlimited*, *The Silver Surfer*, *Fantastic Four*, *Venom: Nights of Vengeance*, *Superman & the Silver Surfer*, *They Call Me . . . The Skul*, and many more. His other work in book illustration includes *Spider-Man: The Venom Factor*, *X-Men: Siege*, *The Ultimate Spider-Man*, *The Ultimate Super-Villains*, *The Ultimate X-Men*, and *Untold Tales of Spider-Man*.

NOW AVAILABLE IN HARDCOVER
THE GRIPPING NEW THRILLER
SPIDER-MAN®
WANTED: DEAD OR ALIVE
BY NEW YORK TIMES BEST-SELLING AUTHOR
CRAIG SHAW GARDNER
PUTNAM